Carmine
Copyright © 2016 by Alan Janney

@alanjanney
alan@ChaseTheOutlaw.com

Second Edition
Printed in USA

Cover by Damonza
Artwork by Anne Pierson

ISBN: 978-0-9962293-9-5

Sparkle Press

 Created with Vellum

For Sarah
For Always

Carmine
Rise of the Warrior Queen

"Lovers don't finally meet somewhere.
They are in each other all along."
- Rumi

"What's past is prologue"
- *Tempest*. Shakespeare.

THE CAST OF CHARACTERS

Infected - Pure-born Variants
    Blue-Eyes - Secretary of State / President's mistress
    Caleb - a runaway
Nuts - mechanical genius
The Outlaw - masked vigilante
PuckDaddy - internet hacker
Samantha - sniper working with the Resistance
Tank - dangerous drifter
Walter - terrorist living in the northwest
Carter
China
Pacific
Russia
The Zealot

Kingdom Variants
    Becky - scavenger
    Carmine- Queen of New Los Angeles
    Kayla - Minister of Communication

Mason - leader of the Falcons

OTHERS OF NOTE

The Cheerleader - mysterious recluse
Dalton - bodyguard
General Brown - military commander
The Governess - supervisor of New Los Angeles
The Inheritors- ???
Isaac Anderson - leader of the Resistance
Miss Pauline - Orphan Overseer
The Priest - Law Keeper Overseer

PART I

May, 2019

In visions of the dark night
I have dreamed of joy departed
But a waking dream of life and light
Hath left me broken-hearted.
-*A Dream*. Edgar Allan Poe

I exist.

A consciousness surfacing from the dark.

My universe endures. I'm still here.

And I'm hungry.

Time is gradually coalescing into meaning. Hunger is substantial. Hunger marks the passage of time. So does the incremental increase of light.

I see.

I walk. I stumble around. And I have been for some time, possessing only a dim grasp of self. Operating on instinct and lower brain function. Cognition is finally warming up, fighting through layers of vegetative residue.

I'm in an abandoned Walmart and I'm safe. Other than hunger, those are the primary notions piercing my delirium. The store is empty, and I'm safe. Over and over. Hunger. Abandoned Walmart. Safety.

Then I discover my reflection.

The mirror is attached to a rack in the clothing department. A full-length mirror, which I approach curiously. My reflection is so unsettling I drop the juice box and bag of granola I'd been holding. Despite the vague awareness of wearing no clothes, I am shocked by my stark nakedness. I am *thin*. And my skin has lightened. Or at least, I think it has. I've matured since...since last I looked in a mirror, whenever that was. Am I only eighteen?

I struggle to remember what I should look like. Where did I get the number eighteen?

And why am I in a Walmart?

The store is pitch black but I see perfectly well. Darkness is no veil to my eyes. A single IV cord dangles from the inside of my right elbow. I tug it out and notice I'm wearing a UCLA Medical Center bracelet. It reads <u>**Katie Lopez**</u>, but in my frazzled state I forget the name immediately.

This place is a disaster. The store's proprietors must've taken the valuables and fled. Followed by looters ransacking the rest. About a quarter of the original merchandise remains, the cheap stuff. Hobos are sleeping in the rear of the shopping complex. I smell their unwashed bodies, and hear their snores. Perhaps a dozen of them sleep on plundered sheets, and I snort their stench from my nose.

Where is everyone else?

My hands shake with hunger. I finish the granola and drain the juice box, but I need more. The food sits on my stomach like a bomb about to erupt, like I haven't eaten in forever, so I choose the least moldy loaf of bread on the shelf. The stench of rotten meat in the deli is atrocious.

Strangers are cautiously creeping through the store's front doors. I'm aware of them the same way I'm aware of wind or a car horn or thirst. I can't see the strangers yet, but I know these newcomers aren't hobos heading to bed. They smell powerful. On some subterranean biological level, I realize the strangers are looking for me. I *Feel* them, which is a startling realization. I quickly hunt for clothing. Pickings are slim. I settle on off-brand athletic leggings and Reeboks.

The fabric of a neoprene shirt rips as I pull it over my head. I find another, carefully tug it on, and inspect my fingernails; the keratin is rock hard and the edges are sharp as a razor. Dangerously keen.

I return to the mirror and, no longer distracted by my body, I notice my hair. Or lack of hair. I see my scalp. I step closer and begin to tremble. I look like a Q-tip with thick brown fuzz. That's...that's not right. Is it? I shouldn't look like that. My hair is...was...long?

What *did* my hair look like?

What did I look like?

What does...who...

I'm thunderstruck with realization. I am... I was... I have no idea.

Where is everyone??

Why is my hair cut off??

Sudden ignorance pummels like physical fists. Facts slip through my mind like water when I grasp at them. I can't stack information, no way to scaffold understanding. Why is this store abandoned? Why was I wearing a hospital bracelet? My stomach heaves, like I'm off balance.

While I reel with unanswerable questions, a silent host of watchers surrounds me. They are men and women about my age. Some of them are tall and strong and powerful in appearance, and others crouch like animals. Half are well-dressed, and the rest appear to have no use for clothing. To my eyes they glow in the darkness, a faint illumination just under their skin, bioluminescent blood pumping. Their existence makes an impression on mine, like spirits smashing.

They *glow*?? I do not remember people glowing in the dark.

A man speaks. "Are you her?" he asks. He is one of the strong. He takes care of himself, but he is wary and scared. "He's gone," the man says, "and we need...someone. Are you it?"

I don't answer. His words are meaningless. In the back of my mind, a storm is brewing. Distant thunder between my temples. I can't deal with these people, not now when I can barely deal with myself. I need space to think. In the school supplies aisle, I find a little pink backpack and rip out the paper stuffing. I shove in a change of clothes. Much of the medicine was looted but I locate generic pain relievers, antiseptic, and ointment. Also, dried fruit, granola, beef jerky, and two bottles of Gatorade. Water is nowhere to be found.

I'm panicking. Can't breathe. I run. No, that isn't what I do. I *Run*. I accidentally crash through the glass doors and careen down deserted streets. The trunk of a palm tree cracks when I collide with it, bruising my shoulder. Far-off objects leap closer. Moving this quickly is impossible. So is breaking a tree trunk with my shoulder, but it happens again. And it doesn't hurt.

Faint echoes of explanations carom in my mind, just out of reach. There was a disease. I'm instantly certain of this fact. A virus caused this eerie absence of people. A pandemic, but I didn't have the disease.

Did I?

No, I didn't. I'm almost positive. Certainly I would remember...

I arrive at an intersection. All the lamps are out, but I can read street names. Ohio Avenue. Where on earth is that? No way I'm in Ohio. There are too many palm trees here. A block farther I see signs for the University of California, Los Angeles. UCLA? That's out past Beverly Hills.

Lightning strikes my mind. I sprawl across the blacktop, struck down by a vicious headache no longer distant. My elbows ache. My wrists throb. Knees hurt so badly I can't stand. I crawl into an abandoned Toyota and close the door. No cracked windows; I want my scent contained.

I hunker down and suck on beef jerky through the long night, wondering what happened to the planet.

Two

I don't sleep a wink, and when the sun comes up I'm famished. Behind a nearby stucco house I pick plums and apples, but no amount of food completely quells the hunger. My nails sink easily into the wood, and I climb like a squirrel. That's new.

There are people on the outskirts of Brentwood. Real people in various stages of relocating. Hastily jettisoning extravagant mansions. So the world is not empty after all; I'd started to wonder. Government trucks rumble through the streets, bringing gasoline to stragglers. Children cry. Cars are overloaded.

Smoke rises to the south. The men and women glance that way often, like they're afraid disaster is coming closer, and it might be for all I know. I should talk to the remnants of humanity but I have no desire to. They stink. They smell of anxiety and sweat and fear. The adults are preoccupied and the kids are unsettled. They don't glow. They move too slowly and yell at each other. I don't want people. I want quiet.

I break into an abandoned electronics store, take a cheap smartphone and extra battery, and connect to the public wifi. The internet still functions. I orient myself with Google Earth, capture several screenshots for future use, and hike out of town on San Vicente Boulevard. I need space. And peace. Besides, I have no home to visit. None that I can remember, at least, which is a lonely thought. Very few cars pass, and none pay me any attention. Frequent rests are necessary as I move into Will Rogers State Park, because I have zero stamina. My muscles already quake from fatigue.

The Hyper Virus! That's the name. But I don't have it. Other people did, not me. Not me. I gulp air but can't get enough. Not me. I *didn't* have it, I'm positive.

No. No no no no no, I don't want it. What happened?? I fight for balance, for sanity, for oxygen. Could I have it? Just keep walking. I'll remember. I'll simply keep walking and figure this whole thing out.

What happened to all my friends? Did I have friends? Of course I did, but who? Where?

I'm exhausted five miles in and I halt on a small rise beneath a copse of evergreens. There are no jet contrails in the blue above. No hikers below. I'm alone. And asleep in seconds.

- Three -

A man is here. I heard him approach but I didn't budge. He kept his distance until now that I sit up in the late evening. He draws closer.

I hate him instantly. He glows to my eyes, but he's not like my powerful pursuers at Walmart. He's not curious, not peaceful. He's arrogant and hostile. He is dressed in cargo shorts and an unbuttoned dress shirt, white sneakers, gold necklace, gold bracelet. His blonde hair is slicked back. He watches me and smirks. "You're new," he remarks.

"Go away." My voice sounds harsh and dry, almost alien. I haven't used it since...who knows.

"I can smell it. You're fresh. And your head was shaved not long ago. You just wake up? Leaving the cradle?"

I stand and hitch the backpack high on on my shoulders, and bite into a harvested apple. "You're boring. Don't follow me."

"He's dead, you know."

"Don't care."

"The Father. Our Creator? He's gone."

I set off down the hill, away from the sun. I want to plunge deeper into the park. But the man is fast. Faster than a human should be. He *Moves* and plants himself in my way. "He's dead. Which means," he sneers, "it's every man for himself."

"Or herself."

"Haven't you noticed? The people are terrified of us and they're all leaving. We're in charge now. We can do whatever we want."

He is attractive, in an overly muscular type of way, and he knows it. He says, "You pluck that apple off a tree? You just take it? Take what you want? The apple has no say. You want the apple, you take the apple."

I'm growing angry. Blood gathers in my face and my skin is changing. My muscles are annealing to rock, which would be astonishing if

I could think straight. Emotions swell inside like a wave, and the urge to hurt him is intense. "Move."

He crosses his arms and mocks me. "Move? I've been Variant for over a year. I know you're strong, pretty girl. Stronger than most, but I'm more powerful than you can imagine. I was one of the Father's warriors. Now take off your backpack."

I strike him before he's ready. Hard. I create a direct line of force between my back foot and my right hand, stepping into the attack, driving with my shoulder and putting my fist into his chest. He responds as though he's been crushed by a wrecking ball, swept away with its pendulum swing. His body cartwheels into the brush below and disappears.

Hitting him is exquisite gratification. A release of tension, so good it hurts. How did I do *that*? "So long, warrior."

I glance at the map photos to aim myself, the man quickly forgotten, and I march northeast. Night falls. No matter. Despite the tumult of small animal sounds, I'm unafraid. In fact, night brings a heightened sense of existence, of pleasure. I belong in darkness, as though I'm nocturnal. Slow and steady. I use rhythmic footfalls to help process information. I have the disease. Forcefully I tell myself over and over, I have it. There's no other explanation. Despite having little recollection of the previous months and of my prior self, I know *this* isn't it. My body's changed. I couldn't previously throw grown men around the forest.

Memories vanish like mist in my fingers, leaving me with only emotion. I remember safety, possibly a bedroom. Warmth. A familiar school building. Happiness. Love.

I had a boyfriend. I can't remember his face, but he existed. I flush in embarrassment at the strong emotions swirling around him. A powerful reaction, and my body longs for his. To be held. And then, in an instant, he passes. So do the emotions, lost in fog. So frustrating.

Just keep walking. Keep going.

The Father. That idiot mentioned a Father, and some primal compulsion tugs at me. The Father. Who was the Father?

My march lasts all night and I trek into the forested hills of Topanga. My food supply dwindles but I don't care. Getting nutrition won't be an issue.

As a new day nears dawn, I head towards a clearing I spotted half a mile distant. Anywhere to lay down. Inside the clearing is a small cabin, and I make a complete circle around it, reconnaissance from within tree cover. No paved roads, just a beaten path and small ATV tire tracks. Probably an illegal shelter within the state park. Someone was here recently but now it's vacant. Cold stove. Bottled water. An iron skillet. So tired. There's a bed. That will do.

Four

The cabin's rightful owner returns before noon. I pretend to be asleep. He is startled to find me but keeps quiet. He appears to be about sixty, full beard, dressed in jeans and a flannel shirt. He noisily loads supplies into an underground storage unit reached from the cabin's west wall.

I rise, grab my backpack and walk out to meet him. His brown eyes are flat and calm, and he nods. "Thanks for the bed," I say. "I'll be on my way."

He shrugs and says, "No rush." His voice is thick and dusty. "Eat before you go. You look mighty thin."

I'm about to reject the offer but my stomach rumbles. We both hear it and he chuckles. "Eat a bologna sandwich, little lady. Then take off."

I nod and he finishes loading his haul. His four-wheeler rests underneath brush outside the clearing. "Thank you."

"You're one of them," he remarks. "Ain't you."

"Them?"

"The mutants."

My heart accelerates to a higher R.P.M. Mutant. What an awful word. "Why do you ask?"

He closes the locker door and fastens it, rises with bread and a pack of meat in his left hand, and points with his right. "Your hair. The scars."

"Scars?"

He watches me uncertainly, a simple man trying to figure a complex situation. He points again. "Scars. On your skull. And your arms. He gave you the disease."

My hand trembles as I inspect my cranium. He says, "Other side." There. A small gap in the fuzz. Scar tissue, and subcutaneous tenderness. I discover four healed incisions hidden by hair, two in the back near the mastoid region. And faint scars on each bicep and forearm. I stop searching, afraid I'll find more. I'm breathing deeply, panic threatening to uncoil in my chest.

"You just wake up?"

I nod and wipe furiously at tears. My emotions are so powerful that I groan with the effort of controlling them.

"I read about his Chrysalises," the man continues. "Nasty places."

"What do you mean by Chrysalis?"

"Don't you remember nothing?"

"I woke up in a hospital. I think." I pause to fight back a sob. "That's all I know."

"A hospital," he repeats. "That ain't a Chrysalis." Another long pause as we both grapple with incomprehension. He turns in a circle, glaring into the hidden parts of the forest. "Well. Better come inside, I guess."

I sit on the edge of his bed, forehead resting in my hands. The man opens the cabin's one window and makes a sandwich. He places the food next to me but I can't touch it. Instead of insisting, he eats his own food with the table manners of a recluse, and then guzzles a half bottle of water. Finally he says, "He's dead. You know that?"

"Who?"

The man replies, "The Chemist." There is a swirl of colors and emotions in the front of my mind. The Father.

"How did he die?"

"The Outlaw killed him."

Instead of a swirl, now there is a hurricane. Fireworks of feelings and passions. Unanswerable questions crash and leave me more confused. The Outlaw. I remember him. No, that's not correct. I remember...memories of him. There are echoes of that man deep in my subconscious.

"Ain't that why you all going crazy?"

"I don't understand your question," I sigh. "I don't understand anything."

From under the bed, he produces a portable television. He powers it on and fiddles with dials and a bizarre antenna. "This ain't the Los

Angeles news," he explains. "The local tower is broadcasting San Fransisco's news. Because LA doesn't have news anymore."

I watch in horror. The world is madness. Every major metropolis is erecting interstate checkpoints. Traffic backs for miles. Electrified fences are built as quickly as possible. Large farms take on refugees willing to work as armed security. So do important manufacturing plants. Los Angeles is abandoned. San Diego empties. Las Vegas burns. So do Houston and Oklahoma City. America's military appears to be at war with itself. And on and on, for twenty minutes.

The screen switches to the Director General of the World Health Organization, a well-put-together woman wearing a suit and scarf. She reads a prepared statement.

"The emergency committee convened by the World Health Organization to address the epidemiological outbreak, nicknamed the Hyper Virus, has concluded its first day of meetings. Our work is just beginning, and we're far too early in the discovery stages to declare conclusive recommendations. However, due to the inflammatory nature of the outbreak, the committee has voted for unusual transparency, and to release initial observations.

"Representatives and physicians from all affected NATO countries have presented their findings, and from this collective we note the following:

"The Hyper Virus is new to medicine. Next to nothing is understood about the disease despite months of research.

"The Virus, which may or may not be ultimately labeled as a true virus, is not inherently contagious. Little is known about the initial outbreak, other than Martin Patterson is believed to be the disease's agent of communication, and following his death no literature or data has been found to aid in our research.

"To date we've found nothing to signify the disease has spread within the last sixty days. There are no indications that the disease is spreading by sexual transmission or blood transfusion. All contagion properties appear to be dormant. Only those individuals who underwent the surgical operation are infected."

"Bah," the man grunts. "They're trying to stop the fear, but it won't work. People think they'll become a zombie or vampire or something. Hard to control mass terror."

The woman drones on for several more minutes and while she speaks the news channel displays images of the chaos and hysteria. The WHO uses clinical terms to hide the sordid truth: the mutants are people manufactured into weapons. Supposed super soldiers gone berserk. I close my eyes when the images become too much, and I only listen. The Director refers to the mutants as experiments of a brilliant transhumanist, and she uses the nickname Variants. The Variants were supposed to be the next phase in evolution, or something else equally grandiose, but it failed. Instead of a utopia full of Variant super humans, we got a dystopia full of freaks. The creations weren't peaceful. On screen, a map shows Variants running wild, radiating out primarily from Los Angeles but also from small stations called Chrysalises around the country. The Chrysalises are empty now, grisly warehouses in which half the patients died from infection.

On screen, the Variants break into a Publix supermarket for food and slaughter the law enforcement when a deputy fires his weapon. I watch this video footage. I can't help myself. The entire Sheriff's Office in Alpine, Utah is wiped out when they open fire on a Variant drinking water at a stream. The anchors repeat viewer discretion warnings as video after video plays of the mutants eliminating enemies.

The pattern is evident; Variants respond to violence with over-whelming force.

Small domestic counter-terrorism teams are forming, the news anchors announce, deploying electroshock and fire-based weapons to capture Variants, alive if possible because the President is paying a million dollars per living incarcerated mutant. The teams are called Herders.

I nearly vomit as the weapons are demonstrated. Instruments of pain, built just for me. Eventually he turns the set off.

"They all have the disease," I say, numb from horror overload. "The Variants."

"Yep," he nods. "On account of a surgery. Man-made mutants. The Chemist brought on the apocalypse."

Brought on the apocalypse? No. Not yet, I think.

He says, "You don't have to worry about me. I ain't turning you in. I don't care about money. Besides, you don't seem harmful."

"I'm not like them."

"Those are just the violent ones, I reckon. No one really knows for sure. The peaceful Variants still live downtown, but they won't let anyone in."

"Downtown?"

"Los Angeles. They haunt the towers. Like ghosts. Barely alive. You look familiar, you know. What's your name?"

I shake my head. "I'm not sure. I don't..."

"Okay. Well. I think I seen you before. My name's Cuddy."

"I'm fairly certain I have their disease, Cuddy. Does that mean Herders will hunt me with those...weapons?"

"Yeah. Probably. You fairly certain on account of the scars?"

"And other things."

"Like what?"

"I can see in the dark. And my nails are..." I hold out my hand. Even in the dim light the tips are lethal penumbra.

"And you're fast and strong?" he asks, and I nod. "There are others like you now and then. In the forest. Wandering. Should I be afraid of them?"

"Most likely."

Five

I remain with the man two more days. His cabin is built near the intersection of Tuna, Topanga, and Malibu state parks, in an unattractive valley with no trails. He's been here for two years without drawing attention. I regain some of my strength and some of my sanity. But none of my memories.

I cannot stay. Restlessness is an animal gaining strength in my limbs. I find an evergreen fig tree overlooking brown hills, and I climb it. Here is the peace and distance I've been craving, space to think and consider my options. A strong desire to find family tugs at my heart, tugs me north. But who is my family? And do they want me back? Los Angeles's skyline rises prominently to the south. Variants live there. Like me. I'd be accepted. Maybe I'd find answers. But a future? No idea.

Behind the eastern mountains is war and madness. And Herders wielding electricity. My skin crawls. I hate them. Without trying, I've developed an affinity for the Variants. A solidarity with those being hunted and hurt by lightning. I want to hunt the hunters. Turn their own weapons against them. A suicidal mission, but possibly worth the risk.

Cuddy returns for dinner. He isn't alone. He leads a scared little girl by the hand. "This is Becky," he says.

On second glance, Becky isn't so little. She's eighteen or nineteen. She's short and she's crouched, and she has the disease. Her eyes latch onto me as she enters the clearing.

"Where'd you find Becky?"

"Two miles south. Poor thing's about to starve."

Cuddy leads Becky into the cabin, but her eyes never waver. She watches me like the pursuers did at Walmart. Fascinated. Expectant. Like she thinks I can help her.

I stalk the clearing, pacing back and forth with long legs getting stronger each day. All those faces at the Walmart...they were mutants.

They didn't appear *mutated*, though. Not distorted or grotesque. We need someone, the man said. Are you her?

That's a really good question. Who the heck am I? For the hundredth time, I wish I hadn't taken that hospital bracelet off.

Cuddy walks out and says, "Becky won't eat."

"Why is she like that?"

"Got no idea. Maybe you can help her? The Hyper Virus damages their brains, we know that much."

Hyper Virus. Damaged brains. Causing memory loss?

Becky walks out of the cabin, holding an uneaten sandwich. She is dirty and small and she is crying. I ask, "What's wrong with you?"

"I...I don't know," stammers Becky. "Help me please..."

"Eat your sandwich," I snap, and Becky jumps and obeys, hungrily devouring the food. Hands on hips, I roll my eyes and groan. "This will be pleasant."

~

I'm still awake at midnight. Every time I close my eyes I see violence. I see people like me being hurt on television. I see people like me hurting others. So I sit on the grass, my back resting against the cabin, and listen to Cuddy snore in his tent.

I hear...everything. I'm aware of a thousand nearby animals, and I can see deep into the pitch black forest, like night vision. Like I'm nocturnal. Earlier I *Climbed* Cuddy's cabin using only the strength of my nails. I cannot escape the raw truth; I'm a science experiment. Specifically, a science experiment that failed. Or perhaps, I'm the only one that didn't?

Now what? What do I do? Where do I go? Who is my family? Why did this happen to me? I don't even know which direction to face.

The silent phone rests in my left hand, unused. I feel the familiar urge to check Instagram and SnapChat. To connect socially with my friends. Those networking websites and apps still function but I can't get in. I don't know my email. Or my name. Or my friends.

Becky sneaks out and watches me from the corner. She stands like a shadow for twenty minutes, until I relent and pat the ground beside me. Becky lowers next to me and takes hold of my hand, like she's a toddler and I'm her mom. A long sigh escapes her lips and she falls instantly asleep, her head on my shoulder.

"We need to make plans, Becky," I say, but she's gone.

Six

I return to my evergreen fig tree the following day and stare in all directions. Time and again, my attention is caught by the glittering Pacific Ocean. Distant waves, and the gentle rising and falling of the entire body of water, drain tension from my neck and shoulders.

I'm staying near the ocean. I want to. If I have family, we'll reunite later. Hopefully.

Becky sits at the foot of my tree, playing with pine needles. The little Variant needs a wash and fresh clothes, but she is functioning at a much higher level than yesterday. Beneath the mud and insecurity and timidity, there are signs of a girl who was once attractive and strong.

"More are coming," Becky says. She stares south.

"More? Mutants like me?"

"No. Mutants like me."

"What's the difference?"

"You're strong," she says.

"So?"

"We're drawn to you."

"I don't get it."

She shrugs, a barely perceptible motion. "I feel better. You're safe. I mean, you feel safe. You know?"

No, Becky. No I don't. My fingers tremble slightly at the implications. Drawn to me. That explains the watchers at Walmart. But I don't know why. I ask, "How do you know they're coming?"

"I feel them."

"Will more like you keep appearing the longer we stay here?"

"Yes."

That settles the debate. It's time to leave. Cuddy doesn't need to be swarmed with failed science experiments like me, or Becky. Becky can barely take care of herself. She needs to wash. Then again, I do too.

She stands and moves aside as I descend the tree and stride into ankle-deep waters of a nearby brook. I sit in the stream and dunk my entire head. The water is like ice. I sputter from the chill, and scrub my scalp with fingers. I splash water on my neck and shoulders, and soon my entire body is rinsed. Becky watches, struck dumb by this ceremony, and it doesn't occur to her that she also needs to wash. "Becky. You stink. Get in here."

I stand in the sun and dry for ten minutes. Becky splashes in the water and does the same, as still as a statue. Eventually she says, "Time to go?"

"Yes."

"Where?"

"Towards the Pacific."

"Good. I like the ocean."

As we approach the cabin, alarms begin to ring in my mind. My body prepares for war, an involuntary response. The forest is calm. I spot the cabin's roof through the foliage and it appears quiet. "Becky, do you feel that?"

"Yes."

"What is it?"

"They are here."

The mutants she mentioned. Like her. Variants. There are traces of disease in the breeze. I fill my lungs with air through my nose. More than one is here. Different odors, different flavors of sweat.

Cuddy is dead. I know this before I see his body. We enter the clearing and four mutants exit the cabin. The muscular blond boy is back, and he tosses Cuddy onto the ground between us. Cuddy's neck is broken. I examine the corpse with a detached sense of loss, of injustice, a waste of resources.

"Why did you do that?" I demand.

The attractive boy shrugs thick shoulders. "I step on ants too."

"I was fond of him."

"Even better."

I'm unsettled by the sight of his death, and my outrage sharpens into purpose. I register the event coldly. Cuddy should not have died, and someone will be held accountable. The muscular boy is violent without cause, and his type of mutant bring the Herders and their electricity.

His three-person Variant entourage fan out behind him. They stare fixedly at me with a mixture of emotion, including fear. Comets ready to attach themselves to whoever wins this crash of planets. They are in much better shape than Becky. They wash and eat and think.

The arrogant boy says, "You belong to me now."

In my ear, Becky whispers, "His name is Nathan. He's strong. But not like you."

"Stay here," I reply and I advance on the boy. He makes fists and his followers tense. I briefly consider arguing with him. Threatening him. Letting him leave. But...no.

"You're strong," he admits, bouncing lightly on the balls of his feet. "But there are four of us. You belong to me now, chica. You and the runt both."

"I woke up a few days ago, and I don't know much about us yet," I say, mostly for the benefit of his crew. "But I know we can't kill innocent people for fun. That's not how this works. We need a better way."

"We—"

"You are sentenced to death for your violence and for your future crimes. An eye for an eye."

"...what?"

I strike. He's ready for it but his movements are sluggish. He blocks my right fist but I anticipated that. With the fingernails on my left hand, I open him from groin to ribcage, like unzipping a body-bag. My nails slice cleanly and deeply, and the boy fumbles at his abdomen in quiet astonishment. He is vulnerable and helpless, and I cut his throat with a quick slash motion. He falls neatly on top of Cuddy and doesn't struggle.

I didn't want to do that; I had to. My stomach doesn't care, however, and I vomit into the grass. No one speaks while I wipe my mouth, careful of the dripping blood. I spit twice and tell the others, "Becky and I are going to the ocean. You can tag along."

The tall pretty girl states, "We are definitely coming with you. You are awesome, and that guy was *ew*." The two boys with her nod in agreement. They don't even glance at their former leader, still warm.

I ask, "Just like that? You want to go with us?"

"Of course."

"Well...okay. We need to bury the bodies," I say and the four Variants obey immediately. I step into the musty cabin to collect my things. The small television is on. A news special, highlighting the domestic counter-terrorist teams. The Herders are corralling mutants. The footage is grim. Shock weapons, bursts of electricity, howls of pain.

Some of us are violent. Some of us should be incarcerated. But not all. I shatter the screen.

I emerge with backpack hitched tight. They've already dug an impressive ditch. "Becky, Cuddy's four-wheeler has a metal cargo basket. Fill it with his supplies. Please."

An hour later we follow the beaten path west towards Wildwood. Becky drives the ATV. I lead.

Seven

We camp at midnight near Highway 27. I don't want to stop but the others are tired. I'd prefer not to light a fire, but they beg. I don't want to talk but they won't shut up. Sigh.

What I really want is to find a boat, sail into the Pacific and read a good book. I almost groan with sudden desire. But these kids would follow me. They're not kids, though, it only feels that way, and I won't be free of them any time soon.

What would I read? I can't remember my favorite books.

They swap histories around the cheery blaze. The tall pretty girl was one of the first volunteers to be injected in Compton. She's so pretty it hurts to look at her. She woke over a year ago and guarded the eastern Downtown boundary as recently as April.

What month is it now? May, I think. Maybe June?

One of the boys, a stout kid with coal black skin, brags that he was a Warrior, one of the Father's favorites. He fought the Outlaw in a tower once and lived.

Longings and fury rise like lava in my heart at the mention of the Outlaw.

The other boy is named James. He's newer and migrated here from a small Chrysalis near Reno. He fled the war when his companions were killed by fire.

Becky doesn't say much, just that she feels better now.

The four laugh at jokes I don't understand, and they use foreign jargon. At a lapse in conversation, I ask, "Where are you all going now?" They stare at me, quizzically, silently. I point at the tall pretty girl and the warrior boy, and ask, "Why were you following that blond kid?"

"Nathan was strong."

"So?"

"So we followed him."

"You're leaving Los Angeles? Why?"

"It's a mess."

The boy nods. "Not like it used to be."

"Explain."

"The Father is dead," the pretty girl says simply. "Walter is gone. Carla is dead. There is no leader."

"Caleb trying to lead," the boy scoffs. "But he isn't a leader. No way."

Walter? Carla? Caleb? I don't know these names, and it makes my head hurt.

Becky softly adds, "Los Angeles is a bad place now."

The tall pretty girl wrinkles her nose. "And the Fire Girl is there. You can smell her a mile away."

"The Fire Girl?" I ask.

"The Cheerleader. She's almost as strong as you."

Frustrated, I ask again, "Where will you go now? You haven't answered my question."

Becky says, "I want to stay with you."

The tall girl chirps, "Me too! Where are *you* going?"

The two boys nod and watch my reaction. I ask, "Anywhere I go, you want to go?"

"Yes," all four answer at once.

I rub my eyes and can't think of a response.

- Eight -

The four strangers sleep.

I do not. I hug my knees to my chest and glare at dead embers for hours, considering my options.

At three in the morning, I shake the pretty girl awake. "Hey. Wake up. Hey. You said Caleb is in charge of Los Angeles?"

"Mmm," the pretty girl moans, partially asleep. She has pine straw in her hair. "What? Oh. Yes. Why?"

"What's he like?"

"I don't know. He's quiet, I guess. Scared. Kind of a wimp, you know? We call him Kid."

"Am I stronger than him? Than Kid?"

"No. But he'll be afraid of you. He'll run away."

"You're sure?" I persist.

"Definitely," she smiles dreamily. "You're like...pow."

"Okay." I sniff, trying to identify a scent that's been eluding me. "Do you smell...sugar cookies?"

"That's probably me."

"You smell like sugar cookies? Your deodorant or something?"

"No. It's me." She covers her mouth and laughs.

"Why?"

"I dunno. But this is my first time sleeping in four days, so...can I...?"

"Sure. Sorry. Go back to sleep."

She does, and I think about Caleb and sugar cookies and the future for the remainder of the night.

Nine

I gain new followers during the night. Six others creep close. I don't acknowledge their arrival and they remain at a safe distance.

At dawn, Becky and the three other original followers stare uncertainly into the trees and back to me. Becky won't leave my side.

I jerk my chin at the forest. "Feed them breakfast. Everyone eats and then we go."

"It's okay!" the pretty girl calls into the trees. "You can come out! She will feed you breakfast!"

Ten. Ten total Variants watch me and feed from the four-wheeler's cargo basket, eating bread and meat and apples. We can scavenge more supplies soon. I eat the final plum from my pink backpack and rub fingers into my joints, which have begun to ache.

Three of the newcomers bear scars, purple and raised welts on their necks and limbs. They relate stories of fleeing from Herders. Men in helicopters with electroshock weapons tormenting them, even though they'd done nothing wrong.

The thought of this makes me want to uproot trees. What will happen to them? They aren't unified, and they can't fight back, not against the entire United States military. They are leaderless. And I don't have a home.

They exchange names. Kayla. Megan. Travis. Adrian. Tray-Von. Becky.

Their collective mood has shifted from fear to enthusiasm, even if it doesn't register in their voices yet. I sense it. I sense it the way I feel sunlight on my face.

The tall pretty girl, Kayla, asks, "So...what's your name?"

What's my name. It was written on the hospital bracelet, but my name didn't seem important at the time. I've forgotten. I long for my name. For my family. I answer, "Carmine."

"Carmine. That's unusual. But pretty."

"It means red. Or crimson," I explain, and all ten sets of eyes drop to my right hand, which is still stained with blood. "Finish eating. It's time we go."

"Go where?"

"We're going to spread out and head south. We'll collect as many as we can."

"Collect what? Variants?"

"I don't like that term," I say.

"The Father said we were Chosen."

"I don't care. I'll think up another name soon. You have a new purpose now. Point is, we find as many as we can. Hundreds. Thousands. And we rendezvous in Los Angeles."

They stir excitedly. Hope rises.

"We need to unify. You need a home." And I need one too. They hang on each syllable. "Follow me. And we'll figure this out. You'll be safe in Los Angeles."

"Really?"

"I can do this. I promise."

- Ten -

Three days later I walk down Broadway at noon, followed by a crowd of three hundred. The Variants in my wake are of all shapes, sizes, and strengths, but they share one common characteristic; they are desperate for leadership and they believe I'm it, based purely on strength.

I don't know what we are, but everyone who underwent the knife is more of an animal now than before. Strong emotions trigger physiological changes in our bodies, and we devolve from rational human to part savage. We're like werewolves without the fur. And without the lunar dependency.

Because of our new primal instincts, strength rules. Might makes right. And I woke up king of the jungle. Or queen. A terrifying thought which steals my ability to fall asleep.

Parts of Los Angeles still burn; there is no active fire department. With the rest of America in chaos, California decided to leave Los Angeles to the Variants. At least they're partly contained here, right? When the dust settles, officials will come back and deal with the city.

Except I'm here now. If they don't want the city, we'll take it.

I watched a briefing from the CDC based in Atlanta, and they call us mutants. Maybe the term Variant isn't so bad after all. Less offensive somehow.

From the Variants, I learned Downtown LA was evacuated in November of last year. The rest of Greater Los Angeles followed suit, slowly peeling away beginning in March of this year. Now the city is empty for fifty miles in all directions, everyone running from the monsters. From us.

Our arrival downtown has not gone unnoticed. Towers are lined with thousands of Variants. They cling to surfaces like spider monkeys overhead, and an eerie silence permeates the once bustling metropolis. I'm shocked by what I see. Several streets are caved in, revealing underground metro lines below. Many of the towers bear scars from some previous battle, and in the distance I see an enormous mound of rubble, clearly a fallen skyscraper. It's a war zone, not the City of Angels.

The pretty girl, Kayla, has already arrived. She and a crowd of two hundred wait at the intersection of Broadway and Olympic.

"See?" She beams and sparkles with excitement, and I'm beginning to realize she's more than simply pretty. Her beauty is enhanced to such a degree it's hard to look away. She smells like a field of strawberries. "Follow me, I told them. Come and see. And they did!"

"Where is Kid?"

"I don't know."

I want this issue settled immediately. There cannot be two leaders. Caleb, the one they call Kid, should have been stronger. With better leadership the Variants wouldn't be wandering away and into the clutches of Herders. Or worse, into Walter's. I'm hearing alarming stories about Walter, a powerful Variant living in Oregon. My head swirls with painful emotions when I think of him.

"Caleb!" I roar. The others back away and give me the entire intersection. "Kid! Come out here!" My voice is a hurricane. I'm shouting loud enough to rattle nearby storefront windows. I pace back and forth, and my voice disperses throughout the city. If he's downtown, he can hear me. "Caleb! Now!"

"The boy is gone," I hear. I turn and I'm startled to see a spry bald man, maybe sixty years old, striding from the crowd. The rest of us are nineteen or twenty, so his advanced age is a stark contrast. He has thick forearms and he's wiping his hands with a greasy rag. "Fled yesterday, like a damn coward. Heard you were coming."

"You're in charge?"

"Absolutely not. Never have been, never will be, got no interest. I fix things."

"That's Nuts," Kayla offers. "He's our genius. And he's Infected."

Infected. My vision swims with distant memories. I've been hearing that term, Infected. Gotta lock it down. That means he's different from me, but I don't know how. "Then who is in charge?"

"You are, and it's about time," he says. "I'm restoring partial water pressure, and haven't slept in four days. Send me some help and it'll cut my time in half."

Send him help. He wants me to allocate some of these people. Just like that, I'm in charge? Just like that, I've got a city to take care of and no one bats an eye at the transfer of power?

"I'm in charge," I announce, but it's a cautious announcement. An exploratory power grab to see who voices disagreement, but not one does. Kayla's so happy she bounces on her toes. "And this is our home now." I'm standing in the intersection, surrounded by five hundred onlookers on foot and by another thousand on the towers, and when I finish speaking they swarm closer. Over a thousand bodies press in to touch me. Kayla grasps my hand, and then so does someone else, a face I don't recognize. Strangers approach and caress my shoulders, my arms, my neck, my scalp, my back, and even my abdomen. Becky gives me a full embrace. I am ritually squeezed and prodded. They cup my chin and my cheeks and then retreat, making room for others. At first I'm startled, verging on claustrophobia, but soon I understand they *need* to touch me. Our skin contact creates a bridge. A connection I cannot explain, other than I experience them differently than I did before. Our bond calms their anxiety and fear.

We are one.

- Eleven -

That night, Olympic Boulevard is lit with small coal fires. Pyres are set in the middle of the street where cars once roared and we gather around in pockets to rest and eat.

We spent the day creating a new life. I divided the workers into five-person teams and assigned missions, such as scavenging enough water and food to last for a week, locating other Variants and calling them home, helping Nuts, clearing rubble, locating resources, mapping trouble spots, and so on.

"Stay together," I warned them. "Safety in numbers." Two Variant teams spent the afternoon patrolling the outskirts of Downtown, *Leaping* from building to building, and they reported small gatherings of survivalists to the south and east. Sturdy Los Angolans refusing to flee. They'll become our allies, if I get my way.

It's a breezy night and my bones ache, but the fire glazes us all in a communal warmth. I sit in a canvas folding chair, Kayla on my right, and Becky on my left. Becky doesn't speak, but Kayla doesn't shut up. She and a kid named Mason do most of the talking. Mason is wiry and powerful, a leader among the Variants, and he keeps saying, "Everything will change now. It's going to be better."

"This is our home," Kayla replies, echoing my words. "It'll be a real home. I'm going to hang curtains. I'm so excited!"

I hear whispers from the outskirts of our firelight.

"She killed Nathan."

"Ripped him open and cut his throat."

As the evening wears on, our campfire population swells. We started with twenty, but soon I see a hundred faces. Maybe two hundred. Maybe over a thousand. All these lonely monsters. Formerly they obeyed the Father, a madman named the Chemist and also their creator. Then they followed Caleb, but he wasn't resilient enough. Didn't have the backbone. Now, me?

Nature hates a vacuum.

"We can be free," Mason says. He can do the trick of spinning a knife around his fingers, transferring it up and down between his knuckles. His hands are heavily tattooed.

"You weren't free yesterday?" I ask.

"There are different forms of slavery," he says. "Slaves to fear. Slaves to ourself. Our uncontrollable wants. But now..."

Someone outside the firelight asks, "What will we *do* now?"

The question is for me. Silence falls. Warriors eager for purpose, listening for orders. A tingly sensation settles over me, like being sprinkled with fairy dust. An immense conviction mounts in my chest, a certainty that we're part of something special. A preordained court of angels, in the grand halls of an abandoned cathedral.

"The world is crashing," I proclaim. "They blame us, and they're correct. To an extent. But not tomorrow. Tomorrow we're the solution. We're going to build a refuge. A safe place. A city we'll protect."

I see the wonderment in their eyes. The hope. Our corner of the world won't break. We'll hold it together.

Someone asks, "What if they stop us?"

"They Herders won't stop us."

"What about the others?"

The others. I keep hearing about the others, mighty Variants like Walter who are stronger than us. I don't understand all the terminology yet, or the hierarchies, but I know everyone in the firelight is terrified of them.

"We won't be stopped," I say. "By anyone. Our purpose is too important. We'll be the light in a darkening world."

They are satisfied with my confidence, and the murmuring begins again. I listen until my ears go fuzzy with exhaustion. The night wears on and I stare at looming towers above. So much empty real estate. So many empty apartments. So many unused resources. Such a crazy, savage world.

Tonight I'm going to find a million dollar apartment in the Ritz, climb into in a king bed and sleep well for the first time in days. Tomorrow our work begins.

Twelve

Ten days later I'm on the roof of the US Bank Tower, inspecting the northern horizon with binoculars. Experimentally I raise and lower the glasses a few times and decide I see better without them. Another side effect of the Hyper Virus; I'm a predator and I have excellent eyesight. "How far away is Rosamond?"

Mason McHale is on the roof too. He is my age. Tall. Dark hair. Dark eyes. Hispanic, like me, but nature built ethnicity more prominently into his features than is evident in mine. Tattoos gleam dully on his hands. He wouldn't be attractive, a little too brutish around the eyes, except for his confidence and perpetual smile. Our hastily cobbled-together society is a whirlwind and he's taken on a team of Variants to act as our provisional police force until we establish a permanent one. He says, "Dunno. Eighty miles?"

"If the smoke rises high enough then we might see it over the mountains." I keep staring. Of all the tragedies befalling our country, this one hits close. The small city of Rosamond was wiped off the earth yesterday. Unfortunate enough to be the battleground between Herders and berserk mutants, Rosamond's gas supply caught fire and *poof*. The town burned down. "We should send trucks. Trucks to pick up the Rosamond survivors and bring them here."

"Should I go? I'll take the Falcons."

"The who?"

"The Falcons," he repeats, with a hint of sheepishness. "That's what I've decided to call my team."

"Why?"

"I like the term."

"Why a falcon?"

"I don't know, Queen Carmine. Don't you like it?"

"You and your Falcons stay here. We have too much to do. But scrounge up a team of volunteers. Send that new guy, what's his name? The Priest. Put him to good use."

"Why do they call him the Priest?"

"No idea. Seems like everyone's got a weird title now. Like the Falcons," I say.

Mason examines his boots.

I say, "He seems eager to help and he has plenty of followers. I don't care what they call him."

"Yes Queen Carmine."

"Stop referring to me as Queen," I snap, but he's gone. With his enhanced body he'll bound down the thousand feet of stairs in only a couple minutes.

I should be able to also, but I can't. I'm still unaccustomed to this skin and often I stumble around like newborn Bambi. If I attempt descending the staircase like Mason, I'll fall most the way.

I raise the binoculars (out of habit) and sweep Los Angeles again. More newcomers are trickling in on Interstate 5 and 10, cautiously venturing closer to see if the rumors are true: the Variants in Los Angeles have gone friendly.

I wouldn't say friendly. Not yet. They're still angry and suspicious (who can blame them?) but less hostile. The scary speculation about them is what keeps us safe from bands of armed looters and rogue military units. We'd win those fights but we're not ready. This part of California is dangerous but we're guarded by hearsay.

Guards. Guardians - I like that. I've been brainstorming termi-nology to use instead of mutants or Variants. Some expression to indicate the Variants living in Los Angeles are different. We're not wild animals, we're under control. You can trust us. You can trust the Guardians. Hmmm. That could work.

I absently run my hand over the short prickly hairs on my head as I think. Everyday I wish for my hair. Everyday I find myself wanting to check Instagram, like an itch I can't scratch because I don't know my name. Everyday I find myself missing...missing someone...

I've reconstructed the events in my mind as best I can from old articles and videos. A man named Martin Patterson (the Chemist) tried to harness the power of an extremely rare disease, creating the Variants here in Los Angeles. His lust for power and his insanity grew out of control and LA had to be abandoned. I was his final project, his pièce de résistance, finished at the end of Patterson's life.

Even more fascinating than his creations was the revelation that Martin Patterson had the disease himself, as did a tiny society of mutants living in secret for centuries. The military couldn't stop him so the secret society did. Patterson was killed in March, but by then there was an unmanageable number of new mutants, including some with powerful positions in the government. All went to hell and I woke up three months later. Alone.

And now the city's empty. It's almost an out-of-body experience, standing on the tower and surveying the city of angels and knowing I'm the makeshift governor. I don't want the job; I'll find some trustworthy grownups soon to put in charge. You handle the stuff like food and housing, and I'll handle the Variants, I'll say to the responsible adults. Assuming we find any who trust us.

Los Angeles is not exactly our playground, but it's close. There's too much work and no time to play, however, so I sling the glasses around my neck and hurry down the stairs. The trip takes fifteen minutes. A cleaning crew is clearing rubble and detritus from the first floor. I'm assigning jobs as fast as possible and giving the workers generic titles, like Cleaners or Cooks. Not original, but it's working. The Variants aren't stable enough to handle mundane tasks like cleaning so I send them out on longer and more strenuous missions.

I'm making this up as I go. There's no manual.

I exit the tower and Kayla falls in step beside me, like she'd been waiting. "Do you know what they're calling you?" she asks.

"Who?"

"Everyone on the outside. On the east coast."

"Why would they call me anything?"

"They're calling you the Warrior Queen," she says, and she's beaming. She's texting and walking and talking and smiling and bouncing, and everyone we pass stops to watch us.

"I don't understand how people know who I am."

"Are you kidding? The whole country is talking about the woman who tamed the mutants. That reporter is here documenting everything."

"What do you think about the term Guardians? Instead of mutants or Variants?"

"I *love* it!"

"Of course you do."

"The Warrior Queen and her Guardians are going to slay the evil Infected Walter! Can I tweet that?" she asks, and she's already typing into her phone.

"Absolutely not."

I'm learning on the fly. Especially about the two types of mutants.

The first group we simply call Variants. We weren't born with the disease. A transhumanist physician nicknamed the Chemist injected it into our veins during a secret surgery, trying to create metahumans. We also received stem cell transplants, gene therapy, and God knows what else. The Chemist *made* us. We were manufactured. Not natural. We surge through life with varying degrees of madness. I have to remind this group to brush their teeth. For whatever reason, I emerged from the coma stronger than most surgical patients, and more able to think clearly.

Second is the mysterious secret group. We call them the others, or Infected. They've been around for hundreds of years, living in shadow and secrecy. Walter is Infected, and there are only ten or fifteen like him alive. This small elite group was *born* with the Hyper Virus, an incredibly rare occurrence. Natural. Pure. Immensely strong. World breakers.

Their names are hallowed. Some of them are legend. The Outlaw. Shooter. Carter.

Some of them are villains, like Walter and the Chemist.

Some of them are unknown by the general public. Like Caleb and Nuts. And a girl named Blue-Eyes who has seduced the President, or so Kayla tells me. She's going to be trouble.

There's too much information and too many people to keep track, like I'm still trying to wake up from a dream, so I'm not even attempting to make sense of it all yet. Today we survive. That's what matters.

I say, "Kayla, remind me that we need to send Nuts more workers. He's securing our water supply and he needs extra hands. Some of the new arrivals are going to become Engineers."

"Yes Queen Carmine."

"Don't call me that."

I spend the afternoon helping move our belongings, of which there are few, into the Olympic tower. When the Chemist died he left behind warriors like Mason but also a support system of servants. They call themselves the Devotees (because everyone needs a title, apparently), and the Devotees have attached themselves to Nuts, and me, and Kayla, and anyone else they deem leadership material. Like butlers, essentially. Some were with the Chemist and his team for years. I can't make the Devotees stop waiting on me, so we're moving into the Olympic tower to appease them. That's where we belong, or so they say.

After the final load I find myself alone in the tower's dusty lobby. I'm twisting the top off a water bottle when I hear a heavy slam and then a muffled sob somewhere behind me. Curious, I force open a door marked 'Authorized Personnel Only' and explore deeper into the bowels of Olympic. At the back of the H/VAC room there's a woman cowering in a dark corner beside an unmarked door. "I'm sorry," she cries. "But the elevator don't work."

The woman is emaciated. She's suffering from malnutrition, her clothes are rags, and she smells awful, like gangrene. I crouch beside her and offer my water bottle. She gulps it down and I say, "Take your time. And then explain what's going on."

"He told us not to come up but we're down to two days half rations." She wipes her mouth with the back of her hand. "They sent me for help. Do you know where's Caleb?"

"Caleb? He left last week. What do you mean down to two days rations?"

"He left?" she gasps. "Well...who..." She starts to cry again. I pat her on the shoulder and debate running to fetch food. She asks, "Who is...I mean, I guess, I ought talk to someone. Someone in charge."

"You can tell me."

"Did Caleb leave you any...instructions? Like a message, like maybe from the Father?"

"No. What about?" I ask.

"About important secrets?"

"What's your name?"

"Heidi."

"Heidi, I'm confused but I want to help. You're starving. You need medical care. Where have you been? What is this special secret?"

"Is the Father really dead?"

"He's been dead for three months or more."

"You heard of the Inheritors?"

"No. Tell me."

"Maybe," Heidi says and she takes my hand. Like holding hands with a skeleton. I help her to her feet. "Maybe I best show you. Cause we're dying."

At Heidi's direction I open the heavy unmarked door. I'm struck by the smell of unwashed bodies as we proceed down a small staircase. Down into her world. She asks me questions but I can't answer. I'm too shocked to speak.

PART II

November, 2019

Here, on this mountain, I and my sons and my chosen friends shall build our new land and our fort. And it will become as the heart of the earth, lost and hidden at first, but beating, beating louder each day. And word of it will reach every corner of the earth. - *Anthem*. Ayn Rand.

One

In November, the sun rises at 6:25am. I am awake. From my vantage, the sun climbs between skyscrapers, rising over San Bernardino. Angry red chroma ricochets off windows.

I watch from inside the shattered 717 Olympic Tower. Once a modern residential high rise, now, like every other skyscraper, 717 Olympic bears gaping wounds, and so do many of its inhabitants. My corner bedroom is missing most of the northern and eastern walls, so essentially I live on a balcony, exposed to the tranquil southern California climate. I'm not inured to my view yet, the vast carpet of our abandoned city, still emptier now than at any time since the mid 1800s. A metropolis built to hold eighteen million now contains eighty thousand.

It is a haunting and heart-breaking sight. But it is my home. Eighty thousand is an amazing accomplishment considering our starting point six months ago.

Someone scuffs the carpet in the hallway outside my apartment. The door handle twists, so I step over the man sleeping on my floor, slip over the side and begin a descent of Olympic's exterior surface. I live on the twenty-second floor, but the high rise offers a surplus of handholds and landing spots. Unnoticed, I *Climb* down and drop on Figueroa Street four minutes later. Streets are still dark with shadow. Perfect. I don't want to be seen.

Only a few of the city's residents are up. Cooks shout and laugh in makeshift cafeterias scattered throughout Downtown. They'll have breakfast prepared by 6:30am for the Fishers, the Farmers, and the Shepherds. Early birds, all of them, selected for their profession based partly on sleep habits. The Cooks will have another meal prepared at 8am for the Engineers, the Scavengers, the Cleaners, and all the rest.

I move north, pulling the blue zip-up hoodie tight against the chill. The air is damp and cool and makes my joints ache. This early, the wide boulevards are mine alone. The once manicured planters now spill with overgrowth beside the streets.

Gardeners. We need more Gardeners. We put people to work the minute they take up residence here, and surely some of the incoming can use pruning sheers.

As I walk past the old Staples Center, home of the Lakers, Night Guardians begin their return from patrolling Koreatown, Glendale, Hollywood, and everywhere else within a two-hour walk. The Guardians don't trudge along the dusty road like I do. They *Leap* from rooftops, screaming like howler monkeys when their adrenaline reaches an unbearable level. Some of them haven't touched the earth all night, consuming as much as six thousand calories during their prowling. The Leapers jump distances over a hundred feet. They flit like red demons in the dawn, and they protect our borders.

I close my eyes and enjoy the effect their homeward migration has on my sensorium. I don't have to see the Guardians; I *feel* them. The herd passes overhead like a thunderstorm.

I've gradually convinced New Los Angeles to call them Guardians instead of Variants or mutants. Our Guardians are blessed in different ways. Some leap. Some are strong. Some climb. Some fight. Some are blessed mentally instead of physically. All are enhanced, but in different proportion. Our city has over four thousand. Because I'm here.

The Discipline Assembly doesn't begin until 10am. I arrive at the old Dodgers baseball stadium three hours early, so to kill time I tour Angelino Heights and Elysian Park. The pretty victorian houses here were the source of bitter arguments two months ago. Some of the rightful owners returned to LA and wanted to live in their own houses again, demanding the new residents vacate. I forget how the Courts ruled. Didn't care then. Don't care now.

I sit on a bench in Elysian Park and slap the dust off my cargo pants and Nikes. Only a small portion of New LA has been swept clean of concrete grime and rubble, so we toil constantly in a scrim of soot. The view of Downtown takes my breath away. The horizon is flat other than the stately tower cluster. Barely visible beyond, the horizon twinkles as sunlight begins glinting off Pacific waves. The firmament rises to eternity in a cloudless blue.

Another perfect day to swell our batteries with solar panels. Another frustrating day for rooftop rain-catchers and Farmers, who must now manually haul water to the top of buildings for their potted gardens.

"We live in paradise," I observe. No one hears me except the closest cow, belonging to a cattle herd which grazes here in Elysian. The park is big and grassy enough to support several dozen.

It's not paradise, though. It's a hive of rebels, working feverishly to create a self-sufficient society. We don't have much time. We reside in the eye of a storm, one which threatens to consume us any day.

My phone buzzes again. I have twenty unanswered texts. I reply, **I'm fine. Leave me alone, and I turn on airplane mode.**

I'm going to get an earful for that.

While I have the device out, I scan through saved Instagram photos. Hundreds of pics of me, in a prior life. Kayla figured out my identity months ago. I used to be a girl named Katie Lopez, but I don't recall taking these Instagram photos. Any picture saved during the previous three years lays beyond my powers of recollection.

Having a destroyed history is like staring into a black hole; memories get sucked away when I reach. Who *is* Katie Lopez? I remember her like I remember an old acquaintance. I force myself through dozens of smiling faces. I *should* know this. I *should* know these people. I feel phantom pain. Swirling emotions without foundation. Like walking through fog.

I turn off the phone as my fingers begin to tremble. The Chemist did this to me. Took my memory. It makes me furious. Deep breaths. Slow the pulse. I'll remember Katie one of these days.

Maybe.

The agitation requires ten minutes to subside, as always. Still an hour before the Assembly, so I wander to the makeshift market erected in the shade provided by the sprawling intersection of the old 101 and 110 interstates. Here Venders set up shop for ten hours a day, displaying the efforts of Scavengers and Farmers and Shepherds and

Crafters and Engineers. This particular market is known for beef. If you want fish then you need to visit a market closer to the ocean. If you want eggs, go anywhere. We have chickens galore, and eggs to spare. There are a dozen such markets scattered around New LA, and our populace can get any necessity here.

Our Kingdom is still new. Only half a year old. And so our system of commerce is still in infancy. Right now, in order to survive, we're all pulling on the same rope in the same direction. You work, you get to eat. That's our commerce. If you run out of food, visit a cafeteria. We're experimenting with digital currency, our very own Paypal. Like bitcoin. No one has physical money but we all have phones. So why not? (New LA doesn't possess an infinite supply of central electricity, but every home has an industrial battery or generator for phones.) The digital currency will be a disaster when it first launches next month, but then we'll tweak. Until then, we all share. It's very imperfect but it suffices. For now.

We're doing about as well as the rest of the planet, I suppose. Better than most.

Both the market patrons and Vendors are well dressed. Designer clothes everywhere I look. Los Angeles was evacuated in a hurry during November of 2018, leaving behind *billions* in retail merchandise and personal belongings. And we haven't scavenged even a third of the greater Los Angeles area yet.

I do my best to be invisible, even holding my breath, and I enter the marketplace. It's not a true marketplace yet. But it will be when we have currency. The Vendors have finished setting tables. Most patrons are Scavengers or Cleaners on their way to work. They take an apple or a wrapped parcel of beef, or browse for new gloves, and then ride off on bicycles. The mood is light-hearted and friendly. Fear of severe consequences prevents overt greed, and the absence of haggling keeps the transactions brisk. The Vendors simply make notes about who takes what, and the Vendor Overseer monitors the whole process.

"Back again, Stas?"

"You know it. Got any safety goggles today?"

"Fraid not. Maybe if you Scavengers would quit sitting on your asses all day."

"Hah! I work myself to the bone while you Vendors stand in the shade."

"Yeah but I gotta put up with ugly patrons like yourself."

"Fair enough."

"Make sure you get a cut of beef before you go. Strips of sirloin today."

I smile. Friendly conversations like this between the two men are the norm. It won't last forever, so I enjoy it while I can.

I don't want beef. I want fruit and veggies and chocolate, so I close the hood even tighter around my face and proceed. The nearest vegetable Vendor is an unhappy looking woman and she glowers when I select a baggie of red and green peppers. She grumbles, "Haven't seen you around before."

I shrug.

She continues, "You aren't circuiting, are you?"

It's a strong accusation. Some indolent drifters try to visit all the markets and build a surplus without doing work. They make a circuit every day. When caught, they spend the subsequent month working to exhaustion as penance.

"No ma'am," I answer, but she reaches for my wrist. I smack her hand away. Her breath catches and she peers hard at me. The adjacent Vendor notices. I don't want attention. I just wanted peppers. But now I'm annoyed. I take several more baggies of food.

"Hey! Maybe I should call the Law Keepers, little thief!"

Now everyone is staring at us. I stride purposefully toward the small knot of children waiting outside the market. I drop food bags into their eager hands, and glare at the shrewish Vendor. "No one goes hungry. The food does not belong to you. We all work. We all eat."

If we have one law, that's it. She makes no rebuttal.

I say, "And do not hassle our Workers. Or you might be assigned to a different job, one more suited to your personality." I storm off, and the market place stares after me.

That was not ideal.

～

Dodgers Stadium can hold 56,000 screaming fans. Today about two hundred will gather to witness the Discipline Assembly. Fifty members of the audience are on the Court, men and women chosen for their good judgement. They are here to witness and vote. The rest are idle Workers, choosing to spend their day off watching the Assembly.

Seven Variants sit over the visitor dugout. The rest of those in attendance provide them a wide berth and stare. Variants are fascinating—sometimes unstable, enormously strong. They eat a *lot,* much more than normal New LA citizens. We have enough to eat, but not much extra. We're a trim and hard city by necessity.

I sit by myself, hidden in a hood. At 10am sharp, the Assembly begins.

Law Keepers brandishing firearms march five prisoners to the pitcher's mound and force them to kneel. The prisoners are big, proud men, ex-military, probably special ops. They kneel, erect with defiance, and they glare.

A man solemnly approaches the pitcher's mound. He is young, maybe thirty, tan, wearing expensive clothes, and his hair is stylishly swept to the side, glistening with gel. I don't know his real name. He's a globally recognized figure known as the Priest, famous from the old world.

The Priest presses a button on his handheld mic and several speakers begin humming. He's either using a gas-powered generator, or he requested Engineers temporarily route electricity to the stadium from our grid. His voice booms too loudly, "We are gathered today to levy sentencing on the guilty. These five were found to be illegal Herders and operating against our Kingdom."

One of the kneeling men, their commanding officer, begins shouting. He receives a crisp blow to the back of his skull and his words cease.

A single Variant (or Guardian, that is) is more than a match for ten unarmed Herders at a time. Maybe twenty. But Herders are big game hunters, employing expensive and advanced electroshock weapons which can only be described as barbaric. And effective.

The Priest continues in a theatrical tone, "These five were discovered in Pasadena, using the Rose Bowl as their base of operations. I personally took the Variants' testimony of the apprehension. Seven of our own were discovered drugged and immobilized within Herder custody. Also discovered were electroshock weapons, and I identified severe electrical burns on the released prisoners. When presented with these facts yesterday, our Courts found them guilty."

The seven Guardians sitting on the dugout begin growling. It is their kind that were captured and tortured in hopes of a large reward. The Priest is calling them Variant instead of Guardians. Whatever. The Assembly would run more smoothly if the mutants weren't here. He should have sent them away.

"Today the gathered Court will vote on sentencing, and witness it's immediate administration."

The Priest is the Law Keeper Overseer, a lofty position and one he lobbied for extensively. His appointment was a controversial one.

One of the Guardians can contain himself no longer. He stands and roars in a voice too loud for a human, "Give the bastards to us! They want to fight? Let them be satisfied!"

The other six Guardians join in. They scream and howl. They are creatures of incredible strength and speed, operating within a constant state of fight-or-flight, riding oceans of adrenaline. The Priest blanches at the show of emotion and his words falter. He is a proud man, an intelligent and persuasive leader, and often he dismisses the Guardians as mere muscle, simple implements incapable of judgement. But all his savvy and bravado vanish when face-to-face with angry and insane mutants. This is one reason for the controversy — he cannot control the Guardians, especially when they're angry.

This isn't going well.

The Priest stammers, "The decision is up to the Court. And

myself. After much deliberation, I present the following judgement for the Court's vote; that the guilty men be sentenced to two months hard labor, working to clear rubble from the underground tunnels."

Our Guardians are instantly displeased. I don't blame them. It's the wrong judgement. Look at the five guilty faces; they smirk in victory. The Priest should now present another option so the Court can vote between two judgements, but he doesn't. He carries on over the protests, essentially providing them only a single choice. The vote is meaningless.

I'm growing more and more aggravated. The Priest wants trophies. He wants our populace to see the prisoners working and to take credit for their humiliation.

He makes a final mistake. He allows the lead Herder to speak to the Court. Absurd. The man's already been found guilty. The big ex-military soldier snatches the microphone from the Priest's hands. I groan and lower my forehead into my hands. So stupid.

The man snarls, "So you vote on our judgement? You are scared and homeless and I don't begrudge you the efforts you take towards survival out here in California. I honor you for your hard, dusty work. But do you begrudge me? The rest of America is being decimated by these...animals. You call them, what? Guardians? We call them mutants. Freaks! My wife and my children and my whole neighborhood were torn apart by these mutants. I do not lie to you. Search the internet and you'll find the stories."

The Priest makes an attempt to get the mic back, but the man dismisses him. His thick muscles bulge as he twists to look at all his accusers. "You judge us? We are officially licensed by the federal government to subdue mutants. We don't kill them. We incarcerate them, and one day we we'll find a cure. Our actions are legal! Let me present you with another option to vote on; release us. Like you, we're doing our best to survive. To keep America upright. We are innocent, guilty only of following orders. Let us go, as you lawfully should."

He tosses the mic back to the Priest, who fumbles it. I scan faces in the audience and I'm dismayed to see they appear indecisive. The Guardians are now on their feet, and there's going to be violence.

"Okay...well," the Priest stammers, "for the sake of democracy and fairness, I suppose, I will allow you to vote between my proposal and the suggestion presented by the guilty."

The seven Guardians rage. Two of them, both males, hop onto the dirt infield from the Dodgers' dugout roof. Law Keepers raise weapons protectively. This is a disaster.

"*Enough!*" I roar the word without thinking. All eyes swing my way. I *Jump* from row E and land halfway between first and second base, causing concentric circles of dust to spread like a shockwave. The crowd silences. I'm so mad I tremble and can barely see straight.

Through the fog of anger, I hear whispers.

The Queen is here!

Two

"Get back!" I shout at the two Guardians near the dugout. They obey, scrambling to stand with their comrades, away from my wrath. "Judgement will be decided by those charged with such tasks. All Guardians are ordered out of the Stadium. At once." My voice echoes and caroms around the arena.

They are Variants, infernos of brute force, but so am I and my strength dwarfs theirs, and my anger burns so bright they can't look directly at me. The mutants don't argue; they flee like gazelles running from a tigress. I am their Alpha.

My blood is churning and it causes my body to harden. I'm frightening when furious; I see it in their averted eyes. The five guilty men flinch like they're being struck with whips as I speak. "You are *innocent*? Your license gives you the right to detain the reckless and the dangerous. Not innocent and peaceful Guardians, like those we found in your custody. You're innocent? Your prisoners bear scars of abuse and torture. You're innocent? We found illegal weapons in your possession. And furthermore, you are not in America. You're in the Kingdom, *my* Kingdom, and we no longer recognize the laws of America."

The Priest clears his throat into the mic and says, "Carmine, my Queen, if-"

I snatch his microphone and squeeze it in my fist, and it bends and melts into a hot clump of useless metal. I want to *Throw* him from the stadium, but instead I address the Court. "You will vote on judgement and I will abide by the Court's decision. But first, let me present an option that the Priest did not: immediate death for the Herders."

My stomach twists and heaves at my own words, but I carry on. I grab the hair of a Herder hiding in the back and tilt his face up. "Do you recognize this one? I do. We caught him three months ago, and foolishly we released him. These are rogue Herders, outside the laws of their own country, and they prey on us. They aren't going to stop. They'll keep returning. They'll keep using their awful inventions to hurt us. And if we make them work, they'll discover means to escape.

"Our lives here are hard. We survive through blood and sweat, and we barely keep nature from consuming us. In the Kingdom, if you don't work then you don't eat. That's how we live. There is no room for pity. Certainly not undeserved pity. Make no mistake. We have enemies who seek to crush us, and these men are their tools. Their forerunners.

"The Priest proposes we make them work. We sentence our *own* to hard labor. These men are not our own. They came uninvited into our land and began capturing and torturing us. Perhaps one day we'll be strong and stable enough to extend mercy. Today we are not. These Herders are cruel men and repeat offenders. They are violent and proud and evil, and deserving of death.

"Vote how you will. Labor or death, and the will of the Court shall rule."

I finish. The Court gathers to discuss. The Priest is furious but dares not show it. I usurped his power. I am not a Queen, no matter what they call me. I share power, rejecting full control, but I'm also fuming and he knows better than to test me at the moment. They'll vote for my proposal; I am a very popular leader in New Los Angeles.

The Court returns the verdict: death. By unanimous decision. We used the death penalty twice before, both for repeat violent crimes. These are savage times. And we're at war in a savage world. And I am SICK of these Herders sneaking into our land. My land.

Camera phones are produced. I was counting on it.

I carry out the sentence myself, immediately, before the guilty Herders can react. I *Move* like lightning and my fingernails are razors, and I open their jugulars. It's messy, but simple and effective. And it's already over.

My hands drip. I don't hide that from the cameras. I want this seen around the globe. The message must get across...

Savage times. And I'm the scariest. And you don't mess with my family.

The Assembly concludes. I find the nearest bathroom, a dark communal lavatory with no plumbing, lock the door, and I vomit into the dry commode. Over and over. And then I cry for the next hour, great shuddering sobs, wiping tears with red hands.

In November of 2018, there were 320 million Americans living in the United States. Today, one year later, there are 295 million. Population researchers predict in the next twelve months we will drop to 260, for a variety of reasons.

First, parents quit making babies. It's too uncertain a world to bring a child into.

Second, due to upheaval, the time, effort, and resources required to unnaturally prolong life with modern medicine are no longer available. Natural causes are taking their toll on the population, an unexpected and ignoble end to the Baby Boomers.

Third, fifty million Americans have been displaced, fleeing from horrors, and another hundred million are voluntarily relocating, and many move to Canada.

Fourth, rampaging mutants.

Fifth and finally, America is in the midst of a civil war. The government and military broke neatly in half, aligning itself with either the federal government (still run by the President and a powerful Variant named Blue-Eyes) or the Resistance (led by a powerful group of military leaders with vast underground support). So far the skirmishes are over territory and resources, and the loss of life isn't devastating. But that will change soon.

In summary, 2018-19 have been nightmare years for our formerly great nation. And I refuse to allow Herders make it worse for our small corner of the world.

Word spreads and a crowd gathers outside Dodgers Stadium. I don't want to face a swarm of admirers so I slip unnoticed over the wall in left field, and I return to the towers with my hood cinched tight, dodging bicycles and the occasional truck. I'm not popular because I'm social; I'm popular because I'm effective. I move quickly and make zero eye contact. After the awful Assembly the last thing I want is to talk. A good book. That's what I need. A book and a nap and chocolate and peace and no disease.

My day is too full to entertain luxuries, however. I need a change of clothes and a bite to eat. I gave my food to those children, so I'm starving. I sneak unnoticed through a small crowd of Workers on the patio and enter my building.

Kayla and Dalton wait for me in the dusty lobby of the 717 Olympic. Dalton is my self-appointed bodyguard. He is a huge, bald, black man, former Navy SEAL. And he hates it when I sneak out.

Kayla's fists are on her hips and she shakes her head at me. Kayla's virus manifested differently than mine; instead of possessing freakish strength, she is statuesque and beautiful and irrepressibly energetic, able to persuade and influence others, and she has a perfect memory. My gifts are less elegant and more brutish.

"My Queen," she scolds, "You did it again."

"That is not my name, Kayla."

"Carmine. Your stunt is going viral." She falls in step with me and I breathe her scent. The disease provides her with a pleasant fragrance, like Mother Nature giving flowers the ability to attract bees. It doesn't matter how she dresses, men can't help but stare. Today she wears designer jeans and a silky white scoop neck, probably once valued in the thousands.

We stop at the bank of elevators. The elevator Worker asks, "The 22nd floor, my Queen?"

I ignore him. "The world is ossifying, Kayla. How on earth can videos still go viral? I mean, I know Nuts has our cell tower plugged into the Resistance network. But...the rest of it?"

Kayla says, "Information is cheap. And yes please, the 22nd floor."

The Worker speaks into a radio and we wait as his collaborators scurry in the floors above. The lift doesn't use electricity. It relies on counter balanced weight provided by human bodies. It's rudimentary but effective; we have plenty of manpower. His radio squawks and he says, "Ready, Miss Carmine."

Kayla, Dalton and I board the lift and slowly rise up the dark shaft. The walls and ceiling of our elevator car were removed for efficiency purposes and soon we see the counter-balance car passing us on its way down to the lobby. Six Workers smile from inside. Kayla smiles and waves back. Her vitality is limitless. She says, "We need to issue a statement, addressing the public execution today."

Kayla is our Minister of Communication, New LA's ambassador to the outside world. Watching her, a spunky nineteen-year-old, negotiate with stodgy old men and women is a source of great joy for me. I say, "The execution was warranted and humane. The Herders trespassed, captured, and tortured our Guardians, and so they were eliminated and the same fate awaits future intruders. Tell the world *that*."

Dalton grunts his approval. "Damn straight."

"Do you want to be interviewed by the New York Times? They're asking again."

"Newspapers still circulate?"

"Some do. On the east coast, of course."

"No. I do not want to be interviewed by the New York Times."

"How about Fox News?"

"No."

"How about—"

"Noooooo. Thank you."

Kayla lays her hand on my shoulder and squeezes. "I know the execution was hard on you, Carmine."

"Get your hand off me or I'll bite your finger."

"Our Kingdom is fortunate to have a leader who shoulders the awful duties and absorbs the agony."

"Stop it."

"And I appreciate you." She beams and it's like being hit with direct sunlight.

I bite her finger and she squeaks in pain.

Cleaners are scrubbing walls and using Bissell Sweepers on the

22nd floor. Dust removal never ends because electric air filters are off and windows are open. The 22nd floor belongs to me and Kayla and Dalton and a reporter named Teresa Triplett. The 23rd and 24th floors house Overseers. General Brown and our military commanders live on the 25th, although they have secondary quarters in the barracks with their troops. The 26th floor is the War Department. The 27th and 28th floors are unusable. Kayla's dog, a little pug named Princess, waddles out of her door and snorts.

I say, "Do me a favor. Tell the market Overseer that an old grouchy woman is harassing patrons near Dodgers stadium."

"Yes Carmine." Kayla immediately begins typing into her phone.

We enter my apartment. Dalton remains outside, arms crossed. Princess sits in the hallway and stares at him. My Devotee greets us with towels. My Devotee is a big, beefy man assigned to fulfill my every wish. Devotees are a residual part of the Chemist's infrastructure, intended to free Variants from mundane responsibilities. I reject the Chemist and his ways, but having Devotees is a tremendous help. Kayla and Mason (the leader of the Falcons) and Nuts (the genius who keeps everything running) and a few others all have Devotees. Mine wears a robe (he insists), cooks for me, keeps my clothing clean, maintains the apartment, sleeps on the floor in my bedroom, and considers it an honor to worship me. Very helpful, but also a little weird.

I growl, "Also, schedule a private meeting with the Priest. Soon." Kayla's not really my assistant but she often assumes that role.

"He's being an irritant again, I assume?"

"He still exists. So yes." I wipe dust from my eyes and ears with the wet towel. The dark-haired Devotee enters with an iPad and I say, "Go."

The Devotee reads from the iPad. "Yes Miss Carmine. You have class with Littles at one. You're meeting with settlers in Santa Monica at three. You're inspecting the southern barracks afterwards. And Nuts wants to show you the filtration plant today, if you have time."

Kayla chirps, "A slow day. Yay!"

"Tell Nuts I'll see his filtration plant some other time."

"Yes Miss Carmine."

I ask, "What is the Governess doing today?"

Kayla shrugs. Her sweet fragrance is subtly saturating the apartment. We might as well be standing in a field of wild flowers, and my Devotee is clearly trying not to watch her. "Doing what she always does. Keeping this place running."

"Any Cheerleader sightings yesterday?"

"I don't know." Her face pales; Kayla is petrified of the the Cheerleader, nicknamed the Fire Girl. She's a Variant who lives around here, a special project of the Chemist's, driven completely insane. From what I hear, even the mighty Infected tread lightly around her. I've never met her, and consider her something of an urban legend. "Would you like me to find her? General Brown might know."

"No. It's fine. Only curious."

"The Priest texted. He asks if you can meet some other day?"

I bite down a snarl and pull out my phone. **Priest, if I have to come find you, you won't like it. 2:30.**

That guy infuriates me.

"Carmine..." Kayla takes my hand and holds it up so we're both looking at it. "Wash your hands, sweetie. This blood is super icky."

"Yuck," I agree. Herder blood.

The Devotee asks, "Miss Carmine, would you care for food?"

I move into my bedroom and answer over my shoulder, "Chocolate. And whatever fruit we have."

My apartment used to be a luxurious space. Two bedrooms, a full kitchen, a living room and dining room, two bathrooms, and lavish furniture. I care for none of it. Now the rooms are cluttered and muddy because I don't let the Cleaners in. I wash my hands as Kayla reads headlines. I partially listen to her news report, and partially wonder how Nuts keeps water running on the 22nd floor of a high rise. The water stains red before draining from the basin. I ask, "Any articles about us?"

She replies, "Not that I see."

I grunt in satisfaction. New Los Angeles is no longer daily news. I used to spot planes and drones circling the sky, but they vanished a month ago. Citizens beyond our borders are fascinated with the Kingdom, but the armies, full of their own trouble, have forgotten us. Maybe we'll survive yet.

Kayla helps me out of the hoodie. "You're in pain. I'll fetch your ribbons."

I undress down to my Under Armour stretch underwear and jogging bra, and examine what I see in the full-length mirror. This is a daily routine, an effort to remember.

My history remains mist and shadow. Periodically I remember distant names and faces, but of myself and my friends and family there is nothing. Katie Lopez is like a childhood story I half-remember, events which happened to someone else. There are swirls of emotion, though, sometimes so intense I can't breathe.

Photos of Katie are taped to the edges of my mirror. She was a beautiful Hispanic girl, happy and innocent judging by the pictures. She had long thick hair, deep brown eyes, and she was soft like pretty girls often are. I would have enjoyed being her.

The girl I see in the mirror now, Carmine, is different. I'm comprised of sharper edges. Stronger, harder, and leaner. My eyes changed to a green hazel. The beautiful brown hair was shaved off for surgery sometime in February. Now I keep the sides short and the top is a tangle that doesn't reach my eyes yet.

Kayla returns and says, "Stop frowning, Carmine. You are lovely. I'd kill to have those abs. Or legs."

I wipe my eyes and shake off the panic which threatens to return whenever I probe my lack of memories. "My hair is growing too slowly."

"You demand too much from yourself, even from your hair."

"I wonder if she'd like me." I pull on black leggings and a tight black tank-top.

"Who?"

"Katie Lopez."

"You *are* Katie Lopez," she smiles to herself. "Just an enhanced version. Arms out."

I stretch my arms and Kayla begins wrapping my wrists and

elbows and ankles and knees with red strips of silk. My joints ache, probably from the surgery and the subsequent growth spurt, and I've discovered that compression helps. Previously I wore thick braces but Kayla protested it made me look brutish and un-ladylike. So now she wraps my joints with layers of red silk, covering much of my forearms and calves, a tight sash for a belt, and even binds my chest with the material. My Devotee comes to help and when they finish I am in much less discomfort. The cool material compresses and secures the aches.

"There," Kayla remarks with pride. "I just love this outfit."

My Devotee agrees, "Very sexy, Miss Carmine."

"It's dramatic. Bold. Fitting for the most dangerous woman on earth."

"It's comfortable," I sigh with my eyes closed. "That's what matters."

. "Can I take a picture of you? For public relation purposes? You look pretty and striking, and it'll help erase mental images of your bloody hands. Please?"

"Under no circumstances." I don't like the way they're examining my body so I pull on a vest too. "I mean it, Kayla."

"Too late. Just did. And you already have six hundred Likes!"

- Three -

80,000 people live in our Kingdom. 9,500 of them are under ten years old, so we're establishing schools and putting Teachers to work. Children attend school two days, work with their parents or guardians one day, and get a day to rest and play. Then repeat.

Again, not perfect. But it's effective. School systems have shut down in other parts of the world, terrified citizens hoping the government will solve their problems and refusing to budge until that occurs. Not here. Here we work. Hard.

Dalton (my angry Navy SEAL bodyguard) and I walk to the Ninth Street Elementary School, a boxy and colorful campus. As usual, we accumulate a following en route. We arrive at the school with an entourage over a hundred strong and Dalton is agitated. I can't have a conversation with a hundred people, so I raise my fist and say, "Stay with me! Stay together! Stay alive!"

It's my common and well-known obeisance to the people of New LA, and they return the salute as one.

I visit schools twice a week and read stories. Students anticipate Story Hour weeks in advance, and compete for the privilege of summarizing previous books for me. Today I perch on a wooden stool in a stuffy cafeteria and face one hundred and fifty students between the ages of four and seven. I read two *Junie B Jones* books to a captive audience which laughs in the right places. I wonder how thoroughly teachers coached the kids on proper etiquette but even if the polite attention is artificial I don't care. It's bliss; a simple story solved in twenty-five minutes. How perfect.

Afterwards I get group hugs, and I praise the teachers until Dalton waves for my attention. Time to go.

The mob outside Ninth Street Elementary has swelled to two hundred. Men and women. Old and young. Black and white and every other beautiful shade. Mixed in with the mass are a handful of mutants; Guardians I detect but can't pinpoint. Dalton rolls his eyes and pushes us through.

Dalton isn't genetically modified. He would die quickly against a mutant. I pointed this out months ago and he said, "I killed Variants once. In a tower. Before you came along. And I'll do it again if I have to." He told me he wouldn't use his pistol; he'd drop grenades. I'm glad he's on my side. As always, today he's wearing a tight red t-shirt, bulging at the biceps, and a shoulder holster.

Most of our followers are in their twenties. Seventy percent of our population is older than eighteen and younger than thirty. Millennials like me. Disgusted with the government, willing to experiment, try something new, take risks, take a chance on our Kingdom, take a chance on the Guardians. On me. Their safety rests on my shoulders like a yoke, and I bear their hopes and fears every day.

Stay with me. Stay alive. Easier said than done. I hope I'm strong enough. Deep breath. Another. I can do this.

We pass a market on the way home, tables full of scavenged goods. One table catches my eye and I stop the entire procession to peruse a collection of books.

"We don't have time for this," Dalton mutters in my ear.

"Text the Priest. Tell him we're running late."

He curses. Dalton hates texting.

I say, "Do you read fiction?"

"I do not."

"Here." I push a Baldacci book into his hands. "It's about war and masculine absurdity and stuff like that. Read it and report."

He curses again, and I spend a few more minutes browsing. Somehow I've picked up a dusty hardback. I didn't mean to. I read the title, "*Cinder.*" A young adult book, kinda girly, not really my style. But. I keep it. Maybe Katie Lopez liked this stuff.

I also select a book on government and a book by John Maxwell on leadership. The awestruck Vendor silently accepts my thanks and I stuff the books into my backpack.

~

The War Department sprawls across the entire 26th floor. It's the one area in the building we allow a constant electrical consumption. Our Techs installed servers and satellites and cable access and computers and televisions and radio antennas and everything else we need to coordinate with the outside world.

The Priest waits for me there, staring at the Maps, hands clasped behind his back. Projected onto several walls are the entire North American continent, America, America's southwest, and our city.

The Great Migration is still underway. Millions flee the increasingly totalitarian, militaristic government. Millions more flee towards the stability and safety it provides. Not since the Civil War have lines been this clearly demarcated.

"So much chaos. A hypocritical nation reaping what it sowed," the Priest mumbles, staring at America. Or what used to be America. Now it's a segmented mess.

The Federal Governments still controls the entire eastern coast, Florida to Maine. The people hide behind their military, spooked and fascinated by the Variants, unaware the strongest of them all hides in the Oval Office.

A maniac named Walter and his band of two thousand Variants and ranks of gunmen rule Oregon, Washington, and Idaho, the northwest corner of America.

New LA, our Kingdom, is sixty miles long and thirty miles deep, from San Fernando to Irvine. Downtown Los Angeles is our capitol. 1,800 square miles along the Pacific Ocean, a little larger than Rhode Island.

The Resistance (military opposing the federal government) is strong in Arizona, New Mexico, Texas, Colorado, Utah, and Oklahoma.

The middle of America (Wyoming, Nebraska, Kansas, Iowa, Illinois, Michigan, etc) is essentially under martial law, the metropolises and localities surviving on their own, building fences and checkpoints as rapidly as possible. Food and water sources are tightly guarded. Semi-trucks travel with armed guards.

A modern day Wild West.

It's not the Apocalypse. But it still could be. The United States, fractured and burning, no longer exists as a single entity. The survivors aren't broken but they're shaken.

I'm not satisfied yet; I've got my eye on San Diego and Santa Barbara, which have both emptied and given control over to renegades. Fine with me. If the residents want to forfeit their resources then I'll recapture the cities from the lawless brigands and turn the land into safe sanctuaries. The people think they'll find safety East, but they only find wars.

"We will survive the chaos. We won't fail." My voice sounds loud in the dark quiet room. The Techs are pointedly staring away from us.

"Admirable confidence, Queen. What makes you so sure?"

"Because, Priest, I *can't* fail. I won't fail these people." I'm frustrated and hissing at him between my clenched teeth. "The price of failure isn't death. It's captivity. It's servitude. For all the Guardians, and all these people. No one is taking New LA from me."

"From you?"

"From me. From us."

"Perhaps if I took a greater role in the management—"

"You weren't summoned here for a promotion, Priest. This is a warning."

"Carmine," he smiles with the look of a patient father. "Let's be reasonable."

"I gave you a position of power because-"

"You *gave* me? I was under the impression New LA was ruled by a three person Council. You, the Governess, and General Brown. And the Council appointed me."

"Interrupt me again and I will dangle you out the window," I snarl. My pulse pounds in my ears. The people follow him because of his supreme confidence, charisma, and conviction. But right now it's just smugness. God help me if I ever come across this way. "I gave you the Overseer position because you brought so many of your followers into our Kingdom. I thought you must be a capable leader."

"Likewise, my Queen."

"But I'm starting to think maybe you had followers because you were simply the craziest patient in the asylum. Understand?"

He makes no response, other than smiling with his hands clasped.

"You made too many mistakes. You don't get to make decisions. We have the Court for that. Your pathetic show in the Assembly today was an example of how *not* to lead. One more misstep and I will personally drive you to our boundary and leave you in the wild."

No response.

"Understand, Priest?"

"You are wise, Carmine, and I will do my best to accommodate your preferences."

I twitch. I am so close to hurling him from the tower. He is a cancer. A weak link. If I was stronger, if I was a better leader, I'd remove him now. But removing him would cause ripples. Ripples we can't afford yet. "Get out."

"I'm returning to duty," he responds as though he hadn't been given a direct order. "Please alert me if you need anything else."

I slam the door behind him so hard it cracks. The Techs jump in their chairs. I hear Dalton's voice in the hall, "We need another damn door. That's the third one this month."

Dalton, Kayla and I leave Downtown on the Ten in a Toyota Land Cruiser. I drive. I always drive, and I can hear my bodyguard Dalton grinding his teeth. He hates riding shotgun. We head west on an interstate mostly cleared of abandoned vehicles. A second SUV full of Law Keepers trails behind, and a third and fourth SUV bring up the rear, hauling supplies.

Law Keepers are our police. They don't have the disease. They aren't modified. But they're former military or law enforcement, and I trust them with firearms. Usually I travel with Mason and his Falcons, an elite squad of trustworthy Guardians, but they are scouting problem spots in south LA today.

We pass thousands of empty houses. Hundreds of vacant office buildings. A mind-boggling surplus of riches. Dalton and I are brain-storming solutions to the growing population of severely mentally ill when Kayla gasps from the backseat. "Whoa! Big news!" she cries.

"What?"

"*Walter* emailed me!"

I nearly crash. There is only one Walter. Born with the disease, bent on burning the world. I control the majority share of the Variants, and he has much of the rest. Walter is the biggest threat to our existence. Intelligence reports indicate the President of the United States (and his Variant mistress) funnel money and supplies to him, bankrolling our destruction. They want to rule the world, and I stand in their way.

"What's Walter want?" I growl.

"He demands a parlay with you. And he's almost here."

Dalton asks, "Almost here? He coming by plane?"

"Train. He arrives at San Fransisco tomorrow and will wait for an escort before continuing south to the station near UCLA."

I muse, "I'm surprised the lines are clear."

"I think a train ride sounds romantic," says Kayla.

"This smells like a trap," Dalton growls.

"How many are with him?"

"He's alone," Kayla replies. "Do you want to meet?"

Gears in my mind begin churning. "He wants to parlay. What about?"

"He doesn't say. Maybe to apologize for being so awful and mean?"

"I'll meet him. Call General Brown. And the Governess. The advanced warning gives us an advantage. Do you have photographs?"

"Not yet. Searching."

Why would he do this? Walter coming alone. It makes no sense. I muse, "We could destroy the train. He's committing suicide."

Dalton says, "Maybe he knows you. Knows you don't operate like that."

My hands tighten on the wheel. "Or maybe he can't be killed that easily. Contact Mason. Tell him I want his group of Falcons on standby when the train pulls in. If they sense a trap, they are to demolish it."

I don't know why Mason chose the name Falcons for his squad but somehow it works for him. He can call his team whatever he wants; the citizens love them and the Variants all want to be a part of his elite group. They're good.

"Understood."

He begins murmuring into his phone, and I ask Kayla, "How do you know Walter's alone?"

"I heard from several sources."

"Who?"

"Just people."

I glance into the rear view mirror. She said it too quickly. Kayla is blushing and staring hard out the window.

I grin. "Is PuckDaddy your source?"

Her patina deepens and she can't fight her smile. "Maybe."

PuckDaddy is the world's most influential internet presence. He is a mysterious and powerful hacker, a god among the cyber community, and powerful ally of the Resistance. Most men who meet Kayla want to marry her, and all the while she crushes on a man she's never met.

"Did you stay awake all night talking with him?"

"No boy is worth talking to all night, Carmine. You taught me that."

"Atta girl. But. Did you?"

"No!" she squeaks. "We don't even text. He sends me messages in chat rooms and on bulletin boards. It's like a game for him, leaving me clues." She is smiling big and beautiful, and her pleasant scent radiates more strongly, like her pores open when she's happy. Even stoic Dalton notices.

I say, "You need to get control of yourself."

"I know!" She shakes her head and rubs her eyes. "I don't know why I'm so into him."

"When is the last time you slept?"

"Couple days ago. I'm not tired yet." Kayla works all night, participating in hundreds of online communities, maintaining a thousand relationships. She's our Minister of Communication but in essence she's a spy. A constant source of knowledge.

Dalton is still watching her in the mirror, unable to resist. When Kayla is smiling and happy she is truly an astonishing sight.

What a mess we are.

"You know—" I start but suddenly I slam the breaks, tossing Kayla and Dalton forward into their restraints. The Land Cruiser leaves a trail of rubber across two lanes. I leap from the vehicle and rush to the barrier. The SUV behind nearly hits me. "There!"

Dalton rushes up, an assault rifle pinned to his shoulder. "What? Where?" Law Keepers pour from the SUV, weapons drawn.

North of the interstate is Memorial, a public park. Sitting in the middle of an overgrown baseball outfield is a tiger. An enormous animal ripping meat off freshly caught prey. My heart pounds with excitement. "Look how big. Look how royal."

"Jesus," Dalton says, glaring through his tactical scope. "That's a big sucker."

Kayla whispers, "I've never been this close."

"Can you smell her?" I ask. The heady, earthy scent of the animal fills my nostrils. "She smells like...muscle and might. And freedom."

The tiger notices us but she's apathetic. We're a hundred yards away and she's gorging herself.

Kayla's nose wrinkles. "What is that she's eating?"

Dalton grumbles, "Probably a large dog. Should we take her out?"

"Take her out?"

He pats the assault rifle's barrel with his left hand. "Eliminate the threat."

"I don't think you could," I grin, nearly delirious with delight. Rumors are, there's two tigers, though I've never seen them together. "She's as big as a rhino. Three times larger than normal, I think. And if you try and fail, she might be up here with us very quickly."

A Law Keeper comments, "How the heck did it get so big?"

I answer, "It underwent the same surgery as the mutants. Has the same modifications. The same disease. Same as me."

The man whistles. "That Chemist was one freaky dude."

Another Law Keeper clears his throat. "So, does this...does this mean the Cheerleader is nearby?"

Kayla echoes, "That's right! She's friends with the tigers, yes? Maybe we should go."

"Just a rumor," Dalton chuckles. "Ain't no way the Cheerleader girl hangs out with tigers."

It's not a rumor. Watching the beautiful animal, I know it's not. I want to stay with her too. The tiger is like me, living how I wish I could live. Free and wild.

"She's here," I whisper. Our group goes silent. "The Cheerleader. I can...feel her. She's not far. Something in the breeze."

"Oh damn," Dalton grunts. "Let's go then."

Everyone hurries to their vehicles. Everyone but me. I watch a few moments more.

I drive to the Santa Monica Pier, parking in a lot beside the aquarium. A pod of five hundred survivalists has recently returned to Los Angeles, having decided this place is as good as any to set up camp. (The Governess estimates as many as two thousand a week are returning, and we convene with them all) I meet individually with this pod's leader, a lean and hard man named Peter who's lost most of his hair. He and his tribe have been through a lot of horrors and hunger in 2019, and he regards me with understandable skepticism and wariness. We chat and his defenses do not lower, but perhaps there is a spark of hope in his eyes.

I stand on the roof of the Land Cruiser and his band of survivors gather. Over their heads I see young children playing in sand and in the calm Pacific. Teenagers inspect the powerless Ferris wheel and the yellow West Roller Coaster.

I speak unnaturally loud, for shock and awe purposes. "Welcome to New Los Angeles. I am glad you've chosen to return. We all are. There is strength in numbers, and you are safe here. At least safer than most of the world."

Nods of agreement. Silence.

"I am on the leadership Council in New Los Angeles. My name is Carmine. I want you to stay here a long time and be prosperous. We need you. We want to work with you.

"However, there are conditions. And our Council sets the conditions. The first truth I want to impart today is this: you are no longer in America. You are in New Los Angeles. A new kingdom. There is no federal government. There is no 911 to call. No police. No fire department. No voting booths. Here, in this savage land, in these hard times, might makes right. At least for the time being. If you want to live here, you are under the authority of our Council."

The crowd shifts uneasily. They cast uncertain glances at one another. Peter's jaw hardens.

"I understand if that makes you nervous. But that's how it must be. You will have more freedom here than you've ever had in a civilization before, but the Council gets the final word. On all matters.

"If you refuse to cooperate...if you refuse to contribute to New Los Angeles...if you cause harm...if you assist our enemies...I will evict you, imprison you, or eliminate you.

"On the other hand. If you work with us, if you allow us to help you, if you accept the terms, we will provide safety. And shelter. And community. And resources. And protection from the outside world.

"You have a week to decide. After that, you will either exist under the laws I set, or you will leave."

A woman in the back, probably pretty and polished many months ago, shouts at me, "But some of these are *our* houses! They legally belong to us!"

I respond, "Legally? In what court? Under whose jurisdiction? How will you enforce your rights?"

She is red in the face. Desperate and exhausted and indignant. "That house belongs to *me*!"

"That house *used* to belong to you. Then you fled and abandoned your home. I took it back. So now it belongs to New Los Angeles. Why? Because I am the strongest."

It's a terrible thing to say. It's awful. But it's the cold truth and we live in a cold, hard world. Tears stream down her face and the crowd is about to turn on me.

"Not very fair, is it? I know it's not. But nothing about the past two years is fair. And I don't blame you for being mad. Or for hating me. But I invite you to consider one fact: the people who live here are happy and safe and fed. Why? Because we protect them. I control the Variants. There is no insane rampaging here, and we keep this city intact. And in order for it to survive, in order for it to thrive, it has to infringe on your rights. For now.

"We don't want five million empty houses. I want *you* to live in your house. I want you to be happy and safe. We want the world to calm down, and we want to give the power back to you. That's my vision. Democracy as soon as possible. But it's going to be an uphill battle.

"I hope you choose to stay. I want there to be people in Santa Barbara again. I want us to have a healthy relationship. As a gesture of goodwill, tonight we're sending you five trucks loaded with food and supplies. You can keep the trucks and you have access to our gasoline reserves, even if you choose to leave. As soon as you decide to stay, our Engineers will begin immediate work on restoring water to this area."

My offer of food and supplies wins the day. They clearly don't like having less rights within the neighborhood they used to own, but it's hard for the hungry to turn down resources and community. Plus, the Law Keepers are already unloading a thousand bottles of water.

Finally, I play the ace up my sleeve. Puppies. I have a soft spot for children and puppies. Law Keepers bring out a dozen sleepy Boston Terrier pups, plus bags of dog food and leashes and water dishes. Instant success. The kids love the animals, and parents smile at the excitement. A potent infusion of youth and innocence, hope and happiness. Life will go on. We're going to make it. I promise.

I take questions from the crowd.

"What laws does New Los Angeles have?"

I respond, "Our Kingdom has a three person triumvirate leadership council. Me, General Brown, and our Governess. Your community will appoint an Overseer to report to the Council. Your community must abide by our Council's leadership and our Court's decisions. You must participate in the work. You will be given a job based on your skill-set. There is no hoarding resources. There is no violence between citizens. If we all work together, we might start handing back individual freedoms next year. Until then, we're one big village trying to survive."

"What about the mutants? Are they dangerous?"

I respond, "We refer to them as Guardians. And yes, they're dangerous. But they are stable and sane while I'm in charge. And they are the primary reason we're safe."

"What about the federal government?"

"We are not under their authority," I say.

"What about the Resistance?"

"We are not under their authority," I say. "But so far they appear to support our cause."

And so on for twenty minutes.

The final question is a shocker. "What about the Inheritors? Are you the Red Butcher? Is it true you killed all those women and babies?"

I don't answer. I refuse to talk about the Inheritors, a topic off limits around me. I stare at the crowd until they can no longer meet my eyes. Then I stare longer before finally answering, "The supply trucks will be here tonight. If you're hungry, visit one of our cafeterias and you will be fed.

"You have one week to decide. Oh, and if you see a tiger...leave it alone."

❧

I meet with the Governess for an hour that evening. She's a brilliant administrator who supervises the city's moving parts. She's the brains of our Kingdom. She and General Brown have decades of leadership experience, while I'm just the muscle and figurehead. I defer to them in everything except the Guardians. I tell her about the meeting with Peter and the immigrants.

She says, "Los Angeles transformed from the most dangerous place on earth to one of the safest. So why are only a few thousand returning? Because they're afraid of the Red Butcher!" she cackles.

I dislike my nickname, but it serves a purpose. They're terrified of me.

I finally get to eat dinner at 7:30, and afterwards I tour the southern barracks. General Brown's troops maintain a tightly run ship and their quarters are immaculate. The Guardians, on the other hand...much less so. I'm exhausted by 10pm and I almost fall asleep riding the elevator. Ironic that people drain my energy but I seem to spend *all* my time with them.

Becky is asleep in my bedroom. She's the only person allowed entrance in my absence. She's put on weight since our encounter in the woods and she's regrown her personality. Nightmares, however, are her continual scourge.

I stand on my balcony and watch Night Guardians leave for duty. They climb towers and jump into the distant indigo, like bright streamers to my eyes. They don't truly glow in the dark; the radiance is simply my mind trying to process disorienting sensory input, but that's what it looks like. Some of them pause at the tower's apex and stare in my direction. They possess a preternatural awareness of me. My strength is a lighthouse. They sit like gargoyles, like guardian angels collecting in ranks until dozens have gathered and stare wordlessly into my apartment.

I know what the world doesn't. The world sees only the massacres, the grisly videos, the rampaging mutants. They don't witness this, the Variant obedience, their docile allegiance to me. Guardians absorb the personality of their pack leader. Soon after I established control, they transformed into an extension of me, throwing off the raging violence of their former master. Now the mighty creatures are defensive instead of aggressive, hell-bent on survival rather than domination.

I raise my fist in salute and they howl in the night, a sudden bright eruption, and bound towards our borders.

That is the reason I'm here. That is my purpose. That is why I lead. The Guardians, tormented and fearsome and abused, are lost souls. Runaway freight trains. They need guidance and leadership. Limits and discipline. A north star.

I provide that.

Below my feet the coal fires are being lit. Nightly the people unwind in the streets around a brazier and laugh until time for bed. Instead of retreating into solitude to stare at televisions, they assemble in small pockets and talk. Such an unusual magical world we've built. If not for the violence, it'd be a fairytale.

I try to read my new books but cannot. The long day is done, responsibilities are satisfied, but I cannot un-shoulder the weight. My duties and worries and nightly whispers follow me to bed.

Why are you doing this, the doubts hiss at me. Life would be easier if you left to locate your past. Why? Why do this job?

Because...

Because I have to. Because of what's at stake. Nothing less than our future. I won't rest on my heels and hope for governmental systems to fix things, because these people are too important.

Because I believe in right and wrong.

Because we all need a purpose, and this is mine. This gives me a home.

Because I'm scared of what will happen if I don't.

But, the voices whisper. But...

Is this job too difficult? Too big? I don't want to fight Walter. I want to be normal. I want my childhood bed.

I'm nineteen, for goodness sake. Who obeys a teenager? I don't know how to lead. Can't they tell I'm faking it? That I'm as terrified as they are?

Will this all crash? I don't understand why this little society hasn't imploded yet. What will happen if we begin to starve?

And yet. I can't shake the feeling of destiny. That our Kingdom was selected for survival. That I was plucked for this purpose. That if God exists then it's not out of control, not going off the rails, and maybe I'm here for a reason. A comforting thought as I stare at the cosmos through my missing walls.

Like last night and the night before, I toss and turn on my bed and wrestle inner demons for an hour. My Devotee learned long ago to leave me alone. He sleeps on my floor because...well, because I get lonely. And actually I enjoy the snores. It means I'm not in total solitude.

Soon my thoughts turn to love and loneliness. I wonder where Katie's boyfriend is now. What would he think of the new Katie? Katie the freak, otherwise known as Carmine? I can't remember him, so it doesn't matter. But it'd be nice to have *someone*. Someone intelligent with backbone who doesn't think I'm breakable. Who doesn't think of me as a scary queen who must be obeyed. But no such men exist in my circles.

Finally I'm drifting, warm at the precipice of sleep when Kayla bursts in with a flashlight. Her eyes are as wide as the moon and her cheeks are flushed. She doesn't speak. Becky murmurs in her sleep.

"What?" I demand. "Kayla, if this isn't important then I'm going to eat your dog."

"The Outlaw..." she gushes. "He's on his way. The Outlaw's coming *here*!"

- Four -

The Outlaw is a boy named Chase Jackson and he's had the disease since birth, one of the others. A mighty Infected. The illness made him so uncontrollable that in 2017 he put on a mask and began leaping around Los Angeles towers. That was the planet's first indication that something was amiss, the first Infected to reveal himself.

I have a vague recollection of this event. It occurred before the surgery and it was a big deal, and my emotions twist when I remember.

Naturally the masked man became a worldwide sensation, but his identity was kept hidden until January of 2019, earlier this year. He's been missing since I woke from my coma.

And now he's coming to New Los Angeles. To wreck everything.

The next morning I travel with Nuts to the Los Angeles Aqueduct Filtration Plant in Sylmar. Life in our Kingdom wouldn't be possible without Nuts. He is kinetic energy personified. He's over a hundred years old but rarely sleeps, like Kayla. His mind works too fast. A diminutive giant among geniuses. He manages every major project that involves electricity and water. And, well, everything else too.

I drive and he works furiously on sketches in the passenger seat, burning through a graphing notepad. Dalton and a squad of Law Keepers trail us.

I swerve around an abandoned firetruck on the side of the interstate and I ask, "What are you working on?"

"Water turbines," Nuts barks. "Need to improve efficiency."

He doesn't like to talk or reveal much information about himself. Or his past, which is frustrating because I want to know everything. And he has the answers to all my questions.

"Nuts, do you remember Caleb? Nicknamed Kid, the boy briefly in charge? Before I showed up."

He grunts noncommittally.

I say, "He's Infected, right? Why'd he run away? What made him so weak-minded?"

Nuts pauses and looks up from his diagram with hard eyes. "Don't matter how hot you cook aluminum. It won't ever be steel."

"Did the Chemist think Caleb was weak?"

"That's why he named him Kid."

I ask, "How did you meet the Chemist?"

"He found me. Back in the 70s."

"Did you enjoy working for him?"

"I reckon that question doesn't matter at all."

"I like you, Nuts."

He grunts again. He briefly worked for the Chemist here in Los Angeles, establishing the infrastructure while committing none of the scientific monstrosities. After the Chemist died, he decided to stay for the challenge.

"I don't know what I'm doing, Nuts," I admit. "I woke up like this. I don't remember the Chemist. Or Walter. Or Blue-Eyes. I don't remember anything. I don't know any Infected, other than you. You've been around a long time, Nuts. You know things. You know about the disease and the other Infected and...anything you can tell me would really help."

"Bah, you're doing fine. Keep it up," he snaps. He sees me like he sees all machines: functional or broken. Right now I'm functional.

"Have you ever met the Outlaw?" I ask.

"I have not."

"Why are you still here? I mean, I'm glad you are. We'd be in trouble without you. Do you have a home?"

"I have a workshop in Germany. A man needs only his shop. All else is superfluous."

"So then why didn't you leave?"

For the first time, he pauses. He searches the horizon a moment. "This is a challenge. Plus, the Blue-Eyed Witch needs killing."

Blue-Eyes. Of the many things I learned when I woke from falling down the rabbit hole was that I have enemies because the Variants follow me. And Blue-Eyes is the worst of them. Possibly the most dangerous woman alive. She is Infected, born with the Hyper Virus. She's similar to Kayla in that her strengths aren't physical. Blue-Eyes produces pheromones and can use her charms to control all those around her. If you're in her sphere of influence, you're in love with her. Especially men. Mind control, in effect. Ten times stronger than Kayla.

She has the President in her grip. She's the reason America's military broke in half; half the generals are under her control and half aren't. And her claws are always reaching for more power. I've never met her. Dalton once said he'd shoot me before allowing us to interact.

I ask Nuts, "You know her?"

"I know our systems will operate better without her. She's an anomaly. Lacks vision. And you might be our last hope for her elimination."

"What about Walter?"

"He's just as bad. Turn north here."

He takes me to a sprawling industrial complex at the far edge of our border. Nuts and his engineers spent the entire month of June at this water treatment facility, installing turbines, fixing overflows, and customizing it for our Kingdom. He guides me on an exhaustive tour, and he inspects and explains things I don't understand. After twenty minutes I quit listening. Engineers gather to watch. I tell them they're doing exemplary work and they flush with pleasure and relief. Like I know what I'm talking about.

"Nuts." I stop him while we're alone on a catwalk suspended over outdoor pools of deep water. "I'm a busy girl. This is overwhelming. I don't understand any of it. And I don't want to. Make this simple for me."

"Bah," he growls and scratches his scalp with knotty fingers. "Fine. Our water spills down the Sierras out of the Owens river in Nevada."

"Okay."

"Our intake is more than enough. We'll never deal with scarcity. And we're using the flow of water to turn turbines and generate electricity. We send the electricity to our power plant in Burbank," he says.

"Got it."

"We've closed down two-thirds of this water filtration plant because we don't have the manpower and we don't need to filter that much water. Our reservoirs are full."

"Okay."

"But look." He gestures impatiently at the big plant. It's a maze of buildings and plumbing. "We're vulnerable. We're at the border and we'll be attacked soon. We have enemies. They take out this plant, we're in trouble three weeks later. Big trouble."

"I see. What's your suggestion?"

"I want soldiers and mutants posted here. A lot of them."

"Sounds wise. I'll confirm it with General Brown. How many?"

His scowl falters a moment and he nearly smiles. Nuts and I get each other. There's too much to be done for indecisiveness. "I'll get you exact numbers."

Kayla swears she told no one, but by lunch time everyone knows the Outlaw approaches. Our hive is abuzz. The Overseers are gossiping. The Guardians are rigid and they stare westward, over the horizon, like meerkats. The Workers discuss events in hushed tones.

I stand in the cafeteria on 8th Street, feet planted firmly on the dirty floor, and glare across tables of lunchers. All eyes are on me. All eyes. They watch and whisper.

"Kayla."

"Yes?" She's behind me, texting so fast she might set her phone on fire. I've seen her texting with a phone in each hand, both thumbs moving like a woodpecker on speed.

"Why are all these people staring at me?"

She doesn't answer. The texting stops.

I say, "I mean, I get it. I get it. I get stared at a lot. But this seems excessive."

She is slow to respond. "Carmine...sweetie, we need to talk."

Back in my apartment, I inspect the horizon through my missing walls like I might spot him. "Where is he?"

"The Outlaw will reach Burbank tonight."

"Hmm." I tap my lips in thought. "What, fifteen miles from here? Fourteen? He might be Downtown tomorrow."

Kayla sits on my bed, long legs crisscross, posture perfect, hair perfect, hands in her lap. "Queen Carmine."

"Yes."

"Take out your phone. And find your photos. Do you remember when I discovered your name was Katie Lopez? And forwarded you all those Instagram pics?"

"In July."

She nods. "Yes. I thought the photos might jog your memory. But I didn't transfer every photo I found. I hid some of them."

"Why?" I take off my backpack and sit on the chair in the corner, and bring up my photo library. "I'm too busy for this. Make it fast."

"Your history is...complex. Find the photo of you and the handsome boy with blue eyes."

I scroll quickly. I know the boy she means. He's in several. Good looking guy, great cheek bones, broad shoulders, big smile. I don't remember him, other than like maybe he was the main character in a movie I saw once as a kid. "You're talking about Katie Lopez's boyfriend."

"Right. *Your* boyfriend."

"I don't have amnesia, Kayla. Or if I do, it's not coming back. I'm a different person. I'm not Katie. This kid is not my boyfriend."

Kayla adjusts her long silky hair and wrinkles her nose and stalls. Anxiety and irritation crash like thunder in my chest, but without a discernible cause. I'm suddenly nervous and I don't know why. She searches the ceiling for answers and shakes her head. "I still can't believe you've never Googled yourself."

"I don't like reading things I can't remember. Plus, I don't fully understand how Google can still even operate. Will the internet function in perpetuity, no matter what happens to the population?"

"Carmine. That blue-eyed boy in the photos? That's Chase Jackson. The Outlaw."

The Outlaw? Really? I enlarge and scrutinize the photo more closely. The boy has his arms around Katie Lopez and their foreheads are touching. I remark, "Katie Lopez dated the infamous Outlaw?"

"Carmine. *You* dated the Outlaw."

"That can't be true."

"But it is."

"But he's one of the others, he's Infected."

"I know this," she says.

"Why am I just learning this now?"

"I assumed you'd eventually figure it out yourself. I assumed you'd investigate your past. I told you your real name, and believed that'd be enough. Little did I know you'd swear off all social networks and news channels. I didn't know you're a recluse."

"Everyone knows?"

"Many do. But how many of the Queen's subjects would dare ask her about her love life?" she says.

"You should have told me."

"You have amnesia, Carmine. I see how the lack of memories affects you. You grow deranged when you realize you should remember something but you can't. You threw a motorcycle once, you were so angry. Much better for you to eventually discover it yourself. Besides, we thought he might be dead. He disappeared."

"When did you discover this?"

"Discover that you used to date the Outlaw?" she asks.

"Yes."

"July. When I hid the photos from you."

"But the Outlaw is...is...he's a world breaker. He's one of *them*. He's insane." Inexplicably, my voice is wavering.

"His insanity is purely a story that Blue-Eyes fabricated for the media. The Outlaw is her enemy. In reality," she takes a deep breath and lets out a dreamy sigh. "In reality, he's perfect."

I place my phone on the overstuffed chair's armrest and grip the fabric. My fingers are trembling and my emotions swirl. I say, "I've seen the videos. The Outlaw killed dozens of Guardians."

"*No*, he killed the Chemist's mutant fighters. The Variants were under strict orders from the Chemist, our Creator. He directed us to beat the Outlaw near death and then subdue and transport him. The Outlaw was never the aggressor."

"Did you ever fight the Outlaw?"

Kayla shakes her head. "No."

"Would you have, given the opportunity?"

"Given the chance, yes."

"Why? This makes no sense."

"Carmine, you never met your creator. I was *built*. I was given a disease and DNA by a madman. I emerged as a new being and then I met my maker. It was the most over-whelming experience of my life. His DNA is inside my bones, and when he spoke my whole being lit on fire. We had no choice but to obey him. Even if we didn't want to, he could turn us into rabid animals." She is shivering and rubbing her arms at the memory. "He was dead when you woke up. You aren't tainted like the rest of us."

"I have another question, one I should have asked long ago."

"Yes, Queen Carmine."

"Why am I a Variant? Did Katie Lopez volunteer for the surgery?" This is one of those seminal questions always hovering in my mind, foundational to existence but too big to confront.

"Oh boy. I feel like I need someone else here for support. Can I go get the reporter Teresa Triplett?"

"Tell me, Kayla."

"Can I record this conversation? I feel like this is a historically important moment."

I lower my head between my knees and start taking deep breaths. It shouldn't bother me. I don't care. But somehow I do. Emotions swirl and rage. "Tell me."

She speaks slowly now, carefully choosing innocuous phrases. "I volunteered for the surgery. I voluntarily became Variant. You did not."

"Explain." I'm staring at the dusty blue carpet under my sneakers, trying to steady the universe. My stomach heaves like I'm car sick. It shouldn't; I'm not Katie.

"Katie Lopez never signed-up for the surgery. She was abducted. You were, I mean. There was a war. The Father...err, the Chemist was hellbent on capturing the Outlaw. So the Chemist abducted you in order to trap him. You were bait, because you were Chase Jackson's girlfriend. You were kidnapped and forced into the surgery against your will."

Voices inside my mind. Far off weeping. My brain pulsates and the room grows dark.

"Are you okay?" she asks. "Carmine? This is another reason I didn't tell you. We have very fragile minds after the surgery. Our brains function like recovering from concussions...Carmine!"

I pitch forward onto my face. As darkness closes, I hear a distant voice in the echoes of my mind...*I was bait and Chase came anyway. He was always silly like that.*

～

Teresa Triplett is here when I wake. She's a pretty reporter who decided to live in New LA and chronicle our lives. I remember her from my past life. A little. I recall her being on television screens.

I'm on my back. My muscles tremble like I've just been sick. I shift uneasily and listen to Kayla and Teresa Triplett chat while Kayla pats my face with a wet cloth.

Teresa says, "I'm surprised she doesn't pass out more often. Most newbies do."

"She still gets the headaches. But she's not like the others," replies Kayla.

"You got that right, girl. You told her everything?"

"No. But most of it. She remembers her boyfriend. But that's it. Not emotional attachments."

Teresa sighs and I hear her bulky digital camera clicking. "I have old images stored on here. I could show her other photographs but apparently they aren't effective. If seeing Chase doesn't help, maybe nothing will."

"Do we want her to remember? I mean, she leads the Guardians naturally."

Teresa says, "I've never been in this apartment before. She lives a simple life, doesn't she. No frills." Her camera shutter clicks three times.

"Hey. No photos."

"Who are you texting?"

"Nobody."

"You're texting the computer hacker, aren't you."

"It doesn't matter, and *don't* write that down," Kayla snaps.

"Do you monitor internet traffic?"

"Of course I monitor internet traffic. I am a internet savant."

"Did you know my photographs of you get so many visits that my website crashes?"

Kayla is silent a moment. I sneak a peek at her. She peers intently at the reporter. "...go on."

"You get more views than Carmine does," Teresa says. "Your pics are the second most forwarded and copied pictures on the net."

Kayla makes a 'humpf' noise. "People are so vain."

Teresa reaches out to tug on Kayla's long-sleeved, form-fitting blue shirt. "Says the girl wearing a six hundred dollar Akris."

"Who gets more views than me?"

Teresa mocks her. "Who cares? People are *so* vain."

Kayla tosses her hair and rolls her eyes. "It's Blue-Eyes. Isn't it? It is. I mean, I don't care. But, right? It's her?"

"Yes. Blue-Eyes get the most traffic."

"Ugh. I hate that woman. I want to claw her eyes out."

I speak for the first time. "Kayla?"

"Yes, my Queen."

"You have issues. And don't call me that."

My Devotee enters, carrying a tray of fruit and veggies and chocolate. My head swims when I sit up, but I eat apple slices and chocolate.

He leaves and Teresa says, "That is a gorgeous man. I don't know how you keep your hands off him."

"He's vapid. Plus, I don't want worshippers. Teresa, you met the Outlaw?" I ask.

"Yes. I used to cover him for Channel Four News and he trusted me. We met several times."

"Did you ever meet Katie Lopez? I mean, did you ever meet me?"

She smiles. "Once. Before you two started dating. Long story."

We're all sitting on the carpet beside my bed, munching on the tray of food. I ask, "How do we make the Outlaw go away?"

Kayla nearly chokes on her orange. "Go *away*? Why would we do that?"

"There's no need for him to visit. He'll be nothing but a distraction. Life is too hard right now. Plus, with Walter here? We don't need extra intruders."

"I...we..." Kayla is blinking and staring out the window like trying to solve an impossible chemistry equation. "I'm speechless. I don't understand."

Teresa says, "I'm a huge fan of the Outlaw, but Carmine might have a point. He'll certainly upset your mutants."

"How?"

"I'm not positive. But he does. He's Infected. Not a Variant like you two. There's a big difference." Teresa finishes chewing a carrot and brushes her hands on her shorts. "Everyone with the disease has... wild tendencies. Like untamed animals. You're all alpha predators. And like alpha predators, you don't get along. What I mean is, you *shouldn't* get along. The Infected tend to hate one another, but the Chemist wanted his army to be cohesive so he messed with your genetics. He tinkered with your DNA and implanted his own. As a result, Variants tolerate each other. The same blood runs through your veins, like you're family.

She continues, "But the Outlaw never underwent the surgery. He's pure. So his body chemistry upsets the Variants. He doesn't have their DNA. He registers as an enemy alpha predator."

I stew on that a moment and ask, "What will happen when our Guardians encounter him in Burbank tonight?"

"Again, I'm not positive. The Chemist didn't reveal everything to me. But I imagine the Guardians will have the same reaction leopards have when a lion wanders into their den. It won't be pretty."

I'm tugging on my lip while I think. Kayla hates it when I do that. She thinks it's unbecoming of a Queen, and now she pulls my fingers away. I smack her hand so hard she yelps. I ask, "Will they kill him?"

"No. I doubt they can. He's quite formidable."

"Okay, so we're back to the beginning. How do we make him leave?"

"You can't." Teresa smiles. "He won't go."

"Why not?"

"He's here for you. He loves you."

I groan in frustration and stand. "That seems aspirational. Kayla, post a message online. We don't need the Outlaw here. I don't want to see him. Katie Lopez is dead."

"No she's not." Kayla is smiling now too. "She's alive. And she needs a sexier outfit."

I hurl Kayla's phone like a frisbee out into space. It spins away, arcing several blocks and falling a hundred feet before smashing into the TCW building. She sticks her tongue out. "I have ten backups."

"Good. Use one of them. We can't risk him upsetting the Guardians. Tell the world the Outlaw is denied entrance into New Los Angeles."

Five

I meet with the Farmer Overseer and Governess to discuss more efficient ways to transport water to our agriculture. The Farmer Overseer wants to use the Guardians. I'm reluctant. I tell her I'll think about it.

My bodyguard Dalton and I leave to inspect the eastern Downtown barracks in Little Tokyo. The Miyako Hotel is a twelve-story slate gray building stuffed with mutants. Most of them are still asleep when we enter but my proximity soon rattles their nerves enough to disturb slumber. They emerge from their rooms and clot the hallways and Miyako hums with energy. We proceed down hallways and up staircases, and I leave my arms stretched wide so the Variants can caress my hands. I don't understand the biology but I know skin contact helps them. I stop in each hallway and issue the same announcement: "You make me very proud. Your service to the Kingdom keeps us safe. It is an honor to work with you. But your rooms are disgusting. We cannot thrive in filth. Clean up your things. Wash yourself. Brush your teeth. You need to relearn discipline. Discipline will help protect your sanity. When I return, I expect improvement."

Becky lives in this hotel. As I exit the building, she follows and holds my hand. "They love you. So much," she says. She's a Scavenger but I have a hunch she skips duty and uses our friendship as the excuse.

"I need to blow off steam, Becky. Too much adrenaline. Let's go for a jog."

"Yes Queen Carmine." She gets her sneakers and we set off west and south. Dalton follows behind us in a truck.

After three blocks, I ask, "Have you heard—"

"The Outlaw is coming? Yes."

"Did—"

"No I never met him. Or fought him."

Becky possesses unusual symptoms. She woke up from the

surgery and was able to read people. And I mean *read* them. Predict what they'll do or say. She says, "You're not sure what to think. Or how to feel, about the Outlaw."

"You got that right."

"He's hot."

"So? Appearances—"

"Can be deceiving, but that's stupid. If he's hot then he's hot."

"Becky—"

She smiles. "You're blushing, Queen Carmine."

"Okay. No more talking. And don't call me that."

By the time we finish, fifty other joggers trail us ten yards back. Dalton honks until they go away. After that, I have two free hours so I go to my office. I pace and stalk and fume and try not to think about the Outlaw. My heart rate has begun slowing when Kayla forwards a call to my phone. It's Mason, leader of the Falcons, a man I trust.

His voice comes over the phone. I can tell he's grinning. "I heard the Outlaw is coming?"

"No. He's not welcome. He'll have to go elsewhere. What's the status on Walter?"

"Did I tell you I fought the Outlaw once? In the Gas Tower. He came in through the window, like three hundred feet in the air. He's so fast, Carmine, it's like fighting an archangel."

"Mason—"

"I was with a squad of, I don't know, maybe ten Variants? He kicked our asses. Like a bomb went off. I might be the only one left, actually, now I think about it. Who else was there that night? I can't remember."

"Mason—"

"I think the others died. He hit me with that stick of his, you know? The one in the photos? Hit me in the shoulder and broke my arm. Knocked me *through* a wall."

I try not to crush my phone. Mason is the most talkative man I know. And perhaps the deadliest Guardian I have, a former gang member. He can't help it, I tell myself. His mouth is too big. "Mason, focus. Tell me about Walter."

"Walter the evil wicked villain? He's on the train, chugging towards the UCLA station. Be there in two hours. He's sitting in the passenger car. Still no signs of duplicity."

"Good. Cars are waiting for you."

"Right-o, Queen. I'll escort him to the Ritz, stash him with a heavy guard, and report."

"Thank you, Mason. Safe travels."

"Queen Carmine?"

"Yes?"

"Don't go meet the Outlaw without me. I want his autograph."

He hangs up quickly before I can yell at him.

My office is the smallest room on the 22nd floor. No beds. No couches. Just a desk facing west and a chair. On the desk is a laptop connected to an industrial battery that my Devotee keeps charged.

I am a student at Stanford. The university is located in San Fransisco, which currently stands strong and resists evacuation. The world might be more unsettled than at any point since World War Two, but Stanford believes future doctors and lawyers still need to be educated. I take courses through correspondence. Katie Lopez had been accepted there, so I simply altered her course load to two online classes this semester. Anthology and Communications.

Kayla once asked me, "Why are you taking college classes? I mean, you're the *Queen*, for goodness sake."

"Because we're trying to have a civilization, Kayla. And I'm not a queen," I answered.

But there's a deeper response to Kayla's inquiry. I'm a student because it helps me remain human. I woke up a hunter, a predator. I'm the chief of a savage tribe, often engulfed by violent urges. The Hyper Virus pushes madness into my processes, causing mania and mood swings. College classes are a deliberate injection of normalcy into my life.

My grades are good. Katie Lopez was intelligent. I remember her high school and experience a flush of pleasure, a recollection of success.

Today, though, there will be no successes. I try working on a research paper, but I can't. I attempt studying for approaching final exams. No use. I'm too full of unanswered questions. After thirty minutes of frustration, I slam my textbook and open up an internet browser. I find an article written by Teresa Triplett, dated two weeks ago.

I scroll through the paragraphs. "Blah...blah...blah." Nothing of interest until the bottom.

...As for the Outlaw, he remains safely ensconced inside Luke Air Force Base in Arizona, progressing through rehab. Here at New Los Angeles, a contingent of Outlaw supporters (including yours truly) eagerly anticipate his long-heralded return, a homecoming which seems more likely after cell phone video surfaced on Monday of the man in the mask jogging laps around the runways. Not even a broken back will ultimately deter him from his task, so it seems. He told me in a private email in July that Katie Lopez was not lost, and that he was going to make her remember. In so doing, he'll rekindle the planet's foremost storied romance. In July, that promise seemed preposterous, but now? I've watched the video of his jog at least a dozen times, and he appears to be a man on a mission. A man in love. A man desperate. So, Queen Carmine, sooner or later the hour tolls for thee...

"These idiots have delusions of grandeur," I growl and rub at the headache behind my eyes. I'm not sure why he irritates me so much, but he does. It's probably his entitlement, his cocksure belief he'll simply waltz back and fix things. That assumption implies I need fixing. That I'm broken. Like all my hard work isn't enough.

Maybe in another life, Outlaw. A prior life which ended six months ago.

Now if I could only calm the passions which thunder whenever I think of him.

∼

That night I stand on the peak of the 717 Olympic. Our high-rise is near the southern boundary of Los Angeles's tower cluster. Directly north is a forest of skyscrapers, mostly empty, mammoth and haunting and impersonal and cratered by war. Last year, the city would have been aglow with energy, brilliant crystal shards thick to the horizon. Now it's black, save for tiny coal fires. The wind sings through antennas over my head and the chill makes my joints hurt.

"Where is he?" I ask.

Kayla is lounging in a deck chair, eyes fixed on her phone. "Who?"

"The Outlaw."

"He's in Burbank."

"I know that. But where?"

"Near the mountains."

"Where?"

"Ugh," she groans. "One second, my *Queen*. I'll find out, my *Queen*."

"Thank you."

She works her phone for a minute and reports, "He and his followers are camping in the Starlight Bowl."

"That's within our borders. Our checkpoints are a sieve, at best. That vexes me."

"I doubt he knows about the checkpoints. They came over the mountains."

I ask, "Why does he have followers?"

"Who has followers?" Mason McHale emerges from the stairwell, walking with his usual swagger. He bows slightly in greeting. "My Queen."

"The Outlaw has followers," I respond. "Is it a coincidence Walter is here and the Outlaw is on his way?"

Mason shrugs and sits next to Kayla. "Maybe not. They hate each other." He turns to Kayla. "Hello angel."

She takes her eyes off her phone long enough to roll them. "My name is Kayla."

I ask, "The Outlaw and Walter hate each other?" but no one listens.

Mason pulls a necklace over his head, and holds it out to Kayla. A diamond ring dangles from it. "Let's get married, my love. Tonight."

"No!" she squeaks. "And quit asking me."

"Never. Did Adonis ever quit chasing Aphrodite?"

"What? I don't know! Shut up."

"Hey," I say, "Why does the Outlaw have followers?"

Mason shrugs again. "Security. If you're near him, you're safe. Well, normal people are safe, I mean."

"He walked here from a military hospital in Phoenix," Kayla answers. "Started a week ago. Stragglers joined him when he passed. Now he's got several hundred. Maybe a thousand."

"Do you think he got the message? That he's not welcome?"

"Yes. PuckDaddy delivered the message himself."

I frown. "How did he do that? Do they know each other?"

"Probably," she says. She's ducking from Mason as he tries to stroke her hair. "Both PuckDaddy and the Outlaw are supporters of the Resistance. At least those are the rumors. Stop it!"

"What do you have against affection, my love?"

"Are you so desperate for it? Go visit the third floor then."

He winks, a strand of golden hair sliding between his fingers. "I get asked there every day. But I wait for you."

One of the many problems I need to solve is the third floor of our tower. Guardians overflow with energy and adrenaline and hormones, and their sentry duties aren't enough to suppress it entirely. Those with less self-control find a release for their urges on the third floor, or in similar spots around the city. Teresa Triplett spoke of it once, saying, "The third floor is pure rampant sexual activity. Like the Olympic Village, which is a fitting name."

Gross.

"You'll be waiting a long time, Mason, if you want me to join you on the third floor," Kayla remarks.

"Worth it."

"I'm leaving," I say.

They both stand suddenly. I'm on the tower's balustrade, staring north, but I feel their concern boring into my back. My heels are on the security railing, my toes protrude into space. I want to fall. It's a longing all Variants feel. The adventure. The unknown. The danger. We clean one or two Guardians off the pavement every week, those who give in to the craving. Just thinking about the plunge dumps endorphins into my bloodstream. Part of the insanity.

"Going where?"

"Burbank," I say.

"Carmine, my Queen," Kayla's voice grows frantic. "I don't...that's not a great idea. Why would you go there?"

"I want to see the Outlaw. And then tell him to leave." Besides, I often go out during the night. We hunt for looters, thieves, Herders, spies, and any other unwelcome visitor. This is my role in New LA.

I've never jumped this high. I've leapt around small buildings but nothing like this. The Apex apartment tower is across the street. I can make it. Easy. I've seen Mason do it, but he's had the disease three times longer than me. It's second nature to him but I'm still uneasy. The longer I stare, the further away Apex tower recedes.

Kayla is mustering up arguments on why I shouldn't go. I don't care. I *Jump*. High. Far. At the pinnacle of my parabola I roll over, weightless for an instant, suspended in silence, and descend toes first. I nearly overshoot my target, landing on the furthest edge of Apex's large helipad, which is painted with a big fading red *15*. The concrete buckles slightly with the impact.

I hear Mason before he arrives. We *Leap* differently. He displaces more air than I do and his touchdown is heavier, but he's more accustomed to jumping and his landings are accurately pinpointed. He can't jump as far however, despite his experience, which gives me a small amount of pleasure. Mason straightens beside me and says, "I'm coming with you."

"Kayla's orders?"

"It's fifteen miles. Will you jump the whole way? I was up there recently and it's no small hike."

"I'll take a car from the northern garage. Meet me there." Then

I'm gone, strong legs launching me into stars. The next landing spot is the TCW, a brown office goliath, much higher than than the Apex. Too far for Mason; he'll pick a different route.

Again I miss my mark. I sail fifty yards like a dart, rotating slowly, arms wide, eyes closed. It's bliss. Heaven. Freedom. Until I begin the descent. I aimed for the top and I won't get close. The cold air is loud in my ears, and the eastern surface of the TCW expands to fill the horizon until I plunge through a window. I skid to a stop on the thin carpet underneath a wreckage of chairs. My face hurts from smiling, and I shake off the glass and dust.

"Ouch," I laugh, almost girlish with enchantment.

I exit from the shattered window and touch down on the Jetro building. Then Ernst & Young. I hop all the way to the Cathedral of Our Lady of Angels. Aerobatic and breathless, moving like a phantom. A clumsy phantom. My lungs burn when I finally land in the church parking lot. So good. I cherish the pins and needles in my chest.

This small section of the city is dedicated to the Guardian's armada. The once vacant lots are now populated with vehicles. Cars, trucks, but mainly motorcycles. Over a thousand of them. Colorful Kawasaki, Suzuki and Yamaha sport bikes. Racing motocross bikes. Honda, BMW, and Harley Davidson street motorcycles. All of them have full tanks, and keys in the ignition. No one can touch them except our Guardians, and only then in case of emergency. Nuts finds the bikes and the luxury sports cars awaiting repairs in garages, and he fixes them when he can't sleep. I climb into a cherry red 2018 Porsche Boxster and lower the roof. Mason slips into the passenger seat, sucking oxygen, and I gun the engine.

We take the Five north. I churn through silky gears and top out at 135 mph. The interstate is void of vehicles and the blacktop flows like liquid under our tires and the only danger is the chance of stray animals.

The Hyper Virus makes us jumpy. We're full of adrenaline, ready to snap, and staying sane requires constant effort. Jumping from towers and stomping the gas is therapy, probably like the release

Guardians feel on the third floor. Except without STDs and hurt feelings and unwashed bodies. When we arrive at Burbank I am significantly more relaxed, my demons exorcised, like I've just eaten a big, satisfying meal.

The Starlight Bowl is an outdoor concert venue built into the side of a mountain near Wildwood Canyon Park. Following Mason's directions, we roar up the peak and park at DeBell Golf Course, a mile from the Bowl. There is a soft glow emitting from over the rise, and we cautiously make our way through the brown brush and scrub trees. Mason chattered the whole trip but now his voice drops to a whisper and then into silence.

We exit the forest above the Bowl. A clearing unfolds below us, two hundred yards away. Fifty tents have been erected, and hundreds of people sleep on the grass and the stage. Embers burn in fire pits. Sentries patrol with flashlights.

I can't go any closer. My feet won't move. My heart hammers louder than the car engine did.

I *feel* him.

The Outlaw's presence looms ahead like a thundercloud. Like a drop in barometric pressure. The disease is thick in his veins, creating a nearly visible aura.

It's intoxicating. It's seductive.

It's frightening.

I am terrified. A new emotion for me. Like I'm standing on the edge of an endless abyss and afraid of heights. I'm overwhelmed to the point of tears.

I manage to ask, "Do you feel him?"

"Of course," Mason replies. "He's an avalanche."

"He can't come into the city. The Guardians would lose their minds."

Emotions swirl inside. I'm drawn to him. Like a siren call, he physically pulls me. And yet I hate him. I do. My whole body is rigid and my jaw is set and the desire to destroy him rises like a wave. I want violence. He's a colossal danger, so powerful that I can't help but hate him.

Suddenly we're not alone. Other Guardians silently slide through the trees and join us on their nightly patrols, drawn like moths to a flame. We all stare with wide eyes at the Bowl and it's occupants.

I ask, "Do you feel it too? The need to hurt him?"

"Absolutely. This is the third time I've been close enough to smell him. My body is...outraged by his."

I shake my head. What is *wrong* with me? Such a strong response. Teresa Triplett warned me, but I assumed I'd be impervious. All the Guardians are standing or sitting with rapt attention, erect backs, and barred teeth. Like wild animals.

There's a strange noise. Someone is humming. Loudly.

"Knock it off," I hiss.

Mason looks askance at me. "What?"

"The humming."

"No one is humming."

I gape. He can't hear that? It's so loud. It's...

It's in my mind. It's a tune in my brain but I'm not controlling it, like speakers activating deep in my ear canals.

He asks, "You okay, Carmine?"

It's a woman's voice.

It has to be Katie Lopez. She is humming in my head! I feel her smiling with pleasure. She's happy and it makes me flush with emotion. I want to rip the Outlaw's head off but she's happy to be near him. This is new. And wild.

"Carmine?"

"I'm a mess," I whisper, shoving Katie Lopez deeper into the recessed halls of my consciousness. I've wanted to remember for so long, and now some small part of me responds at the exact wrong time. The irony would be amusing if I wasn't so amped.

He asks, "What'd you say?"

"Nothing. Pass the word. No one attacks. Not tonight."

Mason obeys and the orders travel up the line of watchers. Maybe I spoke too loudly. Maybe he did. But for whatever reason, one of the far tents shudders. The canvas walls rise and fall. It's him. The

Outlaw. I know it is. All of us do. As one body, we begin an involuntary retreat.

The tent flaps part. A figure emerges. He shines like the sun to my eyes.

"Run," I whisper, half choked. "Before he sees..."

Like scared children, we flee. And Katie laughs.

Six

The next morning, over a thousand people wait for me. They crowd the tower lobby. Throng the courtyard. Line the sidewalks. Skyscrapers block the morning sun, but even so the air is bright with hope and pride. Civilians cheer. Law Keepers hold them back. Guardians perch on wall protrusions and salute.

This is our chance. We don't know why Walter's here, but we'll deliver a message to him. We'll tell him and the President and Blue-Eyes that we will survive. We'll cry our independence to the world. I raise my fist and the tumult increases an octave.

Kayla waits in the rear of the Land Cruiser. She is pristine and manicured. Our driver tries not to gawk at her. Dalton gets into the passenger seat, shifting until his shoulder holster is comfortable. He is furious at the commotion. I slide in back, beside Kayla, and the door closes.

"My Queen. You look...formidable," she says.

"Walter's in place?"

"Yes. He must be positively sick of Mason's mouth by now."

"General Brown is with him?"

"Yes ma'am."

I tap the driver. He speaks into his radio and our caravan rolls.

Walter was raised in east LA. He alternated living between his mother and his aunt, depending on who was sober. He dropped out of school at age thirteen, and spent a total of fifteen months at Los Padrinos for various offenses. During his final stay he was introduced to Al Arrington, a social worker for the after school program.

Teresa Triplett met Al's wife while doing research for her article on Walter. According to her, Walter and Al got along because they both liked baseball. Al talked Walter into returning to school and kicking the drug habit. Soon after he turned eighteen, Walter's debilitating headaches began. The Virus, dormant since birth, arrived and demanded sacrifice. Walter couldn't attend school and failed all his classes, one semester before graduation. His coach kicked him off the baseball team. Al assumed Walter had returned to gang activity. His sickness grew worse and eventually snapped his sanity, triggering uncontrollable aggression. Walter never graduated high school, and he killed Al Arrington one night during a dispute, Al's widow reported.

Walter would certainly have formed his own gang and dominated the territory wars, Teresa Triplett assumes in her article, but the Chemist found him first. Walter was put in charge of the Chemist's security team, though the two men never got along. The Chemist was refined and educated, and Walter is instinct and aggression. Eventually the Chemist was killed and Walter took much of the Variant army for himself. He left to terrorize and seize control of the northwest, away from the Resistance.

And now he's here. Returned to Los Angeles, his home. And I have to face him. I read Teresa Triplett's article last night and consulted with her. She thinks I'm going to die.

The Los Angeles Convention Center is impressive, even for Los Angeles. Over a million square feet of glass and angular architecture filled with pop culture relics from past conventions. It gleams brilliantly with reflected sunlight. Two years ago, tens of thousands gathered for the big Auto Show, or E3, or the Anime Expo, or the Primetime Emmy Awards, or the Governors Ball, and so forth.

Now we store dry goods in the basement.

But as soon as we're more secure in our electricity consumption we might show movies in the theater.

Walter waits outside, sitting at a table across from General Brown in the Gilbert Lindsay Plaza, a broad courtyard scrubbed white for the occasion. He is surrounded by a ring of armed Law Keepers standing fifty yards distant. Mason and the nine other Falcons wait on motorcycles by the palm trees, ready for action.

Kayla enters the ring of Law Keepers, serenely approaches the table and sits without speaking.

I land between Kayla and General Brown, falling from the sky and deliberately busting the concrete slab on which they sit. Walter doesn't react other than a slight smirk.

Walter is a solidly built man. Long muscular limbs. His brown skin is crisscrossed with scarified designs. His short hair is corn-rowed. He wears sunglasses, jeans and a vest. He has a presence, like an evil radiation. A spreading stain on the atmosphere, so thick I can smell it. He is *significantly* stronger than I am.

Most noticeable, however, are the short knives bolted into the bones of his finger tips. He's given himself surgically attached claws. How gruesome.

I'm wearing boots, cargo pants, black shirt, and a jacket. My joints are compressed with red silk. My short hair is a mess. I'm a worker. A survivor. A fighter. Not here to be pleasant.

"Nice manicure," I say. "I came by my nails naturally."

"I wouldn't call it *natural*, sweetheart," he drawls, almost a southern accent. "Remember me? You and me, we go back."

"What are you doing here, Walter?"

"That night on the beach. You remember?" He grins, revealing teeth full of gold and silver. "Heard you lost your memory. You remember the beach? Me comin' to fetch you?"

"I imagine abducting teenagers makes you feel powerful."

"You didn't go by Carmine back then. I found Katie Lopez on a beach. At night. Hiding from me, but not hiding good enough. I took you. Threw you in a car. Took you to the Chemist. To the surgery. You remember?"

I feel like I'm being shocked, small frissons, pinpricks in my mind. Memories flash on my consciousness. A beach. At night. With…? With someone I remember. Katie lurches inside of me. *No. No no no,* she says with such strength I actually hear her. I'm going insane.

"I'm not helpless anymore, Walter. What do you want?"

"Nice place you built." He leans back and spreads his arms like he's stretching. "Impressive colony for such a little girl."

"Wasn't just me."

"How long you think you can survive here?"

"We have a surplus of water. Four aqueducts to choose from, and we only require one. We have gasification generators, gasoline generators, solar panels, and turbines. Plenty of food. And the most dangerous army on earth. We can survive indefinitely."

"Bravo, Ms. Carmine. You a scary lady."

"Why are you here?"

"Doing you a favor."

"What favor?"

"Keeping you alive."

"I don't need your help. We're doing fine on our own."

"Cause the heat ain't been turned on yet. S'only a matter of time. You got enemies you ain't heard of." He smiles and pops some gum into his mouth. Crinkles the wrapper and flicks it onto the table between us.

"This is a waste of my time. Anything else?"

"You sittin' on too much power. The Chemist, see, he spent billions. Billions. Building an army of freaks. And then you come along and think they yours? Well, pretty girl, they ain't. You can't keep'em."

My blood is warming, listening to him talk about the Guardians like possessions. Like manufactured tools to be owned. "They could have gone north. They could have located you. They chose otherwise. They don't belong to you."

"Let's you and I make a deal. Me and you. Fact is, I got a couple deals for you. You can pick which you want." He leans back and props his feet up. "This is me helping you. Helping you stay alive."

"You have nothing to bargain with. You have nothing I want."

"You wrong. I can tell your President to let you live."

Kayla speaks up. "We don't have a president. We declared Greater Los Angeles officially annexed on the fourth of July."

Walter lazily shifts his attention to Kayla. Gazes at her a long moment, face unreadable. Her legs are crossed and she's been pumping her ankle until now. She doesn't fidget. She returns his stare, but I know it takes every bit of her self-control to remain calm. Walter is a frightening man, and Kayla is an outrageously desirable woman. Finally he says, "Irrelevant. I can *officially* declare myself the Pope. But that's got no bearing on reality. You on American soil."

"No. You're on our Kingdom's soil. My soil."

"Your soil?"

I snap, "The President cut off Los Angeles's electricity from the power plants. And cut the phone lines. And medical supplies. And shipping. And trucking. He deliberately tried to starve his citizens. If anything has no meaning, it's the President's claim on New Los Angeles. He lost that right months ago."

He shrugs and laces fingers across his flat stomach. "Don't matter much, I guess. He'll kill you either way. So will the others."

"He's tried. Hasn't work so far."

"The rightful and the legal owners of this fine city gonna get more creative. They want their property back. They got stuff here. You sittin' on a hundred billion in real estate alone."

"Ownership will be returned after certain conditions are met."

He sniffs. "Just so happens a powerful syndicate of owners contacted me. Want to know how they can get you out. You're pissing on billionaires. Walt Disney, he wants Disney Land back. Lakers want the Staple Center returned. Musk, Sterling, Buss, Resnick, Murdock, Spielburg, Redstone...names mean anything to you? You got their stuff. Powerful men and women, money coming out they ears. So mad they could hire mercenaries. Violent mercenaries."

"Tell your grumpy old men they can return. We've made it clear the Kingdom welcomes refugees. But for the moment, I'm in charge."

He turns to General Brown and says, "General. You a respected military leader. Former CO of Los Alamitos. Decorated war veteran. You can't talk sense into these little girls?"

General Brown defected from the American government when the military split in February. Unlike most military officials, he didn't join the Resistance. He and ten thousand soldiers drove trucks laden with munitions and ordnance to our border and pledged allegiance to our cause. He's a fifty-five-year-old, stern, hidebound black man with a buzzed haircut, and his men love him. So do I.

He returns Walter's stare and smiles sadly. "I don't envy you, young man. You're a captive. A hostage of Blue-Eyes, but you don't know it. And you're in over your head with these...girls, as you call them."

"You follow her leadership?" Walter sneers. His metal claws are tapping and scratching the table.

"I'd follow Carmine into hell, boy."

"Let's be clear about one thing. I don't answer to the Blue-Eyed Bitch. I ain't here for her."

I say, "She bankrolls your terrorist operation. You're a simple errand boy."

That gets him. For the first time he shows emotion. His face darkens and his hands clench. He is a viper itching to uncoil, to strike. "Ain't a terrorist," he growls in a low rumble. "Ain't a errand boy. I'm a businessman, like you. 'Cept you ain't even a man."

Then he stops. Angles his face upwards, like he's testing the air. Twists in his chair and glares over his shoulder, towards the glass Convention Center. "She's here."

At first I think he's talking about the Blue-Eyed Witch, but that's impossible. We'd know if she was. He's not talking about her. I say, "You mean the Cheerleader? She's around. Why, scared of her?"

"The Cheerleader," he chuckles. "Hell yeah I'm scared of the Cheerleader. You should be too. She's a fun one, though. She crazy." He sinks back into his chair, clearly shaken. He twitches his shoulders and shifts uncomfortably. "You got allies. I'll grant you that. But she can't keep you alive."

I keep my mouth shut. The Cheerleader is *not* our ally. We simply have no idea how to get rid of her.

He says, "Okay, let's get this over with. I want the Inheritors."

There it is. The bomb I knew he'd drop. Very few things would be worth risking his life for, but the Inheritors are one of them. He travelled alone, hundreds of miles for a chance. I shake my head. "There are no Inheritors, Walter. They're gone."

"You really expect me to believe the rumors? That you really the Red Butcher? That you killed those kids? Give me the Inheritors and you live and you keep your Variant army."

A headache is building, a gathering storm behind my eyes. It takes me a full thirty seconds to find my voice, and it comes out hoarse. "Look all you want. The Inheritors are gone, bodies washed out to sea."

He regards me suspiciously. "Ain't fooling nobody."

I shrug and wipe my eyes. I hate talking about the Inheritors. Something inside me shivers, an involuntary response. *He's the devil. I hate him.*

He grunts, "Okay then. Second and final offer. You leave Los Angeles. Leave the Variants. And I won't come hunt your ass down."

"No deal."

"Maybe you oughta consult with your friends. Isn't your...colony ruled by a three person council? Maybe they be willing to sacrifice you so they can live."

I say, "I'm a third of our triumvirate. I handle all mutant affairs. And you're a mutant. Therefore you deal with me."

"Give me the Variants, little girl. Or I will slaughter you."

A threat. And we capture it on video, insurance against a day we need to prove our goodwill to the public. I stand and lean towards him, resting my splayed fingers on the table. "Now I'll make you a deal. You're going into our jail. We can throw you in quietly. Or we can use violence and *then* throw you in. You pick."

He arches a brow and smiles. "This an, ah...abduction?"

"You're in my Kingdom. And I'm incarcerating you. You will stand trial before our Courts for your crimes."

Walter shakes his head and makes soft *tsk* noises. "And to think, pretty girl. I came on a peaceful diplomatic errand."

"Get up. We have your cell prepared."

General Brown and Kayla are tense. They disapprove of this plan. Said we aren't prepared. Said we can't control Walter, that he was a warrior beyond our reckoning. But I'm not letting this monster walk free.

"You even know how the disease works?" Walter asks.

"I know you slip into and out of ebonics, depending on your mood at the moment. Everything about you is an act. You're a fake."

"The disease evolves us," Walter says. "We get harder as we age. And faster. Your creator, the Chemist, was damn near indestructible. Had to be dropped off a sky scraper onto his head. What I'm saying, Red Butcher, is that there ain't anyone here to contend with me. You're still alive cause I'm trying to be polite."

The table between us is thick and heavy, made from a single cut of walnut. Scavengers found it in a luxury condo. I punch my fist clean through and pull the wood apart. It breaks in half, an eruption of splinters.

The Falcons are off their bikes and approaching. The Law Keepers have been instructed to fire only as a last resort; too many people in a small area.

"On the ground," I order. "Or this is about to get messy." I'm jumpy, like a kid at the doctor's office bracing for a shot. This will probably hurt.

Hit me. Hit me. Go on, Walter. We're recording everything; I want him to be the aggressor. We can't kill him unprovoked, or we'd lose everything we've worked so hard to attain. Not sure we can kill him at all, but I want to try.

He almost goes for it. I detect the rising tide of hate, the minor muscle twitches, the pall of his disease thickening. Can General Brown feel that? He doesn't have the Hyper Virus, but can he tell how powerful Walter is?

Walter makes a show of straightening his vest. Presses the Ray-Bans firmly onto his nose with his pointer finger. Then looks at Kayla. "Mamá, you shouldn't'na come here showing so much skin. Imma return for you. And you gonna be a hard working girl, cause I got them big appetites."

No! I strike like lightning, darting forward and plunging razor nails at his neck. He *Catches* my fingers with his clawed hand. "Told you," he breaths into my face. "You ain't ready yet to play with big kids."

Walter *Hits* me in the chest. I'm lifted up and over Brown and Kayla. Like being smashed by a car and hurled into pavement.

"Come on," he laughs as the Falcons circle him, their fists bristling with knives. "Little warriors, see if you can hit me."

He's enjoying this. My blood runs cold. He's a titan from another dimension compared to us. We're not on his level. The Falcons launch themselves and fall apart. They bounce off or he throws them down. Walter is calloused and skilled from countless fights, some against the Outlaw himself. This was a mistake. Brown's pistol is in his hands but he can't get a shot; Walter is everywhere.

I attack again, and connect with a snap kick that shatters his sunglasses. He's off-balance but he parries the next blow. I slash him across the chest but he *Moves* like a viper. Grabs me by the throat and lifts me. My entire body hangs in his hand, and I kick at his knees and waist but it's like flailing at reinforced steel. His wrist turns to bloody ribbons as I claw but he doesn't budge. He raises his hand, about to remove my face with his knives.

"No!" Kayla screams. Her voice goes straight into my brain. Straight into Walter's too, and her power is obvious. He releases me and recoils, as though she threw scalding water in his eyes and ears. The Falcons reel too, her influence over our bodies passing like a shockwave.

Brown and Kayla were right. We should have let him leave. This could end in disaster. He hits Mason so hard I'm surprised his back didn't break.

We need more Guardians. We need them all. I raise the radio to my lips, but a gun fires. A distant retort, sound without source. I'm coughing on the ground so it takes me an extra second to realize Walter's been shot. He is the only one standing, his opponents all thrown down, and he's holding his shoulder. General Brown's gun is gone, so it wasn't him. *Who?* Walter is glaring at the Staples Center two blocks away. I follow his gaze. There is a silhouette on top, a shooter distorted by rising heat. One of General Brown's snipers?

That was a jaw-dropping shot, connecting with Walter as he flickered among us.

"Coward," he snarls. "An ambush, Red Butcher? Not your style." There's a ghost of a smile as his advanced eyes zero in, a glister of recognition. "Shoulda guessed she'd be here. Bitch hid upwind."

The shooter's rifle flashes in quick succession. Additional incoming rounds. Walter *Moves*, scrambling away as high velocity bullets shatter the patio. Then he's gone, *Running* west. The Law Keepers scramble. General Brown is shouting into a radio.

Mason is on his feet and chasing. So are the other Falcons, but they move like Olympic sprinters at full speed. They'll never catch Walter, who moves like a cheetah. He's gone.

So is the mysterious sniper. The silhouette has vanished. Whoever she is, the girl can shoot. She's female, according to Walter. He referred to her as a bitch. But maybe he calls everyone that. Seems likely.

I lay on my back and gently rub my neck. Kayla scoots over to check on me. "What a charming man," I croak.

Seven

Two hours later, Walter is spotted in a Toyota Tacoma heading north, returning to his stronghold in Oregon. Kayla announces that somehow CNN learned of the showdown and is speculating on scandals and conspiracies. She can release footage of the meeting if we're forced to repudiate rumors of terrorism association. I watch the video; he wrecks us and it's embarrassing, but at least it'd allay fears. I don't want the remaining population of America to turn on us.

Lesson learned. The Infected are not to be trifled with. But I'm furious he escaped.

I need to clear my head so, after I debrief with General Brown and Mason, I jump into the lake at MacArthur Park. The water will turn foul soon, so I don't stay long. Just enough to reset.

I spend the afternoon with a team of Scavengers and Law Keepers, probing the uppermost subterranean lair of our city. Los Angeles's metro is not as extensive as lines in other metropolises, especially in the Downtown district. More concerned with transporting people into and out of Downtown, rather than shuttling within, city planners built only five main tunnel systems. These arteries are clotted with detritus and cave-ins and the hideouts of an underground community. We call them Cave Dwellers, and they are harmless recluses who refuse to work or participate in our governed society. Harmless until recently when they began stealing from warehouses. Today we have no intention of evicting them. We only reconnoiter and plan and draw maps, and we'll present our findings and suggestions to the Council later. Becky is in her element down here, squirming through muddy holes and broken lines, grinning all the while. My presence isn't strictly necessary, but its fascinating and I want to keep my mind off Walter and his threats.

At six that evening, I trudge up the stairs to my apartment. The stairwell is lit with one lightbulb per landing. Dalton stays outside and keeps Kayla's dog away. The Devotee takes my jacket and I sit in the overstuffed chair, enjoying the purpling horizon with a vacant mind. I've earned ten minutes of rest. Ten minutes of daydreaming. Of peace.

General Brown swears the sniper atop the Staples Center doesn't belong to him. I ask the Priest and he seems unsure if he should claim credit, but I see through him; he doesn't know the sniper either. Perhaps it's an old enemy of Walter's hunting him down, and I'm unsettled to have such a powerful warrior in the Kingdom.

I work until ten on the Stanford research paper, snacking on whatever the Devotee brings me. I'll need to visit a library soon. Much of the information once available on the internet is gone, succumbed to power-loss or destruction.

Mason calls and breaks my concentration. He's talking through the headset in his motorcycle helmet. "Just got word that the Lakewood punks are back. Raided Anaheim last night."

His news instantly irritates me. We're too big. Our territory covers too much ground and we can't monitor it efficiently, even with our checkpoints and designated Overseers. Drifters and looters sneak in and cause problems, like the gang which keeps popping up in Lakewood. A peaceful community of five thousand settlers recently moved back into Anaheim, grateful and willing to join our Kingdom in exchange for protection. But the Lakewood gang has thousands of houses to hide in, and thousands of pantries to raid for food, and nothing better to do than harass the community in Anaheim.

"Coordinate with the Priest," I growl. "I want him out there with a squad of Law Keepers. They'll patrol at night and pinpoint the Lakewood hideout. I'm sick of this."

Mason pauses. He doesn't trust the Priest any more than I do. He's too...unctuous. Not decisive. Not a warrior. But this will toughen him up. I hope. "Are you sure?"

I say, "I want him to handle this. It's a simple pack of jerks with guns. It'll be good for the Priest. He and his Law Keepers will locate them and the Falcons will assist in removal. Agreed?"

He sighs. "Agreed. Want me to tag along?"

"Not tonight. Not with the Outlaw still inside our borders."

"Worried he'll sneak into your bedroom?"

I hang up.

I'm manic at eleven. Can't sleep. Adrenalized by my body's overproduced endorphins or dopamine or whatever it is. I don't know much about it. I'm in full fight-or-flight mode, revved up and ready to fly, incapable of controlling the energy.

I sleep five hours on average. I like to be up by seven, but nature made me a night owl. Well, nature or the knife. I grow increasingly crepuscular as time passes. The darkness calls, invigorates me, a seductive beckoning. Some nights I can read to sleep. Some nights I can't.

Come out. Come out and play, little one.

Dance, Katie says. I'm hearing her more and more often and she startles me every time. *I want to dance.*

I want to *Jump*. Leap with no predetermined landing spot. Just see what happens. Dare death to come collect. The fall would be such a rush, a plunge into bellowing black.

But not tonight.

I check myself in the mirror. I'm a mess, dressed in active wear and ribbons, no makeup, and hair a tangled nimbus. Whatever. At my core, when you pare down all the responsibilities and enhancements, I'm just a nineteen-year-old girl. And tonight I want to dance and throw off steam.

"I'm going to the Mayan," I inform my Devotee. "Come if you like."

I leap down the stairs, rebounding off concrete walls like a ping-pong ball. Outside, the ground level atmosphere is cool and fresh, typical Los Angeles, a sky full of stars and a solitary streetlamp burning on every corner.

Most Workers are asleep, exhausted from an honest day's labor. Most, but not all. Our demographics trend towards the young and carefree, and LA still bounces at night in certain spots.

The Mayan is a well-known dance club on Hill Street, not far. New Los Angeles provides no electricity to the club, so dancers bring big batteries charged from personal solar panels baking in the sun all day to fuel the lights and speakers. If I listen closely I can hear it from my tower.

I'm hurrying on bare feet. My Devotee, dressed now in shorts and t-shirt, reaches me at the intersection of Grand and 11th. Apparently alerted by phone, Dalton catches us on Olive one block later.

"Shoulda told me," Dalton growls, hastily tucking in his red t-shirt, and then shoving a pistol under the waistline at the small of his back.

"Come on Dalton," I grin. "Catch me if you can." And I'm off, *Sprinting* the rest of the way, the two beefy men left in the distance.

The Mayan was a hotspot before the crash and still is today, stuffed with survivors, adventurers full of vitality who are willing to work all day and party all night.

The exterior of the club is a mixture of theater and pink Mayan stone temple. No bouncers at the door. All are welcome. Though even if there were bouncers, the Queen could likely talk her way in. The club has a Latin American flair that I enjoy, probably because Katie Lopez is Hispanic. The throbbing music alternates between salsa remixes and pop techno, and walls flash in shades of crimson and indigo and gold. In less than sixty seconds, I'm lost in the rhythm and the crush of dancers.

Music ignites my biological triggers. My soul transmutes into something more beautiful, more elemental, brighter and happier. I smile and laugh for no reason, awakening to pure existence. Perhaps I am most like Katie Lopez while I dance.

The Mayan is one of the few places enhanced humans publicly mix with the un-enhanced. Guardians interacting with citizens. Our society isn't segregated, but people are still recovering from the collapse. We all possess a natural fear of the unknown. And Guardians are very unknown, terrifying when fully lost to their disease. But here, dancing at the Mayan, walls fall. Danger becomes desire. Beauties and the beasts.

Old-world celebrities are here, recognizable from a time when LA was the entertainment capital of the world. Some stars lingered, agreeing to work and remain in their luxury homes. They come to dance, much admired, much sought after by nocturnal crowds, but at clubs like this they are eclipsed by Guardians. The exotic instability and subtle hints of enhancement are intoxicating; mutants dance and move with adoring entourages.

My own two-person cortege follows me. I am most tolerant of my Devotee while on a dance floor. His affection is less cloying after I abandon restraint and surrender to my humanity. We dance intimately, pulsating to the same beats. But the spell only lasts as long as the music.

Wine and liquor flow liberally. One day the alcohol will run dry and bars will be forced to make their own. But not tonight. I don't drink, guided by conditioning, a built-in respect for the old law; I'm not twenty-one yet. Plus my liver would metabolize the alcohol too quickly. And it smells gross. Katie Lopez must've been a major league Good Girl.

Off-duty Guardians notice my arrival immediately. After half an hour, so do the others.

The Queen is here.

The Queen is here.

I don't care. Let them come. Let them assemble and dance with me. Tonight I am not the leader, I am the prize. We are surrounded and engaged. Covetous girls captivate my Devotee, and even Dalton has fun, his scowl slipping for a few minutes. For two hours nothing matters. There is no Witch. No madman promising to kidnap and abuse Kayla. There are no Herders. We simply move.

At one in the morning my biochemical compulsives are satisfied and I'm drowsy, somnolence demanding its dues. I tap Dalton on the shoulder and the crowd parts and watches me leave. Drenched in sweat, I breath in pure air outside and begin the walk home.

As it usually happens after dancing, my body is satiated but my spirit decompresses. The bliss was temporary and unsubstantial, and once again I'm alone. All my ribbons are gone and silence looms. A small crowd follows Dalton and me, groupies hoping to be invited to further festivities. But I have no wish for them. My Devotee has vanished, a severe crime but I won't report him to his Overseer; let him live. I don't envy his profession, and he'll return soon enough.

We reach the tower and Dalton denies our followers entrance. They call and wave and yawn and slink off to their homes. My body has begun a trophic tremble, a hollow hungry feeling in my gut. I need caloric input.

We pass the third floor, which always sounds like a raging party, and the Guardians' ardor hits me like a blast of convection heat, and I blush furiously. The third floor might as well be a furnace. The intensity makes my pulse race, and I hurry up the stairs to escape their influence. What's got them so excited?

"You could be a SEAL," Dalton chuckles as we climb. "Got the discipline."

"Explain?"

"You could have any man in that dance club. But you never do."

"Ah. *That.* I don't need the drama."

"Like you ain't even human. You don't feel the need? The urges the rest of us feel?"

"Dalton, are we talking about sex?"

"Hell yeah we are. You don't need it?"

This is fun. No one has asked me about sex before. No one dares question the queen. I admit, "I experience all human emotions and needs."

"And?"

"It's complicated."

"Always is."

"I think Katie Lopez was a virgin. Which means I am too. And I won't simply throw that away. Not to satisfy a craving." That was more honesty than I intended. Just tumbled out.

He shakes his head in disbelief. "Cravings are meant to be satisfied."

"To an extent. That's why we're in this mess, though."

"Huh?"

"A madman tried to get everything he ever wanted. He was never satisfied, craved more and more power. And then he built humans who can barely control themselves. The world would benefit from a global dose of self-control."

He is silent, the muscle in his jaw flexing as he mulls it over. Then, "So you're just never gonna...?"

We're at my apartment. Dalton follows me in, checking to make sure it's clear. No Devotee. He'll probably sleep on the couch till he arrives.

Dalton is safe. He isn't trying to sleep with me. That's not what he's after. In some ways, he's a close friend and not a bodyguard. I slam a granola bar in my mouth and go looking for more.

So I'm just never gonna...? His words carom in my mind. What am I waiting on?

I want to be in love. That's what. And it's a sudden realization. An epiphany which touches down for the first time; I don't crave sex nearly as much as love. To be loved by someone whom I love. But I doubt that's in my cards. I don't live in a land that lets girls like me fall in love. I'm too...unique. My job is too demanding. My body too freakish. Add it all up and you get one very unlovable girl.

The reading lamp flickers in my bedroom. Other than my phone charger, the lamp is the only electrical pull in the apartment. I glance outside in time to see lights fail in other towers, especially in stairwell windows. Few rooms are using electricity, but those which do are experiencing brownouts. Lights blinking out everywhere.

I say, "The Governess is asleep, Dalton. Go wake her and find out what's happening with the power."

"Aight." He yawns and stumps heavily out of the bedroom.

I'm tired and I collapse onto the bed to wait. But before he reaches the hall door, the Governess herself barges into my apartment. She's a large middle-aged woman who always wears black clothes and keeps her hair in a bun. She's no-nonsense, a former city planner, and I like her. "Queen Carmine!" she calls. "Let go of me, you big beautiful thug!"

I grin. "Let her in."

She hurries into my bedroom, casting an interested glance at my sparse belongings, and she's breathing thickly. I'm sitting on my bed in the dark. She shines her flashlight on me a moment before clicking it off with an apology. "I'm...I'm sorry to bother you, Carmine..."

"Your power flickering?"

"I heard on the radio. The power station. It's...there's...sounds like there are intruders."

A handheld radio is on her hip and it squawks again. Screams and the unmistakable rattle of gunfire burst from the speaker.

We're under attack!

I'm out of bed in a flash, shoving feet into shoes. "Call General Brown and the Priest and wake all Law Keepers! Dalton, get Mason on the phone. I want them at the power station immediately! And find Nuts!"

We're in trouble without central power. The solar panels and gas generators are good for smaller personalized uses, but we're utilizing the Magnolia Power Plant as a conduit and glorified battery and generating enough electricity for places like the hospital.

I jam a bluetooth earpiece in my right ear, shove my cell into a pocket, and grab her radio.

Dalton barks, "The hell you think you're doing? You ain't going out there without me."

Too late.

I *Jump.*

- Eight -

The Magnolia Power Plant isn't far from the Starlight Bowl, from the Outlaw. If he's the intruder, we're going to kill him tonight.

I land like a professional acrobat on Apex tower. Cell phones ring in the nearby high-rises. I detect the sounds with enhanced hearing. Off-duty Guardians are being woken. Calling all cars.

I soar across Downtown, covering vast distances with running *Leaps* and hopscotching roofs, touching down and *Launching* like the night is a fabric I can climb, like gravity has an off switch, until I reach the northern garages. I land in the cherry red Boxster and tear up the same interstate as last night.

Tonight isn't reconnaissance.

Tonight is fury.

I am judge and jury. I am death.

The engine surges beautifully. So does the disease in my veins, and I'll cover ten miles in four minutes. The city is black; a ghost town but I'm the ghost.

I'm wearing only leggings and a tank top, and already my joints begin to protest. I miss the compresses. My headset rings. It's Mason. "Falcons en route," he calls directly into my ear.

"Took you long enough."

"The Priest and a regiment of Law Keepers are loading up, but they'll be thirty minutes. General Brown and the troops are moving even slower."

I grind my teeth and try to remember that not everyone is enhanced. Some people are normal. Normal and slow.

"It's only us, then," I say. "Better move your ass."

Halfway there, my radio burst to life. A man I don't recognize is giving updates from the power plant. His voice is strained, panicking.

-We're under attack!

-Trucks! Guns!

-Herders trapping Guardians!

More gunfire, then silence.

My blood runs cold. This has happened before in other locations. I see it all in my mind. The Herders will have attacked the Power Plant, drawing attention from nearby Night Guardians, and then used electroshock weapons to subdue them. Last time the Herders kidnapped fifteen, worth a fortune. Soldiers for the Blue-Eyed Witch. I bet the Herders are already rumbling away in a truck, laden with unconscious prizes. Smash and grab.

Mason calls me again. "Wait for us, Carmine! We're on the way. It could be a trap specifically for you."

The sky throbs an angry red. I round a bend on the Five and see the blazing Magnolia. It's from a nightmare. Hundreds of gunfire bursts. Blasts of electricity, more dazzling than the sun. Bright coils of fire spiral upwards. The Power Plant is an expansive industrial park, bigger in appearance than the Water Filtration Plant. Metal towers and smokestacks and buildings for acres, and all is chaos.

"The Herders came in force," I snarl. "Maybe a hundred."

"Wait for us," he warns.

"Too late. Trucks are already rolling up Victory Boulevard to the interstate ramps. Get here!"

I couldn't stop if I wanted. I only maintain partial control on my sanity, on my actions. The need, the hunger, the thirst for action is unquenchable.

I can do this.

A convoy is exiting the madhouse in a hurry. A heavy jeep leads the way, gunner on top, preceding an eighteen-wheeler and rear-guard, headlights puncturing the black as they rumble up the entrance ramp at Mile 146. My direction. They can't escape. They have my people. I roar past their ramp, cut the wheel and engage the emergency brake. The little sports car locks rear wheels, squeals in a 180 degree turn, and faces the oncoming motorcade. The leading jeep exits the long pretzel turn and accelerates onto the interstate heading north, heading straight at me. Behind it, the eighteen wheeler is picking up steam.

The jeep is a stripped down Humvee, military grade, camouflage paint, heavy gun on top. I rev my engine, frissons radiating in my fingers, and launch forward. A game of chicken; I don't care if I lose because the eighteen-wheeler will be forced to grind through vehicle wreckage. Bring it on. The distance between is vanishing quickly. The Hummer's high-beams click on, further destroying my night vision, and the machine gun rattles to life. Brilliant bursts of death, and my car shudders. My body can't withstand those heavy rounds so I crouch low under the wheel. The little Boxster is instantly ruined; smoke pours from the hood, and my windshield shatters. But I don't swerve.

I want to crash. I crave the noise. Madness spreads like a fever. Adventure and death are almost sensual in their power.

The Humvee chickens out. He jerks sideways at the last instant, plowing into the concrete retaining wall, throwing his gunner violently forward. One down.

The massive eighteen-wheeler doesn't flinch. He grinds gears and bellows forward onto the wide interstate. I don't flinch either. My Boxster disintegrates into his grill. Tires burst with the impact. Steam and fire erupt from his undercarriage, covering the road. The big truck's engine breaks and front axle snaps. Men scream.

I neatly soar over the truck's cab, fifteen feet high, my luxury car left to melt alone. I alight and slide across the slick trailer roof, and the big vehicle's death throes vibrate through my shins. I shove fingernails into the roof's surface and peel the layered metal back like a giant can of tuna.

It's a trap.

Inside are Herders, picking themselves up from the collision. This convoy is bait, intended to capture more Guardians. Or me. A man on the floor squints at my silhouette above and fires his gun. I'm hit in the shoulder. It feels like being struck with a sledge. The slug doesn't penetrate because the disease dumped enough adrenaline to temporarily transmute my muscle to rock and my skin to tough hide. But it hurts and I'm knocked off the truck. I land hard on the road— my ankle pops and I lose my air.

The second Humvee can't brake in time and it slams into the rear of the smoldering eighteen-wheeler. Injured men groan and scramble clear. A destruction illuminated by fire.

Herders. I despise them. My hands itch to open the truck's gas tanks, to incinerate the men inside. But I'm not like them. I don't destroy the defenseless. This fight is over; I'm needed at the Power Plant.

I turn to run. A Herder rises from his smoking Humvee and fires a high-powered, riot-control net gun. The net is metal chain and it hits me from behind. I'm covered as if by a blanket, and the small battery releases its charge. A snap of sick blue light and I'm electrocuted, struck down in the middle of Interstate 5.

"Got her! I got the witch!"

The shock isn't lethal. Maybe if I hadn't been wearing rubber soled shoes? But the electro-muscular disruption overrides muscle control and singes my skin. The men howl and encircle me. They have electrified batons, electric cattle prods, net guns, and (the worst) lightning poles.

It's hard to kill Guardians. The easiest way is fire and electricity, but flamethrowers are too volatile and lightning guns only exist in science fiction. Lightning can't be *shot*, like bullets can. It has to transfer between termini with a strong differential in electric potential. So the Herders travel in pairs with charged poles and throw lightning back and forth.

Their mistake is giving me too much time to recuperate. My muscles cease twitching as they surround me. I'm shot again, this time by a shotgun. Agony. My body curls in on itself. But again, no permanent damage.

"No, no! Don't kill her! I got this."

A man approaches with a sizzling cattle prod. It's deadly, delivers a much bigger payload than the net. I'll be rendered insensate and wake up immobilized.

He nears. I cry and they laugh in response.

I will enjoy this.

Closer. Closer.

I *Move*. I'm off the ground before he can blink. The net spins into two men with electrified batons, enveloping them. Metal mesh connects the batons to their skin. The circle completes and electricity releases into flesh.

They scream. Their skin melts.

I disarm and fry my closest attacker with his own cattle prod. He has no chance to be surprised.

We're all lucky it isn't raining.

I hate this. And I crave it. The violence makes me sick, and fills me with disparate rapture. I used to be a girl, now a monster built with one purpose; demolition. I vanish within the melee. My fists are hammers and I drive them into my enemy, crushing bone. My nails are razors and I open their bodies, slicing cleanly through armor. I'm not good at fighting yet. My movements are clumsy and I'm inefficient at high speeds, but to my un-enhanced opponents it's like battling the wind. I'm hit only once, a lucky elbow to my jaw. The bones in his arm break.

Suddenly the night explodes with lightning, freezing the scene in my eyes. Herders scramble and throw heavy bolts of power between them, a lethal game of catch using batteries and rods. The proximity causes my hair to stand on end. It's mindless and desperate and they can't control the lightning. Nature is too powerful a force to command safely. I'm living proof. I am a wraith among them, a demon, and they shoot and sizzle each other instead. It's disgusting slaughter.

And it's over. Two dozen men lay groaning or dead on the pavement. I am burnt and hurt and furious. The smell turns my insides and I roar as a lion, as a dragon, as a goddess would. My voice will be heard for miles.

Abandon hope, all my enemies. I come for you.

The men wear suits and helmets. The helmets have cameras attached, transmitting a live feed. I pick one up and glare into it.

"Your men shatter against me. Come yourself, Witch. Let this be settled."

No time to catch my breath; another convoy is approaching. Jeep, truck, jeep, in that order, like the last one, banging around the entrance ramp at thirty, forty, fifty miles per hour. I bet this one isn't bait. It's gotta be full of wounded Guardians, struck down with awful weapons. I'm too tired. Too injured to stop it. I cast around for something, anything. There is a mounted machine gun on the Humvee's roof, however I'd be a sitting target.

The oncoming mass of machine won't be stopped by me. But I have to try.

All at once, the flight of Falcons screams out of the dark. Their headlights blaze to life and they swoop in elegant formation beside the Herder motorcade. Eight Falcons, flying together on motorcycles.

The cavalry has arrived.

The foremost enemy Humvee swerves to miss flaming wreckage. Three Falcons converge and *Leap* from their black motorcycles. They swarm the jeep like wolfs taking down big game. The gunner is dispatched, doors ripped off, and driver yanked out, a fast devastating attack so gorgeous I almost feel bad for the men inside. The Falcons jump off before the Humvee t-bones the far barricade.

The next wave of Falcons conducts a similar attack on the big eighteen-wheeler, except Mason hauls himself into the cab and jams the brakes to avoid a crash. Tires scream and dissolve.

The rearguard accelerates, the last Humvee's heavy gun rattling and chewing up the pavement. The final two Falcons jump aboard and the gun silences.

Surviving Herders spill from all three vehicles, heavy with armor and equipment. These are expert hunters and former special-ops, men trained for years, hardened fighters, and they are shredded by the Falcon Variants. You can't hit what you can't see. Mason and the Falcons *Move*, too fast, and they strike with long knives, and the Herders have no advantage of surprise. The cowardly Herders make their living through ambush, and without it they fall before us.

Afterwards, the Falcons scavenge through bodies, taking ID and weapons and valuables. I break the lock on the trailer. Before I open it, Mason asks, "What about the survivors? The Herders? Some of them live."

"Let them limp home," I say. "Let the world see what becomes of our aggressors." Perhaps we should execute them, but I have no stomach for it. Too much blood tonight. Plus the Herders are already wounded and the message might connect more solidly when they return home scarred.

I swing open the doors. Within the darkness, twenty Guardians are trussed by heavy chain and elasti-cuffs. All of them unconscious. All of them caught by surprise, bearing fresh electrical burns.

"Mason, assign a sentry. Call for Law Keepers and Medics to tend these Guardians."

Mason nods and slaps a hand on a Falcon's shoulder, a man taller than himself. "Yes ma'am. Chris will handle it. What about us?"

"Back to the power plant. We are needed."

Half a mile away, an inferno is melting the western corner of the Magnolia Power Plant. Gunfire has stopped within the vast complex.

Mason and I find our Engineers hiding behind abandoned trucks in the parking lot across Magnolia Boulevard. Their faces glow with flame and fear.

"Report. Tell me everything, quickly."

A wizened, shaggy man gulps air. "Yes Queen Carmine. They arrived in three trucks and approximately five hummers. They have guns. The fire started in the offices and warehouse. They shot at us to pin us down," he pants. "They captured all the Guardians who went in. Sixty seconds ago, they quit shooting."

"Three trucks? I've only seen two."

"Yes ma'am. The big one is still in there."

So the enemy is still inside, securing more of our fallen family. I won't wait. I press my radio into his hand. "Call for firetrucks. Got it? Update General Brown. And tell Nuts to hurry."

In times of stress, the Guardians operate on instinct. Pack animal mentality. They wait by my side, quivering, muscles trembling, hounds yearning to be unleashed. I bolt across the street and they sprint at my side. This is why the Blue-Eyed Witch and Walter want them; the Guardians would follow them as they follow me, blindly into combat, an unstoppable force moving as one.

The Herders have retreated deep into the complex and are piling into the largest truck I've ever seen. It's an armored troop transport capable of moving hundreds. More of a long tank broken into two locking segments, like two wide train cars, moving on twelve reinforced wheels taller than I can reach.

"Dios mio," Mason grunts. We stand on the second floor landing of an exposed metal staircase, watching the beast belch diesel smoke. "What the hell is that thing? Must've cost fifty million to build."

The army-green transport rumbles forward. The drivers peer through thin slits in the cab, probably steering mostly from camera feed. My people are inside that dragon.

From our second-story perch, we have to jump *up* to land on the transport's roof. There are no defenses because the tank doesn't need them. We're powerless against this overwhelming machine. We kick and pry and pull and don't even dent the thick steel. Our knives break when they strike the tires. There's no weakness to exploit. Can't get in. Can't stop it.

"What do we do?" Mason asks. We stand on top as it rumbles out of Magnolia. It takes up two lanes and carelessly crushes any obstruction.

"We can't stop it." My bruised hands are on my knees and I'm sucking wind. "We need rockets to break the engine or puncture the tires, but General Brown won't get here in time."

The dragon is picking up speed. Ten miles per hour. Fifteen. Twenty. It turns left on Front Street and thunders north. Our hidden Engineers stare with wide eyes from the parking lot as we pass. We'll be on the interstate in two minutes.

I was stupid not to have a stronger guard here, armed with heavy munitions. This is my fault.

"Mason, you and the Falcons find your motorcycles," I call over the groaning engine. "Get to General Brown and grab all the armor piercing weapons you can carry. I'll stay with the transport and guide you over the phone."

He shakes his head. "You'll be twenty miles away by then. Alone."

"This is not a debate, Mason."

"Look!"

"*The Outlaw!*"

We turn to see a man fall from the sky and land heavily on the transport's nose. He is dressed in black pants, black vest, and a red mask which covers his eyes and hair and ties in the back, like the pirate from *Princess Bride*. The crimson mask is theatrical and dramatic and stupid, and somehow it looks great. It's the most well-known costume...ever. He carries a heavy metal rod in his hands, slightly longer than a baseball bat, and he drives it down through the driver's thin viewport, puncturing the dragon's eye.

There's a small explosion of fire and sparks. The engine's drone increases in pitch, and its drivetrain lurches sickly. The Outlaw has wounded it. A sudden change in direction throws the Falcons off the sides, and I barely cling on. The rod must have gone straight into the dash, pulverizing controls. The behemoth barrels over a fence and across railroad tracks, moving like a drunken, charging grizzly bear into an abandoned lumber yard. The Outlaw drives his bat through the second viewport, splitting steel and rending the dragon uncontrollable. His jaw is set and he ignores the mayhem. The truck storms through tall stacks of lumber and the engines smoke heavily. We push the growing mountain of destruction ahead like a plow, careening into old cargo trucks.

Too much strain. Too much electrical damage. Gears shred. The engine blows, rupturing oil and steam, and the beast shudders. The churning wheels cease laboring, and we settle on slackening hydraulics. My ears ring with sudden silence.

Enemy soldiers shout and pour from the rear gates. Dozens. They meet the Falcons. They meet me. They meet death. Forked lightning jumps. Men fall. Five minutes of hell.

We suffer one casualty. A Falcon catches a bolt of energy through his chest. He will not rise, and I *Feel* his death. The rest of us are shot. Burnt. Bleeding. Exhausted. Sick. But alive.

I sit in the lumber yard, side by side with Mason in the carnage.

This is why we were created. Built with bones of iron. Thick skin. Lethal nails. Snap reflexes. Built to kill. But I hate it. I want to leave the field of strewn bodies but I'm too tired.

Mason is spitting sweat and blood from his lips as it drips down his nose. "This sucks. When are they going to learn?"

"When is *she* going to learn," I say. "This is the work of one woman."

"The Blue-Eyed Witch? You're sure?"

"She attacks with Herders. Walter would use Variants."

He waves vaguely towards the steaming dragon. "Looks like twenty Guardians are stashed inside. Tied up."

"General Brown should arrive any minute. He can transport them to the hospital."

"Look," he says and nudges me. He points to the roof of the lumber yard's warehouse. A man. In a mask, watching us. "Your guardian angel. Good thing he was nearby."

"Coincidence?" I ask. "Or planned?"

Mason laughs and stands. "You really can't remember, can you. He would never plan this."

He offers me his hand. I take it and haul myself up. I sneak another glance.

The Outlaw is gone.

- Nine -

"What are those?" I ask.

Kayla responds, "Sneakers. Your Devotee brought them." She didn't sleep last night yet she's fresh and exquisite in a white babydoll dress, alacrity personified.

I'm standing in my bathroom, examining scorch marks from last night. Only one would require intense medical treatment if my skin wasn't enhanced. An electrical burn that fused bits of black fabric into my chest. It'll heal in a few days, two or three times faster than a normal person. An advantage of being mutated.

The Falcons and I require new shoes. The extreme speed and instant changes in direction grinds off the tread in a single night. "But those are pink."

"So?" Kayla asks.

"The Devotee brought pink sneakers?"

"Well. He brought several. I selected the pink pair. They're cute. Try them on." The sneakers are Saucony, pink with rose colored laces.

"I don't like pink. You're not my haberdasher, Kayla."

"No one knows what that means, Carmine. But you've got great legs and these shoes will draw attention to them."

"But-"

She beams and clasps her hands, and her sudden flush of excitement hits me like a tanning bed lamp. "If you don't like these, I have a pair of white platform peep toes picked out. I've been saving them for weeks."

"High heels? No thank you. How much were they?"

"That doesn't matter. They're Valentino and have rosette details. And I have a matching skirt—"

"No! I'll take the pink sneakers." I dress and she helps bind my joints. My bones ache and my head is pounding to the extent that I down a handful of ibuprofen, though it's never helped in the past. "What have you read online about last night's attack?"

"Very little. No one knows much. PuckDaddy is apologetic he didn't see the attack something."

"Would he have warned us?

"Of course, Carmine. He worships you."

"He *does*? I thought he worked for the Resistance."

She shakes her head, causing fulgent silver shimmers in her hair. "One day you'll realize how important you are. And that you're not alone. He does work for the Resistance but he is also our supporter. And also, I don't think you should date the Outlaw."

Whoa.

"Excuse me?" I say around the bite of chocolate in my mouth.

"Dating him could be a disaster. My advice is to stay away."

"I thought you loved the Outlaw."

"I do! But it could endanger everything you've worked for. Did you know one of the Falcons attacked him instead of the Herders last night? The Guardians simply can't control themselves around him. Our Kingdom is surviving, but barely. We can't afford anything which might upset that."

I grab a broom and start sweeping dust and dirt out of my room, tossing gathered piles through the missing walls to be redistributed by the slipstream. I don't allow Cleaners in here, and boys are awful at dusting. "My love life is none of your business. But rest assured, I have no romantic interest in the Outlaw."

"Yes you do."

"No. I don't."

"Carmine. You're wearing that silly smile when you think about him," she says, and she covers her grin with her hand. I shoot a glance at the mirror. I'm *not* smiling. That is not a smile. That's...I'm... squinting. She continues, "You're still Katie Lopez. Whether you like it or not. And according to the legend, Katie and Chase Jackson have been sweethearts since their pre-teens. Part of you still loves him."

The broom cracks in half. I didn't break the wood intentionally, it just happened. "Don't you have a job to do?"

"I'm doing it now!"

"Then you're fired."

"You're really sensitive about the Outlaw." She's glowing behind her hand, her pheromones filling my head with visions of flowers and the ocean.

I snap, "How could this possibly be your job? Your job is to be a transcendent annoyance?"

"The Outlaw wants to meet with you! I'm helping you prep."

I throw the broken broom at her and stomp out of the room. "Tell him no. Or I'm re-assigning you to Sanitation."

The victims from last night's attack are being treated at Good Samaritan Hospital. The building is fully functional, operating at maximum power. The Kingdom has a full staff of Doctors and Nurses and Medics, and storage rooms overflowing with supplies. Injured Guardians won't be here long; the Hyper Virus will knit them together. Doctors set their broken bones, treat infections, and pump them full of nutrients. The Engineers and Workers will require extra care.

I walk the halls and visit the injured. The Guardians perk up as I enter their rooms. Such a sad state of dependance they were re-born into, requiring another (me) to lead them. They experience hope and despondence in exaggerated proportion, based on their relationship to me. Their proximity to me. I visit Becky, who happened to be nearby last night. She suffered only minor burns but still she fights tears when its time for me to go. She grips my hand fiercely and says, "Sorry...it's just...easier when you're around."

They need each other. They need me. My gut churns when I think about Walter getting his hands on them. Or on Kayla.

In addition to the injured, three Guardians (including one Falcon)

and eight Workers died. Per our customs, we hold a ceremony for them on the piers at Redondo Beach, and their bodies are sailed to sea and sunk. It's a somber affair, a grisly reminder that we have enemies and they are relentless. I lay flowers on their corpses and cry. Supposedly the deaths in battle are the easiest to bear because we can blame them on the enemy, but I don't feel that way today. Today I hurt. I sense the weight of all eyes, wondering how I'm going to ensure their safety.

Good question. I toss and turn at night wondering the same thing.

Workers bury the eighty dead Herders in a mass grave inside La Tuna Canyon. Kayla attends and takes pictures, documenting the unnecessary slaughter. She's at war with the American president, with Blue-Eyes, with Walter, and her weapons are media. *This is a disaster*, she'll say. *Look what your leaders are doing.*

Nuts reports that we got lucky last night. The fire at Magnolia damaged mostly non-essential equipment. He and the Engineers are hard at work pilfering from other power plants, and he thinks we'll be back at full strength in three days.

The Priest is sweeping northwest LA with Law Keepers. We have spies. Insurgents. Traitors working for the enemy. Some hide in our ranks, and some hide in the capacious empty residential neighborhoods, probably in Reseda and Northridge. The Priest not so subtly blames me for last night, a failure in intelligence, in planning, in defense, and states he should be given more power. More responsibility, more control. He might be right, but I'm too stubborn to acquiesce.

I spend much of the day with General Brown, touring our boundaries, identifying weak spots, examining maps, and arguing over how best to allocate our resources. He doesn't need my assistance. In fact I get in the way more than I help, but I can't do nothing. Kayla told me this is a character flaw of mine, that I'm a micromanager, that I work too hard, that I don't trust others to do their job. But if I don't, people might die. At four in the afternoon we're bickering inside the tower's hot war department. He stands and stretches and says, "Carmine, your help is appreciated. But it's time you go."

"Why?"

"You need a break. And you're denting my table."

My whole body is tense and my fingers have imbedded into the table's plywood. I tug them out and mutter, "Sorry, General."

"I know a thing or two about leadership. And I know you got a hard job. The most difficult on earth, my opinion. So I'd like to give you a word of advice. Then I'll keep my peace."

"Anything. Absolutely, by all means. I have no idea what I'm doing."

He removes his cap and runs a hand over his trimmed pate. "Just this. You built this community through the force of your leadership. People naturally trust your conviction and your work ethic and your strength. Don't fall into management mode. Learn the difference between management and leadership. Because you're a natural leader, and that's what we need. For our little world to prosper, we need Carmine to lead, not manage. You point the way. Trust me, they'll follow."

Five minutes later I'm in my apartment, staring at the Maxwell book on leadership. I don't know what General Brown means. I'm in constant crisis mode; is that leadership? Somehow I don't think leadership can be learned from a book. Besides, any free moment I find is spent reading the *Cinder* book, which is shockingly enjoyable.

My phone rings. It's Mason.

"Guess what I'm doing?" he whispers.

"I'm too tired to guess."

"I'm tailing the Outlaw."

I collapse on the bed and close my eyes, pushing against my headache with thumb and forefinger. "If he catches and whomps you, you deserve it."

"I stumbled on his trail and tracked him. His scent is...it's hard to describe. He smells like a bright day. Like the sun."

"That makes no sense."

"Want to know what he's doing?"

"Not really." That's a lie. I very much want to know.

"He's in Glendale. I think he visited your old home. I mean, Katie Lopez's old home."

I sit up so fast I slide off the bed and land heavily on my butt. "How do you know?"

"I stuck my head in after he left. Found pictures of a girl that looks like you. But with longer hair."

"Give me the address. I'm on the way."

Mason is sitting on his motorcycle outside a brick apartment building near the entrance to a neighborhood, one mile off the Five. Memories stir as I climb from the truck. Or echoes of memories. Kayla could never find my address, so I never visited. The daylight turns amber as the sun drops, and I'm struck by the familiarity of the shade as it crawls across evergreens. "I know this place. I think..."

Mason says, "Go through the sliding glass door in the back. Dalton and I'll wait here."

"Where is he?"

"The Outlaw? Took off. Went north. He has a motorcycle too." He smiles with pride, absently patting his bike.

It's just an apartment. An empty one. No reason to be nervous. But my heart hammers as I push the curtains aside and step into the dim room. The walls and bedspread and pictures are shades of pink. Maybe I do like pink?

My home! Katie Lopez responds to the bedroom, and her voice is freighted with passion. *This is where I live!*

The Outlaw *was* here. And he does smell like sunlight. However there's more than just him. The various scents are a full-on assault. Each inhalation is a memory. I remember buying that perfume; Burberry. And the scented tissues. And this! I would scrub my hands and legs with this cheap lotion whenever a boy came over. Pictures flash in my mind. More than one boy. Kissing. I remember kissing. But I can't summon the faces.

My breath won't come. I lower to the bed as my head swims, and I anticipate the squeak of springs. The pillow smells of stale shampoo when I lay down. Dust motes dance in the fading light. This is a small bedroom, but I think it's perfect. I bet I did all my homework at that desk. My mother would cook and I'd leave the door open so we could talk. I can almost smell peppers. After several minutes with my eyes closed I realize my ears have been waiting for the familiar click of air conditioning.

The closet's been ransacked, but a few items incite a swirl of pleasant emotions. I lock the door, strip, and try on outfits. I'm taller now, but I knew that. The shorts are indecent and the tops are positively scandalous. The bra clasps won't connect but the shorts button without a struggle. Hah, small victories. I grin, picturing Mason's face if I walked out wearing these jean shorts and white tank top. I run the brush through my hair and marvel at the length of the strands I find coiled around bristles. Katie Lopez had great hair.

And the sandals fit! Katie loved these. Almost positive. I'm keeping them. I find two old backpacks and stuff them with perfume, the lotion, a teddy bear, shoes, jewelry, some old diaries, and...I cover a sob as I shuffle through a stack of photographs. Katie Lopez, so full of life, so happy. Smiling with her mother. My mother. Another of me hugging a boy. I recognize Chase Jackson. More photos of Chase. Katie is kissing his cheek. Katie and Chase stand on a football field, maybe for prom? That night...that was a special night.

I drop the photographs and cry. My hands tremble and I can't stop the flood of emotion. Katie Lopez's soul is in agony and I hear her raging somewhere inside. Her passions come pouring out of me and I'm helpless to prevent her pain. This isn't fair to either of us. Me, a new creation with no past; and Katie, a real person trapped inside a...a robot. A cyborg. That's what I am. A programmed machine. I'm nothing.

The past few months, history has become more fixed in my mind. Everything sharpens into focus except me. I can't make the facts connect with *me*. I'm a stumbling phantom, blind, being crushed by emotions without source, without warning. Why am I weeping over this prom picture?

I pack the photographs after three minutes of crying.

Mamá. Where is she?

"No," I say. "Sorry Katie. I can't deal with her right now." My voice is shaky. I look at the closed bedroom door. Beyond lies the rest of her apartment. The kitchen. Her mother's room. *My* mother's room. "We'll come back. Okay? It's been an exhausting twenty-four hours. I can't. Not today."

Katie goes quiet but she's unhappy. I feel her inside like a tight ball of discontent. I can't blame her.

On my way out, I notice the flowers. I must've knocked them off when I fell on the bed. A bouquet of godetia. My favorites. They are freshly cut, bound with string, and the stems are wrapped with a wet washcloth to keep them healthy. I breathe in their fragrance with my eyes closed. Katie does too, and she sighs happily.

The Outlaw brought me flowers. He knows what I like best. He knows me better than I know me. No. No. I will not cry again. Deep breaths, keep it together.

I force myself to leave. The day is all but gone. Dalton and Mason wordlessly take the backpacks from me, casting glances at the flowers. Mason sits on his bike and points down the street. "He used to live down there."

I'm numb but I follow the direction of his eyes down an idyllic street. "The Outlaw? You investigated?"

"I remember."

"Remember? You came before the Evacuation? When Chase lived here?"

Mason takes a while answering. His mind is far off, like wading through thick waters. "We are bound to you, Carmine. The Guardians, I mean. You've become *part* of us. And it used to be that way with the Chemist. But much more so. We follow you because we choose to, because we love you. But we followed the Chemist because that was life. Our entire being was serving. He had gravity and we just fell after him. The Chemist could stir us up, make us so angry, rabid. Almost feral. We'd go onto a mentally catatonic state and become animals, like werewolves, hell I don't know, but we'd wake up later with these awful memories. The Chemist sent us here. To the Outlaw's house to kill him. I remember now."

"What happened?"

He grins suddenly. "This is a fun story."

"Why?"

"Because you're in it. So we ambushed Chase Jackson at his house. Hundreds of us. Somehow he got away but we wrecked his place and then chased him here. He is faster than us. And stronger. My clearest memory is of you driving a truck and he's in the back, fighting us. Him and someone else. A girl with a gun, maybe? It's all hazy. But I remember you. How funny, right? Now here you are again."

"I was driving a truck?"

"You don't remember? Yeah, right through here. Tore up these bushes. That's my clearest memory. He came here to warn Katie, because we were after both of you. We ambushed him. But you two made it to a truck and escaped. We chased you up the Five! Hah. Forgot about that. A lot of us died. But I didn't care about them."

I sit in the passenger seat and rest my head on the dash. Katie is holding her breath. She remembers the truck escape, though I don't. This is all so...I don't know how to deal.

He brought me flowers.

"Mason."

"Yeah?"

"Call Kayla. Tell her we'll meet with the Outlaw. Tomorrow."

Ten

I'm still awake at one in the morning. I clutch Katie Lopez's teddy bear and rub her lotion into my hands for the fifteenth time and sort through the accompanying olfactory nostalgia. Nostalgia without memories is disorienting, and the result is I'm homesick without a home.

Finally I kick off the covers with a huff, dress, shrug into my backpack, and *Climb* down the outside of Olympic. I borrow a sturdy ten-speed and pedal west on the 101 towards Hollywood, entirely alone in the darkness. I ride hard for ten miles, reaching my destination in forty minutes.

The Griffith Park Observatory sits on Hollywood Mountain like a huge white-walled castle. There's good hiking inside Griffith Park, as well as the old zoo and golf course. The Observatory's great domes and stately main hall are still exquisite but the green lawn needs a trim. If I was a resident of New Los Angeles, instead of one of it's leaders, this is where I would live. I'd sling a hammock on the east terrace, sleep in the west alcoves when it rained, bring water and food up with me every day after work. However I'd probably feel less confident at night without all the enhancements.

I lay a thin blanket near the solar system lawn model and sit crisscross. After a few minutes, my pulse slows and my body unclenches. Relaxes. Almost melts. My eyes close and I cast myself outwards, a trick I've learned over time. I rummage through the Observatory grounds with my senses, like a predatory mammal would, and expand beyond. I *Listen*. I *Smell*. I *Feel*. I map the lives I find. Two owls perch in silent observance on the limb of a sycamore. A family of mule deer also watch, alert and ready for flight. There is a romantic couple frolicking on Roosevelt Municipal beside the embers of their fire. A thousand animals rampage with tiny footfalls through the bracken. A pack of gray foxes rest near the Hollywood Sign. Soon it becomes too much and I'm overwhelmed, but that's okay. As my awareness is subsumed by nature, so is my scent cast from the mountain and distributed through the trees and streets. My body makes a strong impression on nature when I allow it.

The Outlaw is nearby, only a few miles distant. Most likely he will detect me. But will he investigate? Part of me hopes so. Part of me desires him, driven to complete distraction by him. But he won't come. He's denied entrance until tomorrow and he won't risk the insult. I force him from my mind as Katie begins stirring restlessly from the catacombs.

Still I wait and allow my scent to travel. Two hours go by before I open my eyes. They are here. They have come silently, stealing through the scrub forest, sneaking up the drive, tentative reconnaissance.

They are the wild Variants living nearby, creatures enhanced and broken on an operating table. As yet unsure of me. Of each other. They aren't part of my pack and so they've hidden in fear. Men and women my age in various stages of decay and superhuman might, surviving as outcasts in this new world without a master, without a creator. Tonight there are twelve. A week ago, only five. We need them and they need us. They need a home. They need companions. Security. A purpose. And the purpose I offer is healthier than Walter's. Lost sheep in need of a shepherd.

"Don't be afraid. I am Carmine." I extend my hands so they can touch me. "Follow me. To your new home."

PART III

November, 2019

I sleep, but my heart is awake; It is the voice of my beloved!
He knocks, saying, "Open for me, my love,
my dove, my perfect one."
- Song of Solomon 5:2

The following morning, the Priest bursts into my apartment. My Devotee doesn't like him so he pushes him back with thick hands.

"Carmine!" he snarls. "I just heard. You can *not* meet with him."

I'm bone tired, sitting crisscross on my bed and reading old Teresa Triplett articles about the Outlaw. Doing my homework.

Homework! I've been neglecting school. I'm so behind on my papers. Ugh.

Teresa Triplett met with the Outlaw on several occasions. At the time she didn't know he was a boy in high school. The nighttime interviews are fascinating; she was clearly crushing on him, and the reports are anything but objective and balanced.

"Carmine! Are you listening to me?"

Teresa will request permission to attend today's meeting. She probably has valuable insight into the Outlaw. I stare hard at her words, vainly trying to focus, to slow my pulse. He's just a boy. Relax.

Kayla enters the apartment. Her humming stops when she sees the Priest. "What are *you* doing here?"

"I'm being treated like a second-class citizen, that's what." I hear the sneer in his voice. "She can't go."

His voice compounds my headache. I drop the articles into my lap, rub my eyes, and say, "Let him in, Kayla." Then maybe he'll go away. They both walk in, followed by Kayla's Devotee carrying two armloads of clothing. I groan, "What is that?"

Kayla flourishes her hands like a model on the old *Price is Right* gameshow. "Merely the first load. Two more on the way. I raided every boutique within ten miles."

"I'm not dressing up. You're wasting your time."

The Priest looks like he spent two hours getting ready this morning. He's so manicured he's almost effeminate, and I can't imagine what the women see in him. Right now he's red in the face and seething. "Carmine—"

I interrupt him, "Kayla, would you call Teresa Triplett? I want her advice."

"She's waiting outside. So are General Brown and the Governess. Just arrived."

"Carmine!" the Priest snaps. "I've dealt with him before. *Listen* to me. He's a heretic. A madman. But a powerful one. I forbid this encounter. He is *after* you."

"I'm not going alone, Priest." My voice is cold. If he wasn't so respected by the people this would be the day I terminate his employment within our Kingdom. Don't want the ripples yet. Can't upset the balance. "We all are."

"He'll seduce you." The Priest is spitting his words, pacing back and forth. "He's been gifted by some evil power, bent on blasphemy. A freak. An arrogant, law-breaking freak."

"I will not be seduced. Calm yourself."

"He has no respect for authority. He wants attention and power, and he'll usurp your control over the mutants. You cannot go. I *cannot* allow it."

Kayla wrinkles her nose at him. "You're not nice. And you spit."

"Be quiet, silly girl. Leave the talking to the grownups. If we need a pretty picture, I'll call."

"You are dismissed, Priest." I signal my Devotee and the Priest is bodily hauled from the room against his outrage and protests. In his place comes Teresa Triplett the reporter, the Governess, and General Brown. The three of us are rarely in the same room, because for a while the American military was spying on us with satellites and we worried they might drop a missile on the triumvirate. "Did everyone get my note? You approve?"

The Governess offers a snap nod. "Decisive and simple. I have set the Overseers to scampering. All should be prepared."

General Brown sits in my chair and picks lint from his pressed pants. "Seems like a straight-forward operation. We convene, the man gets to say his piece, and I'll escort him back to the boundary."

"You'll have snipers in place, General?"

"I will not," he replies and I'm surprised. "They'd be useless. Besides, Ms. Carmine, if there is one man on earth we don't need fear it's him."

"Forgive me if I don't share your confidence. From what I've read he's going to have a strong affect on the Guardians. What if he uses them?"

"He won't." Teresa Triplett is in the corner, typing notes as fast as she can. The details of this meeting won't be published unless the triumvirate approves, which we won't. "It's not them you should worry about, Queen."

Kayla selects tops and dresses from her collection of clothing and holds them up beside me. She squints and shakes her head and tosses them into a discard pile.

"What do you mean?" I ask Teresa. "You know the Outlaw. You anticipate this meeting derailing?"

"No. I anticipate you derailing."

I growl in frustration and scrub a hand through my hair. "Why does everyone assume he's going to seduce me? That I can't control myself? Maybe he'll seduce Kayla."

"He's not in love with *me*," Kayla responds, and I smack the red dress out of her hand.

"I have no interest in this man."

"Good," the Governess says. She's a woman used to wearing authority and she speaks loudly with strength and conviction. "Because I agree with Kayla. You cannot fall in love with this man."

"I'm not! What...why is everyone so concerned with my love life?" I'm shouting. I try to lower my voice but I cannot. "I'm not Katie Lopez! The Outlaw will have to find someone else. Besides, what would be so wrong about dating him? Why do you all care?"

General Brown answers in a calm voice, "The heart is a deep ocean, Miss Carmine. Hard to predict. Hard to control. I watched both my daughters fall in love. My oldest dropped out of college to chase her minor league outfielder around the east coast. My youngest is pregnant in Alabama with my third grandchild. What I'm saying is, the best-laid plans are wrecked by romance. We're at war, and our most powerful ally is in love with you. You can understand our concern."

"No. I cannot. You're married, General. What's the difference?"

He and the Governess share a look and slight smile. Infuriating. "The difference is I'm no longer young."

"So?"

"We're all wild in our youth, Carmine," he says. "That's what it's for; learning from mistakes. And getting involved with him would be a mistake."

"What would be so bad about me dating him?" I'm just being surly now. The Outlaw and I have no future, but I'm chafing against their intrusions.

The Governess throws up her hands in exasperation. General Brown says, "Do you realize what we've sacrificed to follow you? Everything. We threw our lives and careers away because we believe in your vision to build a refuge for the Variants, who are the real victims of the Chemist. You're the leader. So much depends on you, and we believe in you. But you're about to tangle with a dangerous man."

"But isn't he good?"

Kayla mutters, "Good *looking*."

"My first two husbands were good," the Governess scoffs. "Doesn't mean they weren't dangerous."

Teresa Triplett, Kayla, General Brown and the Governess are all staring at me. Might as well have hands on their hips like four protective parents.

"Like I said before," I say through clenched teeth, "Katie Lopez is dead. We're going to meet the Outlaw as a professional courtesy and send him on his way."

With that they let the matter drop and we discuss details for ten more minutes. Then all but Kayla leave. I stand at the edge of the broken wall and stare north for a few minutes. "No harm in arriving early. Should we go?"

In response, Kayla holds up a mirror. My heart sinks at my reflection. I look awful. Like an exhausted zombie. My clothes are dirty and there's an actual twig in my hair. "Queen Carmine, sweetie, when was your last shower?"

I screw up my eyes in thought. I've forgotten what month it is. "I can't remember. I swam in the lake last week. Does that count?"

"Wow. Okay, never mind. My goodness. What I meant to say is, get your beautiful butt in the shower. I have soap and shampoo and a razor."

My filth requires forty-five minutes to eradicate entirely. Three cycles of shampoo, conditioner, and body wash under a tepid spray. Got to admit, the stuff she selected smells great. I emerge refreshed in a towel and find Kayla has assembled an entire makeup workshop.

I say, "No."

"Carmine-"

"No makeup."

"But-"

"No!"

"Compromise!" she shouts back, and her words sink straight into my muscles. She's using her gift of persuasion, hitting me full force with her eyes like a Cheshire cat. Its effective even when I know she's doing it.

"What compromise?"

"Just rouge, lipstick, eye-liner, blush-"

"No deal."

"Fine! Honestly, Carmine. I'll highlight your cheekbones. And use mascara on your lashes. That's it. Deal?"

I sit on the chair and she hovers over me, doing stuff to my face. The Outlaw probably doesn't have to go through this facade before meetings. This close, her breath smells like sugar. While she works I notice the outfits she's picked out.

"I'm not wearing a dress."

"You're a *Queen*."

"My jeans and jacket are fine."

Her hand falters at my eye. "You can't."

"Yes. I can."

"I threw them out the window."

I slump back in the chair. She's probably lying but I'm too stressed to search the apartment. "Meddlesome."

"What?"

"That's what it'll say on your tombstone. After I hurl you off the tower. You died because you're too meddlesome."

"You say the most ghastly things, Carmine. But good news, I'm done!"

"Kayla. Here's the deal. I'm exhausted. And worried about this meeting. I don't know why but I'm feeling antsy. And I'd feel a lot better if I wore my favorite jacket."

"Aw! You have first date jitters!"

"You said I couldn't date him!"

"You can't! And stop shouting at me. You're going on this date to break his heart. It's not even a date. We just want him to want you. Make sense?"

"It absolutely does not. This is a meeting of allies. I'm not wearing any of this crap." Clutching the towel with one hand, I toss the pile of clothes onto the floor one piece at a time. "Too girly. Too pink. Too fluffy. Too see-through. Too stupid. Too girly. Too small." My hand stops at a pretty green top.

Kayla gasps. "Do you like that one? It's darling! It's an off-the-shoulder, silk Armani tunic. Loose fitting and sheer, so you'd need to wear something underneath. Unless you *really* want to get his attention..."

"Can I wear jeans with it?"

"Of course! I brought several. And I have the perfect leather booties to pair with them."

Kayla's exuberance wins the day. She dresses me, pokes and tugs and examines and finally announces it perfect. I inspect her handi-work in the mirror and am startled by the stranger within.

Oh! It's me! There I am.

Katie is pleased. I'm amazed. My cheekbones look great and my eyes are bigger and I wouldn't mind wearing this outfit again. I didn't know I could look pretty.

"Can you find this tunic in other colors? I don't hate it." I walk out of the bathroom and she's waiting for me with a small, glittering, and jeweled gizmo.

"You're a queen." Her voice sounds hesitant. "And I found this crown..."

Two

We arrive at the baseball field ten minutes before the Outlaw. Dodgers Stadium has a capacity of fifty-five thousand and the blue and gray seats are stuffed with Guardians and Workers. As Dalton, Kayla, and I walk onto the field the crowd erupts and cheers, an overwhelming avalanche of sound.

I'm not wearing Kayla's crown. I broke it in half. She told me it cost half a million dollars. We settled on dainty silver hair clips, barely visible but Kayla insisted they'd catch the sunlight. Will he notice? And why do I care?

I feel like we're at the bottom of a funnel, walled in by spectators and noise. Not a cloud in the sky so the angels can watch this circus.

"We scheduled this meeting last night," I growl. "How on earth are fifty-thousand people here?"

Dalton, wearing a red t-shirt and furious scowl, shakes his head. "Security's gone to hell in this place. A tactical nightmare." Law Keepers and soldiers line the walls, but according to the General they'll be useless.

We ascend the raised platform placed over second base. The Outlaw wants to meet with me? Fine, but it'll be on my terms. He'll have to look up, giving me the height advantage. The platform is wide but crowded with the three of us, the Governess, General Brown, Teresa Triplett, and the Priest. No need for the Priest to be here, but he'd never miss an opportunity to be in the spotlight. I can feel anxiety leaking from everyone's pores and they fan out, placing me at the center. We're a far more impressive welcoming committee than is necessary.

I say, "Nuts should be here. He's Infected, the most powerful among us."

"I asked him," General Brown chuckles. "Man said he's got no time for damn meetings."

"Forget him," the Governess states. She's wearing her usual black skirt and button up shirt. Her hair is in a bun. Why didn't Kayla pester *her* about wardrobe choices? "We must focus."

Mason radios Dalton. The Falcons are outside the stadium, Outlaw in tow. Dalton glances at me and I growl, "Bring him in. Let's get this over with."

The stadium speakers blare and the Outlaw is given some honorable introduction. I don't listen. I can barely think. The first Falcon appears in the doorway of the right-field wall, and I'm panicking. If this is like that night at the Starlight Bowl then his presence is going to invade the stadium. His aura or whatever will go straight into our nostrils and ear canals; we'll breath him in and the Guardians will lose their minds.

The Outlaw himself comes into view, encircled by Falcons. The crowd is dead silent. "This is a bad idea," I hiss.

Kayla whispers back, "What! Why?"

I'm on the verge of bolting. As soon as the virus in me detects the virus in him, I'll lose control. My body is hardening in preparation for battle. "He can kill us all. Why are we doing this?"

"Just like we planned," General Brown says and his voice is calm, soothing. "Everything is fine."

I'm gulping deep breaths but not getting enough oxygen. He's coming closer. I'm terrified. I'm terrified of being terrified, like I was in Burbank.

I can do this. I can do this.

Chase is wearing the red mask, Katie says. *He always was too theatrical.*

He's taller than I thought he'd be. Wearing the infamous black pants and vest combo, and the rod is shoved down the back of his collar. His legs are rangy and his arms are well-muscled. Tattoos glint on his left shoulder, bicep and forearm.

Tattoos. That's new. I think I like them.

"Shut up," I growl.

Kayla squeaks, "I didn't say anything!"

Is he limping? Or strutting? He's not arrogant. Not really. Silly boy. But he's limping?

It's almost comical, the Outlaw walking within a circle of men who dress in imitation of him. The Falcons wear black pants and vests too, and I wonder if Mason is embarrassed. Chase Jackson does appear to have a minor limp. Every few steps.

His processional reaches the platform and the Falcons step back. His eyes are locked on mine and our gazes shatter like fireworks. He bows low while I scramble for words.

"Welcome to New Los Angeles, Outlaw," I announce. I speak loudly as to be heard in the upper decks. "We're honored by your visit."

He grabs his mask with a fist and tugs it off. He's a perfectly made specimen of man, though his dark hair reaches his ears. Too long for my taste. His eyes are strikingly blue. He's my age, about twenty, and his jaw is peppered with a day old beard.

"Hi Katie."

I know his voice. A familiar timbre. His eyes walk over me, and I can't blame him; his girlfriend's body has changed. He's fiddling with the mask in both hands like he's nervous. He opens his mouth to speak but thinks better of it, and simply smiles instead. Such a smile my heart leaps.

He's better looking than I anticipated, and belatedly I realize it must be my turn to talk. But before I can, Teresa Triplett surprises us all by hopping off the platform and hugging him. He laughs and returns the embrace, and then they're both wiping away tears. The crowd applauds and whistles.

What just happened? *I'm* the one who's going to derail? I'm not the one pawing him.

"I haven't seen you since...wow, I don't know. That awful night, I guess," she says and she's sniffing. Her pretty and plastic face has lost all composure.

"I'm glad you're still here," he says.

"They wouldn't let me visit you in the hospital."

She's so sweet. I always liked her, Katie thinks. But I want her out of the way. I feel an undeniable stab of jealousy.

Then Dalton jumps down. The two men hug and pound each

other on the back and laugh about something and the Outlaw is thanking him and I'm so confused. Never once has Dalton mentioned he knows the Outlaw. Chase is sneaking glances at me and I feel tingles of electricity each time.

I'm not terrified, I realize. I don't *feel* his overwhelming strength like the other night. The Falcons are erect and tense, eyes locked on him, so they must be sensing something. The Variants sitting in the stands are frozen, rapt, many squatting on their haunches, straining forward. Like hunting dogs who've spotted prey.

Chase bounds up to the platform. My pulse races. We're too close. But he moves to General Brown and salutes him.

Brown cracks a smile and returns it. "Good to see you, boy."

The Outlaw replies, "Congratulations on your promotion. You're the finest General on earth, in my opinion."

General Brown knows him too? I'm growing livid. All these prattling, over-bearing twits giving me advice? My blood boils.

He needs to cut his hair. And why is he limping?

Shut up Katie.

"Thank you for being here, General," Chase says. "For keeping Los Angeles safe. I know you took a huge risk. Please thank your men for me."

"You're welcome. I'll give you a tour and you can thank them yourself."

"It'd be an honor."

Hypocrite. General Brown is a hypocrite. I'm going to skewer him. And Dalton. I'm so mad I tremble.

The two men shake hands and Chase compliments the Governess on her management of the Kingdom. He speaks specifically about certain operations he admires and she flusters and reddens and waves off his praise.

Good heavens. I roll my eyes and huff. I think Katie does too.

Kiss him.

Katie. No. The Outlaw very pointedly does not speak to the Priest. He stops in front of Kayla, whose eyes are wide. I'm not sure she's breathing. He produces a small red rose from his vest and presents it to her. Her hand trembles, and he says, "A gift. From PuckDaddy. He is your biggest fan."

For a moment Kayla borders on fainting. She grabs his hand for balance, and I swear I smell rainbows. She asks, "You know him? You know PuckDaddy? I mean, I know you do, but...do you?"

"I do."

"What's he like?"

"He's one of my closest friends. He's a good man, and he's listening to this conversation through my ear piece."

"Oh...really?"

Chase nods and grins and it's magnificent.

Kiss him. Kiss Chase. Kiss him. Katie Lopez is thunderously invasive and I can't concentrate.

Kayla's voice fails her temporarily. She clears her throat and speaks into Chase's ear, "Hi PuckDaddy."

The Outlaw answers, "Puck says, 'What's up girl.'"

She laughs and brings the flower to her nose.

Kiss him. Kiss him. Kiss him.

"Kiss me," I say.

Everyone freezes. Holy sweet sugar, did that just come out of my mouth? Kayla is aghast. The Governess throws up her hands, disgusted with me as usual. Even Katie feels stunned. Chase Jackson has said hello to everyone else and now finally he moves in front of me. We're too close on this stupid tiny platform and at this intimate range the force of his power is intoxicating and fearsome. He gives off heat. He's too dangerous. No one should be this impossibly strong. I want to rip his throat out for the sake of us all, but the urge is simply an animal instinct, a battle for food chain supremacy. I'll use words instead.

He's at least six inches taller than me and twice as wide, and rock hard. This close he's quite intimidating. Height advantage has been lost.

If I could get my hands on Katie, I'd strangle her. I clear my throat, and say, "That was unfortunate." He arches an eyebrow at me.

"What I clearly meant to say is...*Excuse me*, Chase, but we have business to discuss."

He's examining my hair, my eyes, my mouth. "How much do you remember? Of me?"

"I have no memory of you." It's a partial fabrication. I need distance between us. I need space.

His face falls and he nods. "I heard. Just needed to verify." His breath catches and he has my arm in his hand. Then he has both my arms and he's running his thumbs down the scars on the inside of my forearms. I want to jerk my hands away but his touch is magic. The omnipresent storm behind my eyes, the headache, is suddenly gone. His hands radiate warmth, tingles washing away the joint aches. I feel better than I have in months. Katie groans like she feels the relief too. "You still have the scars. I put lotion on them for weeks. I thought they might go away."

He's crying. Or at least he's trying not to cry. Put lotion on my scars? "I don't understand."

"I tried to keep the Chemist away from you. But you still ended up with his scars. And I'm sorry." He releases me and steps off the platform. At the release, my body instantly misses his.

Chase.

He shakes his head and wipes his eyes and says, "Sorry about that. Didn't mean to...you know."

Dalton and Teresa return to the stage, appearing reluctant to leave his side. I say, "That's understandable. I know you and Katie were close."

"I commend you on New Los Angeles. This is an impressive reclamation project. The Variants are in great danger, and the sanctuary you've built is incredible."

"Thank you. We've worked hard to make it so."

"But you should never have let Walter in here."

A rebuke. I'm stung and indignant and temporarily at a loss for words.

The Priest scoffs and speaks for the first time. "He was under guard the entire time, Outlaw. My men are highly trained, and he was lucky to escape with his life."

"Walter is a nightmare. He came on a recon mission. He walked these streets and measured your strengths and weaknesses. Have you been to his strongholds? Have you seen his forces? Now he has a tremendous advantage. You don't let the enemy into your home."

General Brown is silent. He's not sticking up for me, and he shouldn't. It was my idea to let Walter in because I handle mutant affairs. And the Outlaw is correct; it was a disastrous mistake.

The Priest mutters, "We almost had him."

"I've seen the video. Your leaders are only alive because the Shooter intervened," he replies.

I gasp. "The Shooter? *The* Shooter? That was her? On the roof?"

"I asked her to monitor because you denied me entrance."

I'm reeling. And torn. The Shooter is legend, a woman even greater than the stories about her. She took down a squadron of helicopters with only a rifle, and she was here watching us. If I have an idol, she's it. But we didn't invite her. And I need to be strong.

"I'd be a fool if I was anything other than grateful to be alive. Clearly our encounter with Walter didn't go as planned," I say carefully. "But I'm concerned to learn that the Resistance is sending unwelcome soldiers into our Kingdom."

He grins at something funny I don't understand. "The Shooter doesn't get sent anywhere. If I ask politely enough, sometimes she says yes. And sometimes she hits me."

"You sent her? I thought you said the Resistance did."

He shrugs. "The Shooter and I are allies of the Resistance. Sometimes our purposes intersect."

"Is she still here?"

"No."

"Where'd she go?"

He pauses and frowns. "Good question. Puck, where is Samantha?" He waits, clearly listening to someone speaking into his head. We have that in common.

I ask, "Well?"

"Puck says to tell Katie he likes her new hairstyle."

Kayla snickers and I'm ready for this charade to end. He continues before I can kick him out, "Somehow I picked up a thousand followers on the way here. Do you mind if they move in?"

I'm caught off guard again. My mouth works soundlessly, so the Governess answers. "Of course. We welcome all."

"Thank you. The reason I came here is to alert you that Walter is moving his troops. He's been here, scouted your territory, and he's preparing to attack."

"We'll be ready."

"No. You won't. You've accomplished the impossible, and New Los Angeles is unreal. You've built a peaceful paradise and I love it. Now you're a ripe target. And even with General Brown's considerable help, you're not ready to face Walter's army of Variants."

"We refer to them as Guardians here in the Kingdom. And our Guardian army outnumbers his two to one."

He shakes his head and gestures towards the stands. "You bring Variants here to heal. To learn to live again. Walter gathers Variants and gives them weapons. Trains them to fight. Drills them into a mighty army. Your superior numbers won't be enough."

"You're suggesting we form an alliance with the Resistance. But we are independent. We've fought and clawed our way here, and we'll continue to do so."

"Then let me help. I'm capable of dealing with Walter. The Shooter and I—"

"The Kingdom is grateful for your help. As I am too, personally. But you and the Shooter have been too tainted by the disease to remain here. I'm confident we can maintain a partnership and assist one another when possible, but it must be done so at a distance."

"Why?"

"The Guardians cannot tolerate you."

"And you?"

"I cannot tolerate you either."

He nods and his eyes grow distant. There's a shift in the quality of his stillness. No one speaks. The lull lengthens and he chews on his lip, searching for answers. Finally I can bear the silence no longer.

"We thank you for the privilege of your visit. General Brown will escort you to the boundary."

He takes a deep breath and lets it out in a frustrated blast. "And there I will remain."

"Explain?"

"I'll honor your wishes. I won't enter your Kingdom. But I'm making camp just beyond. I'll only enter if Walter or Blue-Eyes comes in person. Thanks for meeting with me. Goodbye, Queen."

He turns to leave without another word. The Falcons scramble to catch up and General Brown follows.

Kayla and Teresa and the Governess and Dalton are incensed with me. Their displeasure roils off in waves. So too is the fifty-five thousand gathered host of witnesses. What? You told me to keep my distance, I want to say. But I'm not happy with me either. I'm hollow and hurt by the Outlaw's dismissal.

Chase...

Three

General Brown and the Outlaw are driven to the border in a stripped-down army jeep. Brown and Chase talk for five minutes, Brown returns to the jeep, and his driver motors back towards Downtown on the Glendale Freeway.

I am waiting for them in the middle of the highway near Glendale's Community College, a particularly abandoned stretch of road. The driver brakes to a halt, and General Brown knows better than to speak first. We glare at each other through the windshield.

"I have two questions," I say. I'm angry beyond reason, and I don't know how to stop. "If you lie, I'll know."

General Brown nods once. His driver swallows and sweats.

I ask, "Have you been communicating with the Outlaw during the past five months?"

"I have not."

"Have you been in communication with the Resistance during the past five months?"

He opens his mouth. Stalls. Tries again. "...Carmine, I—"

I get my fingernails under the jeep's front bumper. General Brown shoves the driver from his seat and dives to the road. I *Hurl* the jeep's front axle towards the sky. The vehicle rotates upwards with a groan of metal, landing and balancing temporarily on the rear gate, perpendicular to the ground, all four wheels spinning lazily in the air.

"You're a *spy*."

"No Carmine, I am not," he shouts back. "I am a General in a war and I communicate with my allies."

"The Resistance is not our ally."

"The Resistance provides us more help and support than you realize."

"And what do they get in return?"

"So far, nothing. They help because it's the right thing to do." He stands and brushes himself free of dirt. The driver scoots further away from me. "We have too many enemies. Let's not turn away our friends."

"You send them information about me?"

"Perhaps it's better if you read the reports yourself."

"You send them information about me?"

"I send them updates, yes, and you're included. But they have no input into our lives here. Read the reports. I'll provide you the password to my account."

"You should have told me."

"Maybe. Maybe not. I don't demand total transparency from you in your dealings with the Guardians. I trust you. My opinion, you're the most important person on earth. And this stretch of ground is our ark. Our best hope through the coming disaster. And I'm doing everything I can to help you, including coordinating with allies."

"I can trust no one, Brown. No one. Not the Resistance. Perhaps not even you. I expect your password sent to my phone in the next five minutes."

I turn and stalk down the Freeway, leaving the General and his driver wondering how to tip the jeep onto its wheels.

Dalton is waiting at the Olympic tower doors. Kayla and Teresa and the Governess are all inside, watching through the glass.

"You." I jam my finger at my bodyguard. "You showed up in July. Did the Outlaw send you?"

Dalton doesn't answer immediately. He glares, arms crossed over his thick chest. I wait. His lips pull to one side in displeasure. "You don't trust me."

"I woke up abandoned. Betrayed. I've earned trust issues."

"I used to be the Outlaw's security detail, and he asked me to keep you safe."

"Have you been communicating with him?"

"Every week," he snaps.

"Pack your bags. I want you out of the tower. You are dismissed."

He doesn't budge. Inside the lobby, Kayla's eyes are pooling and Teresa Triplett's hands are clenched in her blond hair. Perhaps I'm being unreasonable but I don't care. They're spying on me. Don't trust me. Think I'm weak.

And that's the one thing I can't be.

New Los Angeles has a large population of orphans. Hundreds of them, and they live in the eastern portion of Downtown, in houses surrounding the Utah Street School. This might be the cleanest part of the city and the kids take great joy in gloating to anyone who listens. They go to school, play on the soccer field and basketball courts, and work like the rest of us, tending their own gardens and chicken coops.

The children meet me as I turn off 1st Street onto Gabriel Garcia Marquez. Dozens of them, wearing the widest smiles I've seen in days. I'm coerced into dancing and hopscotch and a game of knock-out. They show me their paintings of me and the Guardians. I speak to them in English and Spanish and when that fails I speak in hugs.

After thirty minutes, Miss Pauline comes to my rescue. She shoos the kids back to their chores or studies. She's a pretty lady, maybe fifty-five with streaks of grey in her curly black hair. Miss Pauline is the former mayor of Compton, keeping much of south LA afloat during the upheaval and exodus. As her citizens fled for greener pastures, she gathered the stragglers and homeless and took care of them. Now she's the orphanage Overseer, working with fifty of her friends to raise the kids.

"Well," she sighs, wiping her hands on a rag. "Look who come to see me. It's Miss Temper Tantrum herself."

"Temper tantrum?"

"News travel fast, sweetie."

I'm not sure why I'm here. I didn't know where else to go. I couldn't bear to face Kayla or the Governess, and to suffer their reproach. Miss Pauline seems to sense my distress so she takes me by the hand and walks me towards her house. I'm exhausted, mentally and physically, and soon my feet have trouble walking in the heeled booties. I'm crying quietly. Carl, Miss Pauline's constant companion, arrives and takes my other hand. Then he's carrying me, though I don't remember being lifted.

Soon there's nothing.

~

I don't know how long I slept. The rays of sunlight filtering through are turning red.

Miss Pauline is at her kitchen table, looking over sheets of homework while two little girls sneak glances at me. Carl is in the back, teaching a boy how to hammer in hinges.

A whisper. "She's awake."

"Mmhm."

"Miss Pauline, she awake."

"Well then why don't you bring her tea?"

"Yes Miss Pauline."

A rattling cup and saucer are placed on the coffee table next to my couch.

I say, "Thank you."

"Miss Pauline, she say thank you."

"I heard. What do you say?"

"Thank you."

"No, child," Miss Pauline says. "You're welcome."

The little girl tells me, "You welcome."

Miss Pauline returns their homework. "You two. Go play. Get."

The two girls, wearing white clicking braids, wave and run out the front door.

I ask, "How long have I been asleep?"

"Long enough. Heard you kicked the Outlaw out. Before he can come see me."

"Do you know him?"

"A little. He stayed with me, back...I don't know. Long time ago, seems. Came for help. Remind me of my Anthony."

I sit up and rub my eyes. "He can't stay in New Los Angeles. He upsets the Guardians."

"I expect he does. Lot of things upset you people."

"Yeah, I guess you're right." I grin and sip the warm tea.

"Suppose it was February. Maybe March. He came to talk. He and the pretty white girl with guns. Forget her name."

"The Shooter? Her name is Samantha Gear. She's famous. I didn't know they came to see you."

"Didn't stay long. But I liked him right off. Carl too, and Lord Jesus knows Carl don't like nobody." She smiles in memory and fans herself with a paper. "Talked about you. The Jackson boy did."

Despite myself, I flush with pleasure. "Chase Jackson did? What'd he say?"

"I guess that don't matter. Seeing as you kicked him out. Then you get rid of Dalton."

"You know him too?"

"Dalton comes around. Think he's a little sweet on me."

I rest my elbows on my knees and my forehead in my hands. Miss Pauline seems like she's everyone's mother. Coming here was selfish. She already has enough on her plate, while I just run around making messes. "Thank you for letting me sleep here."

"About to start dinner. Stay and eat. Skinny little ninãta."

"I've taken too much of your time. I appreciate the offer."

"Gonna push me away too?"

"No, I—"

"We both taking care of orphans. Maybe you and me, we need each other."

My head is still in my hands and I admit, "I don't know what I'm doing."

"Lord Jesus, ain't that the truth."

"It's that obvious?"

"You a baby, Miss Carmine. Still nothing but a newborn, but you been given the whole world to tend. How's anyone going to do that?"

"Good question. I wish I knew."

"Could start by not refusing help." She grunts to her feet and turns on a burner which is connected to solar panels outside. "I pray every night. For you. Need all the help you can get."

"I'm not sure I can trust their help."

"Well. I won't pretend to know. But seems to me moldy bread is better than no bread. To a starving woman." She puts a pot of water on and starts chopping vegetables. Making soup? My stomach growls. "Heard you met Walter."

I sniff. "He's a real treat."

"He used to be in Compton. One of the Chemist's first men." Her knife stops and she stares far off into the cabinets. "Walter used to abuse the woman. Call me the Hag. Come here, Hag. Bring me food, Hag." She shudders and resumes cutting. "I pray for Walter too. Don't know it'll do any good. Glad we're rid of him."

"We're not rid of Walter yet, I'm afraid. I'm working on it."

"Nice pretty girl like you? Better leave him to the Jackson boy. I'm no sexist. I just like you in one piece."

"Yeah," I say, and now I'm sadly staring far off into the cabinets too. "The Jackson boy."

- Four -

It's eight at night when I return to the tower.

Dalton has slung a hammock outside the lobby doors. He stares impassively at me over the Baldacci novel in his fist. I evicted him from the tower, but not the Kingdom. He probably wouldn't have left if I had.

I walk inside without speaking to him. Tomorrow perhaps. The residual embers of my anger still burn right now. Every week, he said. Every week he sent reports to the Outlaw. Ugh.

He thinks I'm weak. But if I'm weak then we're all going to die. I can't be soft. I can't fail. I promised.

My Devotee is overjoyed and relieved at my return, like he worried I'd never come back. Big baby.

Inside my bedroom I examine the reflection in my mirror. I'm still pretty. Why didn't the Outlaw like me? I remove the hair clips and store them carefully; I might wear them again. Kick off the boots; will never wear again. Hang up the tunic: love it, might wear again tomorrow. Strip out of the jeans and lay them on the bed next to a few outfits Kayla left. She removed the piles of girly clothes but left some I might like. She wasn't wrong. I could be convinced to wear these. Especially this white one. All of tops are off-the-shoulder. Are capris in style? Could I wear them with shorts?

I'm wearing UnderArmour spandex shorts and a black tank top. Perhaps my underwear needs an update too. There must be more to lingerie than activewear.

I'm about to remove the red silk ribbon from my knees and feet when I realize a man is standing behind me. He says, "Cute outfit. Black and red are my colors."

He's on me in a flash, before I can hit him. My arms are pinned and he covers my mouth. He's made of iron! I see the Outlaw in the mirror, his red mask, his lips at my ear.

He's wearing the cologne I bought him.

He says, "Katie. It's only me. Don't scream. Wouldn't do you much good anyway. You fired your bodyguard, right?"

I bite hard into the flesh of his hand. He doesn't flinch; it's like chewing leather.

"I got an idea. Let's go on a date. You wanna? I know this great place."

What! I duck my head and jerk it backwards, crushing his nose. Again, into his mouth. Each time earning a sick crunch and a groan.

"Mmmmpfgh!" I scream.

"I'll take that as a yes," he mutters. Before I know it, he's grabbed my hand and we're climbing the outside of Olympic. Actually, he's climbing, and I'm dangling and scrabbling for hand and footholds. It's like he's glued to the building. Far below, the ground swings dizzily. I half climb and half get hauled upwards.

"You *idiot*. Let go," I shout. "Let go of my hand. Immediately!"

"Playing hard to get? It won't work."

"You're not allowed to be here. And how on *earth* are you climbing so fast? I can't climb like this."

"One of my oddities. Almost there."

The top two floors of Olympic are in bad shape. The observation deck was hit by a rocket and the stairs destroyed months ago. He pulls me to the south side and I stumble after. I wish he'd kidnapped me *before* I took off the pretty tunic.

"Let go," I snap.

"Does anything happen when our skin touches?"

"What do you mean?" I jerk free.

"Does your headache go away?"

"I don't get headaches," I lie.

Yes I do.

"Yes you do. Do they go away when we touch?"

"No," I lie again. Katie Lopez is surging through my limbs, threatening to take control. Katie wants to kiss him, and I want to garrote him. "You were banished from the city. Why are you back?"

"Trying to get to first base."

"Be serious."

"I am. I miss you. But also, I need to find out if the disease has broken your brain."

"A waste of your time. I'm more sane than most."

He gingerly touches his nose and wrinkles it. Was he a normal man I'd probably have driven the nasal bone into his brain. "Ooooooouch. You've gotten stronger."

"I'm not Katie Lopez."

"I can tell. You're taller and your boobs are bigger."

I hit him with the back of my hand. It's like striking a statue. "You're *not* allowed to talk about my body." But I'm pleased he noticed.

No. No I'm not. What is *wrong* with me.

He says, "I meant it as a compliment. You used to be short. You look great. Healthy. Last time I saw you, you were waking up from a coma. Not healthy."

I only now realize he's set up candles everywhere and there's two chairs for us to sit on. This would be romantic if...you know...if....something. If I didn't loathe him. The stars look photoshopped. His cologne smells so good that my first instinct is to bite him.

"Don't get the wrong idea." He holds his hands up, palms out. "The candles aren't here for seduction. I wanted lights and you have no power."

"This is not a date."

"Relax. I have no interest in dating you."

"You...why not?" The questions slips out before I consider it. This is going sub-optimally. Humiliating. He pulls off his red mask and stuffs it into a pocket. His hair falls into place around his eyes. Maybe I don't hate that length after all. He's beautiful. I hate him. I change the subject before he can answer, "You were there when I woke up? At the hospital?"

He sits and indicates I do the same. I don't. Instead I make a show of unwinding the compression silk from my knees.

He asks, "What's with the ribbons?"

"They palliate my joint pain."

"Which joints?"

"The majority."

He watches with interest. "That's the virus. Happens to some of us. I could hear your bones grinding in your sleep."

"Do yours ache also?"

"No. Blue-Eyes has bad bones, I know. She can't run."

I could hit him; his guard isn't up. I could retreat, but he might catch me. I could call for help, but do I need it? He doesn't appear to be aggressive.

Maybe I could sit in his lap.

Good grief, Katie.

I clear my throat and ask, "What do you mean you heard bones grinding?"

"During your coma."

"You were in attendance?"

"How much do you remember? Of your awakening?"

I shake my head. "Nothing. My memory starts several days after. In a Walmart, I think."

"You can hold my hand."

"You can keep dreaming."

"My headache was terrible for the first eight months. I bet yours is too. Holding my hand will help."

"No thank you," I say. But maybe. Just to defy General Brown. I sit and ball up the silk from my knees. Before I can argue he's taken my foot and is unwrapping the short section of ribbon around my ankle. My body relaxes at his touch. I think his fingers are trembling.

He's nervous. Precious boy. I've loved him since I was nine. He was a grade older than me.

"Yes, I was there. When you woke," he says.

"Then you abandoned me. I remember that. I was alone."

"I didn't abandon you. And you weren't alone. You were surrounded by Variants. It was freaky, like they coronated you in your sleep."

"We refer to them as Guardians."

"Whatever. They were all over that hospital."

"Were you and Katie still dating at the time?"

"Yes. We were dating." He looks up from my foot and catches my gaze. I wish he wouldn't do that, it's terribly off-putting. Katie Lopez is happy and rattling on about candles and fire and her pleasure makes me blush. I hope he doesn't notice.

I ask, "Where'd you go? After I woke up?"

"To a hospital in Arizona. I think. I'm fuzzy on the details."

"Why?"

He chuckles and it's a nice easy sound. "Because you broke my back."

I sit up straight and he drops my foot. "No I didn't."

"Yes you did. You woke up and panicked or something. You hit me and threw me from a third floor window."

My hand is over my mouth. It's so bizarre that I almost laugh. "You're not joking."

"No."

"Is that why you limp?"

He frowns, affronted. "It's a tiny limp. More of a strut. But yes. Doctors said I'd never walk again."

"I heard about the broken back, but didn't realize... So I broke your back and you're still in love with me?"

Oh no. Ugh. Another sentence I desperately want back. My mouth is out of control. He sits back in his chair with a cagey grin on his face. "Who says I'm in love with you?"

"Everyone. Sorry, I shouldn't have...I should just shut up."

"I'm not in love with you."

"Why not?"

"I was in love with Katie Lopez. You say you're not her."

"That's right." Katie's gone quiet and the silence in my head is deafening. "I'm not her. We're different. Do you know why my breasts enlarged? Why I'm taller? I've read about the virus online but it doesn't satisfactorily clarify anything."

"Yeah we're a secretive bunch. Not much is known. I bet if you asked your Guardians you'll find the growth happened to some of them too. It was explained to me that the disease enhances our natural assets. Guys get taller. Harrier. Girls get prettier. Your friend

Kayla smells better. Stuff like that. You've always been athletic and pretty. Now perhaps even more so."

He thinks I'm pretty. But I don't care.

"Were you and Katie a good couple?" I ask.

"The best. She was everything."

"What was she like?"

He takes a long time answering. This *has* to be surreal and uncomfortable for him, talking to his ex-girlfriend who can't remember him. Or if she can, won't admit it.

"Katie was the one truly good person in a high school full of selfish, overly-rich, vapid consumers. The rest of us had our flaws, but not her. We loved her. She was the fire we all gathered around for warmth. Maybe she still is," he says and he indicates the surrounding city. The surrounding eighty-thousand people. "You may not remember yourself, but you haven't changed much. You're still strong. Determined. Emotional. Intelligent."

Katie is crying. I think most of her higher mental processes are dormant except emotion; she runs on pure feeling. "I'm not the same."

"Yes you are. If you don't remember then I'll be the judge. This is no empty tabula rasa I see. You are Katie Lopez, hardened into a warrior."

I blink the tears away. Her moods must be affecting mine. "Katie sounds magical. But I'm not her. I'm full of anger. Hate. Ambition. I've killed...a *lot* of people. I almost killed General Brown today when I found out he betrayed me."

"You've been through hell. You probably have clinical abandonment and trust issues. You were betrayed by everyone you knew."

"Who?"

"Me, for starters. I left you in the care of a woman who betrayed you. She sold you to the Chemist. You watched me sail away, and you told me then you didn't think we'd see each other again. You watched your friend Cory die. Then your friend Tank abandoned you. Then you spent a day with the Chemist, knowing full well he was going to operate on you. So I think you've earned some trust issues."

We're silent a moment, letting the words and emotions fade. I don't know how to feel about him. He seems genuine, and Katie adores him. As a general rule I don't trust anyone, but there's something to be said for unconditional love. He's right about the headaches; they disappear when we touch.

I say, "You don't feel as strong as you did the other night."

"What do you mean?"

"In the Starlight Bowl. Your presence was overwhelming. But here, and at Dodgers Stadium, it's tolerable."

"You spied on me?"

"Of course. You're a threat."

"No I'm not."

"Yes. You are. Somehow you're masking your biological output, but that only changes how effectively I feel the danger. How do you do that?"

"Hard to explain. I practiced it for months. I can control how strongly the disease broadcasts itself, basically. Like flexing a muscle. I'm doing it now so you don't take my head off."

"How long can you control it?"

"Good question," he says.

"Show me."

"No."

"Why not?"

He grins. "That's more of a second date activity."

"Who says I want to go on a second date?"

"I got nothing better to do than kidnap you every night."

"Release your grip on the disease. I want to see if I can control myself."

He locks eyes with me, deep contact. The air around him seems to shift, and his bioluminescence increases. I feel the heat off his skin. The hackles on my neck rise and my nails dig into the couch. Bad idea. He *is* a danger. A wolf in sheep's clothing.

"Do you see?" he asks.

"Yes. I see."

"And?"

"And I want you to leave. Even if you love me, even if you're a good-looking guy, this can't work. You repel me."

He nods his head, mouth a grim line. I can tell he's bottling up his scent again, locking away the disease as tightly as possible. But it's too late. I feel Guardians below us awaken. They know he's here. We don't have much time.

Quickly, I ask, "Why is everyone coming here? You, Walter, the Shooter?"

"Walter wants to kill you and take the Guardians. The Shooter and I come for a different reason."

"Which is?"

"We think you're worth rescuing."

"I don't need to be rescued. I don't need you."

"Katie—"

"I have an army of Guardians. Men and women who follow me. I have a Devotee who sees to my every need, even romantic needs." It's a lie. The words sting him, as I intended. I want to hurt him, drive him away. I don't know why and I can't stop. I want to finish talking, but my mouth rebels. "You are not necessary. I can do this. Alone."

"Your Guardians are climbing the walls. Can you feel them?"

I snap, "Of course I can. They can't tolerate you. Just as I can't tolerate you."

"Katie—"

"It's not personal. It's biological. And it's why you must remain outside of our boundary."

Guardians reach our floor and begin pouring over the lip of the destroyed observation deck. They're driven mad by his disease. Dozens of them, nearly feral.

The Outlaw doesn't seem concerned. He stands and points at them. Only a finger. "**Wait**," he says.

He doesn't shout but the strength of his voice crushes me. And crushes the oncoming horde. The amplitude is pitched to establish his dominance. They react like they've been struck with a firehose. His body seems to swell, like he gets taller when he's angry.

He controls Variants with his voice. Wow.

He is hurt. I see it in his eyes. I was too harsh. This man has been nothing but kind. I glance at the Guardians and see their hate, and witness myself in the frenzy. I responded the same as they do; too violent. Wasn't I just telling Dalton I wouldn't give in to urges?

"Chase, I—"

There is a pop. A snap and sizzle of electricity. Chase drops, struck down by an electroshock weapon. Who? I search the crowd and see several tasers, brought by warriors who've battled him before. He tries to rise while his body twitches, but the spell he cast over the Guardians vanishes. They surge.

"No!" I cry.

Most Guardians don't listen. They're lost to insanity. Chase is attacked, beaten, and lifted over their heads.

"Stop!" I roar. Finally I have their attention, but it's too late. They launch him far off the tower, flung by strong arms. I scramble to the side, searching the black. He's gone. He'll die. My heart drops. No one can survive that...

No! There! Against the dark sky, a shape streaks away from our tower, stars winking out as he passes. The Outlaw soars on wings in a majestic arc, curving north.

"He can *fly*?"

Finally back in my bedroom. I'm so tired. And confused. I collapse into bed, not caring that a few of the Guardians follow me in, like worried service dogs.

My phone has a text message from an unknown number.

>> so that date didn't go as planned
>> let's give it another shot
>> soon
>> but without all your friends

The following day I invite Dalton back inside the tower on the condition he ceases all communication with the Outlaw. He agrees.

He is lying.

I send a note of apology to General Brown for flipping his jeep, and a promise that I'll read the reports soon. He doesn't reply.

Busy. I need to stay busy.

Packs of wild dogs are becoming a bigger problem, so I prowl Downtown with a squad of Guardians and we eliminate dozens of them. These hounds are rabid, beyond help. We load the broken animals onto a truck and I ignore the poignant symbolism as best I can.

At day's end, the Outlaw still hasn't contacted me.

I don't care. I don't care that he hasn't texted me again. Not even a little. Even though I kick fitfully at my sheets like a jilted lover. I find photos of him taken a year ago, pictures of the Outlaw flying with a wing-suit. The wings fold into his pant legs when not in use. Extremely inventive. Maybe he'll let me try them.

But why would he? I was vicious to him. And my 'friends' threw him off a high-rise. And I didn't respond to his messages. I can't tolerate you, I said.

There's not a single reason for him to text again.

Except I want him too. He interests me. I stay up late reading the book on leadership so I'll be awake. Just in case.

But he doesn't.

Six

I barge into Kayla's room, which is furnished in utter dichotomy of mine. Hers is a maze of lavish furniture and original artwork, all of it flowers and still-life scavenged from the Los Angeles County Museum of Art. Bottles of sparkling waters everywhere. Two laptops. A dozen phone cords plugged into small chargers. Thousand-dollar cashmere blankets. Scented candles. Vases of fresh flowers. Her canopy bed is draped with diaphanous curtains. So is her dog's.

Kayla herself wears a white nighty, fashionable even in her sleep. She's sprawled primly on the carpet, head resting on a lacy throw pillow.

"Good morning, my Queen." She smiles sleepily and stretches. She looks like a bombshell pinup. Her bedroom has two walk-in closets, a panoply of fashion.

"Don't call me that. And he still hasn't texted me."

"Who hasn't? Did you put those ribbons on by yourself? Because we can do better. Did you know that pictures of you taken at the stadium are viral? The next fashion trend will be green off-the-shoulder tunics and little silver hair clips. Simply because you wore them two days ago. This broken country is obsessed with the rebel warrior queen."

"Why are you on the floor? Did you sleep last night?"

"I did not. But I will soon. It's been ages since my last beauty rest."

"You were up all night texting with PuckDaddy, your hacker."

"Among *others*, yes," she says and closes her eyes with false dignity. "I'm quite popular, you know. And I've been keeping tabs on Walter's troop migration."

"Where are they?"

"Hard to pinpoint. Walter's Variant warriors are sneaking away in small handfuls so we can't track them. My informants within the Resistance don't know either. The only thing we know for certain is that his army appears to have thinned by a third in the last three days."

A tight ball of sick dread settles into my stomach. Walter promised he'd return. And I don't know if we can resist him.

"Okay." I take a steadying breath. "Okay. Alert the Guardians. Mandatory assembly tonight in the Disney Concert Hall. After you send the message, take a nap."

"On it," she chirps, and she begins working magic on her phone. "You said someone hasn't texted you?"

"Nobody. Forget I said anything."

"The Outlaw?"

"No."

Her dog Princess lifts her furry head up long enough to examine me. Even that dumb dog can tell I'm lying.

I should text Chase. It'd be polite. He's always been a worrier.

"Were you expecting him to text you?" Kayla has quit working on her phone and she examines me with a piercing stare.

Crud. Coming here was a bad idea. I wave my hand, brushing off her question, and I turn to leave. "Forget I said anything."

"Carmine..."

"Goodbye."

"Are you and the Outlaw engaging in textual relations? Because the Governess forbids it."

I'm at her door when I detect an odor, disparate from Kayla's perfumed palace. A sharp biting whiff. I turn and follow my nose, pushing deeper back into her apartment. It's coming from her open window. What is...?

Katie Lopez knows the scent. I do too. From somewhere. An unpleasant whisper of recognition.

Kayla's window looks south towards Huntington Park. I lose the trail inside her silky curtains. I stick my head out and discover it again. The odor is being circulated by the Olympic's downdraught, and without pausing I climb onto the ledge.

"Carmine?"

I close my eyes, tasting the air with all my senses. The stimulant is faint and probably long gone, but I'm compelled. Up. That's where it is. Up. So I *Climb*, using each level's outcroppings as a handhold. I move much slower than the Outlaw but I reach the shattered observation deck soon enough, and I'm hit by the reek.

It's not an entirely unpleasant odor, actually. Just a potent one. A rich mixture. I inspect the entirety of the roof, and discover the faint traces of a woman's lotion. And the scent of soap. And the disease, a particularly strong strain. And perfume. And finally, the tang of gasoline.

The puzzle pieces fit. The Cheerleader. The Fire Girl. She was up here. Recently. Maybe last night? She climbed down the south face, and I can almost see her trail, an ill-defined impression she leaves on the universe. Without thinking, I follow. For whatever reason, descending a tower is harder than ascending and it takes over five minutes.

I find three Guardians squatting on haunches and staring west down Olympic Boulevard. After the long descent, I squat next to them, catch my breath, and follow their eyes.

All three are boys. Well, boys my age. "What do you smell?" I ask.

"We don't know, Miss Carmine."

"Something."

"Something powerful."

I smell it too; maybe the Cheerleader rested here a few moments. I nod and pat their shoulders. "Better leave this one to me."

Perhaps I should alert Dalton or Mason, but this feels like a journey I must make alone. Before long, I've left Downtown. The trail shoots straight towards Hollywood and Beverly Hills. I lose her track every few minutes so I can't follow in a car or on a bike. She's fast and determined and I'm so focused I don't feel the passing hours. My phone buzzes persistently so I turn it off. Soon I'm in sparsely populated neighborhoods, and I'm alone for all intents and purposes, and still her trail leads ever on.

Why am I doing this? My plate is too full for this insanity.

She hasn't deviated from West Olympic Boulevard, always returning after a handful of blocks on Wilshire. I munch on apples and oranges plucked from trees heavy with ripe fruit. What on earth will I do if I catch her? No idea.

Her trail plunges into Beverly Hills and I pause near the entrance to the ritzy neighborhoods. No official rules were established but sometime during the previous four months these lavish palaces became off limits. One of those cultural anomalies which spring up organically; no trespassing. Ten million dollar homes. At least they used to be, and even now in the decay of society most citizens of New Los Angeles feel uncomfortable here. Homes too rich for our dusty feet.

There's also the fact that many wealthy former owners return periodically, bribing their way through our borders with armed guards to retrieve abandoned valuables. Some reside here permanently, living quiet lives and hoping to escape our notice. Our Kingdom is too big.

Dealing with rich interlopers is on my to-do list. I don't want to kick them out; I want to involve them in our Kingdom.

The Cheerleader's journey takes her north, past Sunset Boulevard and into the hills. These houses are absolute jaw-droppers but I'm wearying of the trek. Maybe she lives in a palace up there, and maybe she'll keep moving. Maybe I'll chase her into the night and still never get a glimpse. I've wasted too much time on this rabbit hunt. It's after lunch and I'm miles from the city.

Some other time, Cheerleader. Time for me to go.

I'm on my way out of the neighborhoods when I see movement below. A person walking, coming around the bend. I slip into the hedges beside a stucco palace and wait for him to pass. Just to be safe. And it's hot and I'm tired and grouchy and don't want to chat.

The biggest man I've ever seen pauses at the foot of the drive. Maybe seven feet tall? He's gargantuan. He is wearing jeans and heavy boots, a tight t-shirt, and white gloves, strangely enough. Across his back is strapped an honest-to-goodness double-bladed axe. Not the cheap costume kind that Lord of the Rings fanatics wear, but a thick tool used to fell trees.

Katie leaps inside my chest. She's knows this man. I do too.

"Tank?" I gasp. "Tank Ware?"

The man tenses, clearly caught of guard, and his hand involuntarily goes for the axe handle. Tank's a Hispanic boy about my age. He sees me and relaxes.

"I thought I smelled you." He grins. "Recognize you anywhere."

"What are you doing here? It's been...wow, I don't even know." We naturally fall into an embrace. He's *so* big.

"Looking for someone." His voice resonates from his wide chest like a sub-woofer. "Someone dangerous. But then I smelled Katie Lopez. How's my baby?"

"I'm not your baby. But I'm very glad to see you."

He hasn't let go. I haven't let go either. Friends are worth their weight in gold in a savage land.

I ask, "Why are you in New Los Angeles?"

"I live nearby. Just outside your border."

"And you never came to see me?"

He takes me by the shoulders and holds me at a distance. "I heard you lost your memory."

"The rumors are true."

"Heard you don't remember anyone."

"Some people. But not well."

"Then why do you remember me?"

His question has me at a total loss. Why *do* I remember him? He's Tank Ware. Memories come back like the sun breaking through clouds. At one point last year, he was the highest rated high school football player in America. Very wealthy. Aloof, but a lot of fun. The further I reach, the more I recall. He used to live Downtown. Nice parents.

"I...I'm not sure. But you're very familiar. I remember you the way friends should."

"That's all?"

"You have the Hyper Virus," I realize suddenly. "That's why you glow."

"I glow?"

Memories keep storming. I close my eyes. I remember dating him.

I remember kissing. I remember... "You're my ex-boyfriend. We dated."

"Damn right."

"You're a Variant, but not like me. You're Infected."

"I hate that term."

"But...you're, like, one of only ten Infected alive. Wow this is... I don't know. I'm disoriented. Why would I remember you and no one else?"

"Destiny, babe. Fate. Pure and simple."

I grin at him. His face and neck bear the scars from old burn injuries. He's not deformed, but the right right side of his face looks melted. His handsome visage is not totally ruined, but it's close. I can't remember what happened...

I say, "Walk me back downtown. You can tell me about your life now."

"No go, kid. Your goons don't like me much."

"The Guardians?"

"Whatever the hell you call the freaks."

"Then what are you doing in this neighborhood? They patrol here at night."

"Like I said. Looking for someone."

"The Cheerleader?"

He nods, his mouth a fixed line.

"I was too."

He asks, "You going to kill her?"

"No. I don't know if I can. I was hoping to drive her away."

He shakes his head and crosses his thick arms. "She won't go."

"Why not?"

"She's obsessed. Fixated on Pajamas."

"Pajamas?"

"Chase Jackson. You know, the little runt?"

"The Cheerleader is obsessed with *Chase*?" I experience a hot flash of jealousy. Katie really needs to cool her mood swings. "Were you going to kill her?"

"I am. One of these days."

"As a favor to Chase?"

"As a favor—" he repeats and then laughs, like thunder rumbling. "You really don't remember, do you."

"No. It's maddening."

He points to his ruined face. "She did this."

"Yikes."

"Yeah."

"Fair warning, Tank. Walter is coming. I don't know when, but he's threatening to kill me and capture the Guardians. New Los Angeles might get a whole lot less friendly soon."

He nods slowly. He's inspecting me, head to toe. A lingering inspection. Almost a leer. "You remember the night Walter took you from me?"

"I don't. He mentioned a giant. Must be you."

"I owe Walter. He's next on my list. After Hannah."

The Cheerleader. Her name is Hannah?

Hannah Walker.

"I need to show you something," he says.

"What?"

"Not today. Soon. Before Walter gets here."

"Okay, what?"

"Give me your number. I'll call you."

I do. We hug again, a lingering affectionate embrace. And it's the closest I've felt to home in months.

Seven

I don't know how many Guardians live in New Los Angeles. Approximately four thousand. The number fluctuates because I periodically add to the pile, and every week some of them surrender to the siren call and they leap to their death. Plus it's challenging to take roll because they find it difficult to sit still.

Tonight they're all here, traveling as much as two hours from their distant sentry posts. Some of them haven't seen me in weeks. Immediately following our assembly, the Night Guardians will leave for their patrol duties.

We pile into the Disney Concert Hall, a big, gleaming, silver geometric rupture of a building. It's built to seat less than three thousand, but the Guardians improvise. They squat in the aisles. Cling to curved walls. Hang from the draped spotlights. It's hot and stuffy with testosterone and adrenaline. We're an array of miscellany; some of us wear jewelry, some of us barely dress at all. We're tall, short, thick, thin, all of us enhanced beyond the limits of accustomed human endurance.

I'm still on cloud nine from my encounter earlier with Tank. Finally, I remember someone. More than that, I know him. Very little of our relationship is missing, just the last few weeks perhaps. I feel quasi-normal for the first time in months.

It helps that he's a big handsome man. With an axe.

They swarm as I enter. I cannot press deep into the concert hall because they need to touch me first. Brief caresses. They squeeze my shoulders. Grip my hand. All four thousand. This is the second episode of our ritual.

My relationship to the Guardians is impossible to explain. We don't have telepathy, but we share a connection which goes beyond physical. "Like ants," Becky once said. "And you're the queen." I'm in a good mood, and so right now they are too. We feed off each other. My head buzzes with the overwhelming collective connection.

Eventually I stand in the middle of the room, surrounded on all sides, and raise my hand. "Stay with me! Stay together! Stay alive!"

They roar in return and it's a heady experience. They need me and I need them, and together we're a living force. A pack at full strength.

"Thank you for coming on short notice. It does me good to see you. My strength returns when we gather," I announce. "I wish we had more time, but our business is urgent. We have enemies and I don't know how immediate is the threat. One day soon, my friends, we will be able to rest. To lower our guard and enjoy peace. But that day is not today. Our safety and the safety of the innocents within our care require vigilance. So our time together will be brief.

"You've heard of Walter's recent visit. You know the man. Many of you fought along side him before the Chemist died." At the mention of the two names, the crowd shivers. Muscles quiver in fear. In hatred. "He has returned. He seeks to enslave us, in the same manner as he has two thousand of our brothers and sisters. Directly to my face he explained that you are manufactured property that belongs to him. And he is coming to claim what he thinks is rightfully his."

The crowd is dead silent, an indication of how seriously they take Walter. How much they respect the threat he represents.

"Listen carefully to me, brothers and sisters. He is *wrong*. You are not property. You are not slaves. We must admit that our bodies react to his. That he calls to us. That he is stronger than us. But that is all we grant him. Not one more inch does he deserve from us. We will pay him no allegiance. In fact, we will resist him to our last breath.

"We will be true to each other. We will be true to our new Kingdom. And we will fight him. It's either that or surrender, because he is coming. He's on the move. And I will die a thousand deaths before I surrender."

They respond to the emotion in my voice with their own, screaming in a single voice so loud it distorts my sensory input. I raise my hand and wait for quiet again.

"We were built for war. Our bodies were. But my soul longs for peace. So what shall I do? I will use my body as a tool to defend the innocent. To protect our home. To protect you. To protect our future. I call on you to do the same. If you cannot muster the strength, go quickly. Because here you will be called upon to support your family. Here we will fight.

"His army advances. So must we prepare. We will work with General Brown and his troops. With the Priest and his Law Keepers. And we will prevail.

"While we wait to see his intentions, we shall train. You will remain at your station, but too long have we ignored our need to harness the strength and speed which consume us. I will circulate among you. Mason and the Falcons will circulate among you. You are powerful beyond imagination, but so are our enemies. They prepare for war, and so shall we. We will begin drilling. Practices intended to sharpen you further, to prepare you for the looming battles.

"So tonight I ask you to return to your posts with vigilance and urgency. To steel yourselves for what is to come. To look for my arrival. And to heed my call for greater discipline, for increased training. A storm is coming. But we will prevail against it."

I raise my fist again. They raise theirs.

"Stay with me. Stay together. Stay alive."

Eight

I'd kill for a Chick-fil-A spicy chicken and egg breakfast sandwich. And hash browns. That might be worth biking all the way to Utah. Assuming Chick-fil-A still exists. Like most days, however, I wolf down a lukewarm fruit smoothie and examine our domain from my balcony.

General Brown and his troops are circumnavigating New Los Angeles and installing cameras and motion detectors. More guards are stationed at armed checkpoints and the mountains are being crenellated. We still can't locate Walter and his vanishing army. Neither can the Resistance, so Brown claims. He and I have been communicating solely through texts.

My to-do list looms. Of paramount importance is training the Guardians to face stronger enemies. Of lesser urgency is the ongoing work to remove dead bodies from the million homes in our Kingdom, those who were too old to flee. The Doctors keep harping on the contagion these corpses could spread. I also need to remove Cave Dwellers from the subway lines. And keep sweeping for wild dogs. And evict the gang near Anaheim. And welcome the thousands of newcomers. And on and on.

A Chick-fil-A breakfast sandwich would solve a lot of these problems, in my opinion.

My phone beeps. A text message.

>> **Hey pretty lady**

>> **What'cha doing?**

It's the Outlaw. Chase. Finally, he texts me. Katie smiles in the back of my skull and tells me that Chase should come over.

Instead, I reply, **I'm working.**

>> **When was your last day off?**

I sniff. July, maybe?

Not all of us live on permanent holiday. I don't get days off.

>> **You need to. Have one day for rest every week.**

I wish. Pure fantasy.

>> Take the morning off.

My fingers hesitate. I've got so much to do...

>> Please. I'm already at Venice Beach

I probably shouldn't. Everyone I know has forbidden it. Plus I'll have to sneak past Dalton again. But he's right; I haven't had a day off in a long time.

And he's cute, Katie says.

I can't argue.

Okay. I'll be there in an hour.

And don't get spotted. Our Law Keepers are on high Outlaw alert.

It takes me an hour and a half. I can't decide what to wear, suffering from a sudden inability to dress myself. I change shorts three times and try on twenty pairs of shoes. I'm not superficial, I'm just bad at this. I want to ask Kayla, Where's the line between perfect and too short? Flats or heels? Flip flops or sandals? But I can't because then she'd know I'm sneaking out. I snort; Queens don't sneak out. I do what I want. I'm simply doing it quietly. After fifteen minutes of frustration I throw a pair of wedges *through* the rear closet wall and I leave the apartment barefoot.

Venice Beach is an eclectic place despite the great evacuation. Its population vacillated between the wealthy and impoverished for a century as gangs and gentrification battled to gain dominance. The current population still reflects this melting pot of cultures. Several dozen off-duty Workers of all shapes and colors lounge under the palm trees which dot the sidewalks like tall lollipops. This is a lazy, care-free place. Much of the community bikes to work instead of living downtown, probably because they dislike living so close to authority. No one takes note of me as I walk across the sand. Slowly. Queens do not hurry. Not for boys.

He's wearing jeans and flip-flops and a tight cerulean t-shirt that does wonders for his crystal blue eyes. And for his torso. And arms.

"Nice outfit," he says.

I don't care. I don't care that he noticed. I refuse to. "You too."

"It feels good to wear normal clothes, doesn't it."

I nod. "And to pretend we're normal people?"

I'm at the ocean. With Chase. A rush of deep contentment comes over me. Katie is at peace.

He chuckles. "I haven't felt normal in a long time. Thanks for taking the morning off."

"It was a worthy suggestion." I walk into the ocean for the first time in weeks. The water is clear and warm, and I close my eyes a moment to enjoy existing. To remember that not all the world is a battle. Some corners of the earth remain solely to feel good between my toes. He takes my hand in his; he feels better than the Pacific, and once again the storm in my temples rolls away.

"Fine," I say. "I admit it. The headache goes away when we hold hands."

"Are you familiar with Maslow's Hierarchy of Needs?" he asks.

"Certainly."

"I'll explain the headaches. The Hyper Virus kills, like...ninety-five percent of its victims. Statistically, you should have died after injection. But the Chemist kept you unconscious for the worst of it, and he surgically reinforced parts of your body so you'd emerge even stronger. He took care of your basic physiological needs, in other words, to keep you alive. Those headaches you feel are the result of your changing frontal cortex. Instead of an aneurysm, you have headaches. Are you following?"

"Of course. A five-year old could follow so far."

"My headaches have mostly gone away, thanks in part to you. Last year, during our senior year, you used to hold my hand even when you didn't understand. You were fulfilling my need to be loved, which is the next level of the Hierarchy. We're very vulnerable as we trans-form, and the more needs we have met the better. Human touch is powerful. That's why when I hold your hand, your headaches get better. More of your needs are being met."

"How did you know I have them? The headaches, I mean."

He says, "No one knows your face like I do. I know when you have a headache. And I can tell your skin has gotten a shade lighter."

He's examining my arms, rubbing his fingers up and down my forearm and bicep. I ask, "What do you mean?"

"I don't think your color has fully returned from the three months in a coma. In retrospect I should have wheeled you outside more often."

"I'm darker than *you*."

He pinches me and says, "Because you're Hispanic. And I'm Caucasian."

"I doubt the nurses would let you wheel a patient into the parking lot to work on her tan."

"There were no nurses during the second half. I could do what I wanted."

"What? Explain?"

He takes my hand again and we start walking south in the surf, like we're a normal couple. In his mind we might be. He's evidently comfortable with my body, enough that he takes my hand and brushes my shoulders while everyone else in New Los Angeles is afraid to touch me. I'm quickly falling under his comfortable spell. Lost in his atmosphere. He says, "The hospital was evacuated, but I wouldn't let them move you. So we stayed by ourselves for a month."

"That's not true."

"It is. The nurses were overrun so I'd been caring for you myself for weeks by the time they left. I'd feed you, change your catheter bags, stretch you, give you medicine, and read to you. Just you and me." I'd think he's crazy, but he's smiling to himself as he recalls those months.

Oh sweet Chase. He's just the kind of fool to throw his life away for me. Poor sweetheart, all alone.

I stop. He stops. I place my free hand over my eyes to staunch the mutiny welling there. "Chase. Before we go on, you need to know that

I cannot control my emotions. At the moment, I'm trying not to weep and I'm not sure why."

"The disease. You have raging hormones."

"If your story about the hospital is true, you have saddled me with a debt I can never repay. I wouldn't even know how to begin."

"No debt. That's what we do. We take care of each other."

"No. That's not what *friends* do. I'm worried you're expecting things from me - things you deserve - that I just don't have to give."

He starts walking again, tugging me after. "Like what?"

"Like reciprocal unconditional love."

"Nah. I'm not expecting that."

But I love him. So so much.

He's taller than me. I'm walking higher up the slope of sand and yet my forehead still barely reaches his chin. He's not as tall as Tank, but who is. I say, "I don't love you. I'm serious. I don't even remember you."

"I know."

"Then what are you expecting?"

"Just a chance. I only want to be around you now and then."

I shake my head and finish wiping my eyes. I'm a gross mess. Good thing I don't care what he thinks... "See, that's the problem. You say hopeful romantic things, like we're in a fairytale movie. But I sincerely doubt that's how this plays out."

"Why the doubt?"

"For one thing, I have a nemesis. A sadistic maniac who promised to butcher me."

"Ah," he says. "Walter."

"Walter."

Walter...

He says, "He's returning."

"Exactly."

"So leave."

I shake my head. "I can't. I won't. I promised myself to the Guardians. Somehow they're my people. They trust me."

"It's a big world. It's not hard to hide four thousand people. I'll help."

"Run and hide?" I scoff. "That's your solution?"

"Is there another reason you don't want to leave this place? A secret you're keeping?"

"No."

"The Inheritors?"

Dang it. First Walter and now the Outlaw want to discuss the Inheritors. I refuse to talk about them. "You don't know me as well as you think you do. I'm not Katie."

He considers me a moment and nods in understanding. "You crave the action. The risk. You need adventure the same way you need nutrition."

"Yes. Well phrased. I feel the need. This burning urge for the world to get loud."

"You're an adrenaline junkie like me. It's so weird. I struggled with the disease for months. Over a year. It wrecked my life and you didn't know what was wrong. Now it's my turn to watch you struggle. And even though I know what's wrong, I'm not sure how to help."

"I know a way."

"Sure."

I say, "Train Mason and the Falcons. They're my best warriors. Teach them to fight, teach them anything they don't know already."

"Good idea. I'll start tonight."

"So soon? That easily?"

"For you, Katie, anything."

Katie leaps in my chest and she groans. *Oooooh.*

Knock it off, Katie. Keep it together. Her passions hit me like a hot flash. "You've got to stop that," I growl.

"Stop what?"

"I know your voice. I remember it. You spoke to me during the coma. Your vocalization has some dream-like power over me. You have the voice of God and it connects straight to my soul."

"If I quote an Emily Dickinson poem, you might hurl yourself at me?" he asks.

"Coming here was unwise. I should go."

"Why?"

"Because, you idiot, we're holding hands in the ocean. This is romantic as hell, Chase. But it can't be. I'm a mess. I have nothing to offer. I don't even know you. But when I'm around you everything inside me feels like it's falling apart."

He stays silent.

"I'm not Katie. Want to know why I'm so confident about that fact? I *hear* her. She's in my head. Like, her actual voice. Thoughts and opinions that aren't my own."

He doesn't answer. In fact he takes a step back and his eyes widen a fraction. His gaze shifts from me to the ocean and back, and he swallows. A slow minute passes and I hurt for him. "What does she say?"

"I think she operates on pure emotion now. She reacts to things that happen to me. She's an optimistic person. She's very positive, and passionate. Especially about you. Sometimes she's so in love with you she can barely breathe."

He laces his fingers in his hair and walks away. For a moment it appears he might keep going, but he returns. The corners of his mouth pull down in tragic, ravishing heartbreak and he cries. What more powerful force in the universe could there be? Love shatters us all. I watch his agony and wonder if I shouldn't have confided that secret. The bottoms of his jeans are getting wet from the surf.

"Yeah," he half-laughs and half-sobs. "She was always optimistic. Upbeat."

"I'm sorry."

He says, "Tell me what you see when you look at me. Please? We grew up together. You're a pillar of my life. I've always known where I stood with you. Part of my identity is who I am in your eyes. And now? I have no idea. Who am I to you? What's going on inside?"

"Chase, maybe this isn't the best time? I don't know you like you know me."

"Please."

I take a deep breath. "I remember you as a boy. The same way I remember other childhood friends. I have strong emotions that storm in my chest when I think about you. But no recent memories. You're a beautiful stranger, one that I'm inexplicably drawn to."

"Drawn to?

I know I'm blushing but I plow forward with the truth. Just this once. "You're the Outlaw, you buffoon. The planet's premiere sex symbol. I feel what most women feel around you, I assume, except I feel it much stronger. Because of our convoluted past."

We start walking again. I think he wants to ask more questions but he's satisfied with my honesty. At least temporarily. What an absolute disaster we are. Most of his longings are emotional while mine are corporeal.

Offhand I ask, "Do you remember Tank?"

"Of course I remember that big dumb idiot. Why?"

"Oh," I laugh, surprised at his strong reaction. "No...no reason."

"Katie."

"My name is Carmine."

"Why are you asking about Tank?"

Oh boy. Maybe I should not talk. Ever. "For some reason, I remember him. Like...completely. Everything else faded but not him."

He stares stonily ahead and his jaw flexes. "Well. Isn't that fantastic."

"I take it you're not a fan?"

"Of course not. He's tried to kill me a dozen times. And failed. Because he's stupid. He dated you just to hurt me."

"And maybe on account of my sparkling personality? And killer physique?" I ask.

"Shut up. That guy is garbage. He's still around. I can smell his stench now and then."

Didn't smell bad to me. I thought he smelled big and sexy. "Do you have any idea why I'd remember him?"

"Unfortunately I do."

"Tell me," I say.

"No. He's ugly."

"Please?"

"The Virus affects people differently. To some, it grants increased intelligence, like PuckDaddy. To others, increased beauty and influence, like Blue-Eyes and your friend Kayla. Increased jumping and strength, like me. Increased coordination, like Samantha Gear the Shooter. For some, it's more of an all-around enhancement, like Carter and like Pacific," he says, mentioning these strangers like I should know who they are. "But for Tank, it's simple brute strength. Nothing fancy. And when the Chemist operated on you, he planted stem cells and DNA into your limbs and your bones and your spine and your brain and God knows where else. The Chemist implanted his *own* DNA. And...also Tank's. Don't ask me how. I understand nothing about this crap. Simply put, a portion of your genes were spliced with Tank's. That's one reason you're so powerful, I bet."

"Fascinating. That explains all the incisions. So I remember Tank because of genetic cellular therapy?"

"Whatever. He's stupid."

"Are you jealous?"

"Of course."

I grin. "What do you see when you look at me? I told you. Turn about is fair play."

"The truth?"

"The truth."

He squints and tilts his head to the side. "A California Seven. Maybe Seven and a Half."

"I don't understand. A California Sev— ...are you joking?"

"What? That's really good."

"That's what you see? On a scale of One to Ten? A Seven?"

He grins. "And a Half! Five is average. You're way above average."

"You've got to be kidding. This shirt used to cost a thousand dollars. And it would be hard to wear these shorts any better. A *Seven?*"

"You're not considering the exchange rate, Katie. A California Seven is a Virginia Eight. A Texas Ten. A Pittsburgh Twelve."

"What is Kayla?"

"Well. That's not fair. She's make-believe, basically. She's a Disney Ten. Like…Ariel or Jasmine."

"You're the worst. I can't believe I dressed up. I even put on a real bra instead of active wear."

"Prove it."

"A Seven." I roll my eyes but can't muster up any real anger. He's clearly teasing. I don't know if he's in love, but he's fond of me. Crazy fond. He listens to every syllable, *really* listens. Like what I say matters. "Would I be an Eight if I hadn't broken your back?"

"And ordered your followers to throw me off a tower the other night? Yeah you're being docked points."

I say, "I found the reports. I shattered your vertebra and sacrum bones. I almost killed you, and still might. Surely you can find another girl."

"Where else would I go? We all give ourselves away. Our life is spent in pursuit of something. Mine happens to be a person."

"You love me."

"I loved Katie," he says. "Are you her or not?"

I grin. I grin out of happiness, and at the sheer lunacy of our situation. "You love me."

"You wish."

"You want to kiss me."

"You wish again," he says.

"I'll allow it, Chase. Once. It might help you."

"Nah."

"Hurry up," I say. "Just get it over with. And we can get on with our lives."

"You haven't earned it."

"*Earned* it?"

"Besides, I can't cheat on Katie with you."

"I *am* Katie."

"Are you?"

"Ugh. You're exhausting," I groan.

"You want me to cheat on you with you? That's messed up. You've got issues."

"And you're the biggest one at the moment. What if this is like a Disney movie? Katie won't wake up until you kiss her?"

"Then where would you go? Katie comes back and Carmine goes...?"

Kiss him Kiss him Kiss him Kiss him.

"I'm trying," I growl.

"What?"

"Katie says you're an idiot."

"She does *not*."

"And she wonders why you'd want to kiss a Seven anyway?"

He says, "Seven and a Half."

"Did you and Katie ever...you know?"

"Sex?"

"Sex."

"We definitely can't do that, Carmine. Not with Katie watching."

"I'm *not* offering," I growl.

"Like right here on the sand?"

"Chase. Focus."

"No. We never did. We wanted to get married soon. That was the last thing we said to each other."

That stops me. My knees buckle and I sink onto the sand. In my mind, this was a game. Pure flirtation. But to him, this is no game. "Wow, Chase, I..."

He sits beside me, and wraps his arms around his knees. "What?"

"That is *so* sad. I didn't know. I can't remember that."

"There wasn't an official proposal or a ring or anything. The world was falling apart and we decided to get married sooner rather than later. Those were the last words you said to me, until a few days ago when you welcomed me to New Los Angeles."

Katie Lopez surges and forcefully tilts my head over to lean on his shoulder. I smell his cologne. I say, "I'm sorry. If you'd have told me I would have..."

"Been nicer?"

"Or something. I don't know. This whole thing has been rough on you. I never think about it from your perspective, you know? I apologize for banning you from New Los Angeles so quickly. You walked all this way to see me and I was awful."

"Okay. Fine. I give in. You're an Eight."

"You're darn right I'm an Eight. At minimum."

"Where the hell you been?" Dalton barks at me when I return to the tower. He's out front, hands on hips, and everyone in the courtyard stares at us. Embarrassing. Kayla is behind him, practically hopping. No, she's actually hopping.

"Down boy," I say. "Sometimes I don't let you tag along because you slow me down."

"You tell me where you're going or I'll tag your ass with a tracking anklet," he says.

"Carmine Carmine Carmine," Kayla chirps. "The Outlaw! He's here."

I blurt, "I wasn't with him."

"I didn't say you were."

"No...he's...I didn't...how do you know?"

"He was spotted five minutes ago. The Law Keepers are hunting him now."

"Hah. Good luck with that." I pause at the elevator while the Worker radios for the car. "Dalton, tell Mason and the Falcons I need to meet with them later. Maybe after dinner? Right now I want to see some of General Brown's upgrades, and then we'll talk with Law Keepers about the underground tunnels. Those are my plans. Happy?"

"Carmine, don't you care the Outlaw broke your edict about New Los Angeles? You banished him." Kayla pauses a moment to examine my outfit, and she says suspiciously, "You look...nice. Why do you look nice? Where have you been?"

"You picked these out. Does this outfit no longer meet your approval?"

"No, but sweetie those are *short*."

Shoot. I knew it.

She says, "And have you noticed how happy the Guardians are? I just saw two singing a duet from that Nicole Kidman musical, you know, the one in Paris? The rest are jumping and smiling and acting goofy. What's gotten into them?"

I am saved by the arrival of the Priest. He storms into the tower lobby in a holy fury and he is trailed by two of his fanatical followers. "Carmine," he rants. "I told you. What did I tell you? That the self-righteous do-gooder is insubordinate. A law breaker. We have photos of him walking the streets in west LA." He takes a breath and admires my outfit. Ugh. Don't look at me. "I have the Outlaw surrounded and he'll be in custody before lunch."

"Glad to hear it," I remark. No chance.

This little man annoys me. He couldn't catch Chase with an entire army.

Right you are, Katie. I continue, "Custody? But we only incarcerate violent offenders. Correct?"

"Justice must be served, *Queen.* I've already called for a meeting of the Courts and—"

"If you catch him, and I'm sure you will, rebuke him thoroughly. But we cannot throw the Outlaw into prison for his first offense."

"His first? And what of the stories passed around? That he visited you the other night in your bedroom?"

"Don't believe every rumor you hear, Priest." Except that one. That one is true. Katie snickers.

"Like you said at the Herder execution," he smirks, "we do not live in a world in which we can grant mercy."

"We don't incarcerate first-time non-violent offenders. Not in this Kingdom."

"Trust me, *Queen,* he'll be back. What do you suggest as discipline for his second offense, Queen?"

Dalton is rumbling beside me. He'd like to break the man's nose. The Priest has backed me into a corner. A corner in which I keep secrets. "I sincerely doubt you'll catch him twice."

"And if we do? Surely the man didn't get to you. Surely you

haven't fallen for the heretic?" He laughs quietly and his breath smells of wine.

I snap, "Kayla, post a bulletin online. If the Outlaw returns again then he'll spend a week in our jails. Happy, Priest? Now it'll be up to you to apprehend him."

The elevator car arrives and we board, leaving the Priest behind. Kayla is already at work on her phone. She pauses and asks in a tentative voice, "Can I post a pic of you in those shorts on Instagram?"

~

Mason is excited about training with the Outlaw. I swear him to secrecy but that might not be enough. Perhaps I should wire his mouth shut.

That night, after everyone is asleep, I sneak off to Glendale to a lumber yard Chase suggested. He is there, and so are the Falcons. I perch on a stack of bricks and monitor the secret training from a distance.

Chase is just...quicker than they are. Smarter. Stronger. I don't know how else to explain it. He moves like Neo from the Matrix, one of Katie's favorite movies. He works patiently with the Falcons, primarily forcing them to slow down. Mistakes are made when you fight out of control, he repeats again and again. How did this nine-teen-year-old boy learn so much? He puts them through drills, forces them to concentrate instead of battling with blind aggression. The Falcons are our best fighters and they can't touch him unless they all gang up.

After two hours of training, the Falcons are thoroughly exhausted and beaten. The Outlaw appears fresh, though he presses a hand to his hip now and then. I experience a pang of guilt about breaking his back. Chase tells the Falcons to meet him again tomorrow night. Before he leaves, he glances my way and winks across the distance.

Nine

The following day I'm in the War Department, staring at maps on walls. General Brown is with me, as are a handful of his commanders.

Brown shakes his head as we scroll along our border. "Ain't no way a large group can get in undetected now, Carmine. Anyone coming here either goes through a checkpoint or sneaks past one at a time. Walter could smash his way in, but we'd know."

I ask, "And the ocean?"

"The Navy hasn't declared for either the Resistance or the Federal Government. Mostly they're sittin' dead in the water, trying to conserve fuel. But their radars still work and we'll know if any troop transport approaches."

"You have men aboard those Navy ships? Spies loyal to you?"

"No. I got spies who are loyal to *you*. And the Outlaw. Walter is no friend of the Resistance. If he tries to crack our borders, the Resistance is prepared to support."

"Do you still communicate with them?"

His hands are on his hips and he nods slowly. "I do. Get used to it."

That makes me nervous. Too many eyes. Too many cracks in our armor. I have serious trust issues; waking up abandoned will do that to a girl. I know I need to get over it, and that it negatively impacts my leadership. But I'm not sure how. "So if Walter can't get in...what's he doing?"

"That is a question I'd very much like an answer to myself."

My phone buzzes. It's a text message. From Tank, my friend the giant from Beverly Hills. Katie has no response.

>> **hey mamita**

>> **come meet me**

>> **got something to show you**

>> **trust me, its worth your time**

"Thank you, gentlemen. I'll get out of your way." I leave the War

Room and close the door behind. Dalton looks up from sitting crisscross on the hall floor, sees me texting, and returns to his novel.

Where should I meet you?

And this better be good.

>> Tell you what

>> I'll meet you halfway

>> In Santa Monica

He gives me an address, which I save into my phone. Now to ditch the bodyguard. I jog down the stairs and return to my apartment. Dalton follows, glances in, sees my Devotee waiting, and assumes his place outside. "I'm taking a nap," I tell the Devotee. I really need to find him a more appropriate outfit, other than a robe. Or a different job. This is kinda absurd.

"Would you like—"

"No, I don't want company, thank you." I close the bedroom door and immediately slip over the side of my shattered wall.

Twenty minutes later I'm in a truck heading west, having abandoned my security detail once again. I never used to do that, and I'm not sure why I've started now. Queens can't have crushes. Can they? I'm no Queen, so... Am I a warrior or a woman? An executioner or a girl with a crush? Perhaps I shouldn't need to choose one or the other, but so far I'm finding that difficult. Maybe this is what happens when nineteen-year-olds are thrust into positions of leadership; we screw things up, including ourselves. In a perfect world I'd be sitting in a classroom, taking notes, instead of trying to save a city and ignore boys.

Santa Monica is inside our borders but just barely. I haven't followed up with the Overseer responsible for the settlers here, but when I arrive I see signs of life. A mom and two children at the beach. Clothes hung out to dry. Three men hauling supplies in a wheelbarrow. Good. This is good. Hardworking people bringing life to our neighborhoods.

Tank's address leads to a dilapidated development two miles inland. The house is falling apart. A big black truck is parked in the drive. My blood is pumping, adrenaline pouring into veins, muscles tensing. This could be a trap.

He's sitting in a dusty recliner, heavy boots propped up on a coffee table, eating graham crackers with white-gloved hands. His double-bladed axe leans against the wall.

Gosh he's big. Big shoulders, big forearms, big thighs, big jaw. He's strong too. The disease gives him a musk, almost like a pleasant sauna, and he glows.

"There's my baby," he grins.

"This house sucks. So far I'm not impressed."

"What about this chair? Looks big enough for two."

"No chair with you in it is big enough for two." There's old Hershey Kisses on the top shelf of the pantry and I help myself. I hear rats scurry behind the fridge. "You live here?"

"Naw. I live outside your sanctuary. Don't need the hassle."

"Where?"

"Houses up in Tarzana. We use Canyonback as our playground. Nobody for miles."

I frown. "Houses? We?"

"Nice to see you again."

I don't reply. Not going to play his game. This guy is trouble. Large sexy trouble. And I'm not sure I want to get mixed up in it.

He points at my arms. "What's with the ribbons?"

"My joints hurt. They help."

"Your skeleton grew funny." He tugs off one of his white gloves and splays his fingers. They're blocky and misshapen, like the bones are too large for his skin. "Mine too. Got that in common." He stands, puts the glove back on, and brushes cracker crumbs off his white button up shirt.

"Tank—"

He hugs me. My voice gets muffled in his chest. He has the audacity to kiss the top of my head. "Thanks for coming, babe. I know I haven't earned your trust. Not after being a rascal in our past lives."

"A rascal? Who says rascal?"

He releases me and plays with my hair. "I like your new look."

"Tank, why am I here?"

"Okay. Down to business. So I found some of your Variant pets wandering in the state parks."

"Not pets. And I call them Guardians."

"Whatever. And these guys have broken brains. You know? Whatever the Chemist did, they don't work right anymore. Got the intelligence of five-year-olds."

"I've seen that before. We have a hotel Downtown where we house Guardians who can no longer function by themselves. It's heartbreaking. I can take them off your hands..."

He chuckles and crosses his arms. "Naw. I like them. We've become buddies. Want to meet one?"

"I assume that's why you brought me."

He tilts his head to the ceiling. "Thompson! Come on down here."

There's a heavy groan of wood, and dust filters down from cracks in the ceiling plaster. Another groan, then another, like rolls of thunder. They're heavy footsteps and each one causes a minor avalanche. Tank says, "Even those of us who got the virus from birth, we don't know much about it. But I'm guessing the Chemist didn't predict this."

"What do you mean?" I ask, gaping at the stairs with mounting apprehension.

"I only find males. So it's probably a testosterone thing."

Down the staircase stumps a giant. Tank is big, but he's within the boundaries of human limitation. Tank is as tall as Lebron James maybe. However, this guy is gargantuan. I backpedal out of the room, into the kitchen, and onto the front lawn. Tank follows, a grim smile on his face, and then the giant unfolds from the door. He's over ten feet. Possibly eleven.

I can't find enough air. "Tank...what..."

"This is Thompson."

"I recognize him. He...he found me in the forest, same time I found Kayla. His name is Travis. He was tall...but not...you know...not like this."

"They go through a growth spurt soon after the headaches drive them from your city. Thompson?" Tank calls loudly at the giant. "Your first name Travis?"

Travis nods. His eyes are fixed on me. He's not just tall, he's thick too. He must weigh four hundred pounds. No, more than that. Over five. He's wearing a tunic (a sheet with a hole cut for his head) and a kilt (a green blanket tied around his waist). What else would fit him?

Tank says, "I figure for some, the virus just keeps growing. Most of them stall around eleven and a half feet."

"Most? How many have you found?"

"Fifty-one. The noise of your Kingdom starts to wear on them, so they say, and they flee into the woods and start growing. Sooner or later they find me."

"Drawn to your power, I bet. You take care of them?"

"They can handle themselves. I mostly...shepherd them. Keep them from wandering off. Help them make clothes. Stop the fights. This group, they have a temper. Worse than mine."

"What do they eat?"

"Everything. Fortunately there's food in every house and animals are creeping back in. These guys are fast and can chase down deer if they work together. Spitted a bear two nights ago."

Thompson is almost twice my height, no exaggeration. I place my hand on his stomach, which is at eye-level, and he smiles. The physical connection brings him peace. "Travis. I'm pleased to meet you again. I'm glad you're okay. And that you're still alive."

Travis laughs, a deep booming cough, and says, "**Thaank youuu, Queeeen.**" The words are leisurely and pronounced with a slow tongue. "**Happyyy to seeee you toooo.**"

Tank says, "None of them talk much. They like to laugh, though."

"I can bring physicians. Are they....do they need medical care?"

"Don't think so. Thompson you need to see the doctor?" Tank shouts, like he needs to reengage the giant's attention. Thompson shakes his head and reaches his hand into the tree top for a bird. "Pretty simple bunch. I'm telling you, like five-year-olds. They get nightmares. Like to play outside. Run. That kind of thing."

"I'm glad you showed me. But I'm not sure how I can help."

"Not asking for help. These big guys love you. Talk about the Queen all the time. They want to help *you*."

"Oh yeah?" I smile. Travis Thompson is no longer paying attention to us. He's peering into the neighbor's second floor window on his tiptoes. "How?"

"They hate Walter. I bring him up and it sends them into a rage."

"I can't use them as a weapon, Tank. They aren't grist for the mill."

"These boys ain't grist," he replies. "Grist has no say-so. The giants have a say-so. A loud one. And they want to tear Walter apart."

"Do you want to bring them into New LA? A secluded section?"

He shakes his head. "They wouldn't go. Guys like Thompson, they like freedom. Plus I want them a secret. The powers-that-be would swoop in for research purposes. Governments would go nuts, you know?"

"I wouldn't let them."

"I don't know if you remember or not, but I was once strapped to the back of a flatbed truck. While cameras rolled." His voice is dark and tugs at a distant memory I can't place. Katie remembers and shivers. "The FBI couldn't wait to open me up once they discovered my disease. They threw me into an electrified jail cell and starved me."

"I don't remember...not really."

"I'm never going back. Neither is my gang of giants."

"Maybe I can send some tailors? With materials for custom clothes?"

"There's an idea. Though these fine gentlemen prefer nudity. Oh, another thing I should mention." He grins, which looks good on him despite the burn marks. "Seeing as how they worship you, I told them you're my girlfriend."

"Tank," I growl. "That's precisely what an inveterate rascal would do."

"What can I say?" He spreads his arms wide, palms up. "I'm a desperate man. And I always thought you were crazy hot. Remember how much fun we used to have?"

I do remember. In fact, it's one of the only things I remember. Which is why I can't think straight.

Ten

I'm driving home, a hundred miles per hour on the vacant Ten. Trying to ignore the memories of kissing Tank in Katie's bedroom. He was not good to Katie; that's easy to recall. As a boyfriend he'd been distant and inconsistent, and Chase's assertion that Tank used Katie is valid. But do people not change? Have I not changed into an entirely new creature?

It'd be easier if he didn't feel like home when nothing else does. If he wasn't comfortable and familiar. If my sudden love life wasn't wrecking the rest of it.

"Come on, Carmine," I scold myself. I pinch the bridge of my nose. I'm not a little girl. I'm not a teenager battling hormones and security issues. "Well...actually...yes, that's exactly what I am."

My eyes aren't on the road, and the truck is veering across both lanes. There's a loud *Thump* from my bumper and the entire chassis shudders.

I've run over something.

"Oh damn it..." My stomach turns to ice. Looks like a person in the rearview. Tires squeal as I fishtail to a halt. "What halfwit was in the middle of the road..."

What halfwit wasn't watching where she was going?

I scramble from the cab. There's an unmoving lump forty yards back. I'm the worst Queen ever. It's a body, lying on the hot road. I kneel beside him. Can't call 911, it's non-existent. On the bright side, so are the general circuit courts. I can't be sued.

"Hey. Talk to me." I lay a hand on his shoulder.

His hand snaps out, catching my wrist in an iron grip. "Gotcha."

This man's very much alive.

It's a trap.

Men burst over the interstate's retaining wall. A net is tossed over us both. I'm too fast. Before it settles, I snatch the center and twirl it in a tight circle, and the mesh twists harmlessly around my wrist and forearm, like a thick glove. I kick at the man's face, the man who's holding my arm. I stomp, intending to crush his skull, but he dodges. Again and again, impossibly fast.

He's Variant. From Walter. Has to be. I smell their disease.

Another net is tossed, much larger. This time it settles around us in a wide pool. I stomp on the man's chest and claw his neck. Blood spurts. He groans and I'm released.

There are four other attackers. Big powerful men.

"Stop," I order. They laugh. How does the Outlaw do that?

I cut the net with my nails but the fabric shifts and gives. At best I've tugged a hole wide enough for my hand to go through. Someone hits me from behind and I collapse under his weight. Laying on my stomach. I hammer an elbow backwards, but he catches it. These are no ordinary men.

"Nice try, witch," he says. "We heard you'd be feisty."

"**Wait!**" I shout, throwing all my willpower into the imperative. He *does*. He even recoils. Hah! Just like Chase. I gather a fistful of net and reach back far enough to pull mesh around his neck. He makes a choking sound as I haul him forward. The situation reverses, and now I'm on top of him. I've got his noose in one hand and I use the other to pulverize his face. Two of his friends grab my arms and pull me off. They're standing on top of the net and I'm under. I jerk hard on the material and the two men lose their footing. We all fall, but they're still grasping my biceps.

I'm lost in the sea of mesh. The net is everywhere, slowly tightening a fierce grip. The fight is silent, ugly, desperate. I head-butt a man through the net. Stars explode in my vision but he lets go. I use my free hand to attack the other assailant but net catches me. Mobility fading fast. Instead of hitting him I roll on top and press my nails into his throat.

There are five of us tangled and trussed. I'm the strongest and I might still win the fight except for the final man. He's not caught in the net. He calmly approaches and sets his boot against my skull. The net has been pulled tight over my face like a mask. He presses down and I glance at him in fear. He's holding a sledge hammer.

"Well, well. We caught a fish." He hefts the heavy hammer onto his shoulder. "Know what Walter said? Go for the head, he said. Newborns are vulnerable to concussions, he said."

I've got a man in my hands, nails in his neck. He isn't moving because he knows I'll severe his carotid artery. But that's not doing me a lot of good at the moment. I'm essentially frozen, caught in acres of fabric. I could break it or rip through with enough time.

"I'd offer to let you surrender, but you know what Walter said?" he continues. "She won't go quietly, Walter said. Don't give the bitch an inch. So. I'll have to use my trusty sledge."

"Stop," I say again, but without much conviction. I can't get full breaths.

"Don't move. I'm serious. I might miss and crush your esophagus and Walter'll skin me. Don't kill her, he said. He really will, you know. Skin me."

"How scary for you," I pant. His weight shifts, and the sledge is hefted in both hands over his head.

Then there is a tiger. A massive beast bounding over the interstate's railings.

I see a flash of teeth and fur in my peripheral vision and the man with the sledgehammer is suddenly gone. Men scream. The net in which we're all caught drags several feet, jerking in short tugs, terrible noises like wet paper tearing. I am wrapped snugly, but pressure eases as the net rips. The men worry me; the tiger terrifies me.

Not tiger. *Tigers.*

There are two. One behind me working on the net (or working on something in the net) and one padding eighteen inches from my face. I pinch my eyes closed and concentrate on not trembling. Play dead, play dead. Dead people don't tremble. Katie is a cold knot of terror sitting on my stomach.

I block out gut-wrenching sounds but I cannot ignore the smells. A coppery scent I can't pretend doesn't exist. Rotten meat. Thick musk. A sweet natural odor, like overly ripe fruit.

There's a final sharp tug on the net. Followed by the sound of something heavy being dragged. After that, silence. The men are no more. I try counting seconds but I'm too frightened. The net is loose enough that I could escape but not quickly. Untangling will require effort and time. I'd rather not be eaten during my getaway. The tigers are still close; I smell them.

I wait.

I wait.

After an eternity, the shocks on my truck groan and squeak in protest. I risk a peek. A massive tiger has its front paws on the truck bed, snuffling. Sufficiently intrigued, he (she? it?) hops fully aboard. He's too big to fit so he rests forepaws and his heavy head on the roof of the cab and remains there, as if expecting a ride. The other tiger is walking towards me. She moves with powerful grace, muscles bunching and pressing in harmony. A well-built and perfectly hinged weapon. Her mouth is a cage of pearlescent fangs. She reaches my prostrate figure and collapses with a *Humph* of air. Thick fur and brawn settle on the net, and she leans against me. Another deep breath like a sigh, and she begins a rhythmic chuffing.

Is she...are we...cuddling?

That's exactly how it appears from my angle. Our bodies are touching. She's pinned me effectively to the interstate. I don't dare move. Do these tigers hate only men? I'm glad Dalton isn't here. I can no longer see my truck, but judging by the noises I'd say the male is bouncing up and down, perhaps trying to make it move. Twenty minutes later a vehicle passes on the other side of the interstate barrier but it doesn't slow. I wouldn't either if I saw tigers.

The morning slowly gives way to afternoon and still I wait. Now, both tigers are laying beside me, basking in the sun. Every few minutes my phone buzzes inside the cab. Hello? Kayla? Hi Kayla. Yeah I'm here with the tigers. Waiting to be eaten. How're you? Worst case scenario, I wait here until Night Guardians begin making rounds. No, that's not true. Worst case scenario, the big cats get hungry before then. Best case scenario, Guardians are nearby already. Maybe I can find them...

I close my eyes. Deliberately I reduce my heartbeat with leisurely breaths. I need to unclench. Relax. Find that point where my body almost melts. Cast myself outwards, utilizing the trick I employ from the observatory. To map the world and allow the world to notice me, possibly catch the attention of Guardians in close proximity —

Both tigers shift uneasily. The animal before me twitches his head, like shaking off pesky flies. Behind me, the other big cat coughs and I'm washed with his warm breath. Their uneasiness is hot and alien in my mind. I experience their irritation as if its my own.

Our bodies are linked through the shared virus. I don't understand its mysterious connections, but I'm unwilling to explore them further at the moment. It's not telepathy, but we experience each other. I close myself off. No reason to upset my would-be devourers. Is this what the Outlaw means? Is this how he bottles his biological output?

And so we remain. For hours. I'm getting a sunburn and major crick in my neck.

Around two o'clock, both animals raise their sleepy heads and gaze north with golden eyes. I hear it too. Singing. A faint melody with no tune I recognize, sung by either a man or a woman with a cold. The longer I listen the more feminine it registers, but harsh, as though issued from a damaged throat.

Both animals slowly press themselves off the road. He yawns. She nudges my shoulders with her terrifying maw. Still I don't move a muscle. The song turns into a whistle and both tigers begin padding away. First one, then the other jumps easily over the interstate guardrails.

The whistling grows closer, probably from the abandoned Alexander Hamilton High School grounds north of the road. I tell myself to count to fifty and then go. When I reach twelve I frantically claw at the netting, free myself, and run like hell.

~

I'm still shaking when I get out of the shower. Kayla sits on my bed crosslegged, eyes wide. "So why didn't they eat you?"

"I don't know. It makes no sense."

"They ate the guys in the net."

"Ate or mauled. I didn't inspect the carnage. But I think the tigers...liked me."

"So that's why didn't they eat you?" she asks again.

"Kayla. I. Don't. Know."

"They just...laid there? Like they wanted to be next to you?"

I nod. She's set out sparkly clothes for me. I ignore them and find some black active wear instead.

"Do you think the person whistling was the Cheerleader?"

I say, "That's my best guess. And I didn't want to be stuck in a net when she showed."

"But why didn't they eat you?"

"Kayla! I don't freaking know! It was extremely frightening and I'd like to talk about something else."

"They don't eat the Cheerleader either. Have you thought about that?"

"Yes," I admit. "That has occurred to me. But then again, they haven't eaten any Guardians that we know of."

"What were you doing out there anyway?"

"Investigating a tiger report," I say.

Liar liar.

Shut up Katie. I'm not mentioning Tank. I continue, "Heard a tiger rumor on the street. So I went."

Secrets secrets are no fun. Secrets secrets hurt someone.

Eleven

The first jet I've seen in months roars over my head. I forgot how loud they are. I'm on Highway 1, a quarter mile east of Los Angeles International Airport, watching. Dusk has settled, but Nuts rerouted enough electricity to power the runway lights near Tom Bradley Terminal.

Anyone claiming that our occupation of Los Angeles is a waste of resources can use the airport as evidence. Dozens, maybe hundreds, of airplanes sit unused. The concourse is herculean in size and it's a vacant wasteland. I'd feel bad about the billions in unused assets but air travel is at a barebones minimum since the gasoline shortage. Kayla said commercial air traffic is nonexistent and even the military operates at 25%. Which means the Resistance is spending a fortune on this jet.

The airplane touches down, tires scream, and lights flash. By squinting I can zero in on the aircraft, which taxies to a stop near our Kingdom's motorcade. A ladder unfolds from the open hatch, and both Kayla and General Brown are there to greet the famous leader of the Resistance, Isaac Anderson.

I will not be joining them. They tried to guilt me into attending this meeting of masters of the universe, but I refused. Kayla said stuff about duty and responsibilities and diplomacy. I responded, "That sounds boring. I'm bored now. Just thinking about it."

Kayla scolded me, "Carmine, if you want to form your own kingdom then you must keep up healthy relationships with your allies."

General Brown had also been there, cornering me in the hallway. "I strongly concur, Miss Carmine. These are important people, flying all this way. The least you should do is meet with them. In order for us to survive, we need to do our homework to ensure—"

"Homework!" I cried. "I forgot my homework. I'm totally going to fail."

General Brown looked bewildered, glancing at Kayla for help. "Fail what?"

"Listen," I told them, edging past in the hall. "I'm a nineteen-year-old girl. I don't want to talk strategy with two old military guys. Even if you two are both awesome. Which you are. My brain can't handle the boredom. I realize that sounds arrogant and insular, but it's working so far. General, you said I need to focus less on management and more on leadership. So I'm going to leave this minutia to you. I've been training the Guardians to fight Walter, and I'll keep doing so. You and Isaac Anderson work out the military details. Whatever you recommend, we'll do. Probably. I'm a weapon, a warrior with attention deficit disorder. Not a planner." That ended the conversation. Neither was happy with me.

Now, I watch them shake hands on the tarmac from my vantage outside the airport, sitting on the roof of my Land Cruiser. Katie stirs between my ears at the sight of Isaac Anderson. Dalton is watching the encounter through binoculars, standing on the hood. He doesn't have night vision like I do, however. He grumbles, "We'd get a better view if we *attended* the meeting, you know."

"I don't wanna."

"Carmine, some days, you're a queen. Tough, and scary as hell, and brilliant. And some days you're a teenage punk."

"Thanks."

He sighs and says, "I hear Beyoncé is a handful too."

"We have better things to do."

"Like what?"

"Reconnaissance."

I climb down and get behind the wheel, and he sits in the passenger seat. I stomp the gas and we head northwest. For thirty minutes the ubiquitous palm trees lining the road flash past our headlights until we reach the Kingdom checkpoint on the Ronald Reagan Freeway. All lanes are blocked off and the adjacent land is rocky and barren. This is the farthest edge of my civilization, beyond which is a world we don't patrol. Our high-beams puncture the dark westward, towards Simi Valley several miles beyond.

The guard is surprised by traffic this late. He exits the guardhouse with a flashlight, other hand on the pistol clipped to his belt. I buzz down the window, and he says, "Help you? You heading out this late?"

"We're driving to the orchards," I reply.

"Holy hell, you're Queen Carmine, ain't you. I mean, pardon my... but, are you?" He's a young kid, maybe eighteen, needs to shave his peach fuzz.

"I am. It's a little spooky out here, isn't it?"

"It is, yes ma'am, and I ain't got used to it yet. The animals get loud after sunset."

"Here," I say, and I place a heavy paper bag in his hand. "We brought you a gift. This job isn't easy and we are grateful for you."

He's floored. He doesn't even examine the goods. "Wow, th-thanks. That's so...but, are you sure about the orchards, ma'am? That's a long drive and it ain't safe so late. You're liable to run into trouble."

I jerk my thumb at Dalton. "I brought my backup. Listen, do us a favor. Don't tell anyone you saw us. Kay? This orchard inspection is a secret."

"Yes ma'am. I understand. I mean, I don't. But. You're the queen and I reckon you can inspect whenever you want."

"Thanks. We should be back in a few hours. Open the gate?"

"Yes ma'am. Good luck, ma'am."

He scurries off to find keys. With my window down, I become aware of the tremendous silence pouring through. This outpost feels like it's on Mars, extremely isolated.

"Carmine, this is stupid," Dalton says.

"Don't you start."

"Gonna get yourself killed."

"Walter's missing. So is much of his Variant army, and our satellites can't find them. All I want to do is check."

He scoffs. "Check? How you gonna check the whole state of California?"

"Not all of it. Just our small part."

"Still. That's impossible. What can you do that satellites can't?"

"Dalton, I'm a mutant. A freak. Trust me."

There's a scream of metal as the gate is opened. The guard stands aside and we motor into the black. The checkpoint lights are soon left behind and for several miles we travel quietly through no-man's-land until Dalton can't stand it.

We're nowhere.

"I did two tours in Afghanistan," he says . "And that place is a lot less creepy than this."

"Eerie, isn't it. The lack of people and lights." We're both whispering so we don't attract ghosts or whatever.

Simi Valley comes into view, a small independent city now abandoned. The houses are cold, windows and doors gaping. Stores abandoned and broken. As though we've discovered sunken Atlantis. Dalton keeps groaning. Two miles in, I turn right onto Tapo Canyon road and drive north. I can't suppress chills as we proceed past a vacant Kohl's department store which looks straight from a horror movie.

He says, "If I was Satan, I'd live here."

"I thought you Navy SEALs were tough."

"Can't shoot fallen angels, Carmine. Everyone knows that. Everyone with some common sense."

We push out of the city and into the mountains of Rocky Peak, farther into the stunted wilderness. Farther from everything. My phone keeps vibrating so I hand it to Dalton. "Read me the texts."

He scans the screen and says, "They're all from Kayla."

"They usually are. What's she want?"

"Nothing good. Girl's a mess."

I laugh. "Tell me. What's she texting me about?"

He clears his throat and says, "She thinks Isaac Anderson is a baller."

"A what?"

"Good looking dude. Like a James, you know? She say he looks like Captain America without a shield."

"You're right. She's a mess," I agree.

"You know she used to dance?"

"What do you mean?"

"*Dance*. Like, adult entertainment. You know. At the Rio, back before everything went to hell. Got the job when she still underage. Needed cash."

"No, I didn't know that. She told you?"

"Yeah. Poor girl, too sweet for that life. Bet she was popular, though. Then the Chemist came calling and she jump at it. Wait... another text. Says both the Resistance and Federal Government are scaling down nuclear weapons. Nobody want a nuke war."

"Good. About time." We're on a gravel road now, tree branches brushing our windows. At the crest of a rise, the road opens into a flat clearing. I kill the engine. "This is good."

He whispers, "No it ain't. What are we doing? It's like we in outer space. This mountain don't even have a name, I bet."

"You stay here." I shove open the door.

"Where you going?"

"To listen."

The night is loud with insects and darkness. A deep black, like a fog that stars can't penetrating. It's dark even to my eyes. I hike a tenth of a mile farther. Up this high I see scattered lights from the north-west corner of our Kingdom, fifteen miles distant. We're *so* alone. All our noises feel amplified. I lay flat on the dusty crown. If Walter or some of his Variant army are nearby, I'll know. The earth and wind will tell me. Our warm bodies are easy to detect if one has ears to listen.

Before I begin meditation and searching, my mind wanders to Kayla and her texts. Both sides dismantling nukes. I'd been worried about that. According to General Brown, we have an impressive missile defense shield and the Resistance plans to augment our armory, but I'm still relieved to learn cooler heads are prevailing. Maybe there's hope for humanity yet.

I don't like this place. I'm ready to leave.

Soon, Katie.

Something is wrong.

The mountain range I'm on stretches on as far as I can see to the east and northwest. Part of the greater Santa Monica range probably. It forms a natural border to Los Angeles. The cabin I shared with Cuddy is thirty miles south, a long hike through the scrub oak, pine, and sycamore trees. So many hiding places, even for a large group like Walter's. Maybe I should send Guardians out here in pairs to search, to look in places the satellites can't penetrate. Maybe I...

Then I see the man. He is sitting motionless in a black walnut tree thirty yards ahead of me. How did I not notice him sooner? I should have; he glows. I was too caught up in my thoughts, too sure we'd found solitude. He's a Variant, not one of mine. I realize that before I cast my attention towards him. He's entirely nude, wrapped around the trunk and glaring. Drool leaks at the corner of his mouth.

He's part of a pack. Now that I'm alerted I become aware of others. Maybe a dozen, hanging from trees or watching from brush. I see claws, sharp canines, long hair. Like werewolves without fur. Part of the forest noises I'm hearing is guttural breathing.

More of them behind, near Dalton. Time to go!

These are either feral mutants, or they're allied with Walter. Either way, we drove straight into trouble. Bad luck. Dang it, I hate when Dalton's right. He won't see the Variants because they don't glow to his eyes. I can't run for it; they'd eat Dalton alive if I did. My hand goes to my pocket. I'll text a warning, start the truck!

But I left my phone in the Land Cruiser. Ugh.

My blood begins to churn, thickening my skin and speeding up my systems. The mutants surrounding me sense it and grow excited. It's no use trying to calm their minds and win them to my side. They're too far gone, too angry, too removed from reason. Madness shines like a beacon in their eyes. Stupid Outlaw only shows up at inconvenient times, never when I need him.

Gotta get out of here.

I stand. They tense.

Are they with Walter? That's important. Gotta find out. I'm here for recon, after all. But how? I step towards the man in the walnut tree, and the pack shivers with energy. Can the guy speak, I wonder?

There's a sudden bizarre noise, a soft scratch. Takes me a second to place it—a squawking radio. Deeper inside the forest I spot another mutant, mostly hidden. A girl, peering around a tree. She's dressed in...looks like armor? And she's clutching a handheld radio.

So, that settles it. Militarized. These Variants belong to my enemy. Walter's forces are arriving.

I greet the pack with a shout, loud enough for Dalton to hear. An alarm. "Fellow mutants! You will not die tonight! Because I won't fight you. I need you to pass a message." No response. Like we're frozen in time. This whole night was a bad idea. "A message to Walter."

At his name, the Variants *Launch*. The group snaps over the crown of the hill like a bear trap. I'm caught off guard and nearly crushed. I can't fight this many growling savages. "Dalton start the truck!" I scream.

The engine howls and lights blare. Variants are already surrounding him. His pistol fires, four gun shots. I *Sprint* down the hill. "Go! Go! Reverse! *Go!*" Tires crunch and squeal and the Land Cruiser shoots backwards. I *Run* faster than he drives. Two Variants come snarling from the trees, and I *Jump* to meet them. They're strong but nothing compared to me. They collide and break against my shoulders and fists. Dalton's truck plunges through the heavy growth, ruining scrub and saplings, but the enemy is faster. They can knock over trees too, when they aren't jumping between them like apes. He'll never escape in reverse, so I grab the front bumper and *Throw* it sideways with all my strength. The truck rotates a hundred-eighty degrees and settles pointed in the right direction. He shifts gears and shoots forward with me hopping onto the rear bumper.

Faster!

"Faster!"

The Variants follow in a pack as we exit the gravel road and leave Tapo Canyon. Wolves tracking big prey. They move on all-fours through the Simi Valley neighborhoods, through yards and over roofs. Hanging onto the back, I pound the window. "Redline it, Dalton! *Move!*" I can probably escape; it's him I worry about.

They wait on the road ahead of us. They're swarming out of Kohl's and over the homes. They're everywhere. I climb to the top, brace my feet against the luggage rack, and scream; attack us and die. Onward they come, *Leaping* and descending, claws extended like a leopard's. I fling them aside and throw their bodies down, time and again. The windshield splinters and Dalton's pistol erupts again. Our headlights are busted. Sixty miles per hour. Seventy. Eighty. Five Variants land at once and I'm hauled onto my back, shoulders pinned from behind by powerful arms. Our truck swerves, dislodging several. We're saved from falling by the luggage rack. The wild girl above strikes me in the face. I wrench one arm free and remove her throat, and she falls. Nails rake me, and I'm choked. The Land Cruiser is overrun. More gunshots.

Dalton's going to die...

Katie cries, *Get UP!*

I kick and swing like a woman possessed, connecting with each strike. They are fierce but stunned by my desperate strength. I break free and attack, but suddenly I'm alone. They're gone. The Land Cruiser is clean. What happened? Dalton floors the gas.

The enemy has given up the chase. They stand in a line at the Simi Valley border and recede into the distance. They are heaving beasts pounding the blacktop with rage. Are they under orders not to leave? We turn a corner and they're gone. I spit blood and carefully lower through the broken passenger window. "Where the hell'd they go?" he shouts.

"Nice driving," I pant. "We're safe."

"Why? What happened?"

"Shhh. Talking hurts."

Dalton curses and I tremble all the way to the Ronald Reagan checkpoint. The guard opens the gate, eyes wide. Tree branches have punctured the rear windows. Our windshield is busted. The engine steams. Headlights gone. I'm scratched to pieces. "I heard...gun shots," the guard stammers. "...are you...what *happened?*"

"What are you looking at? You never seen a black man driving a Land Cruiser before?" Dalton snaps. He rolls through the gate.

I call through the missing rear window, "You hear anything coming, you call for help and get out of here. Understand?"

His face pales.

I'm such a compassionate queen.

- Twelve -

The next morning I return with three hundred Guardians, soldiers, and Law Keepers. In the pouring sunlight we search Simi Valley and find nothing. Of course the enemy fled, but I had to be sure. This place reeks of death. General Brown is at my side, filling me in on the meeting last night. The Resistance is committed to our cause and they're sending recon teams to hunt for Walter in the wastelands.

He says, "Isaac Anderson suggests we relocate you and the Guardians to Hawaii. Like I do, he believes Walter will back down if the Variants are gone."

"I'm staying. Walter is massacring the northwest, and he'll do the same here."

"He suggested you might have an ulterior movie for remaining."

He and I are standing at an intersection near the spooky Kohl's, which is less terrifying in daylight. I ask, "Such as?"

"The Inheritors."

"The Inheritors," I repeat.

"I don't pry into Guardians affairs, Carmine. I do my job, and you do yours. But maybe you ought tell me about them."

"There's nothing to tell," I snap. "They're dead."

"Carmine—"

"Dead."

I storm off and leave him frustrated. Isaac Anderson and the Outlaw both want to evacuate. And everyone wants to talk about the Inheritors, the one subject I refuse to discuss.

I can't, and I won't, abandon New Los Angeles.

I spend hours that afternoon with the Guardians, training, drilling, fighting, and so does Mason. He's exhausting himself at the different barracks, but we need months more to prepare. We aren't ready. The previous evening confirmed my suspicions.

That night I sit on the edge of my balcony and talk myself out of sliding off. My emotional swings are off the charts. I finished *Cinder* and have nothing to occupy my mind, and I'm depressed about nearly getting Dalton killed.

My pragmatism must've evaporated when Chase and Tank appeared. I've been a terrible leader recently. Katie won't stop talking; she's been emotional since Brown mentioned the Inheritors. My adrenaline rages uncontrollably. I'm jumpy and angry and despondent.

An old magazine article hangs limply from my hand. An article about me. The picture on the front is in full color, taken in late July, and is widely considered one of the most powerful photographs of the 21st century. I am depicted kneeling on the 18th green of a golf course. My head is in my hands and I'm dripping crimson up to my elbows. The Red Butcher. I can quote the Teresa Triplett article from memory.

...even from a man given to abominable surprises, the Chemist's final secret is devastating. The Inheritor Project was hidden from all parties, even his inner circle...

The Inheritors. Walter came here for the Inheritors. Isaac Anderson asked about them. Kayla cries when the subject comes up. I wish they'd all forget.

...we should have guessed, in retrospect. The Chemist was hell-bent on world domination, and the man played the long-game. Imagine Queen Carmine's surprise, imagine this reporter's surprise, to learn of the children's existence only when their mothers began to starve and emerge from the tower basements...

My eyes read numbly over the article. Caleb (the Kid) knew about the Inheritors. He ran from them the way he runs from everything. He let me find out for myself.

...perhaps you still don't understand the magnitude of the secret. I didn't at first. Why were these children so special? Why was Queen Carmine shocked into silence for forty-eight hours?

The children were infected with the Hyper Virus, but so what? There were only five hundred of them. Eight thousand Variants already rampaged across western America. What difference would five hundred babies make? Little did I know, they made *all* the difference...

"I read that article," Chase says. I'm so startled I nearly fall. He's sitting on the railing one apartment over. Even Katie is surprised. "Awful photo of you."

"That's not funny."

"You don't like talking about the Inheritors."

"Obviously," I say.

"I know you didn't murder those kids."

"Why are you here?"

He shrugs. "Killing time before I meet with Mason. I thought we could make out."

"No."

Maybe...

No Katie.

I say, "Your friend Isaac Anderson flew in today."

"He's your friend too."

"He's not happy with me. I didn't attend his meeting. I should have, but..."

Then we're silent again. He knows I'm upset. Treading deep waters. "What should I have done?" I ask.

"Huh?"

"With all those kids? The Inheritors. Five hundred of them. They were Infected, Chase. They weren't going to grow up and be like Mason. Or like Kayla. The Inheritors weren't given the disease in late adolescence; they were *born* with it. Injected at birth. They'd grow up and become like the Chemist. Or Walter."

"Not necessarily."

"There are only ten of you guys. You call yourselves Infected, right? Born with the disease? There's only ten of you and you just about broke the planet in half. Imagine five hundred..." I'm having to force my words out through a constricting throat.

"So you took the baby Inheritors to Ranch Palo Verdes. To Trump National Golf Club, to be exact. And you cut all their throats." By the way he's phrasing his sentences and by his tone I can tell he doesn't believe it.

"No. Nuts mixed a poison. Most of the kids drank the poison and just...went to sleep. Teresa didn't report that part."

"The babies drank poison."

"It was mixed in with other stuff. I'd rather not...talk about this, Chase."

He says, "Why didn't Teresa report the poison?"

"After the photo was taken...we thought...it was suggested..." My tears flow freely now. "...that people would stay away...if they thought I was a monster."

"The Red Butcher."

"Right. The poison was effective. I didn't have to do much...by hand. But it was messy. And turns out, made a shocking photo."

"No way. I don't believe you."

"That's because you don't know me. You still don't realize I'm not Katie. That I'm not sane. What would you have me do? Let Walter get his hands on those babies? Or Blue-Eyes? In eighteen years they'd unleash the apocalypse. The Chemist knew what he was doing. He created weapons of mass destruction. So I destroyed them. You wouldn't have?"

"I wouldn't kill innocent kids, no," he says.

"That's a big difference between us. You do what you want. I do what I have to."

"Why Trump's golf course?"

I shrug. "Quiet. Secluded. The surf removed the bodies."

"Apparently there are still courts on the east coast, and I hear Trump is suing you."

That makes me chuckle. I wipe my eyes and nose. "Him and everyone else. I'm eager to be subpoenaed."

He leaps from his railing and lands beside me. I want him here. I want him to stay. But he shouldn't. He takes the article from my dead fingers, and examines the photo. It was snapped as I left the scene of the crime. The weight of the world had crushed me and I collapsed, covered in blood, and Teresa had taken the picture. Murdering five hundred children would've been a bigger deal if the world wasn't heaving, so, instead of outrage, the population shuddered and gave me a nickname. The Red Butcher.

He says, "You're making me nervous."

I shrug.

"Did you really kill them?"

I say, "You should probably go. You'll be thrown in jail if you're discovered."

"You don't want me to go."

"When do people like you and me ever get what we want."

"I *want* to stay." He touches my arm and I'm so surprised that I grab his finger and twist, on instinct. His knuckle pops.

"OOoooooooooOOOoooowwww," he yelps and grabs his clearly dislocated pointer finger. "What the heck, Katie!"

"I broke your finger!" I gasp.

"I'm aware!"

"Sorry about that."

"What's wrong with you?"

"Pop it back in. Let me help."

"No! That'll hurt. I can't believe you're laughing," he says.

"I'm not!"

"Yes you are. After you just broke my finger."

He's glaring and I can't stop...well, I'm not giggling because only little girls do that, but I'm smothering laughter. "It's kinda funny."

"Absolutely nothing about this is funny."

"Big bad Outlaw hurt his little finger."

"No. No. *I* didn't hurt my finger. *You* hurt my finger."

"I was really depressed and this helps. Thank you."

Without warning, he kisses me. Right on my lips. It's warm and soft, and it's over before I can react. My body does crazy things whenever we touch, and now it's going supernova. Our eyes are locked and we both want more. Katie is absolutely groaning with pleasure, threatening to take control of my body. I tilt my head up and he leans down, and the Priest bursts into my apartment with three Law Keepers.

Chase and I leap to our feet like teenagers caught making out. Which, I guess, we are. I grab Chase by the collar and he chokes in surprise.

He kissed me. He loves me.

"Carmine!" the Priest calls. "We heard shouting!" He and the Law Keepers barge into my bedroom and see us. He stops cold. "I *knew* it."

I say, "Look who I caught sneaking around." I give Chase's collar an extra tug and he gags.

"You...*caught*...him?" he asks, icy with suspicion. I'm alarmed to see the Law Keepers are pointing electroshock weapons at us.

"He wouldn't surrender, so I broke his finger."

The Priest examines Chase's hand and the broken finger. He looks back at me, his face a revelation. I broke his own finger two months ago. "Well done, my Queen."

"Run," I whisper, so quietly I barely hear myself. My lips are near Chase's ear. "Go."

More humanity flows into the room. A sleepy Dalton. My Devotee. Law Keepers. Kayla and her dog.

"Chase, go," I whisper in the commotion. "Break free and jump. Get out of here."

He shakes his head. "No."

The Priest is holding forth, bragging to the crowd about his capture. It doesn't occur to him the Outlaw is not truly caught. It'd take a lot more than a mere three men with weapons drawn.

Chase hisses back, "Do you want me to stay?"

"*What?*"

"Might be kinda fun. I'll go to jail if you visit me."

"You're insane."

His finger is grossing me out. Without warning, I grab it in my fist. The bones pop into place. He cries out in pain. Everyone looks at us.

"Sorry." I shrug. "I thought he was trying to escape. So I...hit him again."

"Take me away to jail," Chase calls to a surprised crowd.

I groan and whisper, "What are you doing?"

"Get me away from this crazy lady, who keeps hurting my finger!"

Can't these people tell he's toying with him? That this is a farce? I punch him hard in the ribs. "Knock it off."

He continues, like he's on a high school stage. "I should NOT have come back. What awful decision-making on my part! I accept the punishment. Justice is fair and blind."

The Priest and his Law Keepers close with their tasers and elasticuffs. They look awfully smug for peons about to detain a titan. Chase's hands are carefully bound behind his back.

"Tighter," he tells them. "Who *knows* what I'll do."

I grumble, "This is so weird."

"To the slammer!"

"No one calls it a slammer," I say.

He turns and says, "Remember to visit me."

"No."

"You promised."

"I did *not*."

Kayla and Dalton are glaring suspiciously.

The Priest says, "Seven days. Correct, Queen Carmine? That was your edict? He will spend a week in jail."

Everyone stares at me.

"*Seven*?" Chase sputters. "Seems a little excessive."

Everyone continues to stare.

I could cancel the orders. I could admit I like him. But I say slowly, "Those were my orders...I guess."

The Outlaw is marched from the room. Dalton growls that he only leaves my side for eight hours a day, and apparently that's too much. The Priest leaves. The crowd disperses. The whole tower is abuzz. We caught the Outlaw!

Only Kayla and I are left. She scowls and shakes her head.

"What?" I ask.

"You two," she says, "are into some weird freaky stuff."

- Thirteen -

Kayla and Teresa Triplett wisely decided not to publish the story of us incarcerating the world's first superhero. He's just sitting there, hoping I'll visit. But I'm not. Because of my pride.

And because he's a fool. And I've got a Kingdom to run.

I'm aggravated and grumpy. Angry with both Tank and Chase. But I'm not sure why. Chase told me the virus makes us mean and suspicious, could that be it?

I train with Mason and the Guardians until lunch, and then Dalton and I visit the orphanage and read books to students. I smell Chase's cologne. He's been here in the past forty-eight hours (before the slammer) calling on Ms. Pauline. She appears happier than usual, harboring Chase's visit like classified information. After lunch, we tour the eastern barracks and watch Falcons train Guardians to fight with self-control. Then I have a meeting with Overseers about the incoming flood of settlers, followed by Kayla briefing the Council about Dallas, Texas, which is struggling with wild Variants and violent criminals.

Throughout the day, Katie is chattering in my ears and I can't tune her out. *He's in jail. Just sitting there. Poor thing. He's probably bored.* Chase is playing a bizarre game with me and he's winning. Somehow he's in jail and he's winning. Because I can't think straight. Kayla wants to chat after the meeting but I storm out, frustrated with the world. Chase won't win this game. I'm *not* visiting him.

I eat dinner in my office and work on the Stanford paper. I get an hour into my work before Katie starts chattering again.

I should go visit him. He's probably lonely. Maybe bring him a book. Give him a nice back rub?

I'm not visiting him.

Yes, I want to.

I've got too much to do. Leave me alone.

But he's so sweet.

No.

Could be fun to lock myself in with him.

That might be fun, actually...

I stand, spilling books and papers. Stop! Why can't I concentrate? He's still winning, dammit. Madness. This is madness. Calm down. Calm down, Carmine. After ten minutes of pacing and stretching, I sit back down, ready to finish this stupid essay.

My phone rings.

"What!" I shout into it.

"We need your help at the jail, Queen Carmine."

"What's wrong?"

"There's a...big guy...trying to get in? Like a giant? With an axe?"

Tank.

Of COURSE Tank is trying to break into the jail. Because that's exactly what I need.

The LAPD Detention Center is a blocky grey building near City Hall. I *Leap* my way there. Dalton will arrive soon in his truck. The Priest and his big mouth, that's the problem. He made too big a circus over this phony capture and everyone within fifty miles knows which jail the Outlaw is in.

A small squad of Law Keepers is inside the lobby, barricading a stairwell. They appear...disheveled. Like someone threw them around. Without power, the building is stuffy and dark, especially since the sun is going down. Surfaces are coated with a five-month layer of dust, scuffed by recent footprints.

I demand, "Where is he?"

The Law Keeper says, "Upstairs, Queen Carmine. We don't know how to stop him."

"What's he want?"

"To kill the Outlaw."

I groan. "How precisely masculine and idiotic. Where is Chase Jackson?"

"We've got him housed in the basement. There's still a guard down there."

Most of the Law Keepers obey immediately. Mutants are creepy. Their Overseer asks, "What will you do, ma'am? He can't be stopped. He's Infected."

"I'm going to ask nicely."

"We shot him," he says.

"You *shot* him? What happened?"

Doors slam closed behind them and I'm left alone in the lobby. "Tank!" I yell at the stairwell, and my voice journeys up the stairs and down empty halls. "Tank, you can't be here!"

From deep in the building's upper levels comes a rumbling voice. "Where is he?"

"That doesn't matter. You must leave."

"I haven't seen my old pal Pajamas since he threw me off a boat last March. I just want to say Hi."

"No. Go away. I was in the middle of homework."

He comes stomping heavily down the stairs. Such a big guy. Axe in his right fist. "Homework?"

"Yes. Homework. I'm easily your smartest ex-girlfriend. Now go."

"Homework. That's kinda hot."

"No it's not. It's frustrating. There's an absolute dearth of normal days around here and finally I find two hours to work and you show up. Plus, Walter is coming, and we're training Guardians to fight, and...just go."

I shrug, arms crossed. "He's not here."

"Yes he is. I smell him."

Shut up, Katie. Tank begins to walk past me to the hallway. I put my hand on his chest —his broad, beefy chest— and stop him. He asks, "He down this way?"

"Leave."

He wraps an arm around my waist and hoists me over his shoulder, fireman style facing backwards. "Come on, pretty girl. Let's find him."

Laying on my stomach, bent over his shoulder like an idiot, I shout, "Stop! Put me down. Why does everyone think they should throw me on their shoulder? Tank!"

He ducks through a security door. I grab the reinforced metal doorframe and hold tight with a hand on either side. We're jerked to a halt.

"Tank, this is ludicrous. We're grownups. I don't have time for this."

"Let go."

"*You* let go," I say.

He strains forward. I tighten my grip, digging fingers into the metal.

"Queen Carmine?" A voice I don't know. And I can't see him while I hang stretched between a door and a giant. Must be the guard stationed at Chase's cell, come to inspect the commotion. This is mortifying.

"What?" I shout at the hidden voice.

"What...what are your orders?"

"Nothing. You can go. I'll handle this."

He says, "Negative, ma'am. You need help. I'll call the Overseer."

Tank chuckles. "Yeah. Call the Overseer."

I snap, "I just spoke to your Overseer, soldier. Now go outside and wait."

"Well...okay. Yes ma'am." I can't see him until he's scooting nervously around Tank. He's a big guy, probably twenty-five, buzz cut, former military perhaps, and he's dumbfounded. He ducks under me to go through the door because I won't let go of it. I smile at him. My face is red from hanging upside down. He says, "You want me to—"

"Just go."

"S'okay," Tank rumbles. "Me and her are kinda an item."

"No," I snap. "We are *not* an item. Don't tell people that."

Tank lurches forward. Metal screams and the doorframe twists and breaks off the wall. Now I'm dragging it, like a fool, down the hall past temporary detention cells. "Where is he?"

"Put me down," I say.

"No."

I drop the metal and reach as far as I can. My fingers snatch the back of Tank's pant leg. With one mighty heave, I haul his leg backwards. It bends at the knee and I wrap my arms around his ankle, trapping it. He's standing on one foot and I won't release the other.

"Katie..."

"That's not my name."

He hops to keep his balance. "Don't make me do this. You ain't gonna like it."

"Put. Me. Down."

He leans his axe against the wall and smacks me on the butt. "Always loved this butt."

This is so stupid. I'm so mad. But I don't release. I can't let him go kill a prisoner with an axe.

His fingers curl under the waistline of my leggings. "You sure you ain't gonna let go? Because you're about to lose your pants."

"Tank. No."

He stretches the fabric downwards. If I had to guess, I'd estimate that he just exposed 20% of my rear.

He says, "Oooh. You're tan everywhere? Tell ya what. You don't let me go, Imma take you back outside. And you're gonna moon all your little acolytes."

"You don't even know what that word means." I blow hair from my eyes, a futile gesture.

"I carried a 3.9 GPA my senior year, baby."

"That's *it*?"

He tugs again, further exposing me. I want to scream and laugh and stab him, all at once. He says, "You been working out. Let go my ankle or I'll pull your pants down to your knees."

I release his leg and jam ten razor-sharp fingernails into his back. His skin is tough hide but I penetrate deep enough. His whole body flexes and he shouts in surprise, a noise so violent it shakes the windows. Given room to move, I twist at the waist and bring my knee into his face. Hard enough to bust concrete. If he wasn't Infected it could've caved his skull.

He collapses. I fall with him. One big writhing heap on the floor. I go for his axe. He grabs my calf and hauls me back.

Somehow, someway, my mouth is on his. Kissing. *Kissing?*

I pull back and climb to my feet. "You kissed me!"

"No way, babe. That was all you."

He gets up, holding his jaw. I plant a foot into his chest and kick, my pink Sauconys making solid connection with his ribs. He stumbles and falls into a small detention cell and I slam the heavy door. It locks.

"Hah! I win!"

The door explodes outwards, wrenched from its hinges and bolt. He charges through like a bull, catches me with his shoulder, and we crash through the opposite wall. Dust and debris splash across the security break room. I'm up in a flash and I tip over a tall Pepsi vending machine. It's heavy and it's going to land on him and it's going to hurt. He catches it with his right hand and trips me with the left.

He caught a vending machine with *one* hand?

He throws it to the side with a crash.

I crawl into the hall but he reaches me. Our bodies collide. He's everywhere. This time he's definitely kissing me. I didn't initiate. He stands, his arms encircling my waist. It's hot and my feet aren't touching the floor. My arms wrap around his neck.

I'm such a whore. Look at me. A hot mess.

"Okay, enough," I mumble against his mouth, and untangle my arms from his neck. "No more."

"Why?"

"You need to go."

He drops me. "Come with."

"This was an...astonishing lack of discipline on my part." I'm scooping my hair back in place and trying not to pant. "I got caught up in memories, nothing more."

"You're lonely. Me too."

"You're the *only* person I remember, Tank. And it messes with my brain. But...this can't happen. A lot of people are depending on me and I need to be focused."

He presses his gloved hand against my cheek. "You have a new life, and I'm only a memory. But I'm stuck with the same life and I still think you're sexy as hell."

"Tank," I groan and close my eyes. Focus. I need to focus. I will not allow loneliness to dictate my actions. I'm not pathetic. I'm not weak.

He and I are hit by an unpleasant odor at the same moment. A whiff from the vents. Actually it's not that unpleasant. More of a rich texture...

We realize it at the same moment.

"It's the Cheerleader," Tank says.

"I smell her too. She smells like..."

"Gasoline." His face has gone white and beads of sweat form at his thick hairline. "She's here."

"Let's find her and ship her out of New LA. We can take her together."

"Not in this tiny place. The only way is to catch her by surprise." He turns and pulls me towards the exit. He's panicking and there's real trauma behind his eyes. I resist but my shoes slide across the floor's scrim. He says, "We gotta split. Pronto."

I contort free of his iron grip. "She's here for Chase and he's vulnerable. I have to release him."

"You need to forget about that runt."

I say, "I will not abandon him. Not to that lunatic."

He reaches for me again. "You don't get it, kid. She's Satan. A demon. Come with me. Now."

"Tank. Go. Just go. You're about to hyperventilate. I get it. She messed you up."

He's stuck. He loathes the idea of abandoning me. However the burnt portion of his face has begun to twitch.

A voice drifts through the air conditioning vents. A pleasant but strained sound, and the effect is remarkably similar to a haunted house. She's humming. Tank's knees nearly give out.

"She's above us," he says. "Oh god."

"Go!" I turn and leave him. I locate the stairs and plunge deeper into the detention center. Only two electric lanterns give off light in this dark dungeon. The air is thick and hot, but fortunately Chase is in the first cell. It has a small window at the ceiling. The glass is cracked (maybe he did it?), otherwise it'd be unbearable. He's reclining on a cot, reading a novel. I knock softly on the security door's window.

He doesn't look up.

I knock again.

"Be there in a sec," he says.

"Chase," I hiss.

"This chapter is almost over. Three more pages."

"Chase. Let me in."

He doesn't reply, other than to calmly turn a page of the paperback. He's *trying* to be infuriating.

I whisper, "The Cheerleader is here and I don't want her to know we're in the basement."

That gets his attention. He sits up, novel forgotten. "Hannah Walker is here? You've seen her?"

"Let me in."

"Let you in?" He inspects me like I'm insane. "Just how do you think cell doors work?"

"But I don't have a key."

"And you think they left it with me?"

Argh. I'm not thinking straight. The gasoline aroma is too intense. What do I do? Tank broke a door so maybe I can too. He's Infected, considerably stronger than I am, but it's worth a shot. I take a couple steps backwards.

"Wait." His voice comes muffled through the partition. His cell door shudders and the exterior handle pops off. He jams his fist into the opening, rending the metal outwards, and twists. A click and it swings open on oiled hinges.

Unbelievable.

I say, "You could get out whenever you wanted."

He winks. "But you're worth the wait."

"Why does the Cheerleader smell like that?"

"Long story. Read the articles from February of 2018."

We're whispering. Somehow his hand has slid into mine, and the skin contact immediately lessens my joint aches. He's morphine. That didn't happen with Tank. I ask, "Is she here to execute you?"

"Her brain suffered more than most. I imagine she'd treat me the way Lennie treats puppies."

"So she's violent and obsessed."

"Essentially," he says.

Chase just eluded to Of Mice and Men. *I love John Steinbeck.*

"Lennie? You eluded to *Of Mice and Men*," I say.

"Correct. Did Katie enjoy that reference?"

"She did."

"And as a result, you want to make out?"

"I don't want to discuss it. Let's go."

We hurry to the stairwell on silent feet. He stops me at the base and peers upwards. I'm almost gagging on gas fumes, and I wipe perspiration from my eyelids and lashes. He points with a finger, and mouths the words, *She's at the top of the staircase.*

Holy cow, why am I terrified of this chick? I'm so scared I'm on the verge of hysteria.

We turn and flee the way we came. There has to be another exit, but this dark basement is a maze.

"In here." We return to his cell. His muscles bunch and swell and he rips the window frame from the wall. Chunks of concrete break off, and he yanks out long segments of rebar. The Cheerleader couldn't help but hear *that* tumultuous racket. I leap to the opening and slither through to freedom and fresh night air. He gets stuck. I pulverize the concrete and pull lumps free like a woman possessed. If she grabs him from behind I'll faint.

He asks, "Why do you smell like Tank?"

"He came here to chat with you. The Cheerleader ran him off."

"I kinda miss that idiot. How's he look?"

Like a rugged sexy woodsman?

I grab Chase's arms and heave. He slides through.

We run.

Jerome is our Detention Overseer. He's waiting out front with the other guards, useless shotgun in his grip. They're surprised to see me emerge from behind the building. I order the guards home for the night but pull Jerome after me.

Jerome watches his sentries trudge off and he says, "But...Queen Carmine, the Cheerleader is still in the building."

"Yeah? And what do you plan to do about that?"

"We could...I mean, there's a proper response and protocol, which...I guess..."

"For the present, if the Cheerleader is here, we run. Got it? No one approaches her."

"Yes ma'am."

I haul him by his sleeve around the building to where Chase Jackson waits in the grass, reading his book. "Jerome, this is the Outlaw. He's a substantial pain in the butt. He can escape from our custody but he refuses to."

The Outlaw shrugs, and he possesses the temerity to look modest about it. "I don't make the laws."

"Considering it's late and we're both tired, Jerome, stash him at the Ritz tonight. Hotel room or jail cell, whatever, he could escape either way. So. Who cares. Find rooms at the Ritz. He doesn't need a guard. Get some sleep."

"Yes ma'am." Jerome appears to be as confused as I feel.

"And you." I punch Chase in the shoulder. It hurts. He smiles that wide smile, great teeth, faint dimple, and my stomach flip flops. "It'd make my life a lot easier if you'd escape."

"You kicked me out of LA. The only way I can stay is if I'm incarcerated. Also, if you're putting me in a suite, can you send up a masseuse? My back is killing me. But I require hot blondes."

"No. No girls. Not even girl sentries. I'm the only girl you get to see. And I'm angry with you. If the Night Guardians catch your scent then you'll be attacked."

"I'm becoming adept at bottling it up for longer periods of time. Right Jerome? High five." Chase holds up his hand. Jerome is confused and wishing he was anywhere else other than listening to a pair of idiots bickering.

"If the Cheerleader finds you again, I'm not helping. Good night, you twit." As I turn to go, Katie Lopez surges into my muscles. I almost kiss Chase goodnight. A purely instinctive response, but not mine. We're playing tug-of-war, Katie and I, and she's getting stronger.

One of these days, Katie, you're going to get me into a lot of trouble.

Becky is in my bed when I return. The Devotee was smart enough to let her in. Evidently she's enduring a nightmare, based on the whimpering and kicking. I should continue my Stanford essay but instead I lay beside her and stroke her hair. I don't know the cure. I don't know how to fix her mind. Or anything else.

Also I need new sheets. Mine are dusty and grey. What Queen has old grey sheets? Actually, shut up, Carmine. You're not a Queen.

I'm so tired.

My phone buzzes.

>> My new jail cell is much nicer. How about a conjugal visit?

You have your cell phone with you?

>> And a charger.

You're the worst prisoner ever.

I get up at five in the morning and finish the paper by seven. Suck it, Stanford. I can pass your classes *and* take over the world.

I'm eating a celebratory pear when Becky knocks and enters the office. She quietly sits in the corner and dips apple slices into a jar of peanut butter.

"I'm fine," she says, answering the question on my lips. "Only a bad dream. I was going to proofread your paper but you already submitted it."

I nod. She's creepy sometimes. How does she do that.

"Two Night Guardians are missing," she says.

"How do you know?"

She lifts a dainty shoulder. "That's the gossip."

"Hmm. Who is the Guardian Overseer?"

"You? I don't know. The Guardians don't have a proper Overseer. But we've been taking care of ourselves."

"Where—"

"North. The two missing Guardians were last seen near San Fernando."

"Becky, just because you correctly guess what I'm going to say doesn't—"

"Doesn't mean I should interrupt you. I know."

Hmphf. She can sleep on the floor during her next nightmare.

She says, "He's out there."

I stand and go to the door. I need answers. "Who?"

"Walter. He's close."

"How do—"

"I just know. Even if the Guardians can't express it, they feel him. He's here."

"Becky." I open the door. "Try to be less creepy."

She grins.

I call Mason on my way to the War Department. On the fifth ring, he answers and says, "Just cause you're the queen doesn't mean you should wake people at seven."

"Do you know anything about two missing Night Guardians?"

He yawns loudly into the receiver. "Only rumors. I was out last night and heard those two weren't in position."

"We need a Guardian Overseer. Select a candidate and pass along his or her name."

"Me."

"No. You're a Falcon. I don't want you bogged down with details. Pick someone else. Someone responsible with a stentorian voice."

General Brown is in the War Department. The man doesn't sleep. He's sipping coffee and reading reports on his iPad. Sleepy technicians sit at computers. I glare at maps a few minutes, absorbing information.

I ask Brown, "Have you heard anything unusual from our northern boundary?"

"Such as?"

"I think we may have intruders. Or perhaps runaways."

"Negative. All stations still reporting. I hear anything, you'll know."

"Update me on Walter's forces. And any nearby Herder groups."

"Thought you were a nineteen year-old girl who doesn't like planning." He's smiling into his mug.

"I don't. So make it quick. Use small words."

"There's increased activity at Castaic Lake. About twenty miles past our border. Fifty-five total miles from here. Resistance guesses it may be a staging area." He stands like he's stiff, walks to the map on the wall, and points to a body of water north of our Kingdom.

"Staging area? Like a temporary base?" Our enemies gather, I bet.

"Affirmative. A temporary and local base for Walter. And his Variant army. And complicit Herders, and perhaps mercenaries hired out of Las Vegas. Hell, who knows, maybe even some Federal Government soldiers. We've sent a small recon team to rendezvous with Resistance soldiers...here." He indicate a different spot.

"They're rendezvousing at Six Flags?"

He nods and rests hands on his hips. "It's convenient. And good cover."

"Is that area abandoned?"

"Everything is abandoned within a hundred miles."

"We're alone."

"Affirmative. Only brave interlopers out there, though some highways are still safe for travel."

We're quiet a few minutes, staring at the geography and lost within our thoughts. New LA is an island surrounded by unsafe waters. And somewhere in the surf is a shark. A nasty one named Walter. Brown switches maps a few times, including live satellite feed. Eventually I ask, "Are we too vulnerable?"

"Yes and no. No strike force of significant size can get in without us being alerted. But we're stretched thin."

I say, "The Guardians are antsy. Itchy and eager for a fight. If Walter's forces punch through then they'll have a war on their hands with four thousand angry mutants."

He switches maps to our southern boundary. "If we're vulnerable, it's here. South."

"Huntington Beach? Santa Ana?"

"We're utilizing our resources north. To the south, we're much less crenelated."

"But our enemies are to the north."

"So far." He nods.

"What should we do? About Walter and the gathering forces to our north?"

"Right now, let's wait to hear what the recon team says."

"Waiting sucks, General."

That evening, Kayla, Becky, and I eat dinner in the 8th Street cafeteria. Becky and Kayla tentatively respect one another, even if they're incompatible. Becky is moody and quirky, while Kayla effervesces. Becky can read people, while Kayla changes them.

Becky says, "So Walter is sitting there. Within striking distance. Let's kick his ass."

Kayla repeats herself. "Maybe he's there. Maybe he's not. There are—"

"There are no visual confirmations, but he's here." Becky leans across the table toward us. "He's here."

Kayla shudders and rubs at goosebumps. Sitting at the next table across from us are three members of the Falcons. I assigned them to be Kayla's security detail. She's the only person other than me that Walter directly threatened, and therefore she receives extra protection. With Walter so close, I'd rather be safe than sorry. Dalton sits adjacent to the Guardians.

Becky observes Kayla's discomfort and backs down. She blows hair from her face and mumbles, "Sorry. I forgot he threatened to...you know."

Kayla tilts her head to the side. "You know, Becky, you could see better if I gave you a haircut. Your hair is always in your eyes."

"General Brown advises we wait instead of rushing to attack," I say. "And I trust him. He's a grownup after all, and I'm just pretending."

Becky eats a fried potato off Kayla's plate. "Grownups are the worst."

Kayla continues, "It wouldn't have to be drastic, like bangs. We could...hmm, are you opposed to hair clips?"

"Yes."

"What about—"

"No. Not even side-swept bangs."

"But—"

Becky says, "No. Kayla, hot stuff, listen—no. I like my hair. I don't want yours. I don't want to look like Blue-Eyes. I like me."

Kayla shakes her head and tsk's in frustration. "I still can't find her. No one can."

"Find who?"

"Blue-Eyes."

I pause, a bite of beans forgotten in my mouth. "She's missing?"

"Gross, Carmine, chew your food. You're a *Queen*."

"No I'm not. She's missing?"

"She's been missing for three days. Not even PuckDaddy knows where."

Becky snorts, "So? Good riddance. We have bigger problems to worry about."

"A bigger problem than Blue-Eyes? Like what?" asked Kayla.

"The Queen loves the Outlaw."

My eyes about pop from my head. "I do *not*. And keep your voice down."

"You're always thinking about him," says Becky.

"You don't know—"

"Yes I do." Becky smiles, a mischievous impish smile. "I can tell."

"That doesn't mean I love him. He's a giant annoyance. No one is in love."

"He is. He's bonkers for you."

I growl, "If you don't close your mouth I'm going to stuff it with potatoes."

Kayla stares stonily at me, arms crossed. She smells like a rainstorm. "You promised you wouldn't fall for him."

"I promised *no* such thing, and I haven't."

"The Governess forbade it."

I roll my eyes. "Forbade? No one says forbade. And I don't care what the Governess forbids, I do what I want."

"Like going to visit him tonight?" Becky asks. "In his cell?"

"No. But I can if I want. And it's none of your business."

"You're going."

Kayla groans. "Forbidden love is hot, but I'm so mad at you."

"Okay." I stand with my plate. "You two are juvenile mouth-breathers and I'm leaving. To get away from you."

Outside, the sun is almost gone. Fewer prying eyes. Maybe I should visit Chase's cell just to spite those two...

∾

I stand in front of the mirror, inspecting my outfit with a critical eye. This skirt is *short*. So immodest I'm blushing. It'd look fine if I wasn't tall. Short girls are so lucky.

I'm not tall. Am I tall? I don't think so.

Chase wants to play a game? Fine. We can play. I'll make him beg and leave him unsatisfied. I'll show him what he can't have.

But this skirt though...

I rip it off and somehow I look less indecent. I mutter, "I'm just not a tiny skirt girl. Some girls are, some girls aren't." I'm talking to no one as I tunnel deeper through the clothing pile. Shorts? No, I look twelve. A dress? No, I'm nineteen, not a grandparent. Well, maybe this sexy sheer maxi dress, I think that's what Kayla called it...good gosh it's see-through. Wow, girls wear these out in public? No way. What about khakis? No, I'm not going to a job interview.

Jeans. I settle on jeans. I'm a jeans girl. And a white, loose Hoffman top. The tag says draped front, with a surplice neckline. I don't know what that means, but he should have a hard time not staring. I'm not going to simply win his game, I'm going to crush it.

Wow. I look...wow. He'll notice.

My joints hurt without the comfort of compression, but I'm not wearing the red silk ribbons tonight. My hair looks...meh. I rake my fingers through. Whatever, it's fine, I don't care what he thinks. But maybe I should brush my teeth. And when was my last shower?

I *Leap* to the Ritz-Carlton on Olympic. The Night Guardians are rousing so I move quickly, careful to attract no attention. New Los Angeles is beautiful at night seen from four hundred feet and leaping between towers. Small fires leave trails across my vision. The Ritz looks like a magnificent shard of glass erupted from the ground, soaring high above the Staples Center. Very few of the windows have lights within. I find Chase on the fourth floor. The hallway is dark except for two candles resting on carpet at his doorway. He reclines against the doorframe, novel propped open in his hand. Two sentries sit next to the door. He is reading to them. So rapt is their attention they don't notice my arrival.

He reads, "'But it was not the trolls that had filled the Elf with terror. The ranks of orcs had opened and they crowded away, as if they themselves were afraid. Something was coming up behind them. What it was could not be seen; it was like a great shadow, in the middle of which was a dark form, of man-shape maybe, yet great; and a power and terror seemed to be in it and to go before it. It came to the edge of the fire and the light faded as if a cloud had bent over it. Then with a rush it leaped across the fissure. The flames roared up to greet it, and wreathed about it; and a black smoke swirled in the air. Its streaming mane kindled, and blazed behind it. In its right hand was a blade like a stabbing tongue of fire; in its left hand it held a whip of many thongs.'"

"*Boo*," I say.

Both sentries are so startled that for an instant I worry about being shot. Upon recognition, blood drains from their face and they fall over themselves apologizing.

"Aw, Katie, we just got to the Balrog." Chase is unfazed by my arrival, and I suspect he saw me the whole time. "Come back in twenty minutes."

"You two," I say. "Go get yourselves dinner. Come back in thirty minutes and wait in the stairwell."

"Don't worry, fellas," Chase says. "I'm marking my spot. We're good."

The two sentries depart, deeply ashamed and hangdog.

"The coast is clear," I tell Chase. "Make a run for it."

"No way. Aaron and Jonathan would never find out what happens to the Fellowship. Aaron can't read, you know."

I peer beyond him. His comfortable room is filled with baskets of food and gifts, such as books, clothing, and flowers. "So your cell has a breath-taking corner view. No bars. Not even a closed door. And apparently groupies bring you presents."

"My life is hard. And they're fans, not groupies. Also, I'm aggressively fond of your shirt. Are you missing some of it? If you bend over, I think it'll fall off."

He noticed! He always does.

Katie is nearly delirious. She thinks the empty hallway and candlelight are romantic. Katie does, not me.

"Wanna come in?"

I ask, "Into your jail cell? Better not. People will get ideas." I sit down next to him, separated only by the doorframe. "I don't think prisoners are supposed to read books to their guards."

"Aaron and Jonathan have been stuck here for twelve hours. They're bored to tears. It's the least I could do."

I ask, "Why are you still here?"

He dog-ears a page and closes the novel. "I'm in jail. No means to escape."

"Be serious. Why this farce?"

He nudges me with his shoulder. He's wearing shorts and a t-shirt. I bet the Outlaw getup got hot. "You're making this more complicated than it has to be. Getting thrown into jail is the easiest way to remain in New L.A. And to see you."

I give my head a little shake and tilt my face up towards the ceiling. "Chase, you still think I'll suddenly remember. That I'll morph into Katie Lopez, and everything will snap back in focus. But I don't think that'll happen."

"Maybe. Maybe not." He holds his hand out and I take it on reflex. Our fingers intertwine, and the imputed joy and comfort is more than enough to subdue my headache and joint pain. Like magic. "I'll take whatever version of you I can get. But I have hope."

"Why?"

"Because you keep showing up. I'm a lunatic in a mask, but you're drawn to me for reasons you can't explain. Right?"

My world shrinks. Already forgotten are the cares outside this hallway. Soon the entire universe will fit inside our candlelight. "What if this is all you get, though? It's only me, Chase. Nothing more. What if you have all this hope and you never get Katie back?

What if I'm all there is?" For whatever reason, my words come out in whispers.

"I worry the same thing. What if Katie or Carmine realizes there's nothing more substantive hidden underneath my surface? I don't know how to answer your question. I'm just running on blind faith. Making it up as I go. Besides, I always wanted to stay at the Ritz. Dad and I were poor."

"Katie's family was poor too, right? Just her and her mom? I mean...me and my mom?"

He snickers, a soft sound through his nose. "Yeah, kinda. You called her mamá or mamí. Both our families had barely enough. Usually."

"Was Katie happy? Was I happy?"

"Very."

"Are you happy?" I ask.

The pressure on my fingers increases. "Yeah. I'm very happy."

"I feel...lost."

He asks, "Because you lack memories?"

"And because I lack a future. To borrow your phrase, I'm making it up as I go. I bail water as fast as I can but the ship is still sinking. You know? And there's a shark in the water."

"You should let me handle Walter."

"You'd win that fight? You're positive?"

He shrugs and holds his palm up, like *Who Knows?* "Maybe. I've beaten him before. Twice. Three times? No...the second fight was a tie."

"I can't just launch you at him, like you exist purely as a missile. Besides, I'm the leader. The warrior Queen. If I let someone else fight that battle, I wouldn't be worth following."

He says, "You created a community with only the strength of your will. People follow you without even knowing why, like it's your destiny. It's magic, and it's your gift. You're too valuable to face him alone."

The door at the end of the hallway opens. Two women with a flashlight push in, grinning. I catch the scent of alcohol immediately.

They're shushing each other and stumbling. Dressed provocatively, and wearing makeup and jewelry. Here to entice the fabled war hero. Finally their flashlight lands on me.

"Oh...shhhhhhhh," one girl stammers. Her eyes are wide. "He—hello..."

I arch an imperial eyebrow.

She says, "We were...we're looking for..."

"Somebody else. Not here," her friend says. They turn and flee through the door, which slams after them.

Chase, still in his room and never getting a glimpse, asks, "Company?"

"Do you often receive female visitors?"

"How old were they?" he asks.

"Maybe thirty? And quite pretty. Clearly benefitting from plastic surgery."

"Thirty-year-olds love me. I dunno why. They usually don't run like that."

I ask, "Shall I fetch them?"

"Nah. I'm a one-woman kinda guy."

"You think I'm that one? You're delusional."

"I'm willing to let you audition."

Moment of truth. Time to speak honestly, at least in part. Why else would I come here? I'm the Queen, not a common coward. I don't run. Deep breath. "Chase...you're a Los Angeles Ten. Maybe higher. Any girl would be lucky to be with you. You deserve someone great. But. I'm not sure it's me."

"Do you want it to be you?"

A long pause. Heartbeat like thunder. Holy cow, what a question. "That's not easily answered."

"Why not? Simple question."

"This would be so much simpler if we'd just met. Pure strangers getting acquainted. But we aren't. You're asking me to believe in a fairy tale. Asking me to give myself to a stranger who already loves me. Do I *want* it to be me? Maybe, but I'm not sure I trust what I want.

I want to be Katie again. I want to be in her bed. To remember you. But what good is wishing things like that?"

"I'm not a stranger, though."

"To me you are, but you don't see it that way. I don't know if we get a happy ending, and I'd prefer not to hurt you. If we had no history I could kiss you without the heavy consequences."

We've gotten closer. I don't remember moving. I'm leaning against him now, my back reclining against his shoulder and chest.

I continue, "It's not only that I don't remember. But also that I don't understand."

"Understand what?"

"You. You make no sense. There are so many gaping holes in your story, in your logic."

His breath brushes my ear, my neck. "Give me an example of a gaping hole in the story."

"For example. Why did the Chemist want to kidnap you? Why you?"

"It wasn't only me. He spent the majority of the last two years recruiting new Infected, like Walter and Caleb. He placed a special emphasis on me because, in his vision for the new world, I would lead his armies."

"Again, why you specifically?"

"It's complicated," he says.

"Does it involve you commanding the Variants using only your voice?"

"It does."

"How do you do that?"

"No idea."

"How many Infected are there?" I ask.

"Thirteen. That I know of. Me, Shooter, PuckDaddy, Carter, Walter, Blue-Eyes, Pacific, China, Zealot, Russia...I'm forgetting some."

Those names are legend. Hearing him rattle the list offhand about makes my head explode. I haven't heard of China or Zealot. The plot thickens. "What about Nuts and Caleb?"

"Right, those two. And one more..."

"Tank."

"Ah yes," he grunts. "I forgot the stupidest one."

"Thirteen pure-borns. Does the Cheerleader not count?"

"Hannah Walker wasn't born with the disease. She was the Chemist's most powerful creation. Until you came along."

I trace my finger along the ink on his bicep. "Hannah Walker's name is tattooed on your arm. So are some others. Croc? Shadow? Cory?"

"Friends who died. I got bored at the hospital in Arizona and my favorite nurse is also a tattoo artist. Those are names I don't want to forget."

"Are you friends with the Infected? Is there, like, an Infected email string or anything?"

He laughs, a pleasant noise in our black hallway. "No email string. Infected don't like one another usually. Too suspicious and mean. I'm friends with only Puck and Shooter."

He shifts and his arm encircle my shoulders. Unlike Tank, there is no nostalgia. I wish he was familiar, but he isn't. Just mystery and desire. With a body hard as stone.

I ask, "What's the Shooter like? I idolize her."

"Me too. Despite the fact she shot me a while ago. She's very intense."

I say, "Is the Shooter still here?"

"She is. She visited me earlier today."

"I want to meet her."

"You already have. Katie Lopez and Samantha Gear attended the same school for over a year. You two ate at the same lunch table every day. But you've forgotten."

"She went to my high school?" I gasp.

"Well, she...infiltrated it. Posed as a student. To keep an eye on me. You two became friends."

"Katie was friends with the Shooter." I smother a fangirl swoon. "That's extremely cool."

He laughs and teases my hair, a commonplace action for him but personal and intimate for me.

"You messed up my hair."

"So?"

"The rest of the world is terrified of me, and you mess up my hair. It's nice, though. Being with someone not walking on eggshells."

"Yeah. I'm great."

"I have another question," I say. "You. Shooter. Nuts. Walter. That's a lot of Infected sequestered in our small corner of the world."

"And PuckDaddy is nearby too."

"Why? Why are you all here?"

"For you." He squeezes my shoulder.

"That fails to fully answer my question."

"Our whole world revolves around you, currently. Like I said, we're not some secret society with a common mission. We're a pack of suspicious misfits, but at the moment everything is centered on you and your band of merry men. And women. The mutants were causing a societal collapse before you tamed them, so now we're watching and waiting."

"Hah. I crashed your party. I bet the others are growling about the new kid stomping all over their lawn," I say.

"Carter, who is perhaps the most active and social, wants to buy you and add you to his formidable army of mercenaries. Walter wants to kill you. So does Blue-Eyes. Russia is grumpy but possibly doesn't care that you exist. No idea about Zealot and China. Pacific is insane and most likely hoping you'll start World War Three. Tank is lurking nearby and probably plans on eating you, because he's a troll. Who'd I miss? Nuts respects you. Caleb is terrified of you, I think?"

"And you?"

"Shooter, Puck, and I prefer you alive. And some of us want to kiss you."

I experience a stab of hot guilt. I very much want to get lost in him. Forget everything except Chase for the next hour. But my responsibilities are too heavy to ignore for any extended period. And only yesterday

I caught myself kissing another man, a scoundrel from the past. Perhaps I should be a modern girl and date any number of guys simultaneously, yet I'm not positive I can. Duplicity might be absent from my DNA.

But he loves me. I believe he truly does. And on some ignored subterranean level, I want to be loved. To be with someone who loves me. And I long to love him back.

I'm on the cusp of surrendering, of pushing him into the bedroom and closing the door, when he takes my hand and examines the fingernails. "I saw the video of you executing the Herders."

"I do what I have to do."

"In the past, these perfect hands didn't hurt others. Only healed."

"Soon they'll be employed in the death of Walter."

He shifts uneasily, and runs a fingertip along my nail. "I'd rather you let me do that. Please."

"You said that before, but didn't explain it well. I assume you have reasons beyond sexism?"

"I had two goals during the previous couple years. Keep you alive. And keep Los Angeles standing. I kinda failed at both. I need retribution."

"And revenge," I guess.

"More or less. Plus, he's a force of nature. I don't want you near him."

The door at the end of the hallway opens and two sentries stick their head in. Aaron and Jonathan. "Should we resume our post, Queen Carmine?"

"Come on in, boys," Chase calls.

I'm stung. He'd rather have their company than mine? Did he not see my shirt? I stand and brush the hallway dust from my pants. "I was leaving anyway."

"Come back soon. After you've had a shower."

"Why?"

"You smell like Tank."

PART IV

November, 2019

Alice was a little startled by seeing the Cheshire-Cat sitting on a
bough of a tree a few yards off. The Cat only grinned when it saw her.
- Alice in Wonderland. Lewis Carroll.

One

Kayla's dumb dog Princess scratches at my door from the hallway, as my Devotee cooks breakfast. I ignore her a few minutes but she starts whining. I throw a pillow at the door and the annoyance stops. Stupid animal. Stupid dog and stupid Tank. And stupid Chase.

I still haven't showered. Simply to spite that arrogant jerk.

The Kingdom is *so* close to being self-sustainable. I read over reports as I eat eggs and an orange. We have enough chickens. Enough water. Plenty of fruit, but we need more vegetables. More starches like potatoes and wheat. And sugar. And coffee and fertilizer and salt and so on. We have storehouses ready, but in this time of upheaval I want to be producing everything we consume, not subsidizing from cans.

California provides a vast amount of fruit and vegetables for the world. Or at least it did until recently, but I imagine production has staggered. Finding abandoned fertile farmland and built-in infrastructures shouldn't be difficult. We can do this, but it's all about security and safety.

Our country is collapsing differently than in novels and movies. There is no all-consuming scarcity. Turns out, if there's fewer mouths to feed, there's more for the rest of us thanks to technology and innovation. As long as we're willing to work.

I have a meeting before lunch with the Governess and our Overseers, and I spend a precious hour writing up a list of tasks and items to be prioritized. In reality, she's probably way ahead of me but I can't help it. Our visions of the future need to be unified, and then General Brown will help ensure its protection. When the lists are done, I pack the laptop computer and head upstairs to the printer. Princess follows me, snuffing and yapping as far as the stairs.

"Kayla, come get your dog!"

After printing the documents I check my email. My Stanford paper has been graded and returned, and sits in my inbox. An 88 B.

That's the first B of my entire life.

"More of a B plus, Katie. And I edited it on zero sleep. Calm down."

Everything is falling apart. I never get Bs. And why don't I shower anymore? I like showering.

"Because the water is never hot, and shut up."

My phone dings. New text message. From the Priest.

>> My Queen, you'll be pleased to note I've moved the vigilante to a more secure location. His hotel room was certainly not up the standards you expect us to follow.

>> He is now behind actual bars.

>> And what is more, I had the bars electrified. It is impossible for the heretic to escape.

>> The location of his cell is an absolute secret. Only myself and his three sentries know the whereabouts. I think it best if the location is a secret from your highness as well.

>> It is my pleasure to help you remain above reproach.

That's it; final straw. I make one more note on today's agenda. Discuss a Law Keeper replacement with the Governess. Time for the Priest to go.

The meeting runs smoothly. The Governess relishes the goal of expansion and she's already put into practice many of my ideas. Overseers are moving more chickens south to supplement our fishing boats. Farmers are utilizing additional rooftops and lawns near the ocean to grow vegetables, and Nuts is hard at work establishing an open-air water reservoir for the Shepherds.

She says, "Without oxen, the stable is clean. But from the strength of an ox comes bountiful harvest."

I stare at her blankly. Huh?

She explains, "We're growing. But so do our problems grow." With our swelling population, we're acquiring new headaches. Lazy citizens demanding bizarre rights. Complainers. Thieves. Corrupt Overseers. Bickering communities.

"The farther the community is from me and from the Guardians, the more apt they are to complain. The more freedom they think they have to rebel," I observe.

"Yes. It is so. But also, newer neighborhoods are not as established. More gray area. Still settling. Still scared."

"Then they need to work harder. And so do we. Plus, we need a more robust court system, with greater authority in the south."

She wipes her hands on her dress and gives me a pointed look. "That is the Priest's speciality. And he is good at it."

"Tell that pretty boy to get to work, or he's out."

"He is pretty, that one," she says.

"And alert the Overseers; the Falcons and I will circuit the southern communities and deal with discipline issues soon. We'll drive Greyhounds full of law breakers to the border, if we have to. Anything to get our message across. We have too much to do to suffer the lazy. This is no democracy. Not yet."

She scribbles on her ever-present notepad. "I will. But is Kayla not better at communication such as this?"

"I can't find Kayla. If you see her, send her my way."

The Guardians experience more of the Kingdom than I do. They leave in swarms and return to their hives afterwards, like worker bees. During patrol duties they are deluged with sensory information, like a dog stretching its head from the car window; New Los Angeles imparts itself onto their consciousness. They arrive home with New Los Angeles layered across their being. And something has them uneasy. Even if their distress is subliminal, I feel it. If they're agitated, I'm agitated.

I can't visit all corners of our Kingdom, it'd take me a week. So instead I scale the US Bank Tower, a gargantuan spire providing a clean view in all directions. The tower is multi-tiered with no shortage of foot and handholds. I'm not afraid of heights but as I climb nearer the sky I'm holding on tighter. This is a dizzying, monstrous height, over a thousand feet in the air. Someone's been up here. I don't detect the sharp tang of the Cheerleader, but there is a scent. Perhaps a Guardian. Traces of the virus's power cling to surfaces like residue.

From this vantage I hope to accomplish two things. First, pinpoint the direction of the Guardians' disturbance. Second, spot the Shooter.

I've looked up her photographs a thousand times. Samantha Gear is not classically beautiful but she's striking, like an eagle. Extremely fit. Sandy brown hair cut short. Startling green eyes that suck me in like tractor beams. She looks twenty-two, which for a Variant means she's closer to forty. The virus provided the Shooter with extreme hand-eye coordination, giving her professional sniper attributes. There's nothing she can't do with a gun. Despite the fact that I barely know how a gun operates, she's my idol. She's badass off the charts.

She's close, haunting the rooftops. I'm going to find her.

I walk circles around the tower's helipad, breathing deeply and absorbing the city as a whole. I listen and watch and inhale through my nose, and the Kingdom's ambience becomes more distinguish- able, like stars appearing at night the longer I stare. Lap after lap, the zeitgeist almost develops a flavor.

There *is* a disturbance. After an hour, I sense it. It nags in the back of my mind, like a chore I can't remember no matter how hard I search. This is what the Guardians feel, an impalpable irritation just out of focus, the feeling that evil things are happening over the horizon.

Another hour passes but I get no closer. No clarity. Only a sense of dread. We're still missing two Guardians, and I'm no closer to finding them.

The afternoon wears on and I'm about ready to descend the tower when I spot the Shooter. I know it's her because the Guardians jump from tower to tower like jocund children, but she moves with supreme confidence and precision, a royal arch to her back. She's materialized on the nearby Ritz, stalking the roof. An impressive rifle is slung across her back and her vest is half unzipped.

"She's there for Chase," I whisper. I lay flat on my stomach, peering over the balustrade like a little girl. "But he's gone."

She activates her bluetooth earpiece and talks to someone. Chase? PuckDaddy, the internet hacker? Another Infected? The distance is too great, I can't hear. But I sense she's frustrated. She eats a chocolate granola bar and throws the wrapper in anger.

I need to start eating more granola bars. She makes it look cool.

I pull out my phone to snap a photo but can't zoom in far enough. Kayla and Becky will have to take my word for it; the Shooter *is* here.

But where is Kayla? She hasn't texted me all day.

The Shooter is tired of waiting. She shifts her rifle, synchs it tighter across her chest, jogs a few steps and *Leaps* off the roof. It's so unexpected that I yelp in surprise. She falls fifty feet before calmly attaching her gloves to her pants. She raises her arms and wings snap into place. A wing-suit! Her speed changes to forward motion and she curves around the tower, out of sight.

"Does no one look up anymore?" I mutter, running to the far side of the tower. "How have we not seen her?"

Before I reach the south side, my phone buzzes. A text from General Brown.

>> **Carmine**

>> **I need you at the War Department**

>> **Immediately**

>> **We have a problem**

Two

For the past few days I've lived with mounting anxiety, like walking across thin ice and praying it doesn't break. I approach the War Department with the certainty we're about to be plunged into the deep end. That this is the eruption of ice I've been dreading.

General Brown waits, standing with two of his commanders. Dalton is here with the Governess, and so is Mason. Even the reclusive Nuts is attending. The Priest lurks in the back, and Teresa Triplett the reporter is scribbling things she'll never get to publish. Everyone is here.

"Walter showed his face," Brown barks, fists on hips.

"Where?"

"Castaic Lake. Fifty miles north."

I nod, mouth grim. "The staging area. You were right."

Screens are flooded with various high-definition satellite feeds of the Castaic Lake community. I can't identify much activity on either the wide view or the focused shots. The lake resides in a wide valley, stopped by a dam on its southern shores. Below the dam is a recreational lagoon for use by the nearby neighborhoods.

"His forces are hiding in those houses?"

"We believe so," he answers. "That lake and town are both bigger than they look."

"He could blow the dam."

Nuts barks, "Don't see the point. That reservoir holds less than four hundred million cubic meters of water. The Castaic town would be destroyed but he'd do no damage to us. Plus, that's a big damn earthen wall. Done properly, it'd require tons of dynamite."

I ask, "What about our recon team?"

The General nods at a technician, who changes the screen. A video plays, shot from a camera situated three feet off the ground, and my blood runs cold. Our recon team is tied up in rope, beaten and bloody and being forced to kneel in the lagoon. The water rises to their chins and they tilt their heads up for air. Our two missing Guardians are with them, woozy and secured with extra coils of heavy chain.

They are being manhandled by thugs. There's no better term to describe the degenerates shoving our recon team into the lake. The thugs are shirtless, tattooed, ugly brutes. Like Walter.

Anger ignites inside and my heartbeat throbs like an alarm. "Those are our soldiers?"

"Half ours, half the Resistance."

"If I see our people captured and beaten one more time, I'm going to drive to Washington DC and go on a killing spree," I growl. Wisely no one responds to the railings of a madwoman. "How long ago was this video taken?"

Suddenly, a voice booms out of speakers situated around the stuffy room. "This is a live feed, dummy. Only the best for PuckDaddy."

I gape at the speakers in confusion. So does General Brown and everyone else in the room. Our technicians cast curious glances at one another, hands frozen in the air as if they hit a wrong button. PuckDaddy! Did the infamous internet hacker just answer my question? Could he hear us talking? And did he call me a dummy?

After a prolonged silence, he speaks again. "It's okay. Puck understands your terror. I *am* totally awesome. But our time runs short, so Puck grants you permission to speak."

"You can hear us?" I ask.

"Duh."

"You're PuckDaddy?"

"Indeed. The one and only. I remember you, Katie, even if you don't remember me. You can be mad at this intrusion later, but at the moment we have pressing issues. This is a live feed that Walter is broadcasting. What you see is happening live."

"But. Where are you?"

"I'm everywhere. And no where. I'm not inside New Los Angeles, if that answers your question. Now focus, dummy."

Dalton and Mason bristle at this infidel calling me names, but they have no way to retaliate. General Brown looks as though he woke up in a science fiction movie and he hates it.

I say, "If Walter's broadcasting this video then he wants us to see it."

"Bingo baby. It's a trap."

Katie wakes somewhere behind my eyes. *Those poor people...we have to help them.*

My anger accumulates like the heat of a stoked stove. I feel Mason reflecting and absorbing the emotion. Below me, down the shaft of the tower, other Guardians are wakening and responding to my fury and fear. Soon every Variant within twenty miles will be on alert. "Mason, rouse the Guardians. Get them to the motorcycles, ready to ride."

"Yes ma'am," he responds and begins taping on his phone.

"Don't send the mutants, Carmine," General Brown cautions. "Fools rush to their doom. My soldiers are prepping. This is a snare, probably for you. We can't give Walter what he wants."

He's right. But I don't care. I don't negotiate with terrorists. Nor do I watch hostages die. "I doubt we have time for caution, General. How large is Walter's force?"

Mason grunts, "Isn't Walter enough by himself?"

"We aren't positive," General Brown says. "Best estimate is three thousand."

"Walter has a force of eight thousand." PuckDaddy's voice rattles from speakers. "An unholy mixture of soldiers, Herders, violent criminals, and his freaky mutants. Puck's been monitoring that place for the past week with heat recognition."

"Why the hell does he have our team in the lake?" Dalton grumbles, thick arms crossed over his chest.

"He's going to drown them," I reply. "Slowly. So we'll do something stupid. Like rush to their rescue."

"We're not just going to abandon them, amigo," Mason scoffs. He is anxiously bouncing the phone on his palm. "No way."

Brown shakes his head. "And no way can we waltz into a loaded bear trap. Wars are marathons, and professional soldiers don't jump at bait."

I walk closer to the screen, digesting the displayed environs and shackling system. "It's a gambit. Walter's betting we can't win, and that we'll die trying."

"Bah. This is an acceptable loss," Nuts says. He rubs his scalp with knobby fingers, and waves absently at the video. "Plugged into an input/output equation, their deaths represent nothing significant. Collateral damage."

The Governess nods uncertainly, looking pained. "We are at war. Yes? Casualties are inevitable?"

"Have you all gone mad?" Mason's eyes are wide and he's staring in shock. "That's how the *Chemist* thought. Not us! We don't leave men behind. Or women."

Mason is the same as me. We're the only two mutants in the room. He and I are not only inured to risk-taking, we crave it. I'm close enough to the screen to run my fingers across the captives' faces. My fingers tremble with raw tension. "It'd be crazy to go get them."

"Exactly. Thank you, Queen Carmine," says Brown.

"I prefer crazy."

General Brown groans and the Governess throws up her hands. They like to do that. My ersatz parents. I enjoy their frustration on some stubborn, headstrong level.

The Priest, the pristine prick in the back, clears his throat and says, "My Queen, perhaps you're being too emotional. Too flighty, if I can use the word. See reason. General Brown is clearly—"

I ask, "What do you think, PuckDaddy?"

The speakers reply, "You're going to go, no matter what Puck says. Katie would never let people drown if she could help it. But Puck humbly requests that you go."

"Why?"

"You'll see in sixty seconds. Keep your eyes on screen."

All of the prisoners have been forced into the water. They're kneeling, military uniforms soaked, arms trapped behind their backs, shackles attached to something I can't see. I'm grinding my teeth. What kind of monster—

Walter appears on screen. Like his team, he's shirtless. He's made of skin, bone, and thick cords of twitchy muscle. A reclining chair is set on the sand at water's edge, and he reclines on it. Such a foul man, he's an abomination under a perfect sky. But he's got our attention. Not a sound is uttered in our War Department. We watch and he begins bolting metal claws on the tips of his fingers.

Castaic Lake is fifty-five miles from Downtown, but the route is clotted with debris. Portions of the interstate can be traveled at 150 miles per hour, and other portions will have to be carefully navigated. We can't go by air; we don't have enough helicopters or pilots, plus Walter has surface-to-air missiles. This is a ground game, and he has home-field advantage.

I'm going to peel Walter's skin off and shove it down his throat. While he's still alive.

I feel Variants in the hallway. Clinging to the tower outside. Everywhere. Their essence overflows into our room. Most Guardians are en route to the motorcycles but some are drawn to my anger.

The live feed on screen doesn't have audio, but Walter is overseeing the prisoners. He leers and points and shouts from his chair, and everyone is enjoying themselves. "His servants are released convicts," I observe quietly. Reports indicate that a large number of released convicts have taken up residence in the husk of Las Vegas, causing trouble for the Resistance. Walter has apparently commandeered them.

PuckDaddy replies, "Correct. After much observation, I conclude he uses the released inmates as slaves. His trained army is comprised of Herders and former soldiers, which are fortifying Interstate 5 as we speak. It won't be easy to fight your way in."

General Brown and his commanders are talking in hushed tones. One of his men is on the phone, nodding. His soldiers are mobilizing, but the military is slow to do anything.

PuckDaddy says, "There she is."

I watch in horror as Kayla is dragged across the sand. *Kayla.* Her movements are lazy, uncoordinated, like she's been drugged. Her ankles are chained, her hands are bound behind her back, and she's wearing a gag. They can't afford to let her speak, on account of her influential ability. Even in distress she is heartbreakingly beautiful. She is roughly shoved into Walter's lap. He wraps one arm around her shoulders and lays his hand across her legs, and leers at the camera. He knows we're watching.

"*No!*" I scream so loudly the technicians fall from their chairs, clutching their ears. "*How* did he get her?"

"Now you see," PuckDaddy says and his voice shakes. "That is why I request you go. I'm fond of Kayla."

"Let go of her!" I strike Walter's image, crushing a section of wall. "No!"

"Carmine, our soldiers will be rolling in less than thirty minutes." General Brown has a hand over his cell phone's receiver. "Let us handle this."

I'm raging. Can't think straight. Not Kayla. Take me. Take someone else. Not Kayla. No. No. No! I only have two friends, and she's one of them.

Mason feeds off my wrath. I feel insanity leaking from him. Nuts is too strong to be affected by me, and he merely inspects me like I'm breaking.

On screen, Walter stands. Kayla is easily hefted in his arms, being cradled like a little girl. He kisses her forehead and I almost vomit, and he walks into the lake.

I'm panting. Can't get enough oxygen. "He's going to open the spillway," I groan. "Right? Release water from the dam to flood the lagoon? Drown them all?"

"That's what I'd do," Nuts affirms. "If I was barking mad."

PuckDaddy says, "They've already tried to activate the pumps. I'm stalling them, but Puck's powers are limited. It's only a matter of time."

General Brown's commanders bolt from the room. He tell us, "We're rolling in thirty minutes, Carmine. We'll reach the lake in two hours and engage their forces. We have superior personnel and weaponry."

Mason and I share a glance. Too long. Kayla and our team will be dead by then, and then Walter's men can simply flee north. Brown might be able to help us win a marathon war, but he's useless in our current battle. I'm torn between logic and passion, so dizzy I brace against the wall.

This is for me. They're trying to break me. Weaken our resolve. It might work. They want into our Kingdom so they crack small holes in our armor. Hurt us from the inside.

Brown continues, "Priest. Get your Law Keepers to our borders. We'll need manpower there until our soldiers return."

"If you think that's wise." He dials a number on his phone and raises it to his ear.

Brown continues, "You're too valuable, Carmine. Don't throw your life away. Wait for us. Here."

Wait. Here.

On screen, Walter falls backwards into the lake. He and Kayla both go under momentarily. She surfaces, thrashing to get her nose above the waterline. Walter watches and his mouth opens wide in sick laughter.

"No," I growl. My vision is red.

Go, go, go, go! They're dying!

Mason pauses at the door on his way out. "Carmine, I'm going to the bikes. Sorry General. You're too slow."

"Mason—"

"I will not leave her," I pant. "No one gets abandoned. No one gets hurt because of me. I can do this."

"Carmine," Brown pleads, hands held up, palms toward me. "We need you alive. Don't abandon the city."

Too late. I'm moving. I burst through the nearest window, shattering my way into afternoon sunlight.

Kayla. Walter. I come for you.

Three

The mutants swarm. Their glands produce hormones in overdrive, thickening their skin, sharpening their reflexes, creating a thirst for violence. They flock to our gleaming armada of motorcycles. A thousand Guardians already wait with engines purring.

I arrive and they roar. I select a red Ducati and rev the motor. "Take the bikes! We need mobility!"

Walter wants a fight. I'll give him a massacre.

Mason and the Falcons get to their black motorcycles. They are death and metal. In a span of ninety seconds, every bike is taken, and the Guardians double up. Two on each machine. Four thousand Guardians dwell in New Los Angeles, and three thousand of them are on the bikes. The rest pile into trucks. Due to recent training exercises, the gas tanks aren't full but there's plenty to reach Castaic.

Passions are hot, strengthening our emotional connections. My head sizzles from the overwhelming collective disease.

"Stay with me! Stay together! Stay alive!" I shout as loudly as possible, loud enough to be heard for miles. They witness my fist pump in the air and respond. I tug on a helmet, and so do all the other drivers. We'll communicate through helmet radios.

I open the throttle. Tires scream and I rocket from the parking lot. The front wheel rises off the ground as power surges, like a bucking stallion.

We were built for battle and I thrum with pure existence. Ecstasy, giving ourselves to the virus. All for one. Our cavalcade streams onto the San Bernardino Freeway and merges with the Five. We'll be a motorcycle serpent a mile long. I see General Brown's trucks loading with troops in the Mission Junction. Hundreds of trucks carrying devastating firepower. But they'll be too late. I redline the Ducati's RPMs and hit 120 miles per hour.

I used to ride motorcycles with Chase, Katie says. *I didn't know I could drive one.*

Chase. He's been teaching us about fighting with restraint, and here I am emptying the entire garrison. Madness uncontrollable.

My helmet's bluetooth headset rings. Speakers blare to life and PuckDaddy's voice pumps into my ears. "Walter's ready for you. His men wait in ambush at the Castaic Junction, and then again at the entrance to the lagoon," he says. "Two chokepoints you'll be forced to fight through."

"How do you have this phone number?"

"Puck's been watching you a long time, homie. Plus, I'm awesome."

I sneak a glance at my side mirror. The performance bikes are keeping pace with me, but the dirt and street motorcycles fall back. They'll catch up soon when we're forced to pick our way through obstacles.

PuckDaddy is quiet a few minutes so I can concentrate on driving. I'm traveling at such speeds the world seems to free-fall past. If I had more time, I could have released Chase from prison. Except I don't know where he is. Or I could have alerted Tank and asked for assistance, but it'd take his giants a while to transport. The Resistance pledged their support, but this fight happened too suddenly. We're on our own, as I predicted. This is why I trust no one.

Puck's voice crackles over the speakers, tinged with fear. "Walter manually activated the pumps! I can't stop them. Water is flowing into the lagoon. She'll start drowning soon."

"How soon?"

"I don't know, maybe an hour? Ask Nuts. I'm no engineer."

"Keep her alive, Puck."

"I'm trying! I've cut off all their communication." His ragged breathing distorts his microphone. "But seriously. What are you going to do about Walter's defenses? You'll be shredded going over that bridge."

"I'm going *around* his defenses."

"No way, dummy. It'll take you an hour to circle around from the north. Maybe two."

"Get Mason on the line. I've got a plan."

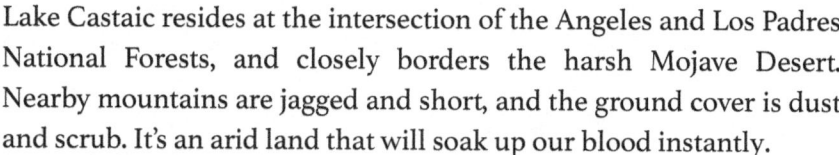

Lake Castaic resides at the intersection of the Angeles and Los Padres National Forests, and closely borders the harsh Mojave Desert. Nearby mountains are jagged and short, and the ground cover is dust and scrub. It's an arid land that will soak up our blood instantly.

Walter believes we have to plow straight up Interstate 5 to reach the lagoon before our people drown. He might be right, but I'm banking we mobilized faster than he predicted, and that PuckDaddy stalled him long enough. We'll take a slightly longer route, a calculated risk.

"Lagoon is swelling. The water level is nearing her chin," Puck warns. "Don't take this the wrong way, Katie, but move your ass. Please."

Forty minutes after leaving the city we bear down on Walter's first choke point at a hundred miles per hour, nearing the entrance to the wide valley. Our rear bikers are still mired in the mess of vehicles at Santa Clarita, a mile behind. I'm the tip of the spear, and directly ahead is the bristling roadblock, a gauntlet of firepower. We could overrun those defenses but we'd suffer catastrophic loses. Some enemy soldier fires too soon. His unguided rocket detonates and vaporizes a donut shop to my left. I'm almost in range, but we swerve off the interstate at the last moment, onto the Biscailuz ramp. We roar across a parking lot, launch from the curb and land on Lake Castaic's old dry river bed, a rough surface that will beat our bikes to hell and which runs parallel to the interstate. Our speed dips to seventy miles per hour, and even that is treacherous. We've caught them completely off guard, taking a slower but safer route. They blocked the road? We'll ride over the dirt. His forces take long distance shots at us but they're meaningless. Our tires fling dust into the air, an expanding tornado of dirt in our wake. We churn north faster than his defenses can respond, and we disappear into the mountains which form the eastern rim of the lake's bowl.

We're here, Kayla. Hang on.

- Four -
The Outlaw

My prison sucks. I *knew* I should have thrown the Priest into the ocean when I had the chance.

Unless I'm mistaken, this is the same prison in which Tank had been incarcerated by the government about a year ago, back when he was a notoriously violent high school senior. I'm in a large nondescript cinderblock room, at the center of which is my metal cage. All four sides and the ceiling of the cage are metal bars, and if I listen carefully I hear electricity coursing through them. It's big enough for me to walk around inside. Nine paces, from one side to the other. The nondescript room has but one window and the Pacific Ocean is audible beyond, further confirming my suspicion I'm at the Federal Correction Institute, near the abandoned navy base.

The afternoon is wearing and Katie still hasn't come to visit. Perhaps I shouldn't have sent her away so hastily last night. Prison is a lot less fun without a hot Latina to hold hands with.

For the thousandth time I muse on the new and transformed Katie. Or Carmine, as she calls herself. Katie Lopez had been my closest friend since elementary school, and then the great love of my short life starting Junior year. But the Chemist altered her dramatically. Katie was sweet, slow to anger, fun, gracious, and soft spoken. All that's gone now. Carmine is fire and determination. Sugar and spice replaced by steel and sweat. The underlying goodness is still present, and so is the relentless work ethic, and the brilliance and the loyalty. The strong belief in right and wrong. Katie was in line to be our valedictorian. Her superlative has shifted from 'Nicest' and 'Most Intelligent' to 'Most Likely to Take Over the World But For Reasons That Are Ultimately For the Greater Good We Hope.' Thankfully, she's still in love with me. Probably. At least I'm fairly certain she is, on some level.

I loved her then. I love her now. And I always will. Come what may.

I wish she'd visit. I only let them imprison me so she'd feel guilty. I finished my book hours ago, and cellphone reception is spotty. Which won't matter long, because I'm almost out of batteries. If Katie isn't here by tomorrow afternoon, I'm leaving. The cell's electricity won't be lethal; I doubt LA has enough juice to spare. I'll surprise her in her tower again. That was fun.

My guard was given strict orders not to speak with me. He sits on a stool near the door, playing a game on his phone. He's about twenty-five and terrified of me. I call him Steve, because he won't reveal his name.

"Steve! When's dinner? I'm hungry," I call from my cot. He freezes, like he always does when I shout at him, but he won't answer. Nor even look at me. A Law Keeper should have brought us both a tray of food by now. "Steve. Steve. Steve. Steeeeeeeeeve."

Nothing. Stupid Steve.

Meh. I might not wait until tomorrow. This is boring. I'm bored now. She has two more hours, then I'm going to find her. The novelty of prison has worn off.

After ten minutes of additional tedium, Steve and I are both aroused by a curious noise. A strange scraping, from the hallway. My sentry and I exchange glances. I shrug, like *I dunno*. Steve stands and moves to the door, right hand going to his pistol. He halts and stares at something beyond my field of vision. Frozen in place.

"Steve? What's up, buddy? What's out there? Steve?"

I'm mildly alarmed. The scraping noise draws closer and still he doesn't move. What on earth? Perhaps it's time I create an egress from this cage. It'll hurt, but only for a...

The most beautiful woman in the world walks into the room. Steve is struck dumb, so wholly enamored that his mouth won't close. She is breathtakingly attractive, a corporeal combination of promise and pain, sin and sex, wrapped inside a tight body and a tighter shirt. Her hair is blond honey, her smile beguiles and bewitches, and her eyes are a shock of rich blue.

This is bad.

Super bad.

Making no sudden movements, my thumbs fly over the phone's screen. I text, **Puck I'm in trouble, blue-eyes is here and I —**

"Stop texting, please, my love," she says, and my hands obey. No! I try to finish but can't. Fingers won't budge. The text is unfinished and unsent.

The woman's name is Mary. The world knows her as Blue-Eyes, or the Blue-Eyed Witch. Possibly earth's most destructive villain at the moment. She sits primly on the stool, her back arched, and smiles at me.

She is Infected, blessed and cursed with dumbfounding beauty, but worse (far worse) is that she produces pheromones. Steve's life is over, and mine will be as soon as I smell her and listen to her voice. Like she's done with the President of the United States, she will rampage over my willpower.

I'm up in a flash, reduced to one option; bust the cell door open and kill her before she hijacks my higher brain functions. Before I bolt, however, another man enters the room, and I recognize him as a Herder. Or is he? That's an unusual device on his back.

He fires what is essentially a water cannon. A blast of water passes through the bars and hits me, creating an instant connection between my body and the electricity. My earlier assumption was correct; it's not fatal, but it hurts. Approximately fifty thousand volts slam into my nervous system. Electro-muscular disruption is one of an Infected's only weaknesses, and I collapse into a twitchy fetal position.

A second man enters, pulling my metal bat behind him. He can't lift it, so both his hands are wrapped around the handle and the far end scrapes and sparks along the floor. Sentry Steve looks curiously at me spasming on the floor, and then glances at my bat. Finally, he sits crisscross at the feet of Blue-Eyes.

Where is Carmine? How did Blue-Eyes get this far into her territory? I need something to throw at her. Maybe my phone? It wouldn't render her unconscious though, and I may still be able to use it, assuming it wasn't fried. I'm recovering quickly from the shock but the Herder stands ready to deliver a second load.

I take a deep breath, hold it, and stick shaky fingers into my ear canals. This is a pose often struck by four-year-old brats, but I don't care; it might extend my life an extra four minutes. If I breath her in, I'm toast. She shakes her head, a playful twist on her lips. Oooh, you silly boy, she says.

This is a nightmare. Electricity and Blue-Eyes, my worst-case scenario.

Withdraw your fingers from your ears, please, she says. I read her lips and shake my head. This is ludicrous. I bet Time Magazine wouldn't have named me Person of the Year if they'd seen this.

Place the Outlaw's totem in the corner, she says. The man drags my bat to the corner and drops it with a loud clang. Thank you. You may go.

He leaves.

Withdraw your fingers or I'll be forced to administer another dose of electricity, she says.

I stick my tongue out. No way, crazy lady.

Very well. Go to the ocean, she tells Steve, and drown yourself, please.

"No! Steve! Don't do it!" I shout, and I am instantly shocked with another round of water and energy. The Herder, an expert with electricity, only releases short blasts so he isn't connected to the power himself.

Steve nods, stands, gives her a final inspection, and leaves. Steve! Stop! He has no chance, so fully ensnared is his mind. The Herder receives a nod from Blue-Eyes and he follows Steve out.

Now she and I are alone. Me, a rat in a cage, and her, the hungry Cheshire cat beyond. She tilts her head to one side, patiently observant. I can hold my breath a long time, maybe three minutes because of the weird virus, but in the end it won't matter.

Can you hear me, she asks.

I nod.

Please release your ears and take a breath.

I shake my head, No.

You are being volitionally stubborn, Chase Jackson, she says. Her voice is only a murmur, but the distant syllables help me codify her lips into words. Even muffled, she sounds sensuous and appealing. I could execute you now, she says. I named myself Secretary of State, did you know? Then she laughs and rolls her eyes, an indication of how seriously she takes the title. Oh dear, she sighs. What fools these mortals be. Why, oh why dear Outlaw, are you so afraid of me? You will enjoy my touch. And my voice. I promise. Are you afraid you'll grow uncontrollably prurient?

I don't know what prurient means, so I shrug.

She smiles, shy and seductive in one blush. I won't mind, she says. We can use your cot.

No. No, I tell myself.

It will be our sordid little secret, she says. Reading her lips has a hypnotic effect, but my eyes won't close. She continues, I've always wanted you, Outlaw, as I presume you're aware.

No no no no no no no. Don't listen to her. My lungs begin to ache.

We've never properly met, she says. I am Mary, the de facto Ruler of the Free World, and you are my new shiny toy. And I am yours, my love.

I wrench my eyes closed. I refuse to watch her sensuous mouth any longer. I can't. I won't. She won't dare get into the cage with me, not until I'm under her spell. So I'll sit here like a stone.

Another two minutes, and my lungs scream and I'm light-headed.

Katie! Puck! Samantha! Somebody! Anybody!

Her voice drones on, even as I near unconsciousness. I will hold my breath until I pass out, but after that I'm depleted of defenses. Survival instincts will engage, and my body will gulp oxygen before I wake. I will breath her, will listen to her, will taste her, will fall in love with her...

...will...will...

...

...will love her...

The most attractive woman in the world is in my cage. I'm lying on the floor. She sits on my pillow beside me and places a hand on either side of my head, and leans over. Her corona of hair tickles my face.

"Beautiful boy," she says. "You made an error. Would you like for me to tell you?"

"Please." I hear myself say the word from a dream. My head pounds and my fingers tingle, but I possess no ability to move anything. She has me.

"You are most susceptible to my charms from within a hypnagogic state. Much easier to be inculcated this way, I'm afraid, my love. Better for you to have grasped the bars of your cage with both hands and simply held on. "

"Maybe I could—"

"Shhhhh." She lowers her face until our mouths touch. With each word, her lips tug on mine. "The planet's mightiest warrior. Insensate and underneath me. Just how I prefer him."

Everywhere I look I find intoxicating blue eyes. Her sweet breath fills my nostrils, and her words warm my ears. She expands inside my head. I'm being saturated.

I could strangle her. She doesn't have a tenth of my strength. One squeeze. But I can't. I won't. Would never.

"I'm not so bad, am I?" she says.

"No ma'am."

"And to think of all those awful imprecations you hurled my way."

"I'm sorry," I say.

"I forgive you. My sweet boy."

"Thank you, Katie."

She recoils in surprise. What? What's wrong? She smacks me, hard, but the emotional pain is far worse than physical. I hurt her somehow and I hate myself for it. "Excuse me?"

"I'm sorry, I don't understand...what's wrong?"

"What is my name?"

"Your name is Mary. Your name is Blue-Eyes."

She takes a deep breath and sighs, a flash of irritation. "I suppose your blunder should be expected. That whelp has you coiled around her finger, and you are not yet lucid."

"Who is a whelp?"

"I've long had my eyes on you, Outlaw. Inspected you from afar. Not another man on earth possesses your bravura in battle. The Outlaw. Defender of Los Angeles. The Masked Man and Infamous Vigilante. You even destroyed my Father."

"The Chemist."

"Yes. I couldn't muster the fortitude for patricide, so I must thank you. You released me."

I know what she's doing. She's binding us together using her pheromones, her voice, her beauty, and even flattery. She is soaking me with her essence, but I don't mind. Maybe once I did, but not now. I can't stop staring at her. She says, "You are the first person in two hundred years that the mighty Infected will follow. We all sense it, you know. The call to be near you. To nestle under your wings. The rest of us are malcontents, despising each other from a safe distance. But you? Oh yes. You shall be my regent. And we shall not let the little pretend princess ruin our destiny. She is a lesser being, far beneath us, commanding only those grafted with the common DNA."

She's talking about Katie. Carmine. A flicker of irritation at this. No one should speak ill of Katie.

She says, "Do you know how we'll defeat her? We'll take away her support. Kill those she loves. Remove her allies."

"Like me."

"Yes, love. Like you."

"No."

"Oh yes. She'll think she's failed, and her resolve will slacken. The little girl will be lonely and broken and vulnerable."

"No..."

"No? Do you love me?" she asks.

"Yes."

"Tell me about the Inheritors, Chase."

"Katie says she killed them all."

"Do you believe her?"

"Maybe. I've looked for the children and I can't find them."

"I've searched too," she says. "And found no trace. If they exist, they *must* be discovered. No cost is too great."

"I understand."

"Tell me about Carmine. Enlighten me."

"Where is she?" I ask, sudden unexpected panic rising in my chest. "Did you hurt her?"

"Focus, my love. If you don't want me to hurt her, I will refrain," she says. It's a lie, but I'm comforted anyway. "But you must focus. What is her agenda?"

"To stay alive. And keep her Guardians safe."

"That is all?" she asks.

"I think so. She's still new. Still raw, and the virus was unkind to her."

"How so?"

"She hears voices," I answer. Or at least, a voice. "She can't control her emotions yet. Suffers headaches."

"Is she strong?"

"Very," I nod. "She and the others like her communicate somehow. They have an awareness of one another."

"An awareness? Tell me more."

"I don't really know. They know if she's angry. They're connected in ways we aren't."

She pulls back a moment, her eyes searching far-off answers, and she sucks lightly at her teeth. "That's an unforeseen side effect." Mary is older and more knowledgable than me, and she'd been a close companion to the Chemist. She perhaps has the world's most complete understanding of the virus. "She and her mutants will be overwhelming in combat, if that's accurate. And you're sure her aspirations go no higher than simple survival?"

"That's what she said."

"Such a foolish, childish dream. Her existentialism and Walter's nihilism are simple-minded. She's a dreamer and he's a common thug. Coordinating with that neanderthal is a necessary evil I can only abide for so long."

"Why do you work with Walter?"

"To get what I want."

"Which is?" I ask.

"Domination without destruction. And, of course, a touch of hedonism. Quite simply, my love, I want it all. But she's a feisty one. That much cannot be denied. Do you love her?"

"I do."

"What a pity. In romance, Chase Jackson, I will abide no competition. Young Carmine must lose her life, then."

"But you said—"

"And you will be the one to assassinate her."

I say, "But—"

"It is time to depart. First, however, I must take precautions." She produces a bizarre collar. Gunmetal grey and black, and an inch thick. I sit up so she can fasten it around my neck. "It's a big snug, but that is your own fault. This collar contains explosives, dear Outlaw, and will ignite if you stray from me. Your head will be popped clean from those broad shoulders. I also have a trigger in my possession. I will execute you, rather than risk losing you. Do you understand?"

"Yes Mary."

"Good. Follow me. We must not be tardy for our flight."

She turns and walks from the cage. I stand and retrieve my phone, which is dry and resting on the cot. I slip it into my pocket, but before I let go, calling upon some hidden reservoir of willpower, my thumb presses the SEND key.

Text message sent.

Katie. Puck. Help.

Five

We abandon our motorcycles on the eastern ridge of Caistic Lake. Walter knows we're here but his troops can't regroup fast enough to form orderly ranks. Their heavy artillery will be too late. Thousands of us crest the rise and sweep across the dam's peripheral structures, which include a small heliport and boat rental shack.

"The water level is over Kayla's mouth," PuckDaddy warns through my bluetooth headset. "Another two minutes and she'll begin to drown. The rest of your troops will follow two minutes after that."

"I see her." I'm at the pinnacle of Castaic's massive earthen dam, glaring into the valley far below. Walter's forces are scrambling from the interstate, tiny soldiers hurrying to meet us. They assumed we'd attack from the south, but instead we come from the north. My hammering heart breaks to see Kayla struggling to keep her nose above water. "I'll reach her in time."

But as I speak, eruptions shake the dam. Deep concussions vibrating through our legs. Mason is beside me. "There." He points to the far side of the dam where dirt is flung into the blue sky.

"What's he doing?" I growl. "He can't bust this dam. It's enormous."

"He's not," Puck says. "Just the spillway. In essence, he opened the floodgates."

He's right. The western spillway becomes an avalanche of water. This is not the work of pumps but rather of gravity, a roaring wall of water. The lake now spills freely and aggressively into the lagoon.

"Set your cameras to record, Puck," I say.

"Why?"

"The world must see what happens when you attack the Kingdom."

As one body, we launch ourselves from the dam and its surrounding ramparts. I didn't issue an order; they *felt* the command.

Four thousand of us. Our nearest enemies are the released convicts who occupy the eastern shores. They witness their death howling down the slopes and they cannot muster strength enough to stand against us. They break ranks and flee, moving in slow motion. There is no hope for them.

Walter's hardened soldiers fire rockets from across the wide lagoon, smoking projectiles which slam the dam's boulders and belch shrapnel into the sky. The explosives are too slow and we evade them like softballs thrown underhand.

I lead the charge. At the last second I issue a war cry, an ear-splitting blast; my enemies cower and I dive into their midst. Their bodies break upon impact with mine. A handful of the brave convicts take shots with assault weapons but they're too late and too few. Our mutated muscles operate at hyper speed and we sweep through them as a wave washes over sand figurines. We have fists like hammers, fingernails like knives, daggers too fast to dodge. The convicts melt before us and we don't break stride.

The Herders assemble into defensive positions near the southern tip. How I despise them. Cowards hiding behind cowardly weapons.

"She's drowning! They all are! Water way over their heads!" Puck reports.

We're circling the enormous lagoon. Kayla and the troops are under water at the far end. Our Leapers begin *Hurling* themselves into the sky and diving under, desperate to find a way to release their drowning friends. Our Swimmers streak across the surface, *Churning* water with webbed feet and herculean strokes.

We can't fail. I can't fail.

The once picturesque picnic and camping park is defiled by violence, as thousands of Herders and enemy soldiers swarm the recreational grounds and brace against our onslaught. The soldiers pour a continual rain of gunfire in our direction but we move like a pack of wolves, too fast for them to pick off efficiently.

A bullet strikes me in the shoulder. No? No it doesn't; it strikes the man to my left. But I feel it and experience his pain. Other Guardians are shot, and each one penetrates my awareness. They hurt, I hurt.

"Destroy the Herders first!" I roar, and then I dive into the lagoon.

The electronics in my bluetooth headset short-circuit immediately. The water is murky and agitated, and silt stirs off the lagoon floor but I see well enough to spot our Guardians. Kayla and the other prisoners thrash against restraints which are chained to a massive poured concrete slab at the bottom of the lagoon. Our Swimmers and Leapers strain to break the heavy links. They're panicking, unable to think clearly, and they aren't doing any good.

Above the surface, one of my Guardians takes a direct hit to the head and he dies instantly. I experience the loss as though a small part of my soul is cleaved. Another Guardian is electrocuted, and I'm hit again with a jolt of pain. The connection we share must be growing stronger. Katie is weeping and heartbroken.

I wave for the attention of nearby Swimmers and I draw them after me to the bottom. My lungs don't burn yet, but Kayla's have to be. Thirty feet under, ears popping, sinuses aching, I plant my feet on the big concrete block and take hold of thick chains. So do my fellow Guardians. We pull, groaning bubbles, braced and heaving against the slab.

A sudden spasm of pain erupts in my muscles. Painful tingles along my skin. And then another blast. The Herders must be shocking the lagoon with electricity, but the body of water is too big. The power diffuses too far and too wide to kill us. Could that have been their master plan? To cook us all in the lake? It won't work. But it hurts.

Pull! Pull! On our third tug, the steel anchors break loose. Chunks of concrete fall apart.

They're free. Kayla's free.

We grab our chained comrades and haul them to the top. Kayla breaks the surface and I tear the gag from her mouth. She coughs and sputters. A hundred drowning soldiers begin surfacing with the assistance of Guardians.

We were underwater less than a minute, but the fight is nearly over. The grass is stained with blood and fallen bodies. We have shown the world our true might. We move as an undeniable force of nature, felling thousands of our armed enemies and losing only eighteen of our own. I felt all eighteen deaths, and my sorrow accumulates like a sudden depression.

"Immunity!" I cry from the lagoon. I'm removed from the battle but the Variants heed my cry. They are tuned to me. "Grant the soldiers immunity! Only the soldiers."

There is no quarter for Herders, who are a special breed of villainy. But I have a soft spot for soldiers sent here by their government, sent here to die without knowing why.

The battle begins drawing to a close. I pull Kayla to shore, where we both lay panting a moment. Her head lulls against the sand, eyes closed, and I begin the task of releasing her. "Where is Walter?" I call.

No one knows.

"Find Walter! This fight isn't over!"

A portion of our Guardians check on their fallen friends, and the remainder round up enemy soldiers who've surrendered. Hundreds of the soldiers granted immunity sit in the picnic area with hands on their heads. They're teenagers, or early twenty-somethings. Scared kids, staring wildly at the enhanced humans. Some of our Guardians are so engorged with adrenaline that they scream uncontrollably or vomit into the grass.

"Where are Walter's Variants?" I ask the captured men. None of them answer. "He was here. Where are his mutants? I don't see any."

This was not an army. This was not a unified military force, but rather an aggregation of confused soldiers and angry stragglers desperate for purpose. They were decoys hurled into a demolition. Savage times indeed.

Finally, a boy with a buzzcut points a shaky finger northwest, towards the far side of the lake's rim. I can't see through all the trees, so I walk back out to the lagoon. Mason follows. He's bleeding from a cut on his face and bullet wound in his shoulder.

Arrayed across the western side of the dam, half a mile distant, Walter's Varients stand like sentries. I now understand the Outlaw's warning; they aren't like us. These are mutants hammered into warriors. They are halloween and hardware, wearing chunks of metal as armor, and holding wicked swords. This is Walter's true army, or at least a portion, and he withheld them from combat.

Mason mutters, "They look like goblins."

"There's less than a thousand," I note. "They don't mean to fight. Not today." My muscles quiver and my stomach heaves, common side effects following a battle. After an hour of hell, the sudden calm is jarring. The warriors on the dam high above us begin turning and disappearing beyond our sight. Retreating. I say, "He sent his Herders and soldiers to die. I don't understand. This makes no sense."

Mason's phone rings. He doesn't recognize the number, but he answers it anyway, listens, and shoots me a bemused glance. "It's our friend the computer hacker. He sounds excited."

I walk out of the lagoon, which is swelling with water and will soon overflow its banks, and I sit next to Kayla beneath a pine tree. "Tell him his girlfriend is safe."

"PuckDaddy says he spotted Walter in a truck. He's headed north, back home. His mutants are following him."

"Wuss." I comb my wet hair backwards. "Walter keeps running from our fights."

Mason extends the phone to me. "He wants to talk. Apparently I don't rank high enough."

I speak into it, "I'm tired and I'm sitting in a field of dead bodies. Leave me alone."

PuckDaddy's voice is urgent. "Blue-Eyes kidnapped the Outlaw. At least I think she did."

It's such an astonishing statement that no response comes to mind. My mouth works uselessly.

He says, "Did you hear me? She's in New Los Angeles."

"Blue-Eyes? She's still there?"

"Think so. Chase sent me a partial text."

I ask, "Where is General Brown?"

"He and his trucks are ten miles behind you. It'll take them over an hour to turn the convoy around and return. But I don't think Blue-Eyes came with an army."

I ask, "How'd she get in?"

"I'm scanning cameras, which is really hard in a city without central power. I'm spotting intruders. Puck thinks she brought seven or eight soldiers with her, maybe? They're searching for something."

"The Inheritors. She's looking for them. But they do not exist. She won't find them," I say.

"Maybe not, but she's got the Outlaw. Which means we're screwed."

I'm experiencing too many emotions to process. Exhaustion. Relief. Anger. Confusion. Jealousy. We're screwed? I think back to my encounters with Chase, and memories flash across my mind. Memories of him falling from the sky and slaying the steel dragon. Memories of him commanding my Guardians with just a word.

PuckDaddy is right. We can't let Blue-Eyes just claim him. If anyone gets to claim Chase, it's me.

"We can't let her get away," I say. "Not with the Outlaw."

"Yes. Exactly. Bingo. She can control him. What are you going to do?"

Good question. I feel like I'm a balloon about to burst. I have no way to get home. I'm two miles from my bike, and an hour's ride from the city. What do I do?

What *can* I do?

Nothing. I think of nothing.

I lost. I can't do this.

Chase. We have to help Chase!

I can't, Katie. I don't know how! "Puck...I have no way to get there."

"You *have* to."

I'm on the verge of tears. I fell into their trap. I'm furious I didn't recognize the danger. "Our bikes will run out of gas. We burnt most of it getting here...what do I do? I'm fifty miles away. There are no nearby cars...I can't...I don't..."

"I'm scanning. You're right, no cars. Wait. Wait, hang on...there's a small helicopter at the helipad."

"A helicopter? I can't fly!"

"Find someone who can!"

I lower the phone and shout to the kneeling soldiers. "Can anyone fly a helicopter?"

No hands go up. Not a single one.

Then, from behind me, "I can. Probably. Maybe. Or at least, I tried a simulator once."

I turn to find a woman approaching, an impressive rifle hefted onto her shoulder. Strong green eyes, Sharp chin. Short sandy brown hair. No extra body fat. Bullet-proof vest. Grenades on her belt.

I realize, "You're the Shooter."

"Hell yeah I am, but call me Samantha."

"You're here," I say. Stupidly. She's the *Shooter,* my idol. The Guardians glare at her, angry and swollen with suspicion.

"I tagged along with your crew. I can't resist a good dustup."

I say, "Blue-Eyes is downtown. She's got Chase."

Her eyes widen a fraction. "That bitch. Let's go. To the chopper. You've got a witch to kill, Katie."

After this calms down, I'm going to fangirl all over her.

Six

The helicopter is a tiny blue Robinson R22, in which Samantha and I barely fit. After five minutes of fiddling with controls and getting advice from PuckDaddy (who accessed an online manual of sorts), and another five minutes of near disasters, we are pointed south and traveling at ninety miles per hour. Before we can exit Castaic, Samantha clips two trees, narrowly misses a telephone pole, and briefly dips our landing gear into the lake.

I shout through our thick headsets, "You said you could fly!"

"I *am* flying!"

"This isn't flying, this is ricocheting!"

Puck is in our earpieces, talking loud enough to be heard over the thumping of rotors, and he notes, "She's doing remarkably well for her first time."

"*First* time?"

"The simulator was much easier than this," Samantha grumbles. "And it always looked so simple. But the pedals are tricky."

We pass General Brown's caravan on the interstate. Half of his motorcade, nearly a hundred jeeps and trucks, are in the process of executing an about-face. Mason has apparently updated the General on the abbreviated battle at Castaic and the threat now within our borders. Brown was correct; emptying the Kingdom of all Guardians was ill advised. I should have listened.

The nose of our chopper keeps rotating to the south, drawing us off course. Samantha swears and works controls at her feet until we return to the appropriate heading. The engines surge like a roller-coaster, thrusting us up into azure skies and subsequently dropping again as she tries to manage our power. At the apogee of our surges, the whole of New Los Angeles unfolds; Mount San Antonio on our left, stately towers in the hazy distance, and a carpet of commerce and houses as far as I can see. My home. A visual reminder of what's at stake. Nothing less than everything is jeopardized if she escapes with the Outlaw. A man who can frenzy the Variants and lead the Infected.

Samantha asks, "Puck, how'd Blue-Eyes get to Chase so fast?"

"No idea."

"The tunnels," I answer. "Metro lines. The Guardians have been uneasy for days, and it's because the enemy was creeping under our noses. Has to be."

Samantha grunts an agreement. "Makes sense. As we rode away, they popped out. But she won't use the tunnels as her escape route. Too slow."

"Puck's been monitoring the Pacific Ocean," he says. "No nearby yachts appear to be waiting as getaway vehicles. That doesn't mean they can't hijack an abandoned speedboat at one of the docks, though. The Marina still has a couple left."

Samantha says, "I doubt they'll take to the sea. Too unpredictable, and the Navy hasn't declared allegiance to her."

"*Watch* where you're going! Less talking, more piloting," I shout.

"Whatever. That house is too damn tall."

The internet hacker and I fall silent, sharing the understanding that my pilot needs fewer distractions. Where could Blue-Eyes go? Speed is essential, she knows, else we'll catch her. She brought a small force for a smash-and-grab burglary, not for combat. Our border checkpoints are still intact, and she'll want to avoid them. Possibly the ocean, but doubtful. Her best option might be to head south towards our least protected flank.

"Hmmm. This is interesting," Puck says in our ears.

"What?"

"Katie is receiving text messages."

"My name is Carmine," I snap. "And my phone is dead."

"I recently began to monitor your messages and phone calls," he says, off-hand. "Even if they haven't been delivered to your device yet."

This is so stunning, so intrusive, so infuriating that I can only growl.

He continues, "And right now Tank is messaging you."

"Tank!" Samantha barks. "That big dumb handsome Infected kid? What's he want?"

"Possibly none of your business." I hate everyone. I hate the world. Monitoring my phone calls. I should choke PuckDaddy with his own power cord.

"Don't be mad at Puck," he says. "Chase told me I could."

"Chase told...so *what*? Who gave Chase *that* authority?"

Katie murmurs sleepily, as though she's just waking up, *Puck-Daddy would do anything for Chase. They're best friends. Puck used to be alone, operating as a machine. No friends, just business partners. Chase changed all that, the way he changes everything.*

There are too many voices in my head!

Katie starts droning about her junior year in high school and I forcibly tune her out as Puck sputters through various reasons he should be allowed to monitor my device.

"Anyway." Samantha rolls her eyes. "What does Tank want?"

"Tank texts that they caught a car speeding south on the 405. After threatening to have them stepped on, Tank learned that both men are Federal pilots, and they'd been heading towards the airport. He has detained them."

"Towards the airport?" Samantha wonders. "No plane has landed there in months."

"No, but dozens are ready to take off," I say. "That's it. Blue-Eyes is going to fly out. It's easy and fast. Even if Tank captured those two pilots, she'll have a backup with her. I bet those two were insurance."

"You're right," Samantha announces. "Changing our heading. Due south towards the airport. We're ten minutes out."

"Your bodyguard Dalton is texting you too," Puck reports. "He's not happy either."

"Can you respond to Dalton? Update him on the situation."

He mutters something about not being my secretary, but he agrees.

Samantha wonders, "Tank used the word *they*. Who is he working with?"

"Giants. It's a long story. And I'd rather you focus on not crashing," I say.

She grumbles under her breath, "You better not be sneaking away to make out with that oaf. I don't care how great an ass he has."

It's easy to miss Los Angeles International from the air. Other than the Downtown spire cluster, the city is flat and gray. Exactly like the airport. No lights illuminate the airport anymore, and because we're flying so low the runways are beneath us almost before we see them.

Samantha has come to a more cohesive understanding with the helicopter, and she pulls up so we have a better vantage. A dozen jumbo jets rest like slumbering whales at the many terminals. Sprinkled around the tarmac are smaller planes. There's too many.

Samantha has a reluctant edge to her voice. "Should you authorize General Brown to shoot down any plane that takes off?"

"No!" I sputter in surprise. "The plane could be carrying the Outlaw."

"That would be brutal, I know, and Chase is my friend. But, it's better he die than to—"

"Never. Absolutely not."

"The longer he's with Blue-Eyes, the more control she'll have. Eventually Chase will cease to exist, and he'll be a mindless zombie for her. I've seen it happen. And she'll send him after us. One by one he will hunt and kill us."

PuckDaddy remains conspicuously silent. Samantha sets her jaw and pointedly doesn't look at me. I won't kill Chase. I don't care if this is war. He's important to me. Katie stirs uneasily between my ears.

"This place is massive," I say. "They could be in any plane, and take off a mile removed from us."

"If I know Blue-Eyes, and I think I do, she'll want a private jet. Public transportation is beneath her. There. Right there, see? Those business hangers on the south side. So we —"

PuckDaddy interrupts us. "Warning! Rocket launch detected! Surface-to-air! Move!"

"She's shooting at us?" I ask.

"Affirmative!"

"Time to ditch our ride!" Samantha shouts, and I swear she *wants* to crash. She thrusts our nose downwards and punches the engine, and the slate tarmac begins plummeting closer. "Prepare to jump!"

I see the rocket a half second before detonation. Samantha's evasive dive prevents a direct hit but the payload erupts near our tail rotor. I'm struck deaf and blind for a half second. The jarring explosion knocks the blue Robinson sideways, and the force of our sudden roll flings me up and out of the cabin. Sudden roaring silence. Nothing but the rush of wind as I flail arms helplessly. I fall end over end, the sun and earth revolving in Carmine-centric orbit, until I smack the deck of a 747's starboard wing. I skid across the hot surface and thud to a stop against passenger windows.

Samantha is also flung from the helicopter. Directly downwards. She hits the runway, a violent collision which would shatter normal humans. She only has time to raise her head before the flaming wreckage of our small Robinson lands directly on top of her. She disappears in the twisted metal. Heat and flames flair outwards from the impact. Rotors splinter and launch in every direction. The helicopter, still carrying leftover velocity, pivots off her and turns three full rotations before resting.

Samantha isn't moving from her fetal position. Maybe because she can't. She's not on fire, though. Small blessings.

Well. We're here. I have no phone. No headset. No backup. Nothing except fury and a body intact.

Blue-Eyes brought Variants with her. I see three Leapers bounding in our direction from southern terminals. Two men, one woman. They're my age and dressed in military combat fatigues, *Hurling* themselves skyward in grotesque bounds. They advance at breakneck speed, carrying knives and tasers, and they converge on the smoldering chopper. I detect something other than their disease...a madness I'm unaccustomed to sensing. A trace of Blue-Eyes?

Samantha lays crumpled on the tarmac and I leave her as bait. My enemies arrive, their eyes naturally drawn to fire and the body. They don't bother searching their surroundings, which is their final mistake. I fall on them from the wing. Their bodies are thick and hard, bones reinforced, skin tough, but even so I remove the closest man's throat on contact. The woman spins at the sound but I'm ready, and I shove her own taser into the soft flesh under her jaw. She seizes and drops.

"Stop," I order the last man. Not a man. He's so young. He doesn't stop but he pauses, a natural response to orders from someone with authority. He pauses long enough to die from his own knife, the one I snatch from him. I don't want to execute Variants. I know they've been through hell and are barely capable of functioning. But these mutants in the employ of Blue-Eyes are brainwashed and rabid for their master.

The sky is high and blue and salted with small cloud clusters, and the wind whips through our aviation graveyard like it's peeved. Across the runway I spy activity at the Atlantic Aviation terminal, a newer construction on the LAX campus. Those are privately owned aircraft, sitting on a recently poured blacktop tarmac. She's there. Has to be. The planes are thick at that terminal and she's hidden beyond. A couple guards keep watch, crouching behind tires.

"Gotcha," I whisper. I circle to the south, bolting between structures and airplanes, staying out of sight but running like hell. They know I'm coming, but they can't stop me either.

This might go terribly wrong. The plan was for me to confront the Witch and for Samantha to shoot her from half a mile distant. However, that was before a helicopter landed on her head. Ideally I'd have help. Mason. General Brown. Kayla. Somebody. I'll be forced to resist mind control long enough to crush her skull.

I've become a monster. Only savages survive.

I hear the whine of engines as I get closer. A jet warming up. Not much time. Her guards are vigilante, two Herders, but I'm fast. They don't even see me before I hit them with a scavenged iron wrench. I drop their limp bodies to the ground and proceed.

Blue-Eyes is here. She waits for me on a comfortable chair stolen from the Mercury terminal. She sits, legs crossed, in a wide clearing encircled by abandoned aircraft. She's even more breathtaking than her picture because here I can see the breeze toss her hair, because I can smell her scent, because I can hear her heartbeat. She is smaller than I expected, cozied on the chair like a cat. There is another chair situated opposite hers. For me. For our showdown.

Chase sits at her feet. A macabre collar is fastened around his throat. His face is buried into knees drawn to his chest, and he clutches tufts of his hair into fists. Like he's in pain. Or like he's straining against something. My heart breaks for him. For us.

"Hello Carmine," she says, and my name is beautiful on her lips. My body lightens and I experience a spasm of pure euphoria. "Please have a seat."

Her getaway vehicle is a pearl HondaJet, small and sleek with a blue nose. Looks as though it holds seven people max. The engines are idling and the stairs are down.

I'm startled to realize I'm sitting in the chair she indicated, ten feet from her. When did that happen?

I say, "Chase? Can you hear me?"

She answers, "He can hear you. But he chooses not to respond. Credit where credit is due, sweet Carmine. I never suspected you'd face me yourself. Most cowardly world leaders sent diplomats, but you? You are preternaturally brave, my dear. And apparently ubiquitous. Recent reports placed you elsewhere."

"Likewise," I say. Speaking requires effort. Adoring her would be as natural as gravity, and I'm fighting against it. "Next time call first, so you won't be forced to sneak through sewers like a rat."

Her face pales a shade and for an instant she's speechless. It's been a long time since someone insulted her, I bet. "I hope you didn't harm the poor men keeping me company."

"Release the Outlaw," I say.

"The Outlaw remains, I'm afraid. Not an hour ago he professed his love for me."

Chase tenses and shakes his head.

"Chase," I call. "Wake up."

She casually raises a small device the size of a thumb drive. "He warned me you might intervene. That your understandable jealousy runs wild. So he wears a collar, and I hold the trigger. Once pressed, the trigger cannot be released. Or perhaps, *should* not be released, is more accurate phrasing. As long as I maintain pressure, he lives. If I release the trigger...well, let's not dwell on such butchery."

Mary's words are battering rams I have to fight through. She is everywhere and everything.

"Do you have a weapon?" she asks.

I don't answer.

Blue-Eyes says, "Find one. And use it. On yourself, please."

Kill myself, she means. Without hesitation, I stand. Those two guards each had a firearm and an electroshock weapon. That would work. I can kill myself with one.

What! What are you doing? Sit down.

Katie's words are loud and angry and they shatter against Mary's. I'm reeling, holding the chair for support. *I will not kill myself! She's holding Chase hostage. You need to snap out of it.*

I sit.

"Carmine," Blue-Eyes says. "Now. You are dismissed."

No. We stay. Do you understand me? We stay.

"I'm staying."

She sucks lightly at her teeth while considering this. "You have backbone. Not so easily overmatched? Very well, let us barter."

"I think instead I will simply kill you," I say.

"You cannot, sweetie. What a factitious story you must be telling yourself."

She's right. I cannot. If I had a gun, I wouldn't shoot her. This is a problem.

The HondaJet is behind her. A man emerges from the cockpit and descends the stairs. "Madam Secretary?"

Mary angles her head to the side and speaks casually over her shoulder. "Yes, David."

"We require more fuel. This jet was never prepped."

"Then. Get. Some."

"Yes ma'am."

The man is wearing combat fatigues, and he scrambles to a nearby fuel truck and drives it closer. There are two other fuel trucks nearby, nestled in among the abandoned aircraft. He fiddles with the mechanism, clearly unused to civilian machinery. She cannot see either the jet or the fuel truck, both are behind her, but her agitation mounts. "David, how long?"

The man says, "Five minutes. Maybe ten."

She turns her attention back to me. "Let us barter. I will trade you. You keep the boy. And I'll take the Inheritors."

"The Variant children?" I ask.

"Yes. The Variant children. The Father's final subterfuge. He never confided their existence to me."

"I killed them all. There are no more Inheritors."

"Killing children requires an unsound mind. It is the pursuit of a sociopath. You could never commit such an atrocity. You're soft. Intrinsically weak minded. Tell me where they are."

"I do what I have to do. They are dead."

"You cannot protect them." She is irritated. Her words grow clipped, losing their dreamy sensuality, and they. "Tell me."

Don't answer that. Say nothing.

She says, "You cannot protect everyone. I will find them. And you will fail."

"I will—"

Quiet. Keep your mouth closed.

She says, "You are powerful, sugar. I will grant you that. If not for the recent surge of Infected, you'd be the debutant of the decade. The prettiest girl at our ball. However, your timing is poor."

I'm desperate for options. She's pinned me to the chair with her eyes. I can't think of anything to do other than keep her talking.

"Can't you and your presidential boyfriend not handle your own affairs? Why abduct the Outlaw?"

"Can you feel him? The Outlaw radiates power. This is why the Father coveted him so." She closes her eyes and tilts her head upwards, and breathes deeply. It's slightly easier for me to think when her eyes are closed. She says, "You are merely an invention, Carmine. A manufactured tool. But the Outlaw is pure born. His body is saturated with the disease, and it calls to us. Can you feel it?"

"I feel it. His power repulses me."

"That's because you're a simpleminded demagogue. A cute wool-gatherer, at best. You perceive him as a threat. But the gods of this age, the Infected, we see him as our future."

"Do you always speak in histrionics? Must be exhausting at the dinner table," I say, and I'm about to continue but I notice something odd—Mary's pilot is lying face down on the tarmac and gasoline is gushing freely from the hose. How'd that happen?

"I'm undecided, sweet little girl, concerning your fate," Blue-Eyes says. "A place in the new aristocracy must be earned, and you simply have not done so."

Without breaking eye contact, I search the peripheral for movement. *Something* is happening. Her pilot didn't just fall dead for no reason. My skin crawls, and there's an odd tang in the air. The pool of gasoline expands, now a small pond beneath her HondaJet.

It's her! It's Hannah, the Cheerleader. Where is she?

Oh crud...

The Blue-Eyed Witch continues, "Our world shall be rearranged rapidly in the coming years. Bifurcated between the powerful and the weak. Those with the disease, and those without. In other words, you have worth, young Carmine."

"I'm relieved to hear it." I shift in my chair and risk a quick glance to my right. A second fuel truck is hemorrhaging gas. The two bodies of liquid spread closer to connecting. On further inspection, one of the smaller jets is also leaking. Petroleum drizzles down the fuselage and the rear landing gear. The hot blacktop warms the liquid and radiates its sharp fragrance. I look to my left. Those planes are leaking too. Gasoline is pouring from everywhere.

The Fire Girl is here.

Somewhere...

She's come for the Outlaw. Followed him by scent. Tank told me the Cheerleader is obsessed with Chase. I'm stuck between two earthquakes of insanity. Powerful women hellbent on getting what they want. But then again, what am I?

Blue-Eyes is too caught up inside herself to notice my distress. She is too self-involved to smell the gas. To notice I'm suddenly sweating. Where is the Cheerleader? Is she behind me?

"I think perhaps I'll leave the decision with you," Mary is saying. "Would you prefer to die, Queen Carmine? Or join my menagerie of beautiful creations? I can find room for you, I believe."

I look in every direction. All three fuel trucks are leaking, and so are several airplanes. Mary, Chase, and I sit on a shrinking island surrounded by an ocean of gasoline. My heart pounds so furiously it hurts.

"Carmine? You will listen to me, little whelp, this instant," Mary snaps. "This conversation itself is beneath me."

"I doubt it. Considering it'll probably be your last." I stand up and scan our surroundings like a woman possessed. Where is she?

Mary prepares a retort but her face goes slack, her focus shifting to something beyond my chair. I spin, following her gaze.

The Cheerleader is here.

She is pretty in the way a barbie doll is pretty. She's perfection crafted from plastic. Her face was either melted and reattached, or it is constructed entirely of skin grafts. The result is not unattractive, but it is not quite human either.

She's athletic, like a girl who's practiced gymnastics for sixteen years. Her hair is a short shock of platinum, approximately the length of Chase's, longer than mine. She's my height, tall for a girl. Maybe 5'10. She wears a stylish skirt and strapless blouse, tight and white and worth thousands, something an actress would wear to the Academy Awards.

Her eyes don't quite focus. Like she considers everything at once. Like she can't concentrate. Like she's unhinged.

"Oh my god," Blue-Eyes breathes. I back away from the Cheerleader until Mary and I stand shoulder to shoulder. "David, it's past time we depart," she calls.

"David's dead," I report. Both our voices shake.

"I can't control her," Mary says. "If I can't control you, I certainly can't stop that freak."

Hannah Walker, Katie pants. *The Cheerleader. Don't leave Chase. She's here for him. Hannah's insane. I watched her die. We have to help!*

The Cheerleader walks barefoot through the gasoline and stops next to a gushing hose. She crouches next to the hose, a surprisingly feminine motion, and collects a small pool of gasoline by cupping her hands together. She splashes her face with the gasoline, and then her shoulders, her chest, her legs, and finally drenches her hair with handfuls of the stuff.

Fully soaked, she stands and walks our way. Petite, girlish footfalls. Brown fuel drains from her hair, streams from her skirt, clings to her eyelashes.

"Katie," she says in a husky rasp. "You found Chase. Thank you. You've always been a good friend to me." Her words scrape, the result of damaged vocal chords.

"Hello Hannah Walker," I say. Probably a bad idea to admit I have no memory of her.

"Sit down Hannah," Blue-Eyes orders. Her voice is so full of magic and desperation that I nearly obey her. "Sit down *now*."

"No, I don't think so," the Cheerleader answers. "You've never been my friend."

Blue-Eyes says, "Carmine, please remove the intruder."

No. No. She's using you. Stay.

I don't move, but I feel as though my soul's tearing in half.

Blue-Eyes hisses, "Carmine! Stop her!"

Hannah reaches into a small pocket at her waist and retrieves a Zippo lighter.

Oh no.

I say, "Hannah, no. You'll kill us. There's too much gasoline. You'll kill Chase."

How fast does fire travel through gasoline? I could make it, most likely. I could get clear. But not without Chase, who still sits cross-legged near the chair.

"I will not kill Chase," she says. "I've come for him. We belong together."

Ugh. There's a lot of that going around.

"Mary, let her have Chase," I whisper. I can recover him after we escape the gasoline lake. After we get off this bomb.

The Cheerleader won't be consumed by fire. Her story is legend. She nearly died in an accident during the Chemist's attack on Los Angeles, but she was re-born from the flames and the Hyper Virus in February of 2018 after the Chemist saved her charred husk from destruction. I read about it online because of Chase's prompting. Over six agonizing months, the virus rebuilt her body and provided immunity from fire.

I don't have that immunity. Mary and Chase and I will burn alive and die. Painfully.

The Blue-Eyed Witch raises the device in her hand and depresses a trigger. The device emits a soft beep. So does the collar around Chase's neck. "If I release this trigger the explosives at Chase's neck will count down from three," she announces. "And then neatly sever his head. You comprehend this, Cheerleader? I am not to be trifled with. I'd rather he die."

Hannah Walker flicks the lighter and a small yellow flame begins dancing on the wick. The air is so thick with pungent fumes that I'm a little surprised we don't instantaneously combust. She says, "Chase comes with me. He kept me safe during the flames. During the darkness. The nightmares. And so I will do the same for him. Chase must transform in the fire. As I did."

"Hannah, no. You'll kill him." Summoning nerves I didn't know I possess, I move to stand between her and Chase. His collar has a small locking mechanism. It's not meant to be permanent and I could rip it off. Maybe. "Let's find another way, Hannah. No one needs to die."

"Katie. Move." The Cheerleader speaks through a yawn, and she rubs her eyes. Like a tired three-year-old would. She doesn't know what to do with me.

"Come with me, Hannah. Come home with me. We're friends, yes? Let's go home and talk. Please?" I say.

"I'm tired," Hannah says. "So tired."

"Come with me. You can sleep in my bed. I promise."

"Chase comes too," she says. "He comes to my bed too."

"Yes. Yes, Hannah. Chase comes with us."

"No," Blue-Eyes says simply. "No he does not. Your little parlay is adorable, but the Outlaw leaves with me. Now. Hannah, sit down. Immediately."

The Cheerleader doesn't budge, as still and as solid as marble, but her eyes shift to Blue-Eyes. They are tinged with menace.

"Chase does not belong to you," she says. "Chase is mine. Always mine."

Oh no. Oh no. It's about to happen.

"Sit down, Hannah," Mary orders. Her voice and her scent are whips, thrumming with power. Does the Cheerleader not even feel it?

"I hate you." She advances on Mary, small deliberate steps. "You're not nice. You take things which do not belong to you. You steal."

"Chase," Mary calls. "Chase. Stand up now, please, and take your possessed ex-girlfriend away. Take her beyond the gasoline and destroy her."

No. Restrain him. He can't control himself.

Chase stands and sways. His eyes are bloodshot and they lock on mine. His face is blue like he's holding his breath. "Help me, Katie." A harsh whisper. "I can't stop. Please."

I touch his face. His eyes close, and he presses against my hand, and he groans. I say, "Stay here, Chase. With me."

"Chase!" Mary shouts, verging on panic. "Now!"

Two things happen at once, so simultaneously they might have been choreographed.

Dalton, my sweet wonderful beautiful bodyguard, rises up from the fuselage of the plane dead ahead. Pistol in his hand. Fury in his eyes. He takes careful aim. At Chase.

And Hannah tosses the lighter into the gasoline.

"No!"

Dalton fires. The locking mechanism on Chase's collar shatters. "Move!" Dalton roars.

The Zippo lands with a small splash in the fuel. There is no sizzle. There is no slow spread of flame. Instead, our entire world detonates. Heat unimaginable. Fire unquenchable. The nearest fuel truck doesn't explode outwards; it explodes upwards, like a NASA rocket.

Before the Zippo splash, Blue-Eyes backed near the gasoline lake and fuel truck. The eruption emits something like a shockwave, and she is flung across our small dry island. She vanishes into a rising wall of fire.

The collar at Chase's neck emits an alarm. Mary released the trigger! It's going to blow. One. "Chase!" Two. I rip the metal free and *Throw* it directly upwards. Three. Small explosives activate like a shotgun blast and the metal collar rends out of shape a dozen feet over our heads.

Heat singes my skin. We're going to die, possibly when the next fuel truck blows. Chase's eyes are fixed on the spot where Blue-Eyes disappeared.

"Chase!" I smack him in the back of his head. "Wake up! We need to go! I can't carry you fast enough—"

Something crushes me from behind. My collarbone, which is a reinforced chunk of of hard collagen, snaps in half, and I fall.

The Cheerleader is transformed. No longer a nubile cheerleader, she is a volcano erupting. She is engulfed in fire, a brilliant camouflage of yellow and black. She burns and her flames lick ten feet in the air. Her pretty blonde hair twists and melts, and her skin crackles but does not dissolve. Her clothing burns to nothing.

"Chase comes with me!" Her voices roars like air from a furnace. "We will transform, and we will be together!"

"Chase!" I scream as loudly as possible, loud enough to burst mortal eardrums. "You big idiot, wake up!"

He blinks his red eyes and looks around, as though only now realizing we're stuck in an inferno. "Katie?"

That's not my name, but whatever.

Hannah Walker, an embodiment of madness, a human-shaped torch, reaches to wrap Chase into a final embrace. A hug from which he won't wake. To bake him alive inside a human oven.

Stop her!

I am! I grab her calf and haul backwards. My shoulder grinds and screams, and the skin on my hands sears. Like placing them on a hot stove.

The plane behind us shatters. Fire reaches its fuel tanks and the frame bursts. Chase and Hannah stagger from the blast. My eyes are about to melt. Chase is too close to the fire, and he's falling. I release Hannah and grab the bottom of his vest with my good arm to prevent him falling into the flames.

Dalton lands next to me. His pants are on fire and his arms are burnt. I would die for him in that instant. He has a grenade in each fist.

Hannah regards him cooly from within her conflagration. But that changes when he releases both safety pins. Even a crazy person recognizes live grenades. Hannah may be immune to fire, but apparently not from shrapnel. "I'm here for Chase," she says.

"You wanna hug someone? Hug me, bitch." He charges her. She hesitates. Would this man really commit suicide? Clutch her until the grenades tear them both in half?

Sanity, for the moment, prevails. Hannah flees. She runs through the mounting wall of fire, and he plunges in after her. Gone.

"Dalton!"

A second fuel truck detonates. Chase and I begin to die. Smoke chokes out the sky, and our island of relative safety is baking. The air has to be over four hundred degrees and rising fast.

"Katie," Chase says. He kneels beside me. "You're here."

"That's not my name, you idiot," I groan.

He gathers me into his arms, like I'm an infant. "You came for me."

I will always come for you, Chase, as you always have for me. Katie is delirious with relief. I want her to shut up so bad. I say, "And your crazy ex-girlfriend broke my shoulder."

"I can't remember."

"I know the feeling. Can we go now?"

He kisses me, a soft brush of our lips, and says, "For you, Katie, anything."

I'm not a Leaper. I can't leap buildings in a single bound. But he can, and we are *Launched* up and over the wall of fire. The air above is agony but it's brief.

Our touchdown is remarkably gentle. He carries us a safe distance and sets me on my feet. I'm exhausted and my shoulder throbs and I've ingested too much smoke, so I lay down and soak in the cooler air. He sits beside me and hacks hot soot from his lungs and tries to remember where he is.

Dalton is alive. He staggers up and collapses next to us. More planes explode. Above us there is no sky, only ash.

"Where'd she go?" I ask. "The Cheerleader?"

"Don't know, don't care," Dalton growls. He needs serious medical attention. Boils are rising on his neck and face, and he's wheezing. "She ran. Fast. I threw the grenades and stop-drop-and-rolled. My ass is fried."

"And Blue-Eyes? Anybody see her?"

"No sign," Chase coughs. He's shielding his eyes against the bright flames.

"Let me know if you do," Dalton says. "Still got some bullets left."

Chase says, "She's crafty. She'll escape. Anyone she meets will fall in love and smuggle her out. We missed our chance."

"No thanks to you," I say.

He grins, which is weary and beautiful. "Yeah. No thanks to me."

He indicates the fire with a wave of his hand. "Samantha will be sorry she missed this."

"She's over there," I say. "A helicopter fell on her."

"A *helicopter* fell on Samantha?" He laughs, but ends up hacking again. "She's going to be so pissed."

"Assuming she's alive," Dalton mumbles.

"She is. It'll take more than that to kill Samantha Gear."

"Both of you be quiet," I murmur. "I need a nap. I've earned it."

Smoke rises over New Los Angeles, but for the moment the Kingdom is safe. So are we. In the distance, firetruck alarms are wailing. The Outlaw gently holds my burnt hand and we don't move for a long time.

Seven

Somehow, someway, Walter, Blue-Eyes, and the Cheerleader all vanish. Like mist carried off in the breeze. The Priest and General Brown cast wide nets and search forty-eight hours straight but come up empty. I'm irate if I dwell on it too long. So close to victory, and yet so far.

The terror of that awful day quickly subsumes under the work demanded by New Los Angeles. The Kingdom doesn't care that we're beaten and battered and burnt; chickens still need to be fed, children need tending, and borders need protecting.

Three days after being carried from hell, my burns have faded. The following Monday, I remove my arm from the sling and experience no pain.

Dalton will require much longer to mend, unfortunately. He is covered with second degree burns but refuses to take a day off. He sleeps on my couch and I bring him food and coffee in the morning, and I will cherish him the rest of his life, which he finds aggravating.

Kayla doesn't sleep much, but when she does it's in my bed. My room smells like strawberries afterwards. She can't remember much of her abduction, but the brilliance of her day-to-day life is diminished by the trauma. Mason even successfully railroads her into accepting a full-time bodyguard: himself, as often as he has time to spare, or Chris, his most trusted Falcon.

Blue-Eyes is photographed a week later in Washington, D.C. wearing a hat. Most likely all of her hair was cooked off. No mention of her excursion to California is made by the news. She appears to pick up where she left off, slowly brainwashing the leaders of the free world into war. She and I will lock horns again soon.

The Cheerleader has disappeared, though Tank reports that he caught her scent near Thousand Oaks. She hasn't gone far, but she's more of a thorn in Chase's side than mine. We're friends, so Hannah said. Friends who break each other's collarbones.

~

Three weeks to the day after the Walter/Blue-Eyes attack, I climb the Bank Tower again. I'm not ascending the spire to spy on the Shooter this time. Nor am I climbing to pinpoint the source of any disturbance. All is quiet on our western front. Simply put, I need a moment of peace. My apartment used to be a quiet sanctuary, but no longer. The door hardly closes.

I lay on the tower's warm helipad and smile at the sun, eyes closed. Crisp sensual silence, the first I've experienced in days. For a moment I consider stripping down and sunbathing, however I've learned that a certain nosey internet hacker has no qualms invading privacy. The last thing I need is PuckDaddy emailing scandalous photographs to Chase.

The Outlaw left an hour after firetrucks arrived that day at the airport. Samantha Gear wasn't dead, but she wasn't healthy either. He borrowed an ambulance and a medic and drove her twelve hours to the physician who'd treated him. I admire his loyalty, but I also miss him. He texted me that Samantha has already made a full recovery.

My new collection of friends (the Outlaw, the Shooter, and Puck-Daddy) are an impressive array of allies, even if they're quirky and mysterious. They seem content to leave me in peace while I'm safely inside New Los Angeles. However, I know they'll return immediately if I ask, so strong is their connection to the girl once known as Katie Lopez.

I have no new memories of her, but I suspect Katie is discovering ways to influence me. I've read two Young Adult romance books during the previous two weeks, and nearly wept when Stanford issued their semester grades. I received a B in both classes. Hardly worth crying over, and yet I did. She grows increasingly chatty as days pass. Right now she's happy. Enjoying the sun and the peace.

After thirty minutes of resting on the helipad, I open my phone and scan news articles. Hostilities between the Federal Government and the Resistance boiled over into open conflict in Lubbock, Texas yesterday. The beginning of major bloodshed, experts forewarn. In other parts of the continent, a harsh winter pounds the population and this year's flu is going to be particularly devastating thanks to the upheaval and lack of coordinated medicine; millions could die. Stock markets are frozen to prevent values from plummeting, and there's a citrus fruit blight predicted. England has terminated diplomatic communication with America (or what used to be America) and all of EuroAsia withdraws into itself.

Gloom and doom and more gloom, much of it caused by mutants. Evil Variants breaking the planet, giving the rest of us a bad name.

Frustrated, I'm about to turn off my phone. But first I get a text message.

>> **lookin fly girl**

I smile and reply, **Thanks PuckDaddy.**

But stop spying on me.

>> **never**

>> **its what puck does**

>> **in case i haven't told u recently...**

>> **thanks 4 saving kayla**

You told me.

And you're welcome.

When will you come visit her?

>> **good question**

You better. She's expecting you.

>> **stop it! u making puck all nervous!**

I smile, click off the phone, and shove it into my pocket.

"Reading about yourself online?" the Outlaw asks. He is striding up the metal staircase. He's wearing the vest but no mask.

I sit up and wrap my arms around my knees. "You startled me."

"I'm sneaky."

"I never google myself. The articles are rarely positive."

"It's not all bad. I read the beginning of some fan fiction that involves you and me trapped alone on a deserted island."

He grins. "Pervert."

"I didn't read far. It got steamy in a hurry."

"Why are you in New Los Angeles?"

"You."

"Took you long enough." I'm smiling and that's okay. I'm happy he's here. I won't pretend otherwise. The new Carmine can take over the world *and* admit she likes boys.

"I can't stay, though. Only passing through. There's going to be trouble in New Mexico. Santa Rosa."

"Blue-Eyes sending soldiers to start fights with the Resistance?"

"She's been in a bad mood for almost a month now. I wonder what ticked her off."

I smile. "Probably getting half killed by a simple cheerleader."

"We may have accidentally started World War Three."

I'm relieved I decided not to sunbathe. It would be challenging to dress frantically and maintain my dignity. I stand and slap the dust from my pants and shirt. From up here, the line of traffic into Downtown is visible, vagrants flocking to New LA by the thousands. I ask, "You'll fight at Santa Rosa?"

"Maybe. Samantha Gear and I go to prevent the fights. If we show up, the other side often backs down. And if not, we operate like a special forces unit behind enemy lines." He moves closer and takes my hand. The faint headache behind my eyes dissipates and Katie begins to hum. "You're still wearing the red ribbons."

"My joints still hurt."

"Have you missed me?"

"Have you missed *me*?"

"I asked first," he says. Our faces are close.

"I've missed you."

"Good."

I say, "You're thinking about kissing me."

"You're correct."

"We're not kids, you wimp. We're allowed. Just do it."

Kiss him kiss him kiss him.

He asks, "What's your plan? What happens next in your Kingdom?"

"Expansion. I want San Diego."

"You're never satisfied. Katie would be happy with Los Angeles only."

"I'm not Katie."

He asks, "Are you dating Tank?"

"I am not."

"Are you two just friends?"

"Basically. It's...complicated."

He kisses me. Finally. But it's more powerful than a simple kiss. We collide like two planets striking and breaking and melting into one. I experience the swirl of emotion, a powerful vortex of pleasure and memory. Katie surges into my hands and wraps my arms around his neck.

The Outlaw loses control over his tightly bottled strength. He relaxes and his power radiates into my pores and nostrils. His disease is *so* strong. He's an alpha male beyond imagination, but Katie doesn't care; she strengthens her grip and so does he. I'm terrified of him, but I think I've decided that's okay. He's a terrifying man, but he's good. And he loves me.

Eventually he presses me away and holds me at arms length. Katie is out of breath, but not as much as him.

"Your Guardians are coming," he says.

"I know. A lot of them."

"They're climbing the tower stairs."

"And up the exterior walls," I say.

He brushes hair out of my eyes. "Your protective watch dogs. They don't seem thrilled that I'm here."

Tell Chase I love him.

"Katie wants you to know she loves you."

"And you?"

"I'm crushing pretty hard. And I hope you return soon. When you can stay."

He walks to the edge of the helipad and hops the short distance to the retaining wall. I'm not afraid of heights but his precarious perch makes my stomach flipflop. "I won't be gone long. You've pissed off some powerful individuals. We'll face them together."

"We can do this."

"You're right. We can."

The penthouse door crashes open and febrile Guardians rush through, like angry german shepherds searching for an intruder. Others come pouring over the wall. Chase is spotted, and they howl and converge.

"I love you, Katie. And I always will," he calls, and he allows himself to fall backwards into nothing. The Guardians don't reach him in time. He plummets several hundred feet, engages his black wing-suit, and begins a majestic curve to the north.

"That's not my name. My name is Carmine."

The End

EPILOGUE

The girl once known as Katie Lopez wakes early on a Thursday. In December, the sun rises at 6:55 but she is gone by then, having stepped across a man sleeping on her floor and slipped over the exterior wall.

She walks her motorcycle from the parking garage, straps on an extra canister of gas, and motors south on the 110 as Cooks began serving breakfast to Shepherds and Farmers. To be safe, she refills her tank at a manual pump in Long Beach and eats a grilled fish at the Queen Mary market.

She climbs back onto her bike and sends a text message before continuing.

Kayla. Don't call me. I need a day off. Back later. Be nice to Dalton.

>> okay!!! have fun!!! xoxoxo love you! xoxoxo

Carmine smiles to herself, envisioning Kayla and PuckDaddy messaging all night and into the morning. She powers the phone off because otherwise Puck would track her.

The drive south along Highway 1 and Interstate 5 is still one of the prettiest journeys on earth. She decelerates through Sunset, Newport, and Laguna beaches so she can enjoy the views of the Pacific. Here not everyone recognizes her and she feels unencumbered enough to wave at smiling children playing in sand. The last interstate guard station is at Dana Point, but the sentry doesn't bother looking up. After San Clemente, she punches the throttle and passes the next thirty miles in twenty minutes, arriving in Oceanside breathless and windburned.

This part of California is mostly abandoned. Without central power or law, it's a realm that belongs to brave survivalists. Further south near San Diego, a criminal warlord has taken up residence and declared sovereignty. He will be dealt with soon enough. But for now, she turns inland at Lawrence Canyon and motors up vacant Route 76.

Nestled into the scrubby hills, and bordered by nearby Camp Pendleton, is a monastery. The Prince of Peace Abbey is well-tended and modern in appearance, sitting on a long campus that backs up to Camp Pendleton's unoccupied military housing. She and Nuts came here in July and oversaw the drilling of two water wells and the tilling of four acres of farmland. Nuts also personally connected the monastery to a neighboring photovoltaic solar panel farm, providing the monks with unlimited electricity, even though they rarely use it. Camp Pendleton, now vacant, didn't notice the reduction in power.

The girl once known as Katie Lopez hasn't visited since October and she's pleased to see a community bustling with work. The number of monks swelled during the evacuations, which means more mouths to feed but more workers to tend crops.

Two guards at the entrance wave her down, but then quickly motion her through after glimpsing her face. She parks her bike and surprises Father Frost in his sparsely decorated office.

"Miss Carmine. What a pleasant surprise." He stands, claps his hands, and politely inclines his head. Father Frost is approaching seventy-five but still has a full head of silver hair. His beard is trim and his eyes are bright.

"It's been too long, Father. I apologize for being away."

"Not at all. Our lives are simple and busy and we have everything we need. What cause is there for apologies?"

Carmine and Father Frost sit and discuss the world for twenty minutes, after which time he presents Carmine with a short hand-written list of supplies that would benefit the monastery. Father Frost seems embarrassed by some of the items, which he calls lavish and unnecessary. Items such as sugar and an air pump.

"I'm surprised the surrounding neighborhoods don't have a surplus of these items," Carmine notes.

"I'm sure they do but we prefer not to take them, in case the owners wish to return home in the near future. Thou shalt not steal, you understand. I'm loathe to set a precedent of easily satisfying our wants with local spoils."

Carmine understands his sentiment. She's read that looting is addictive. "This is not a difficult grocery list. I will personally drive down a truck soon."

"We are grateful."

"Unless there's anything else, I thought I might spy on your charges," she says.

"Of course. They've taken a field trip. To Del Mar Beach. Do you require accompaniment?"

"No. Thank you. Once again, Father Frost, you are a lifesaver. I don't know what we'd do without you."

Carmine quickly tours the monastery and adds additional items to the 'lavish and unnecessary' list. Light-duty work gloves, for example. She returns to her bike and motors five miles to Del Mar Beach, which is an eclectic mixture of paradise and Camp Pendleton's abandoned amphibious assault school. She parks near the eight yellow school buses, climbs on top of one, and peers down at the world's worst kept secret.

The Inheritors.

Five hundred women are on the beach and in the water. To quote the nursery rhyme, they are red and yellow, black and white. And tall and short, thick and thin, each of them a young mother. The five hundred young mothers are each caring for a toddler. Some toddlers sleep. Some splash in the water. Some dodder around sand castles. Others eat. Many are crying. Each toddler was chosen by the Father in 2018, directly after their birth, and injected with the Hyper Virus.

Originally there'd been a thousand Inheritors, but the disease has already claimed half.

He selected only young, poor, unwed mothers. No strings. And no freedom.

Carmine stares at the toddlers, the Inheritors, and chews on her thumbnail. She still doesn't know what to do with them. She tricked the world into believing the babies had been murdered, but her enemies aren't sure they buy the story.

More of the children will die when puberty starts. And then even more when they turn eighteen and the aneurysms begin. The virus is brutal and unforgiving. How many will survive? Nuts did the math on his notepad once and predicted a hundred and fifty would live past their twentieth birthday.

A hundred and fifty as powerful as the Infected, of which there are only thirteen. A hundred and fifty like the Outlaw, and Shooter, and Walter, and Blue-Eyes. Will even a scrap of society survive such mayhem?

The children must be kept as safe as possible. She and Nuts have been musing on possible islands to which the Inheritors could be relocated. Far away from Walter. Far from Blue-Eyes, and far from the Resistance. Who knows how long they'll be kept secret and safe at the monastery.

Not long, most likely. They'll be found here eventually. And then?

Most days Carmine is comforted by a sense of destiny, a feeling that perhaps she and the Kingdom were *selected* to weather the storm. Her cosmic and holy purpose.

But on days like today, when she watches the toddlers laugh and play and she admits to herself that they're fated for madness and world breaking, she puts her hand over her mouth and tries not to cry.

The adventure continues!

Book Two of the Carmine series, now available

From the Author

I hope you enjoyed Carmine. Your Amazon feedback is coveted, good or bad.

If you'd like to read Book One of the Outlaw series, I'll send you a copy for free. Click here —> http://eepurl.com/b95Bgj

Many thanks to everyone involved —
 my beautiful bride Sarah for her patience
 my two boys, Jackson and Chase.
 beta readers (especially Therin, Sarah, Kelley, and Jana)
 editors (Debbie, in particular)
 Damonza for the cover
 Anne for the Carmine illustration
 Polgarus for the formatting
 Text me and let me know what you think of Carmine.
 (260) 673-5450 I'll be in a coffee shop, head down, working on the next book, and I enjoy the texts. I respond to as many as possible.

Colossians 2:2-3

www.ingramcontent.com/pod-product-compliance
Lightning Source LLC
Chambersburg PA
CBHW020227180626
46810CB00006B/2069